PRAISE FOR *HINTON HOLLOW DEATH TRIP*

'Twisty-turny and oh-so provocative, this is the type of book that will stick a sneaky foot out to trip you up … As always with Will Carver, I couldn't begin to guess how it would end, so didn't even try, I just enjoyed the ride. If you like something just a little different then *Hinton Hollow Death Trip* is an original, thought-provoking and hugely entertaining read' Liz Robinson, LoveReading

'Unusual and original … For those who don't mind their crime fiction a little dark, it's a brilliant book' Craig Sisterson

'This is a thriller in the most unconventional and welcome sense, unique in style and perspective … A dark, evil, humdinger of a tale and I absolutely loved it. Brilliant' Chris Scotland

'How do we cope with a small town falling apart at the seams? Why don't we simply heed that warning right at the very start and find something else to do? The answer lies somewhere in the heart of Will Carver's writing, because he is trying to help us. I think' Live Many Lives

'A highly entertaining, thought-provoking read … Chilling, sinister, dark and festering, I only hope that Evil and his plans won't pay a to visit our towns and cities anytime soon!' Miriam Smith

'There are the touches of Stephen King here … *Hinton Hollow Death Trip* made my blood pump, my heart race and my hands sweat … absolutely breathtaking' Reflections of a Reader

'Truly original and brilliant … I absolutely loved it' Emmaz Book Blog

'A completely unique story that will blow your mind' Me Loves Books

'I now know what kind of book a child would produce if his parents were Stephen King and Bentley Little' Mrs Love to Read

'Addictive, disturbing and unsettling … be brave, take the trip … Creative, immersive and complex writing that hooks you with a mighty grip. Read it!' Books.tea.and.me

HINTON HOLLOW DEATH TRIP

ABOUT THE AUTHOR

Will Carver is the international bestselling author of the January David series. He spent his early years in Germany, but returned to the UK at age eleven, when his sporting career took off. He turned down a professional rugby contract to study theatre and television at King Alfred's, Winchester, where he set up a successful theatre company. He currently runs his own fitness and nutrition company, and lives in Reading with his two children.

Good Samaritans was book of the year in the *Guardian*, *Telegraph* and *Daily Express*, was shortlisted for the 2019 Amazon Publishing Readers' Award for Best Independent Voice and hit number one on the ebook charts. It's follow-up, *Nothing Important Happened Today*, was longlisted for both the Goldsboro Books Glass Bell Award 2020 and the Theakston Old Peculier Crime Novel of the Year Award 2020.

Follow Will on Twitter: @will_carver.

The Detective Sergeant Pace Series:

Good Samaritans
Nothing Important Happened Today
Hinton Hollow Death Trip

HINTON HOLLOW
DEATH TRIP

WILL CARVER

ORENDA
BOOKS

Orenda Books
16 Carson Road
West Dulwich
London SE21 8HU
www.orendabooks.co.uk

First published by Orenda Books 2020
Copyright © Will Carver 2020

A catalogue record for this book is available from the British Library.

ISBN 978-1-913193-30-0
eISBN 978-1-913193-31-7
Hardback ISBN 978-1-913193-43-0

Typeset in Garamond by typesetter.org.uk

Printed and bound by CPI Group (UK) Ltd, Croydon, CR0 4YY

For sales and distribution, please contact info@orendabooks.co.uk

HINTON HOLLOW DEATH TRIP

For nothing

Choice is free but seldom easy.
—*A Clockwork Orange,* **Anthony Burgess**

PROLOGUE

Where you will be introduced to:

A boy on a train
A detective
A pig hater
A food lover
A window breaker
and your narrator.

DON'T READ THIS

You can leave now, if you want. Don't even bother finishing this page. Forget you were ever here. There must be something else you could be doing. Get away. Go on.

This is the last time I try to save you.

Go and work out. Cook yourself something from scratch instead of ordering in. Binge on that TV show everyone is talking about. Enrol yourself in that night-school photography course. Because you will think this is strange. Then it will make you angry. Then it gets worse.

I know what you're thinking. Who am I to tell you what to do?

Okay. Don't listen. You weren't, anyway.

It's a small story. That's what you're getting here. A small town with small lives that you'd never have known about if you'd left when you had the chance.

Hinton Hollow.

Population 5,120.

There's a crossroads.

You can see the park from the woods. And the school rooftop just beyond. There's a bench in between now. Where it happened. The golden plaque screwed into the wooden seat is for the young boy. The message, from his older brother and his father.

The mother isn't mentioned.

Of course.

It's less than a minute to drive into the centre of Hinton Hollow but people in this town tend to walk. That will take seven minutes at a brisk pace. Ten minutes on the way back because it's slightly uphill and you often have a bag of shopping. It takes Mrs Beaufort twice as long but she is much older. And she had that scare. With her chest. When it all happened.

The summer had seemed to stretch on for an extra month, keeping the skies light and the air warm. Parents had no need for the autumn cardigans that lined the racks at Rock-a-Buy but, still, they bought them. Because that is what you do in Hinton Hollow. It is the same reason there is still a bakery on the high street, though bread is much cheaper in the supermarkets of neighbouring towns, and it lasts longer. And there's one pub that everybody goes to – The Arboreal – and Fourbears independent bookshop, which refuses to go out of business.

Hinton Hollow was safe. It was exactly the same as it had always been. A place preserved. Existing in a time that has long since passed.

Then I came. And I didn't care about any of that.

It took five days. Small time for a small story. But long enough to touch every path and shopfront, to creep through every alleyway and caress every doorstep. To nudge almost all who lived there as I passed through.

I'm not sorry.

The more awful people become, the worse I have to be.

It's getting harder to be me.

So, if you're not at the gym or boiling some pasta or scrolling through Netflix, it means that you didn't go. You didn't take my advice. You're still here.

And I'm still here.

That says it all, doesn't it?

You want to know.

You want to know about Evil.

THAT THING AROUND HIS NECK

You will think she is an awful mother.

You will judge her.

Judgement has been around for as long as I have, but I find, in recent times, judgement comes quicker. And it is louder now.

Little Henry Wallace is eight years old but looks like he is six. And that boy is more than one hundred miles from home when somebody finally talks to him. They ask him where his mother is. But he doesn't answer. He's not allowed to talk to strangers.

That buys him six miles.

It's another mile before anybody notices the thing around his neck.

The mother wasn't always mad. Something to do with the father walking out one day. He left a note. And some unanswered questions. Quite the scandal in a place like Hinton Hollow. It changed her. People looked at her differently.

Little Henry Wallace, on the train alone, is still. He doesn't seem frightened at all. Just doing what his mother told him. He is to sit in the carriage and not talk to anybody. Not until they ask him about that thing around his neck.

While travellers are more vigilant in current times – they are often drawn to a person of a certain age, sex and ethnicity when a backpack is left on a seat – they are not looking out for a boy, eight years of age, who only looks about six.

You may tell yourself that you would have talked to Little Henry Wallace before this point. But you, too, would have waited. It doesn't look right, does it? That's what stops you from approaching.

🌹 **A NOTE ON BYSTANDER BEHAVIOUR** 🌹
You wait because you think somebody else will help.
You hope they will.
You are scared because you don't know the outcome.
You want to feel safe.
You are the most important person to you.

Henry has an older brother. The mother didn't put him on a train with something around his neck. She kept him. She kept him with her in Hinton Hollow. One hundred and seven miles away.

And now there are four people around her son, on a train bound for the north of England and the elderly woman has grabbed something hanging around the boy's neck.

'What's this?' She is not asking Little Henry Wallace or her fellow passengers, she is thinking out loud. Then, within a few seconds, she is reading out loud.

'"My name is Henry Wallace. I am eight years old. My mother put me on this train to get me away. I can't tell you where I came from until I have had seven sleeps. Please take care of me until then."'

The elderly lady looks at the young boy's face. He's not afraid. She turns to the three passengers who have also taken an interest in the boy's welfare.

Then she moves back to the boy and turns over the brown label in her hand that hangs on a string around Little Henry Wallace's neck. This time, she reads in her head.

Please take care of my boy. I'm scared. Something is coming.

ONE THING TO KNOW ABOUT
THE ELDERLY WOMAN
She does not stand by.

RED HORNS AND A PITCHFORK

A drunken uncle at the bottom of the bed. Aeroplanes flying into skyscrapers.

G o s s i p.

Cancer. See also: *disease, politics, the Western diet.*

Being nailed to a cross. Guilt. Animals in cages.

Children in cages.

A naked nine-year-old Vietnamese girl, screaming in agony, running from her village after it is incinerated in a napalm attack.

Lies.

H o n e s t y.

Some other ways that Evil may present itself:

Propaganda. Television talent shows. Telling another person who they can and cannot love. The school caretaker who informs the news there's a glimmer of hope about finding the missing girls that he knows he dumped in a ditch four days ago.

Harold Shipman. Racism. The dairy industry.

Nine people with ropes around their necks jumping off Chelsea Bridge.

Black flames.

I LIKE IT THERE

I have bigger stories. Of course. You think of wars and famine and plagues, I was there. If you believe in Jesus then you believe I was at his crucifixion. But I am not Hitler. I am not influenza. I am not Judas. I may appear to some with red horns but I am not Him.

I do not hold the knife and I do not pull the trigger.

People do that.

My job is to caress and coax and encourage. But I am not Harold Shipman or pancreatic cancer. I do not administer the lethal dose of morphine and I do not press the button that releases the napalm.

It is people that do that.

I am not Death, with his skeletal face and robe and scythe, and his tap on the shoulder.

I am Evil.

I am the killer-clown nightmare. I am the deviant sexual thought. I am your lack of motivation, your disintegrating willpower. I am one-more-drink, one-more-bite, one-more-time. I do not stab. I do not rape. I do not pour the next gin. But I am there.

Are you still here?

This is difficult to explain with the big stories. That is why I have chosen one of the smaller ones. That's why I chose Detective Sergeant Pace.

I had been with him, watching him. Gently manoeuvring him into place. He was not inherently evil, that is rarer than you think. But, like cancer, all of you have the ability to develop into something darker and more cynical. I can bring that out in you.

I brought it out in him.

With every case, I chipped away, making him question his own involvement with each event. He blamed himself more and more with every subsequent victim he could not save. Then I appeared to him. Burning across his walls and over his ceiling. I trapped him in his paranoia and danced black flames around his life until he snapped.

I didn't fuck the wife of a serial killer. I did not handcuff somebody to a tree and leave them to die. No. Because only people can do that.

Detective Sergeant Pace left. He packed one small case and took the first train home. Home to Hinton Hollow.

And I went with him.

I like it there.

This was my second trip.

DON'T HATE THE MOTHER

Maybe her tea leaves fell in a certain way.

Or she drew the Ten of Wands in the *future* position in her *spread* – this can indicate that you are about to experience the very worst of something, you must prepare for sudden change and disruption. Or The Moon card, which can represent uncertainty and emotional vulnerability. Maybe even The Hermit. An innocuous-looking image, but can be interpreted as a harbinger of future strife and turmoil.

Or her crystal ball turned black.

Perhaps she lit a candle and somebody who had been dead for years spoke to her but only managed to reveal the first letter of their surname. Like that's a thing.

It's easy to be sceptical about all that *medium* crap but that armchair fortune-teller got one of her kids away fast. Too fast. She tied a label around the boy's neck and ditched him on a train before I even arrived in town.

The Wallace woman couldn't say for sure that it was me who was coming but she had faith in her tea leaves or Tarot cards or rune stones or whatever she used.

One of the worst things I see in people now is how easily they believe in something. Anything.

Little Henry Wallace escaped me. One boy. Gone.

One boy. Safe.

Hinton Hollow.

Population 5,119.

More than enough to infect. To test. To darken. Dampen. Devour.

So, don't hate the mother. She wasn't choosing between her children. She didn't pick her favourite to stay with her. She didn't give one away. She got in there before me. She made a decision that day so she would not have to make a choice once I arrived.

She picked them both.

She saved them both.

The locals think she is mad. Mad for the way she dresses. Mad for the way she wears her hair. Mad for the way that she talks to her children, kisses them goodbye, for the food that she buys and the hunched way that she walks. Her spirit makes them uncomfortable.

And they will think she is mad because she put her youngest son on a train by himself and told him not to talk to anybody or say where he is from until a week has passed.

I see her. I watch her.

SOME THINGS TO KNOW
ABOUT THE MOTHER
She is not mad.
She is good.
Better than them. Better than you, even.
I like her.

As long as the rest of the town behaves as I expect they will, there will be no need to taint the Wallaces.

THREE THINGS

Little Henry was one hundred and seven miles away when I arrived for my first sweep of the old town. I just wanted to get things moving before Detective Sergeant Pace arrived. Nothing fancy. A couple of disturbances, perhaps. To get the ball rolling.

It's not quite as simple as finding someone and making them evil. That is not how it works. I can't just pick a person and turn them into a killer or a fraudster or have them create Facebook. I have to massage what is already within them.

Sometimes I get adultery or shoplifting or cheating on a school test.

On that first breeze through the town I got three things:
– Some salted pork
– An angina attack
– A broken window

SALTED/ASSAULTED

This was an easy one. Just to get going.

Lazy, old Evil.

You can't be around so much death, all the time, every day, and not have it affect you in a negative way. A way that makes you act out of character. A way that shows you have become so desensitised by what you see, things you once may have found disturbing are now your normality. You may even take some pleasure in those terrible things you do in order to afford your rent.

Darren merely needed a poke towards evil.

I don't care that Darren left school at sixteen with limited qualifications. He wasn't a smart kid. He wasn't even average. He wasn't naughty or disruptive. He tried hard enough and he did as well as he could. He can read. He can write. He doesn't know how to calculate the circumference of a circle but, like almost everybody, he has no real need for that information. He works in an abattoir.

That's what I care about.

Slaughterhouses employ people of a certain psychological make-up, background and level of education. There is a high staff turnover. And a high rate of employee suicide.

It was almost cruel of me to pick Darren out.

His workmates driving the truck opened the doors and the pigs started to run out into the open. Some were clearly excited at having some space; they jumped and bucked. Some fell over and couldn't get back up. Others were injured inside the truck, while many were coaxed out with a whip on the snout or an electric rod in the anus.

This part is nothing to do with me.

This is what people do.

Darren's job is to round them inside where they are stunned, slit open and dipped into boiling liquid to soften their skin and remove any hair. He has worked there long enough that the sound of the animals squealing and crying doesn't even bother him any more. He can't even remember when it last had.

One of the pigs was acting like it knew where it was heading. It refused to leave the truck. It was whipped and probed and shocked. It ran around the courtyard, avoiding the doors that would lead to its death.

I blew past Darren. A split second. An inaudible whisper in his uncultured ear. And the thing inside him burst out.

He kicked the animal towards the door. He shouted at it and punched it in the face. Then kicked it again. He dragged it inside and grabbed a handful of salt, which he pushed into the cuts of the pig's snout. It screamed. Darren couldn't hear. He was already grabbing another handful of salt to shove into the animal's anus.

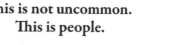

TWO THINGS YOU DON'T
WANT TO KNOW
This is not uncommon.
This is people.

He stunned the pig but did not slit it open. The conveyor dragged it to be dipped in the boiling water while it was still alive.

Only the other workers saw it. And they don't care. They've done the same. They've done worse. It is not on the village's radar. That's not what this visit is about.

Darren's actions will sink in over the next two days.

Darren is changed.

ATTACK/REWARD

There are only fifteen steps, it should not have been that challenging. And she probably deserved some kind of let-up for walking to the shops rather than driving there. Instead, wheezing-through-her-fifties Dorothy Reilly had me circling above her and sprinkling her with a taste of trouble.

That determination she had to be more physically active began to dissipate after six steps. I can do that. As I said, I can increase your apathy. She could feel her chest tightening, like somebody was standing on it.

The final nine steps seemed to stretch off into the distance, but Dorothy eating-her-way-to-heart-failure Reilly still had enough gumption to lift those weary and heavy legs, one at a time, as she plodded towards the summit. And she only stopped once more with three steps to go.

Three.

Two.

One.

She probably could have done with some respite for her efforts.

She was trying, at least. This had gone on long enough. Eating wasn't bringing her mother back to life, it wasn't tearing Bobby away from his new girlfriend and it certainly did not make her feel less alone. She was trying to change, make an effort.

Instead, she had me behind her, pulling at the elastic waist of her trousers as she tried to propel her weight forward.

Then she threw up at the top. Into the plant pot next to her front door. A neighbour's light flickered on and she rummaged quickly for her keys to avoid any kind of confrontation or concern. She pushed through the door, shut it behind her and leant against it. I was just outside, listening as she tried to draw in air with those short, sharp breaths.

She dropped both shopping bags onto the floor then collapsed to her knees. The stabbing in her abdomen forced her to hunch over. She thought it was because she had just been sick, because she felt exhausted from climbing the stairs to her flat.

It wasn't. It was because of me.

Me. And the fact that her coronary arteries were narrowed by fatty deposits as a consequence of her diet and lifestyle.

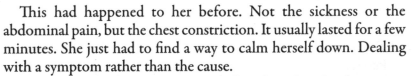

A NOTE
10,000 steps a day is not a target.
It is your minimum requirement.

This had happened to her before. Not the sickness or the abdominal pain, but the chest constriction. It usually lasted for a few minutes. She just had to find a way to calm herself down. Dealing with a symptom rather than the cause.

She sat with her back against the wall and tried to slow her racing mind. I sat with her. Her breaths grew longer and deeper, and the pain eventually evaporated.

Dorothy Reilly, sick on her breath, was thankful for the let-up, the let-off, and decided that she had earned a reward. With her back still pressed against her hallway wall, she reached her left hand towards one of the shopping bags and pulled out a bar of chocolate. She ate it and felt happiness for about six seconds.

Just one more…

I knew that a slightly heavier push from me could have more impact the next time I saw her.

SMASHED/BROKEN

Three minor misdemeanours seemed an adequate start. You can't always tell where that first touch of evil will lead a person. There are people who remain unaffected. There is something inside them that can be worked with but the good in them far outweighs the possibility of any corruption. I find this less and less. Everything moves so fast now that the general population are easy to manipulate because they're so confused by trying to keep up.

Annie Harding was at home, drinking red wine, flicking through a decorating magazine while her husband drank the other half of the bottle and zoned out to the television. Their daughter was upstairs asleep. I could have given her a nightmare but I didn't.

I sat downstairs with the Hardings for a while and watched their odd lack of interaction. The house was neat. Too neat. The furniture had mostly been upcycled with a Paris Grey chalk paint and was accessorised with a vengeance. Everywhere, a splash of colour. Each fleck, some faux personality.

Ordered.

Too ordered.

Perfect.

But too perfect.

And the room was too quiet.

So I waved a hand over both of them and waited to see what would happen. Not enough that one might kill the other or that anything would get heated enough to awaken their child. A prod. A nudge. That's all it took.

The worst I could do that night was to make them talk. Make Annie ask her husband some questions about working late and what he's been doing and where he's been going and who he's been talking to. I had squeezed her insecurities and let her run with it.

Suspicion is fun to play with.

The discussion was pointed but not heated. Annie was calm.

Too calm.

I couldn't tell where it was going to go, if anywhere at all.

Then she laid down her magazine, swigged the last mouthful of her wine, stood up, went to the front door, put on her shoes, grabbed the car keys and a large rock from the front garden and drove off.

Her husband had to stay at the house because he couldn't leave the child. But I followed her. I did not feel I had done enough for her to leave her family.

Annie Harding drove her car into the centre of Hinton Hollow that night, she waited at the traffic lights on the crossroads though no cars seemed to be travelling through in any direction, and she pulled over at the florist, exited the car and threw that giant rock straight through the glass front.

This would be the first window that she would break.

HOME

'How old are you, Henry?'

'I'm sorry but I don't know you, and I'm not supposed to talk to strangers.'

'Did your mummy tell you that? Is she the one who put you on the train?'

The kid was not scared at all. Four grown adults around him, over a hundred miles from home and he refused to disobey his mother's instructions. The old woman was not threatening but she was becoming increasingly frustrated by the boy's lack of cooperation.

'Henry,' – she kept using his name because she thought it would present a veneer of familiarity – 'I'm going to have to call the police because we don't know where you live and we need to know how to get you back. Do you have a train ticket?' Then, aside, she says, 'Why has nobody checked our tickets?' The three men shrug.

I could interject, get the old lady angry, start an argument somewhere else on the carriage to put some fear in that kid with a label around his neck but, sometimes, I watch. To see if things really are worse than ever. Part of me has to respect Henry's mother. What she did was crazy but I'm intrigued to know how it might turn out.

The elderly woman was good as her word. She borrowed a mobile phone from the man opposite and spoke discreetly to the police, explaining what had happened.

'Okay, Henry, the police are on their way. They are going to meet us when the train stops again. Are you hungry? Do you need a drink? It's about ten more minutes away.'

He shook his head but I knew that he wanted both food and drink.

THINGS TO KNOW ABOUT
LITTLE HENRY WALLACE
He is polite.
He is brave.
He does what his mother tells him.
He is so good that I have nothing to work with.

They sat in silence until the train hissed to a stop. The man opposite Henry Wallace kept his head down the entire way so as not to make eye contact with the eight-year-old, who looked only straight ahead.

'Okay, Henry, the police will be waiting on the platform.'

He shook his head at the kind, old lady.

'Come on, boy, up you get, we're only trying to help,' the man with the phone chipped in. Henry scowled at him.

The woman put her hand out as though to hold off the man. She sat back down and told them all to leave and that she would stay with the boy until police came aboard. I waited with them as people got up and moved on with their journeys. I watched her. She wanted to put a hand on the child's knee, to reassure him. She stuttered and thought better of it. It was the right decision.

I didn't like the way the man with the phone had become so angry so quickly. The boy was so fearless. I made a note to visit that man again. From the look of the blood vessels in his cheeks, it would not be too difficult for me to push him into one more drink, one more time.

When the police arrived I left them to it and went back to find Detective Sergeant Pace burning something in his fireplace and packing his bags for home.

HOW'S ANNIE?

How did I appear to you in those first three stories? Was I a pig's scream or a bloodied anus? Or was I Darren? Was Darren evil? I think, if I had not shown up, he would have treated an animal in that way at some point, anyway. I was a catalyst. Selfish, really, but this is my project.

I need a win.

What about Dorothy? To her I am breathlessness. To Dorothy, I am Type 2 Diabetes. I'm a punch in the gut and a weight on her chest. I hardly did anything to sixty-percent-body-fat Dorothy. If I pushed her too hard, we would be talking about a death on my preliminary sweep of Hinton Hollow. And that is not the plan.

Detective Sergeant Pace would not travel home to that.

And how's Annie? What do you think Evil looks like to her? How does it appear to Annie Harding? Is it an image of her husband bending the local florist over their marital bed? You think she sees this reflected in the shop window, and that's why she has to break the glass? I left before she was arrested. Before she was questioned and could come to no reasonable explanation for her actions.

Before the town began to talk.

G o s s i p.

I am not murder or adultery or stealing. I do not dishonour your father or your mother. I do not covet your neighbour's house, wife, slaves or animals. I am not a Lord's name, taken in vain. This is a list of the things that people do.

I am not people.

I am not a person.

I'm trying to explain what I am, what Evil is. Is it making you angry yet? Because, from here, things get horrible. I really get to work, go to town – so to speak. So you can turn back now and there will be no hard feelings. I know that I said it was your last chance before, but this really is it. I mean it.

Once we hit day one, you will see the evil in this world.

People die and they cheat and they kill and they steal and they break windows and they cut themselves and they lie to one another and they keep secrets and they make bad decisions and they disappear. And I move around bringing these things about. I appear as an impossible choice and a shadow and heart failure and a cloaked demon and the darkness of the woods. I can make people act in a way that does not seem like themselves, but there is no acting, the behaviour is always in there somewhere.

I don't want to ruin it. But the guy doesn't always get the girl. The sick do not always heal. Order is not always regained after chaos.

This is it.

Last chance to turn back.

Take a minute to think about it.

THAT WAS NOT A MINUTE

Still here?

Well, here it is.

Welcome. I am Evil.

And this is the small story of how I took five days to destroy Detective Sergeant Pace and the town of Hinton Hollow.

The town would recover.

The detective would not.

DAY ONE

Where you will encounter:

Childhood sweethearts
A town elder (or two)
Our detective's girlfriend
The Brady family
and an Ordinary Man.

THINGS ARE BLEAK

You may think that the events that took place in Hinton Hollow over those five days were awful. Too much, maybe. Unnecessary, even. The problem is that to be good is now too easy.

Because *average* is now good.

It used to be that you had to be Mother Teresa to be seen as virtuous. Now, another driver letting you pull out in front of them when they could have sped right past, is seen as altruistic. Benevolent. It can make your day.

The bar has been set to its lowest level.

The behaviour that was once expected is now revered. Manners and politeness and giving your time/energy/support, these simple ideals are seen as going beyond the call of duty.

You call your parents on the phone once a month, they are so pleased that you remain in contact with them. You offer a friend a lift to the airport and they don't know how to accept your offer because it is far too generous.

Average is now g o o d.

And that makes doing something good, easy.

Which makes being Evil difficult.

And that's who I'm supposed to be.

Things are bleak out there. You probably think that's what I want from the world. But, you see, with everyone so depressed and downtrodden and disconnected and disassociated, the world is an evil place. It means that I have no choice but to be worse, if only to balance things out.

INCIDENTS AND ACCIDENTS

Let's jump straight in.

There are many people to be introduced and each of them have their own part to play in the downfall of the town, but the thing people remember from that first day is that a kid died.

The incident with Jacob Brady is the part that stands out in this dark week of Hinton Hollow history. That's what they still don't talk about. There's the bench and the brass plaque and the flowers and the anniversaries and the missed birthdays.

The problem is that nobody else was there.

The two Brady boys, Michael and Jacob.

Their mother, Faith.

And the man with the gun. The Ordinary Man.

They're the only ones who can piece the parts of the incident together. They saw the same scene, the same events, from different angles, from different perspectives. They had different lives and different histories – some of them not particularly long. But I was there, too. I had to be.

I saw everything. The darkness, the innocence, the decision.

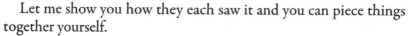

SOMETHING I HAVE LEARNED
FROM HUMANS
Your entire life can change in a moment.

Let me show you how they each saw it and you can piece things together yourself.

Once you have heard from each of them, I'll have something to tell you.

THAT DAY IN THE PARK: MICHAEL BRADY

Faith Brady stuffed the trainer into Michael's backpack and they finally left the school grounds. Nobody else was around. She carried both boys' bags in her right hand to begin with. Jacob held her left hand while Michael walked slightly ahead, his heels scuffing against the concrete of the school playground.

'Pick your feet up, Michael, come on,' his mother instructed. She wasn't telling him off, he knew that. He did as she said.

'Can we go in the park on the way home, please?' asked Michael.

'We're already running late because we had to look for your shoe.'

That was not an answer.

Michael looked at his younger brother, who took his cue.

'Oh, please, Mummy. Just for a bit.'

Faith Brady looked down at the five-year-old boy by her side, then at the seven-year-old a few feet ahead of her, and she smiled. Michael smiled back. She knew what they were doing. Ganging up on her. Running a routine to get what they wanted. She thought it was funny. Cute, even. Brothers should stick together like that. She let it go.

'Sure.' She rolled her eyes comically as though she had no choice. 'But just for a bit, okay?'

'Okay,' they responded, in stereo.

Michael didn't look back but he was smiling.

Jacob let go of his mother's hand and ran forward to catch up with his brother. His hero. Michael ruffled the back of his brother's hair when he arrived at his side, congratulating him on a job well done.

After exiting the school grounds they had a road to cross but it was residential and the flow of traffic was light at the most, particularly after the school had emptied.

'Hold hands and wait,' Faith called to her boys from behind.

The two boys did as they were told. They held hands and stopped at the edge of the pavement, looking both ways until their mother reached them and tapped their backs to signify that it was safe to cross.

Once on the other side, the boys released their grip and sprinted to the wooden fence on the outskirts of the park.

'Not too far ahead, boys. Wait for me.' Their mother was still smiling. Her sons didn't *always* get on, that's normal, but she loved their bond, and Michael was a real help with Jacob on those days when everything seemed too much.

'Maybe we should ask if we can go in the woods,' Jacob suggested in a hushed voice. Smirking. Scheming.

'What about the monster?'

'What?'

'You don't know about the woods monster? Maybe you're too young,' Michael teased.

'Ha ha, Michael. There's nothing in the woods. Nice try.' Jacob looked over at the trees and didn't know whether he believed himself or his brother.

'Ask Mum,' said Michael, then he ran off further down the path.

Jacob stared at the woods for a moment and told himself that there definitely was no monster.

Michael stopped suddenly on the stony pathway and crouched down to see something on the ground more closely. A large black beetle lying on its back, its legs in the air, motionless.

'Jacob, come and look at this,' he shouted.

His little brother came bounding towards him with all the enthusiasm of a puppy.

'Ah, Michael, that's cool. It's massive.'

'I know. Touch it.'

'No way.'

'I've already touched it,' he lied.

Jacob squatted down next to the beetle and pointed a finger at it. Edging it slowly closer so that he could prod it with his fingertip.

Just a little closer. Go on...

Michael was ready to scare his brother. Prepared to make a sudden movement or noise as he got a few millimetres from touching the dead bug. He did this kind of thing to him all the time. He was smiling.

'Michael,' his mother called out in a shriller-than-usual voice.

Mum, you've ruined it now, Michael huffed.

He turned around to see what she wanted. Jacob turned around a fraction after his older brother.

There was a loud noise and Michael heard a thump before his brother's legs seem to lose all strength and give way beneath him. A man in a long dark coat was running towards the woods. His mother was screaming, the most deathly, terrifying howl he had ever heard. She was running towards her youngest son, then dropping to her knees and scooping him into her arms.

The man with the gun reached the line of trees in the distance and looked back over his shoulder. Michael's mother did not notice; she was too busy rocking Jacob and holding her hand to his chest.

Michael saw. In shock, he sat down calmly on the grass a few metres from his wailing mother and bleeding brother. He didn't say anything. His eyes were open but he wasn't really looking at anything. Not in the real world.

He was in shock. Yes. But he had deliberately withdrawn inside himself. There was only one thing in his mind to focus on now. And that was the face of the man who had killed his little brother and would rip his family in half.

SURFACE TOWNS

I've witnessed many deaths.

Have you ever noticed that it always seems to be the funerals that bring people together? Feuds can be put on hold for the duration of a ceremony, grudges can be forgotten while a body is lowered into the ground. It's the weddings that cause all the trouble. The pressure of perfection. That burden just isn't present at an occasion where the guest of honour is decomposing in a box.

It is death that unifies people.

Almost everybody in Hinton Hollow thought it started in the park with the Brady kid, that he was the first victim of that dark week in their town's history. Initial insights suggested an outsider, a freak occurrence, some maniac passing through their sheltered idyll. Perhaps a tearaway from a neighbouring village. There always seemed to be a little more *noise* coming from Roylake. Perhaps a disgruntled resident of Twaincroft Hill, a marginally more affluent village to the east that boasts luxury riverside homes but a high street in decline, overrun with estate agents. Isn't it always one of those *surface* towns where nobody is a suspect and everyone should be?

They were wrong.

This didn't begin with the death of young Jacob Brady. And Detective Sergeant Pace was not an outsider; he was born here. His GP was Dr Green, like so many of the folk that still live in Hinton Hollow, the ones that stayed while that young overachiever was tempted by the pulsating thrum of city life. Pace was a stranger, sure, but he belonged.

It didn't begin with him, either. It opened, as is so often the case, with love and that most formal and public declaration of commitment. The entire village was invited and all were involved with the proceedings in some manner. From the florist arranging gerberas, to the bakery stacking tiers of sponge, to the mediocre local cover band who refused to improve with rehearsal.

But Oscar Tambor went missing, and for two days, nobody took his fiancé seriously. Because a five-year-old boy was killed that day and that case dominated. That is what clawed at the members of the Hinton Hollow community. That is what dampened spirits and wrung hearts. It wasn't Liv Dunham pestering the police about her absent husband-to-be. They didn't believe that Oz Tambor would simply walk out on Liv this close to the big day. But it seemed even less likely that he would have been taken.

It's the weddings that tear people apart.

NOT THAT KIND OF PLACE

He romanticised London inordinately, despite the necessity to escape. That is one of the reasons he sat facing backwards on the train. He wanted one last look, to hold it in his view for as long he could, drinking in the place he had loved before everything turned to shit.

Detective Sergeant Pace was apprehensive about returning to

Hinton Hollow. It had been years and, though he knew the village and its people would not have changed significantly since the date of his departure – it's not that kind of place – he understood that he was never getting back to being the person he had once been; the person they all thought they knew.

The train journey seemed to end too near the point at which it had begun. They were less than an hour from London, and Hinton Hollow was the next stop. It wasn't even necessary to change lines at any point. Hinton Hollow has a quaint but historic station on a route between two major cities. Pace wondered whether it would have made a difference to his life if he'd simply commuted. He could have worked in the city that had attracted him in the first instance but had an escape at the end of the day. The security of his hometown.

He still would have seen those people jump from Tower Bridge, though. And no amount of freshly baked bread or civic conviviality would have been able to make him forget.

The woman opposite him had distractingly smooth legs. *City legs*, he thought to himself. Nobody in Hinton Hollow could possibly have legs like that. Her hair was straight, mousy, stroking lovingly at her thin shoulders. Her gaze was fixed on the pages of her book as Pace's was on her calves. It was a novel he'd never read but instantly dismissed as some unrealistic crime story. He breathed in that reality and it was nothing like the books or movies portrayed.

Pace flicked his eyes up but the woman was still engrossed in her fiction. She was either reading slowly or pretending to read because she hadn't turned the page in the last ninety seconds. He noted that.

I was next to her. Gently caressing her interest so that she would play with him, tease him.

Pace looked out of the window to his left; the buildings had been getting smaller the further he journeyed from London. Even the large telecom company buildings surrounding the last train stop seemed humble in comparison to the adopted home he was running from. He had reached the part of the journey where the concrete gave way to the crops and waterways that led to Hinton Hollow.

He imagined the playful fake reader opposite him was commuting to the city at the other end of the line, and for a moment he thought that she was lucky.

Facing the capital also served the advantage that he could watch where he was coming from. He'd notice if someone or something was following him. He could keep an eye on his own shadow; looking out for the darkness. He had no idea I was right there with him.

The carriage gently urged his travel companion's chest forward as the train began to slow for his stop, Pace took the opportunity for one final innocent dalliance with the sultry pretend bookworm. He wasn't going to see legs like that for a long time. And he wouldn't get a smile like that from a stranger in Hinton Hollow. Because nobody was a stranger.

I put a hand on her back and she produced a coquettish little smile, a knowing look. And Pace put his hand on his right trouser pocket to check for his phone. He'd have to speak to Maeve at some point and some point soon. She'd be wondering where he was. He knew how she would react to him leaving so suddenly. They'd woken up together the previous morning.

Detective Sergeant Pace could have his back turned to his hometown all he wanted. And he could tell himself that it was for his own protection – that he was preserving the people he had known and edged uncomfortably away from. But all it meant was that he couldn't see what was coming.

HEADING OUT

I was all over town. Everywhere. If you are still here, listening to my story, you will also be everywhere.

Try to keep up.

Liv had been talking to Oz Tambor about Maggie when Detective Sergeant Pace's train pulled in to platform two: there are only two platforms at Hinton Hollow train station, one heading to London, the other to Oxford. Maggie was the daughter of the flower arranger who had prepared the wreath for Oz's father's grave four years previous and had woken up that morning to a broken shop window.

'She's certainly got her mother's eye,' Oz had proclaimed, feigning enthusiasm for the subject once again.

He wanted to marry Liv Dunham. He loved her. He had loved her for years. They'd become a couple in secondary school and neither had strayed in that time. Neither had lived. It was an inevitability that this day would come. They knew it. The whole town knew it.

OTHER THINGS THE WHOLE TOWN KNEW
Oz and Liv were perfect for each other.
Their love was so true it was almost enviable.
They were stable.
They were predictable.

Oz was posturing, rattling out some line he'd picked up from Liv and her friends about the *autumnal colours being reflected in the flowers* and how *it would be a continuation of the forest*. Bringing the *outside to the inside*.

He said these kinds of things because he knew it made Liv happy to think that he wanted to be involved in the planning. She had her notebook and her stickers and her colour-coding; he had his nodding agreement.

What a team.

SOMETHING THE WHOLE TOWN DIDN'T KNOW
Stability can leave a person yearning.
I can work with yearning.

Oz was aware that the series of planned moments were important to her, that the spectacle of that one day had become her drive. It was now a project. Though Oz was not hugely interested in what the ceremony looked like, it was important to him because it was important to Liv. All he wanted to do was marry the woman he had always loved.

They had agreed to take the week off work so neither would be stressed with the balance they'd have to perform in the run-up to their vows.

It hadn't worked like that for Oz.

Everything had become about the wedding. It's all they talked about. It was only day one and he had already started to miss the office.

'I don't think it's worth worrying about now, Liv. Everything is in hand. We should just enjoy this week together.' He bit into his toast, the crunch punctuating his sentence.

'I know. I know. You're right. But I'm only planning on doing this once, I don't want to drop the ball now.' Liv was standing waiting for the kettle to boil while Oz sat at the kitchen table. She took half a slice of his toast and started to eat it. She'd always done this, claiming she wasn't a breakfast person; a morning coffee would suffice. It didn't annoy Oz that she did this. It was another of her quirks that made him smile and give that *every single morning* shake of the head.

'I get it.' He swallowed his food before continuing. 'The whole town is in on this; they won't let anything go wrong. Nothing will go wrong.'

A conscience would have made me move on to one of the other 5,019 people left in Hinton Hollow. If, in any way, I had found them interesting, I would have danced my way around somebody else's kitchen that morning. But this was too perfect to pass up.

The kettle clicked as though it had an idea at that moment. Liv poured the boiling water onto her two spoons of instant coffee, stirred and took it over to the table, where she sat with her relaxed husband-to-be and the gnawed triangle of toast she, apparently, didn't even need.

'Surely it's not against the rules to talk about our *preward*?' She smiled. She even winked. She always winked when she said *preward*. Another of her quirks. Making up words. She was an English teacher at the same school she had attended as a teenager, the same school where she had first got together with Oz.

The school that Jacob Brady would never be old enough to attend.

The honeymoon was to be their reward for the hard work of organising a wedding. Their combined wage wasn't high so they had chosen Paris and Provence. A simple trip. Liv wanted Paris due to its literary and romantic connections, then a move on to Provence would provide the quiet relaxation and seclusion expected of such an excursion.

Both places began with P. It was their reward. Hence, *preward*. The word usually made them both grin like idiots – small town, small things – but not on that day. Oz's eyes simply widened and they both stopped chewing.

I found this irritating. It made Liv come across as sickly. And false.

So I danced. I danced around that kitchen and covered it in worry.

Looking back, it's easy to say that the quarrel that followed was, perhaps, where this all began. Oz had never been abroad; he'd hardly been out of Hinton Hollow, so he'd never thought about filling in a form and sending off his birth certificate. Liv was annoyed because it was the only part of the organising that he was solely responsible for: ensuring he could leave this country and enter another.

'I'm heading out for a bit.'

That was the last thing he said to Liv before he was taken.

Before that, he'd told her to calm down. That these things can always be resolved. He'd told her there was an office you could go to in Wales that would sort it for you on the same day. She argued that he was confused and was thinking about the process for obtaining a driving licence.

It all went nowhere and became too much.

My real work had begun.

But it hadn't all started with this confrontation about a passport, as you know. Nor did it begin when he walked out of their front door.

And it would not end on day five when that sixth bullet was due to hit Oscar Tambor in the face.

THAT DAY IN THE PARK: JACOB BRADY

You can't blame Michael. He's just a kid. And he'll be blaming himself forever. Sure, if he hadn't misplaced his shoe then they all would have left school at the correct time, the Bradys would have been a part of the crowd.

So, blame the man with the gun.

Blame the mother.

Blame me.

It wasn't Michael's fault.

And that is not how Jacob saw it at all.

On his hands and knees, five-year-old Jacob Brady scampered around the dusty floor of the changing area, checking beneath every bench, hoping that he would be the one to save the day and find his big brother's missing trainers. Yes, they argued sometimes and they fought about the most insignificant things and they could've shared a little better at times, but Jacob thought that Michael was *the coolest guy in the whole world.*

He never got a chance to tell him that.

They shared a bedroom. Even though there was another room upstairs in their house. Their mother thought it would be a good idea to keep that other space as a playroom. Somewhere that didn't necessarily have to get tidied at the end of the day. Full of toys and paints and superhero costumes.

Their bedroom was smaller than the playroom. They had bunk beds. Michael got to sleep on the top bunk because he was older, but Jacob didn't mind. His brother always hung over the edge at night to talk to him when they were supposed to be sleeping or being quiet. Jacob loved that about him.

'Here's one,' Jacob shouted, proud of himself. 'I don't know where the other one is yet.'

'It's okay. I've only lost one. The other one is in my bag. Well done. You saved me. I thought Mum was going to kill me.' And he did that thing where he ruffled Jacob's hair in a playfully patronising way to disguise his affection.

Jacob didn't mind. He kind of liked it. He knew what it meant. That's why he never flattened it back down.

'Look, Mum,' Michael said, 'Jacob found it. Under the bench.'

Jacob was still smiling.

'Well done, Jacob. Shall we get going now, we'll be the very last ones out today, I think.' His mother started towards the door and the boys followed.

Outside, they ran through a well-rehearsed skit that they used to get their mother to do what they wanted. Michael told his brother once that she couldn't refuse politeness. Especially from Jacob.

She was a sucker for her hazel-eyed angel.

It worked. Jacob's mother agreed that they could cut through the park and play for a bit before returning home for dinner.

'You will eat everything on that dinner plate.'

The boys didn't really pay attention to that last remark as they ran off down the path.

Then Michael was saying, 'Go on. Touch it.'

And Jacob knew his brother was trying to scare him.

Go slowly.

Jacob Brady didn't even have time to be frightened. He turned around to see why his mother was calling Michael and was assaulted by the sound of the gun firing. Before he even reached the top of his flinch, his heart had been ruined.

There was no time to spot the horror on his mother's face and no time to turn to his big brother for help. He didn't even get to touch the beetle.

No time for goodbyes.

No more bad dreams to wake Michael up with in the middle of the night or ideas for new games they could play in the day.

And no opportunity to tell his big brother that he was right about the monster in the woods.

INVISIBLE SHADOW

Pace wanted so much for it to feel like home. To make his time pass more simply. He had missed Hinton Hollow in some ways and hoped he'd somehow find a place to slot back in.

He recognised all the town landmarks immediately. It's possible to see right down into the heart of the village from the station platform. A straight line that leads to the crossroads, where life glides along, holding hands with decency. Unlike the city, where existence seems to thump around corners, scratching at weakness and temptation.

His shoulders slumped slightly but noticeably as the train pulled off, taking the attractive book woman away to Oxford. Pace thought about turning back for one last shared glance. I held her interest in that flirtation until she was out of sight before switching my focus back to the detective. I let go of her and she went back to reading.

The mobile phone vibrated in his pocket.

Maeve.

They needed to talk. He wanted to. So that he could explain his departure, so that he could explain what had happened on that last case. But not at that moment. Not right then. He'd just got back. He was Hinton Hollow. Maeve went back into his pocket and through to voicemail.

With his back to the track, an invisible shadow stretching out behind him, Pace started his walk into town. He could see RD's Diner at the bottom of the sloping street, bustling with trade, its glass front still in one piece – for now – still displaying the dated, American diner-style signage; it offered free refills at a price any of the coffee chains would charge for half a biscotti, if you ate it outside.

The police station was close but Pace was hoping he could avoid that for as long as possible. They were expecting him. To them, it was a temporary transfer, to Pace, it was a sabbatical. A break. An escape. He wanted to announce his own return. To spread the word himself, on his terms. The darkness I had brought to his town was moving slowly but deliberately, even downhill, but, in Hinton Hollow, word has no choice but to travel fast.

His plan was to hit RD's place first, sample some of their legendary homemade cake and drink coffee – no refill necessary on this trip. He'd move on to the corner grocery and pick up a few essentials, give the locals a few minutes for g o s s i p. That would only leave Rock-a-Buy, across the road on the adjacent corner, where Mrs Beaufort would undoubtedly already be expecting him. Then he would go to work.

It was important to visit the old lady, because if she welcomed him back with open arms, he knew the rest of the village would fall in line.

That was Pace's plan.

Mine was to chaperone him around. Make sure his paranoia did not flare up. Not touch him. Keep the shadow off his feet and flames from the walls. Let him meet the various pillars of his former home and remember them as they were.

Then I would change them so that they were unrecognisable even to themselves.

SAMARITAN

Maeve Beauman woke up alone.

After her husband had died, this had been a novelty. Something new to embrace, to try. But getting together with Pace had changed that. She'd convinced him to stay the night before, but he had sped out the door the next morning to work on his case. He hadn't told her too much about it but she'd seen the news. A suicide cult with no leader. People getting together and jumping off bridges to their deaths.

She hadn't asked him too many questions, she didn't want to push. It was the same with their relationship. She liked him more than he liked her. That's what Maeve told herself. So, the things she often wanted to say or feel, she held back.

But she needed to hear his voice.

She called. It went to voicemail.

'Hey, it's Maeve. I just wanted to check in with you. Make sure everything's all right. I'm guessing you're busy. I've seen the news so you must be tied up with all of that. Looks crazy, I don't know what this world is coming to, you know? Why would someone do that? I suppose you're more used to it than I am. Look, I just wanted to talk. You left kind of suddenly. I know you had to get to work but we had such a great night before that. We were close. It's just hard for me. I guess I'm being overly sensitive. Felt a bit like you fucked and ran. I know that's not it, obviously. It just would've been nice to have a little more of a morning together. Difficult, of course, with everything going on. I totally understand. I just ... Can you just call me when you get this, please? Let me know how you're doing. Maybe you'll be around later? Anyway ... call me back or drop me a text if you're tied up. Speak soon.'

The message was relaxed. Maeve was not.

More feelings locked away.

It would not take a lot from me to open up the detective's girlfriend. To make her true.

CRUMBLE

The bell tinkled lightly as Detective Sergeant Pace pushed through the café door. There were locals in there but not enough to make it uncomfortable when the faces turned to view the dark figure that had rung his entrance. RD spotted him immediately, his eyes smiling a greeting that was gratefully received.

RD was in his early sixties. His hair had not thinned but was short, silver and parted neatly to the right. He'd added a few pounds since Pace had seen him last but that was to be expected in a place like this. It was a wonder he wasn't bigger.

Just one more slice...

Pace had only ever known him as RD but some of the older folk occasionally called him Rick. There was a rumour that it wasn't his real name, he just wanted to sound more *Yankee.*

Another way that evil may present itself: *rumours.* See also: *Chinese whispers, viral marketing* and *self-promotion.*

'Well, look what the cat dragged in,' he announced, resisting the urge to deliver in some kind of Southern American drawl.

His wife emerged from a door at the back as though that was her cue. RD ran the room, she ran the kitchen. And she *was* big. Just the way RD liked her. He always said, 'Never trust a thin chef, cos they ain't tasting what they're serving.'

'I guess you want one of those fancy city coffees with the frothed milk and whatnot? I've got black and I've got white.'

'Black's fine, RD. Thanks.' Pace smiled, puffing out a sigh that was disguised as a laugh. I hadn't seen him like this. Relaxed. Relieved. Resigned. Everything was as he had imagined it. People were pleased he had returned, yet reticent about the suddenness of his arrival.

Pace ignored another vibration in his pocket.

RD spoke as he poured. 'It's been a while. This a flying visit?'

His wife tinkered in a glass cabinet behind the counter before emerging next to her husband with a plate of something that looked like a plum crumble and smelled like Christmas. She nodded at Pace before disappearing back into the kitchen.

I could have made RD's old football injury start to throb. I could have constricted the airways of his obese wife until she blacked out. I could have danced black flames across the walls and crushed Pace's spirit. But I did none of these things. I swivelled on the diner chair and let it play out.

'Longer than that. Back for a little while but couldn't really put a time on it.' The idea of moving back there turned his shoulders cold and he shuddered.

'Missed us, did ya?' RD produced a fork as if by magic and placed it next to the plate of pie.

'Something like that,' Pace replied, eyebrows raised.

'Well, that's on the house. Welcome back.'

'RD. There's no need, honest—'

'It's on the house.' He raised his right hand slightly as though pushing away the idea that Pace would be paying. Then he, too, sloped out the back. No doubt to discuss things with his wife and call Mrs Beaufort to prepare her.

The plum crumble made Detective Sergeant Pace lean back in his chair and look at the ceiling towards a God he had lost faith in. It was that good.

The Christmas smell was cinnamon and the spice complemented his coffee.

It was perfect.

It was Hinton Hollow.

He had hoped to announce his return on his own terms but it was obvious to him that they'd been waiting. The cinnamon had given them away. And the fact that all the diners had resisted the urge to even look at him. This was some kind of clandestine welcome-home party and everyone was invited. It made him feel less nervous about visiting Mrs Beaufort, at least.

Pace finished his crumble, downed the last of his cheap, delicious coffee then stood up, deliberately scraping his chair against the floor so that he could watch nobody acknowledge the noise for fear of giving themselves away.

RD came from behind the counter to collect the empty plate.

'Good?'

'My compliments to the chef. I'll definitely be back.' Pace held his hand out and RD took it in one of his own giant, grey bear paws.

'And I will happily accept your money next time, detective.'

Pace nodded and left. He pulled the door shut, the bell rattling behind him like some Pavlovian cue for RD's customers to finally relax.

I tapped a few of the locals on their shoulder as I left. One of them was Darren from the abattoir. He had ordered two bacon sandwiches for his breakfast. When they arrived, he pulled out the meat, licked off the sauce and ate only the bread.

He was different.

NOTHING IMPORTANT

Maeve second-guessed herself the moment she hung up.

She'd given too much away.

She'd seemed desperate.

Faking it through.

'Me again. I knew it would go straight through to voicemail. It's okay, I'm not a psycho. It's just that my secretary reminded me about a thing I'm doing after work, so I won't, actually, be getting in until later. Maybe you'll just want to crash after a day like today but I should be back no later than eight, if you wanted to stay with me again. I have wine. I would've eaten but there's plenty for you if you need something. Either way, it's fine. Just drop me a message. I worry about you, that's all. Okay, well, hopefully see you later. I have to go to a meeting now.'

 TWO THINGS ABOUT MAEVE
She did not have to go to a meeting.
She always feels alone.

You cannot fix falsity with deceit.

PASSING THROUGH

Pace watched a young mother jaywalk with her toddling child. Traffic was light and there was no real need to walk up to the crossing and wait for the green man to start flashing. She looked left, right, then left again before dragging her son across at speed.

Pace did the same thing.

He looked left, right, then left again. A black BMW eased through the village centre crossroads from the direction of neighbouring Roylake. Just passing through.

He crossed. His eyes focused on Mrs Beaufort's shop. And he looked back over his shoulder. *Right at me.* The paranoia was still there. But he saw nothing. *Not that he really knew what to expect. A darkness? A sensation? Cold? I blew in his ear to unnerve him and disappeared across the other side of town, leaving him alone.*

I would come for him eventually. Of course I would. I came for everybody that autumn.

I watched.

And I waited.

And I went for Oz Tambor.

THAT DAY IN THE PARK: FAITH BRADY

A mother always knows more.

She sees more.

The world certainly looked different through the eyes of Michael and Jacob that day. To them, it was unprovoked and instant and it ruined the chance to play in the park or touch the beetle. For Faith Brady, it was a moment that would last forever. It was the end for more than just the youngest of the Bradys. And it started long before a shoe had been misplaced.

A woman in her husband's office had picked up the phone, informing Faith that Owen was in a meeting for the next couple of hours. She didn't bother leaving a message. She didn't have anything significant to say; she just wanted to kill some time that day while walking to the school to pick up her two sons.

She hung up, wondering who that woman was at the end of the phone. Owen had never mentioned her before. She wasn't even sure what she would have talked about on the phone. Nothing important had happened that day. It was her regular routine. Drop the kids off, wait for the online food shop to arrive, drink coffee, get all the sports kits from the weekend into the wash, pick the kids up and make dinner.

She flicked the oven on and set it to pre-heat so that she could throw something in when she got back.

It would be on all night. Cooking nothing.

She collected her youngest son first and asked him the obligatory questions about his day at school, though she was less interested at the start of the working week than she was by Friday, usually. He told her he'd done *nothing*, anyway.

She held his hand because there were a lot of people about. Mothers. Fathers. Children taller than Jacob. They headed to the other side of the building, where Michael and the older kids were waiting. Jacob smiled when he saw his brother; they both looked like their mother when they were happy.

'Ready to go?' she asked Michael, but it wasn't really a question, it's what she always said.

R o u t i n e.

What she meant was, 'Come on, let's get out of here.'

The oven was on.

Michael was looking through his schoolbag. Faith was feeling impatient. She thought that he had drawn her yet another picture that she would have to keep for longer than she wanted – before surreptitiously disposing of it on recycling day.

'I can't find one of my trainers,' he informed her, worried but apologetic.

She was, at once, relieved it was not another scribbling for the fridge door but irritated that he had been so careless.

'You haven't had them that long. When was the last time you saw them?'

'I wore them earlier when I...' He trailed off but something clicked. 'The sports block. They must still be in the sports block. I had them last in the changing room.'

He started to head off in that direction.

'Wait, wait. We'll all go, eh?'

They found it underneath the bench where Michael had changed after sports. The boys turned the task into some kind of treasure-hunt game that Jacob ended up winning. They were always doing that kind of thing. Making everything about play. Faith stood in the background, allowing them to complete their mission. She watched and wished she still had that kind of energy.

Looking at the two of them, how they interacted and looked out for one another, she was proud of them. And herself for being a major part of the way they had been brought up. She mentally patted herself on the back; they were growing up nicely. They were polite and thoughtful.

They were Hinton Hollow.

Her friends said that boys were worse when they were younger and that girls were harder to deal with once they hit their teenage years. Faith hated those kinds of generalisations but hoped this one was true.

I shouldn't have any issues with these two as teenagers, she thought.

Well, maybe Jacob has the potential to get a bit rowdy.

He was holding the missing trainer aloft as though he had dug up a golden nugget. Michael took it from him and rubbed his hair with a rough affection that she melted into.

It was her favourite age, so far.

Every age had been her favourite.

The boys thought they had tricked her into agreeing that they could play in the park before going home, but Faith didn't really mind. It was easier when they wanted to play with each other; it's when they wanted her attention that she wondered what she had done before her caffeine dependency.

Her sons ran off ahead. Michael found something on the ground that he was showing to his younger brother.

Faith put the bags on the floor and checked her mobile phone to see whether Owen had called back despite her not leaving him a message. There was nothing, of course. He was still in his meeting, talking in numbers and acronyms, while a man emerged stealthily from the woods, undetected by a single member of the Brady family.

The phone went back into the pocket of her jeans, the ones that accentuated the shape of her thighs. She picked up the boys' schoolbags once more, one in each hand, but was stopped before she took a step.

A large hand reached around her from behind and covered her mouth. Something hard, cold and metallic poked into the nook at the top of her neck. She had never seen or felt a real gun in her life but she knew that is exactly what was pressed into the ridge of her skull.

'Don't scream. Don't you dare.' His voice was a whisper. Calm and venomous and full of promise. He pronounced the 't' in *Don't* but still he sounded local.

Fuck. She cursed in her head. *What is this? The boys haven't even noticed.*

Run, boys. Get out of here. She screamed with her eyes.

But she knew not to make a sound otherwise her sons would be picking parts of her skull and brain from their hair.

'Very good.' He spoke slowly and clearly but it all happened so fast in Faith Brady's mind.

What do you want? Don't rape me, her mind raced.

Michael, take your brother and sprint.

His hand smelled like cigarettes overpowering peppermint. They were not sweaty or clammy despite the situation. He was not afraid. Nor was he nervous, though he had doubtlessly seen many a mother pass by that he could have pounced on and subdued.

Why me? I'm nobody, her brain rattled.

Her eyes widened like they were shouting at her sons because her voice had been taken away, but Michael and Jacob continued with their fascination with whatever lay dead on the pathway ahead; another of their games.

Their stupid fucking games.

The gunman's breath tickled Faith's right ear. It felt so wrong. So sinister. His hushed tone informed her that everybody dies but she did not have to. He explained her situation and why she was standing there with a weapon pointing at her brain, and she couldn't believe the words he was saying; she could not fathom that something so evil existed. That someone so unhinged and deplorable would ever find their way to Hinton Hollow. To that park at that time with only that family around.

She cursed the quietness of the town.

'Are you ready?' he asked, and she sensed that he may have been smiling behind her.

Time sped up.

He momentarily released the pressure of the pistol on the back of her head and the strength of his grip waned.

Michael. Get Jacob out of here. Her stare burned but the air outside had started to cool.

She remembered their births, both very different, and the many milestones of their lives that had led to that point; Michael, being older, having slightly more of those moments and the added bonus of doing everything first.

In her mind, she screamed his name. To warn him. To get him to hold his brother's hand like he always did, and run, not looking back until they reached the front doorstep.

But that is not how she said it.

'Michael.'

He turned to look at his mother.

The gun appeared over her right shoulder and fired at the other boy. The small one with the hair that was sticking up at the back. The one who was always smiling and falling for his brother's pranks. The one who wouldn't get to touch the beetle.

Her ears were ringing from the explosion next to her head.

And it was all she heard until the detective with the shadow pulled her away from her dead son.

She would never tell anyone what really happened that day in the park.

YOU DIDN'T CALL

Jacob Brady was not the first victim that week in Hinton Hollow. The most shocking. The most public. But it didn't start there.

Oz Tambor arrived at his mother's house. It was a four-minute walk from his own front door but he felt it made more of a statement to Liv about his intentions that he had taken the car. He was being proactive. He was getting things done. This would all be resolved very soon. She could relax for the rest of the week, which would mean that Oz could relax. She could steal toast and combine unrelated words. And he could nod and love and not talk about weddings.

Oz was never able to park in his mother's driveway. There were only two spaces and they were occupied by her Micra, which she never used – people walk in Hinton Hollow – and his father's old Jaguar, which his mother refused to get rid of. It had sat there for four years, since his dad had passed. Of course, she'd thought about selling it or giving it away, she even came close once, but Oz offered to give it a clean – on the outside, at least – and she had regressed into nostalgia. He parked up the street and took the long walk up the front garden to the house.

OSCAR TAMBOR'S FATHER
If he ever scored a bargain, the item he
purchased cost him 'a threepenny bit'.
One summer, he rang the bells at the
Church of the Good Shepherd every Sunday at noon.
His favourite song was 'Night and Day' by Cole Porter.

**When Dr Green told him he was ill, he refused any treatment
and he never mentioned it to his wife
or son until he was weeks from the end.**

Then Oz knocked on the door, not realising that I was watching his every move.

'Hello, dear. I wasn't expecting you. You didn't call.' May Tambor was surprised to see her son standing on her doorstep in the middle of the morning. It wasn't the correct decorum for a visit. Luckily, she was already immaculately dressed and made up. She'd been up for hours and had made cookies, there was some bread baking in the oven; Oz could smell it from the doorway. It smelled like *home*.

'Sorry, Mum. Something's come up. Nothing major.' He kicked his feet against the doormat and his mother moved aside to let him in.

'I'll put the kettle on.'

He waited in the lounge for his mother. The curtains were almost drawn. It was cave-like, but a strip of sun shone through the gap, picking up particles of dust on its way to the carpet, though May Tambor had polished all the furniture that morning. It shouldn't have been so bright at that time of year but summer was still holding on to Hinton Hollow with the tips of its fingers.

'Here you go. A cup of tea. If you'd have warned me that you were coming I could have made the biscuits earlier, they're still cooling.' May just couldn't let it go that he hadn't called ahead.

Oz ignored her prod. That was the best way to handle her. She'd forget it eventually.

**SOME THINGS TO KNOW
ABOUT MAY TAMBOR
She never blamed her husband for the way
he had handled his illness.
She wished she'd had a little more time;
she missed him.
She was waiting to see him again.**

They spoke about nothing for a while. Oz asked what she'd been up to, though he knew it was trivial. Cleaning the house that didn't need cleaning. Baking food that wasn't going to be eaten. Reading books that should never have been written. Worrying.

Then she brought up the wedding.

'Plans all sorted by now, I imagine,' she asked, though it was more of a statement. 'Exciting.'

'Well, that's why I'm here, actually, Mum.'

May Tambor placed her cup on the saucer that was resting on her occasional table with the upturned romance novel. She was expecting bad news. The wedding was off. He'd left Liv.

If only it had been that simple.

'The preparations are fine. Everything is sorted, but you know Liv.'

She did know Liv. She had known her since she was a teenager. She loved Liv. Her husband had been particularly fond of her. She was a local girl. She'd always been pretty. And smart, though she preferred to play that down, for some reason.

'So what is it?'

'The honeymoon.'

'What's wrong? You need some money?' May had money and no mortgage. And she wasn't spending much because she hardly left the house.

'No. No. It's all covered and paid for. Thanks. It's just ... I haven't sorted out my passport yet. Have you got my birth certificate? I think Liv is about ready to kill me.' He smiled but it was nervous.

May Tambor didn't say anything. She stood up from her chair, walked over to the cupboard beneath the stairs, got down to her knees and clicked open the metal box where she kept her important files.

When she returned to the room with a piece of aged paper, folded into perfect thirds, she did not sit down in her seat but next to her son on the two-seater. She looked him in the eyes and poked the birth certificate in his direction. Oz grabbed it between his thumb and forefinger. He pulled but she did not let it go.

'Mum?'

She looked straight into his eyes. She didn't blink.

Oz pulled again and she released the document. She had spent the last four years trying to let go of her husband and now she was relinquishing her son. That's how it felt to her, anyway. Liv would look after him now. Who did May have? What would she be left with?

That's the problem with small-town life. Sometimes you never leave. And that shit can get you killed.

They talked seriously for the first time in years. They needed this talk. They should have had it a long time ago. It was a relief for May but the absolute wrong time for Oz.

He left the house in a hurry, shutting the door himself while his mother remained in her dimly lit lounge. He thought about Liv. The birth certificate was in his right hand. He was getting things done. He should call her. Tell her that.

There hadn't been enough time to dial her number.

The door slammed behind him.

He took one step forward.

And was taken.

WHOLE GALE/STORM

When it's not the people, this is how it works.

Think of it in terms of the Beaufort Scale, where zero is complete calm, five is a fresh breeze, eight is a gale and eleven is a violent storm.

0. Calm. I am watching you. Stalking you. Understanding how you operate. Discovering what evil may lie within you. You appear to other people in the way that you always have. Your inner turmoils remain your own. I have not even had a look inside for myself.

3. Gentle breeze. It's a test. A taster. I want to see how you react to a gentle prod from Evil. This may result in a broken window or tightness in the chest or throwing a handful of salt into a pig's

bloodied face. This is not how people always see you but it may be a part of who you really are.

6. Strong breeze. Your moral compass is twisting, trying to locate which direction is north. What is right? What is wrong? Just one more drink/pill/biscuit/fondle. You post a lie on social media. You are not yourself. You start to lose who you are. See also: *becoming who you really are*. Many people do not return from this.

9. Strong gale. You are angry. You wonder what it might feel like to thrust a knife into someone's stomach or whether you could push them over the edge of a building. What would it feel like to fire a gun? You may think that other people deserve harm because you feel personally hurt about something. You want to inflict suffering. Making somebody else feel worse will make you feel better.

12. Hurricane. Mania. Chaos. A mother makes the worst decision of her life. Selfishness. Sexual promiscuity. Depravity. Taking someone's life. A child, perhaps. A family. More. Breaking *all* the windows. Animal cruelty. Torture. Six bullets to the face. Plunging an entire community into a haunting, distorted darkness that is either the deepest depression or the absolute truth.

This is the part where you give in.

Because you have no choice.

When Oz Tambor was taken, in order for the plan to work, to take away the sunshine and light that had lingered in Hinton Hollow for too long, I had to create a storm.

A GOOD BOY

If you're worried about Little Henry Wallace, please don't. Not yet.

They took care of him.

Two uniformed police officers – one male, one female – entered the train carriage and they teamed up to find out what the hell was happening. The sight of them altered the passengers' moaning-at-being-held-up into whispering g o s s i p. See also: *the damage of conjecture*.

The female constable was responsible for trying to get Henry to talk, to gather some information about where he was from and what brought him so far from home. But the boy did not give over any particulars. He was a good boy. He did as his mother told him.

Her male counterpart took on the elderly lady. She explained how the boy had been in that very seat when she got onto the train. He was next to a woman in her late thirties for about forty minutes. She spent most of the time on her phone while the boy was quiet.

'The only thing that struck me as odd was just how well behaved her son was while she buried her face in one of those ghastly devices.'

'You didn't think of saying something when she got off? She didn't say *anything* to the boy as she left?' He had so many questions: *Could she have been the boy's mother? Do you remember which station she got off at? What did she look like?*

The elderly lady was the one who had acted. Eventually. She read the label around his neck. She alerted the police. She waited with him until they arrived.

She cared.

But what she did should not be seen as *good* – the bar is set too low – it was normal. Typical. Ordinary, even. To me, it is nowhere near enough. It is unexceptional.

She felt beaten down by the officer's questions and let down by her lack of action.

G u i l t.

Nothing came from the questioning. The boy gave zero and the elderly lady had played her part in the pantomime.

'What will happen with the boy? Is there anything I can help with?' She was desperate to atone for her mistake, though it would not have made a difference if she'd called the police straight away, the boy was out of Hinton Hollow and that was all that mattered.

'You've done enough,' the policeman offered. Then added a 'thank you' to try to take out some of the obvious bite in his tone when the old woman's shoulders slumped even further. 'We can take it from here. We will make sure he is fed and watered and has a roof over his head while we get to the bottom of this.' He forced a smile. She didn't buy it.

So, you see, you don't have to worry about little Henry Wallace. Not yet.

He was with the police.

And, as long as he kept his mouth shut for seven sleeps, he wouldn't be able to go home. Home was about to become a horror story.

SOME WAYS IN WHICH EVIL PRESENTED ITSELF*

An old woman lying on her side in a shop.

A boy lying on his back in the park.

Another boy rocking back and forth with his arms folded around his knees.

A mother. Screaming.

A man in the boot of a car.

Another mother lying in the hallway with her brains spread across the wall.

A detective smoking.

*After Oz Tambor was taken.

THAT DAY IN THE PARK: ORDINARY MAN

Oz Tambor was supposed to be his last.

That was the only part he had to plan.

Before, there had to be the mothers. The research. Though he hadn't really planned anything. This was not thought through at all, in fact. It was the start of a rampage. Passionate, yes. But without pattern. The kind of case that has detectives frustrated by its apparent randomness. A killer who is not looking for notoriety, is not trying to be caught. They are not looking to outsmart the investigating officer.

They are doing it for themselves.

Or worse, they don't know why they are doing it.

Worse still, they don't realise.

Sometimes, an ordinary man can simply snap.

He lit a cigarette and waited in the woods near Hinton Hollow Primary School for the children to be dismissed and collected by their parents. He didn't think that the puffs of smoke acted as a beacon to his whereabouts. The dangers of a naked flame in a wooded area had not crossed his mind. He had felt empty since stepping past that very first tree. There was a great nothingness there, and that complete detachment was exactly what he needed to commit the heinous crime he had in his mind.

He wanted to kill another mother.

He wanted to be right.

The first twenty minutes, he viewed children up to nine years old running from their parents towards the grassy area, or racing to the swings for a two-minute play. He saw a father ask his daughter what she did in school that day and her enthusiastic response with regards to mathematics.

There were scores of mothers who used this time to engage with each other rather than their children, and there were slightly older kids who walked home alone or in small groups.

None of them were right.

The monster in the woods knew that he could not walk out into the middle of a crowd and start shooting.

Don't blame Michael.

He needed strays. Stragglers. The lame and wounded antelope that can't keep up with the herd. The weakest link. He heard the woods whisper to him.

You are a predator.

It wasn't the woods that whispered. It was me.

Then nobody came for three minutes. He was left with the trees

to think. But he couldn't think in there. It would get in the way of
what he had to do.

Michael Brady rounded the corner, followed closely by Jacob,
smiling in that way that he did.

He had a couple more minutes left to play with his brother, to talk
with him, laugh and get teased by him. He didn't know that he was
about to die. But neither did the man in the woods.

Faith Brady was not far behind. Her legs were long and lean,
hugged by dark but faded denim. He stared at her thighs, then her
calf muscles. There was an excitement there that he hadn't felt before.
But he wasn't himself – I'd made sure of that.

This is how the shadow saw her.

Instinctively he moved to the right as the boys powered ahead of
their attractive but dawdling mother. He didn't notice her doting
eyes because he didn't care. He just wanted to get behind her. He
wanted to blow her brains out.

The man with the gun was not thinking about the children she
would leave behind.

He just wanted to be right.

Faith dropped the bags by her sides, fished around the tight jean
pocket for her phone and that man, the one who wanted to shoot
her in the back of the head, emerged from the trees unnoticed. He
was safely behind her now, out of her line of vision, he could've
grabbed her but he waited until she picked up the bags again. She'd
have her hands full. He didn't even look at the boys. He thought they
were safe.

This is it.

'Don't scream. Don't you dare.' He whispered in her ear the way I
had whispered to him. And he pushed the gun hard into the back of
her head. The bullet aiming somewhere between her cerebellum and
the occipital lobe.

She was rigid but he sensed that her arms were shaking, still
clinging to the boys' bags.

She'll take the bullet. She will.

The unknown shadow moved his mouth closer to her ear.

'Shh. You don't have to die today, miss,' he told her, but she didn't believe him. He was looking at her sons.

Faith Brady's eyes began to water. She didn't want to die but she didn't want this man to know that she was scared.

He knew she was scared.

I knew. I know fear. See also: *the dark, propaganda, lack of education, social-media likes.*

'Which one is your favourite, miss? Which boy would you keep with you?'

Trying not to make any sudden movements that might make him pull the trigger, Faith Brady shook the back of her head across the width of the muzzle of the gun.

'You are running out of time. Call the boy's name you want to save.'

She won't choose. She is a mother, the man told himself. And he believed it.

She will take the bullet.

I've been around for too long to have had his level of belief in humankind.

THIS IS WHAT I THINK
You are doomed.
There is no way back for you.
The fight is there but you fight for the wrong things.

He held her for a few seconds more, allowing her to mull over his ultimatum. She wasn't trying to fight him off. He loosened his grip of her mouth. He thought she would say nothing. That she was taking one last look at the boys she had given birth to. The good boys. The ones who would be no trouble as teenagers.

Well, Jacob had the chance to be a little rebellious.

And she had known Michael longer; he was more of a person, somehow.

Why was she reasoning with herself?

Then Faith Brady shocked the man with the gun. She called out. But it wasn't in warning. She was not telling her sons to run. She was not saying one last goodbye or stating that she loved them both.

She was choosing.

'Michael.' She spoke loud enough that Michael could hear her. She only said his name but what she was really saying was, *I choose Michael.*

I choose myself.

And she knew it was wrong immediately.

But it was too late.

Michael turned around first to answer his mother's call and the Ordinary Man with the gun knew the child that she had chosen. He moved the gun from her brain and pointed it over her shoulder at the boy deemed *not enough* and he shot that poor child in the chest.

At least he'll never know why, something whispered.

Incidents and accidents.

The man ran back towards the trees, the shriek behind him curdling the cooling Hinton Hollow air. He panted as though ready to cry but as soon as he was within the woods, his emotion evaporated once more. He looked back over his shoulder at the boy she'd chosen and he didn't understand how she could do such a thing.

She's his mother.

She's a monster.

She is to blame.

The woods were not what they seemed.

He could have stayed there and been safe. The woods held in the darkness. They protected it. They knew things.

But he hadn't done that. He'd shot the Brady child, run off to the woods, walked a path straight through and emerged on the other side where his car was waiting.

He couldn't believe she had said that.

He couldn't believe it was true.

This was Faith Brady's fault. That ordinary man was not to blame. He'd need to try again.

WHAT PEOPLE DO

Now you've seen it. From every angle. From everybody who was there. The ones who lived. The one who died. The one who fucked everything up.

So, let me tell you this:

I did not go anywhere near Jacob or Michael. Children give me very little to work with. Jacob had no political stance. He had not developed the true capacity for hatred. He had a Daniel, a Xi-Shu, a Kasheeni, a Naveed and a Roisin in his class at school and, if you asked him who was who, he would choose the colour of their jumper to tell them apart.

I can't do much with innocence.

There was something with Michael. He had a couple more years under his belt. He'd been picked on at school from time to time. He'd been chosen last for sports. He'd been reprimanded by teachers. He'd seen the way his parents were, sometimes, with Jacob and had interpreted it as preferential treatment, which manifested itself as resentment.

But not enough for me to use.

And I didn't want to.

The woods, the man in the woods, they were different. He harboured a lot of anger. Those trees held in the darkness. There were secrets in there. There was history. And there was fear. That can all be used. It was used. To rile him. To give an ordinary man some courage to commit a heinous act.

I do not choose the act.

That is what people do.

I am not an ultimatum. I am not a gun, nor am I the bullet that pierced Jacob's chest.

The boys were love. They were learning. They were ruffled hair and enquiry and practical jokes and teasing and laughing and running so fast that their legs couldn't keep up.

And I do not choose them. But I cannot be held accountable for what happens to them and I can not be forced to care.

And here is the only thing you need to know about what happened in the park that first day in Hinton Hollow: I did nothing to Faith Brady. I did not touch her, whisper to her, brush past her shoulder or run fingers through her hair. I did not tap into the evil inside of her. I did not pull on her inner struggles and force her into anything.

I was with Mrs Beaufort.

Faith Brady came to that decision all by herself.

A strange man snuck up behind her while she was loaded up with schoolbags and coats and the shoe her son had lost that afternoon. She was smiling and doting over her two sons playing so contentedly together. She was exhausted but happy.

And I did nothing to her.

I watched.

I was watching everyone.

He came out of the woods, put a gun into the nape of her neck and gave her a choice. One of the two people she had brought into the world could die. Right there. In front of her eyes. Or she could take the bullet and let them live.

Her. Faith Brady. Exhausted. Unhappy. Failing at life and love. No sex drive. No ambition. Her priority in life had boiled down to one thing: she was a mother. Everything was about being a mother. That's what she told herself.

I did not go near any of the Brady family that day. My energy was with the ordinary man and the woods.

Faith Brady chose to kill Jacob all by herself.

I do not kill children.

I do not choose to take one brother away from another.

People do that.

Faith Brady did that.

And she deserved what was coming in the following days.

JUST UNDER A MILE AWAY

Mrs Beaufort was the town grandmother. The heart of Hinton Hollow. She ran a small store in the centre of the high street called Rock-a-Buy. It sold second-hand kids' clothes, toys and accessories. She had lived there her entire life. A part of Hinton Hollow lore.

And I was with her when it happened.

I helped her to hear.

Mrs Beaufort had not heard about the Brady shooting when I visited her shop. It had only just happened. But she *was* Hinton Hollow. Any change in its landscape, any alteration in its culture, any fluctuation in its mood, she felt it first.

When the bullet passed through Jacob Brady's sternum, it echoed through the town.

And Mrs Beaufort heard.

Another three bags of unneeded clothes had been donated to Rock-a-Buy. The shop had not changed its name since the days when Mr Beaufort ran it as a record store over thirty years ago, when the *Rock* in Rock-a-Buy was associated with guitars and beards and long hair rather than cribs and cardigans.

The elderly lady, pushing steadily towards her nineties, had seen the men and women of Hinton Hollow as young children buying the latest Simon and Garfunkel record, lowering their heads as they purchased something by The Who, hoping 'Mr B' would not mention it to their parents. And she had witnessed these same kids flicking through the winter coats section of the new Rock-a-Buy, hoping to snap up a bargain for their own children.

Mrs Beaufort took the first item from the top of the donated black sack. She sniffed at it to determine its cleanliness then folded it neatly and placed it on the desk next to the cash register. She repeated this for every item in the bag, sorting clothes into different piles according to age, sex and season. Anything deemed to hold odour was thrown on the floor next to her sensible orthopaedic shoes. She would take the pile home and wash it that evening.

There was only one customer in the store at that time. She knew them. Of course. They exchanged pleasantries when the new mother entered, but Mrs Beaufort waited before engaging in deeper conversation, as she always did. Everyone talked to Mrs Beaufort, though, whether there was a queue of people or not. She was kind and selfless and respected in the community. And loved. Nobody had ever been witness to her wicked tongue and her spite. She herself had never experienced it. But Hinton Hollow was not yet fully changed.

Then, just under a mile away, somebody was shot in the park.

The gunshot was loud but not enough to be heard in the centre of town.

Not behind the double-glazed windows of Rock-a-Buy.

But, it was that exact moment that Mrs Beaufort held her hands to her frail chest, dropped to her knees, then fell sideways onto a pile of unclean baby clothes.

When the heart of Jacob Brady gave way, so did the heart of Hinton Hollow.

TWO ROADS INTERSECT

The wind pushed through the leaves and soothed him; I made sure of that. He forged on through the shaded copse and thought only of what lay ahead, not what had already passed. He didn't care.

The gunman, once so ordinary, was confused at the outcome, but that merely made him more determined. He got into his car and drove it down the hill to the crossroads. A mother was kneeling somewhere behind him, rocking a dead child in her arms.

He told himself that *she* had killed that boy. Not him.

Not us.

He turned the ignition of his unremarkable car, a silver Volkswagen, and it started first time. The engine did not sound hurried. He did not screech the tyres and power away from the scene of his crime. He popped the car carefully into gear, checked his mirrors for other vehicles then released the handbrake before slowly crawling away down the hill, checking his mirror again with a quick glance as he pushed it into second.

He should have been feeling some kind of remorse but he, too, was in a state of shock at the outcome. It was a different feeling to when he had shot the first mother.

He never gave her a chance.

She didn't have a choice.

The man who had shot Jacob Brady stopped at the top of the hill where two roads intersect. He'd be long gone before the authorities were speeding through this crossroads, one ambulance heading up the hill towards the park by Hinton Hollow Primary School, the other whizzing in the direction of the town centre to Rock-a-Buy, where a beloved local woman had collapsed in pain.

Turning right would have led the gunman back to May Tambor's side of town. To the left was Mrs Beaufort. The road straight over led to something new. An area untapped, not yet touched by the malevolence creeping steadily around the back roads of this preserved-in-time Berkshire town. There he would find another school. Another mother. Another opportunity.

Another choice.

It would bring him a step closer to that final bullet meant to erase Oscar Tambor.

And lead him out of Hinton Hollow. Back into the light.

He looked left. There was no traffic.

He looked right. There was no traffic.

That ordinary man drove straight across the intersection.

He had a question for one of the mothers who lived over there.

METROPOLITAN LIFE

Two calls came in at the same time.

'Shot,' the paramedic said to his female colleague. 'A shooting. In Hinton Hollow.'

The sirens blared.

The lights had been used before, but it was rare that an ambulance made a sound in this town. Emergencies were few. A generation of expected heart attacks and strokes but nothing that severe. Drunken antics were the height of crime, usually.

'Fuck. And they think it's a kid. It can't be. That can't be right. I can't even believe that somebody has a gun, let alone that they'd shoot a fucking child with it.'

They were silent for a moment. Running through the residents of the close-knit community they had both been a part of since birth. Their collective unconscious flicked through a handful of unsavoury characters, nobody too pernicious – the anti-social farmer, the quiet widow, Mrs Wallace and all her voodoo – but their directories both stopped at the same point.

Detective Sergeant Pace. Word had already spread. He was back.

He had only just returned to Hinton Hollow, and now this had happened. They told themselves there couldn't be a connection. They were thinking of anything other than the prospect of a dead child to attend to. Of course, they knew Pace, everybody did, but they hadn't seen him since he left for a more metropolitan life. And he was unrecognisable from the boy that once kicked a ball against the wall or rode a bike down the street. They'd need an introduction, a reintroduction, but that would only confirm their suspicions.

They would see a blackness.

The sinful dark purple of a troubled shadow.

I'd make sure of that.

The ambulance tyres screeched as they whipped around the corner, passing over the spot where a murderer had sat only minutes before, deliberating which way to indicate. There was no traffic for the paramedics to worry about.

Then they reached the woods.

'You'll have to drive up the kerb.'

'I know. It all seems a bit much. Like all we've done is arrive sooner to a dead kid. I don't want to do this.'

They were scared. Afraid the child may still be alive. That they would have to fight, knowing the outcome was inevitable.

There was nothing for them to worry about.

Jacob Brady wasn't coming back.

He was too broken.

HOME

This was not why he came back to Hinton Hollow. This was exactly what he had been trying to escape. Instinctively, Pace peered backward over his shoulder before rounding the corner, hoping to catch a glimpse of the horror he felt had followed him.

Maybe then he could stop it.

But there was nothing there. Nothing that could be seen. Because I do not want to be seen. Evil cannot be seen. It can only be felt. Though some have suggested the smell of sulphur on occasion.

Pace pulled the front of his coat together as he picked up speed on the hill. At least he'd have other officers in the city, to bounce ideas off, to share thoughts and theories with, concerns. He tried so hard not to think of that. In Hinton Hollow, he was alone, and his memories were the worst company. The things he had witnessed could not be unseen.

And that thing he had done.

He'd imagined a return to his childhood home would be an escape. Hinton Hollow is so separate from the depravity of the world. A place whose values and ethics had been preserved in time, unspoiled.

He'd been wrong.

Pace snapped himself from the melancholic reverie that had become almost routine over the last few months and picked his feet up a little, accelerating towards the bleeding boy and the woods. Running in the opposite direction of the man he should have been chasing.

Welcome home.

Hinton Hollow. Population 5,118.

TWO PEOPLE

You see what I'm saying now, don't you?

She picked one of her children.

How am I supposed to exist in this world when a mother would choose to live and let her child die? Let her child get shot in the chest. Let her other child witness it.

Let me watch as it all unfolds.

How am I supposed to preserve the balance of evil when people will do something like that, all by themselves?

Jacob Brady. The little boy with the hole in his heart. He saw the man who killed him. But the last thing he remembered was his mother's brown eyes, so big they seemed to take up her entire face. She was crying. She called out Michael's name and both boys turned around from the dead beetle. Jacob was a little slower. Even though Faith Brady had called his brother's name, Jacob could see that she was only looking in his direction.

He didn't even have time to be confused about that. The bullet hit him and he dropped to the ground. And then his mother rocked him and pushed his chest, trying to plug the blood that was pouring out of the wound. He knew she was desperately trying to put things right; to turn back time and fix it all.

But there was no turning back.

What had she done?

She had broken his heart.

And then put a bullet through it.

SOMETHING UNFATHOMABLE

Holding her hand over the hole was not going to help.

The paramedics could have told her that.

But they didn't.

Her five-year-old son had a bullet through his heart and putting pressure on the wound was not going to save him. She'd had that chance and she blew it.

She didn't even react when the sirens came blaring around the corner, the blue lights rotating on the roof of the ambulance. She just continued to rock back and forth on her knees with her youngest child dead in her arms, her eldest son sat cross-legged ten feet to the side on the grass, not speaking. Not moving.

In shock.

The paramedics could have told her that, too.

But they didn't say anything. This was a mess. The aftermath of something unfathomable in a town like Hinton Hollow. People were standing agog on their doorsteps in front of doors they had been known to leave unlocked. Some had entered the park, what was now a crime scene, and didn't know what to do. Should they have stopped the distraught mother from rocking her injured child? There may still have been enough time to rescue him from an eternal darkness. What about the other boy? Was he hurt? Why was he not moving?

They knew who *she* was, of course, from the town meetings and the school playground and her lack of attendance at the Church of the Good Shepherd.

Faith Brady paid no attention to the gathering crowd. She couldn't hear the hiss of confused whispers. She didn't even know how much time had passed since Jacob had dropped to the ground and his cowardly murderer had fled without even glancing back at the circus left behind.

She knew Michael was near her but she didn't want to see him right now. She hated him for being alive.

What was Owen going to say?

Her hand was soaked in the blood of her innocent, oblivious son. But she pressed harder against the deep black circle that had spread out into a pink, deathly rose against the white, long-sleeved hooded jumper that Faith only bought from Mrs Beaufort the week before.

Between the redundant male and female paramedics, ahead of the spot where she continued to rock and press and curse herself, a figure emerged. She noticed him because, at first, she saw the man with the gun. A long-coated silhouette. She held her breath.

It couldn't be.

As he neared, his frame became bigger than the light behind him and his face came into focus. Stubble washed his skin to a bluish grey; a cigarette hung from the right of his mouth. His hair was ruffled and dark and his walk was languid and almost uncaring. Detective Sergeant Pace had never really fit in to Hinton Hollow. People said he was too urban. There was a darkness around him.

Faith Brady continued to rock her half-sized cadaver, ignoring her other son, who had not seen the man approaching, and she waited for him to speak.

He introduced himself to the paramedics initially.

It's not him, she told herself.

That's not his voice, she confirmed to nobody who was listening.

I'd know that voice.

A member of the onlooking horde offered Faith's name to the detective.

'Mrs Brady?' She just looked at him. Rocking. 'Mrs Brady, you are going to have to let the paramedics take a look at your son.'

She heard him. She shook her head.

'I'm sorry, Mrs Brady, but you have to let them do their jobs. They just need to take a look at him.' His voice was calming and reassuring but she still did not budge.

No one will touch you again, Jacob. Over and over.

I'll protect you this time. I promise.

The detective's tone changed.

'I'm afraid you don't really have a choice. We have to check the boy.' Pace stepped forward and took her wrist in his giant hand. She felt his strength immediately and tried to grip her son harder but lost out. This was the second time a man had overpowered her today.

The paramedics stepped in as if the move had been rehearsed. They took Jacob and laid him on the ground. Faith screamed and kicked out. Detective Pace said *shh* in her ear repeatedly. It was the same thing that other man had said before he shot her son. But Pace's words contained no venom.

It's not the same voice. It's not. Faith Brady had to convince herself of that fact so that something made sense.

She relented and fell, dead-weight, back into the willowy detective. He held her up and they both watched as the paramedics performed needless tests on the boy with a space in his heart where his mother's love should have been. The male paramedic gave a sideways glance to Pace and shook his head, his face screwing up to say that it was obvious.

'He's gone, Mrs Brady. I'm sorry. I know this is difficult but I need to know exactly what happened here.' Her weight became too much and she dropped to the floor between the feet of the detective.

Pace moved around to face the mother, crouching down to her level.

'What happened here? Who did this? Which way did they go?' Each word was spoken clearly, exaggerated enough for a lip-reader to understand from a hundred yards away. He didn't blink. He didn't inflect his words with any emotion.

He wanted answers. He wanted to catch this bastard. He pushed her and pushed her, hoping to snap her from the haze she had dropped into when the bullet hit and the killer ran off.

But she was unresponsive. She appeared to be in some kind of waking coma. Pace saw her mind was active, probably running through the incident again and again, wondering what she could have done differently.

He wanted to tell her that he understood. That she would have to learn to think about other things. All the time.

'Mrs Brady. I need to know exactly what happened here today.' Pace held her steady by her shoulders, resisting the urge to shake her.

'Do you know the person that shot your little boy?' That was most likely.

Still nothing.

Why didn't she answer? Pace thought she might be protecting someone.

He stood up. Faith Brady rested in a defeated heap on the ground at his feet, watching the female paramedic prod parts of the son she was supposed to protect with her life.

Detective Sergeant Pace thought about changing tack. Being comforting. Telling Faith Brady that it was not her fault. But something stopped him.

I stopped him.

Faith Brady was as silent as the boy sat a few feet to her left.

She couldn't tell him the truth.

She couldn't tell anyone. That truth would have to stay between her, the ordinary man, the woods and me.

She needed more time.

GETTING ANSWERS

Detective Sergeant Pace was angry.

Detective Sergeant Pace had been touched by Evil.

Detective Sergeant Pace was contagious.

He knew he should not have manhandled Faith Brady like that but he didn't care much for protocol when it stood in the way of getting answers. It may not have been the way that things were done in Hinton Hollow but he had been away. He had witnessed a world where neighbours do not talk to one another. Where independent, family-run stores like RD's were obsolete and in their place were chains of soulless companies with no personality, no individualism. Nobody knew your name or that you would love the plum crumble.

They rented their houses. They wanted more than they had. They couldn't settle. They moved around. But Pace was home now. And he had brought me with him.

Jacob Brady looked beyond resuscitation but Pace had seen things. He had watched men with cuts across their throat refuse to die. He had seen women overpower men a hundred pounds heavier than they were because they refused to lie down and allow death to take them.

It had changed him. That was part of the reason he had returned to Hinton Hollow. A small part of why he came home.

And now this.

Pace and I squeezed past the mother you are judging. She was no longer on his mind.

'I'm Detective Sergeant Pace. Are you hurt in any way?'

The boy shook his head.

'What's your name?'

'Michael. Michael Brady.'

'Okay, Michael. I know you say you haven't been hurt but I'd just like to let the medic check you over while we talk. All right?' He beckoned the female paramedic to join us.

Michael dipped his head in a nod that was somehow sad and courageous at the same time.

'Now, I need your help. Can you tell me what happened here today?' Pace's tone was friendly, non-threatening. The boy was doing him a big favour. He was being brave.

'It all happened so fast. But I can try.'

The sun, on day one, plummeted behind the houses the Bradys were heading towards before it happened. The shade hit the woods and the wind shook the trees. And the leaves sounded like they were laughing.

FOR BALANCE

I could see it.

Too frightened to cry, Michael had slipped into a quiet state of disbelief.

I could feel it.

Telling himself that this wasn't happening. That it wasn't real. A game. Just one of their silly games. Michael had not been as successful as his mother at fooling himself.

He had repeatedly pinched the skin on his left forearm with his right hand, starting lightly with his fingertips, eventually getting to a place where his nails were digging into his flesh like pincers and drawing blood. The paramedic spotted the wounds while she examined the boy who had lived to tell the tale.

Part of it.

He had merely been trying to wake himself up from the nightmare.

'We had just finished school and Mum had picked us up. Like she always does. I couldn't find one of my trainers so we were late getting out.' He seemed too coherent for a seven-year-old who had undergone a stressful and shocking event. He seemed removed from it, somehow.

 SOMETHING ABOUT CHILDREN
Children are brave.
It comes from their innocence.
Not knowing the horrors the world has in store for
them means that they have less to fear.

ADDENDUM
Bravery can also be achieved through experiencing horror.

'So there was nobody else in the park with you?' the detective asked.

'I don't remember but I don't think so. Everyone left before us. If I hadn't lost my shoe...'

'You're not to blame for any of this, Michael. None of this is your fault.' For the first time, Detective Sergeant Pace was forceful in his tone with the child, the way he had been with the boy's mother. 'What happened when you got to the park?'

'We were just walking home like we always do. Jacob was holding Mum's hand but I was in front of them. Then he came next to me because there was a dead beetle on the floor and it was massive.' Michael stretched his thumb and forefinger apart to indicate the size. 'We were looking at it. Then Mum called my name. I turned round. There was a man behind her and he shot a gun.'

Michael looked over at his brother then and tears filled his eyes. He started to cough and they fell down his cheeks.

'You're doing really well, Michael,' Pace reassured him.

'Then the man just ran off through the woods and Jacob was lying on the floor. And Mum was really screaming a horrible scream.' He took three consecutive, deep inhalations trying bravely to get through his story, but it had brought too much back. He was no longer detached from his surroundings. Everything became loud. Light became unbearable. The paramedic gave Pace a look that suggested he should pull back a little; the boy was, understandably, not dealing with this.

'Thanks, Michael. That's enough for now. Are you okay to stand up? It might be an idea to take a seat in the back of the ambulance, eh?'

'Is my mum going to be okay?' he asked gallantly, with genuine concern. Pace nodded reassuringly, though he suspected otherwise.

It's the kids. I can't help but like the kids. And there was something about the Hinton Hollow children – Michael Brady, Little Henry Wallace – they were so brave, so thoughtful. A pureness that not even I could corrupt. Nor would I want to.

Good people make my job easier.

The better people are, the less evil I have to be. I will always be there, a necessity, for balance, but with things the way they are, I have to be worse. People make me worse.

The paramedic wrapped a blanket around Michael's shoulders as he sat looking out of the ambulance's rear doors. His younger brother had been covered over, his mother still refused to look at her living son, and the detective was completely still, strong-looking. He was surveying the scene, maybe looking for clues, but his eyes fixed on the wooded area that the attacker had run to after firing his gun. I made him do this. I stroked his paranoia just enough to let his focus wander to the trees.

Michael stared at his mother, hoping that he would catch her eye at some point.

What did that man say to you? he was asking.

Why did you let him kill Jacob?

When the dust settled and reality returned, there would be more questions for Michael Brady. He was the only person to have seen the killer's face and lived.

But, to the boy of seven, he had just looked like an ordinary man.

YOU HAVE TO SLOW DOWN

Mrs Wallace had been right.

Something was coming.

The effects of the events I had brought about travelled faster than a slanderous rumour across that town. Mrs Beaufort's right shoulder rested on a white baby-grow, aged six to nine months.

It needed a wash.

Her eyes never closed. She was nowhere near ready to go but her thoughts were not with herself. They were not even contemplating the prospect of joining Mr Beaufort. She knew that she had one customer in her store. She knew the woman, Katy Childs; she had known her since birth. She knew her parents. She knew her mother, sweet but firm, and her father, more firm than sweet. Too firm.

The Rock-a-Buy owner knew the hardships that Katy had endured, and emerged from them a stronger person, but she didn't want her to have to suffer the anguish that would come with a closed-eyed Mrs Beaufort.

So she fought.

Mrs Beaufort battled against everything her body was telling her.

The pain in your chest is severe.

You can't go on like this.

You have to slow down.

Her mind took over. It told her that she *was* Hinton Hollow. If she went, the town would be lost to the gloaming. She had to protect it. So she battled the cramps in her heart and she forced her eyes to remain open while she waited for an ambulance. She did it for herself. She did it for the new mother, panicking in the shop with her baby swaddled close to her breast. But mostly she did it for the town she loved, the place she had always called home.

The shop-front window turned dark and Mrs Beaufort's open eyes widened further. Katy saw fear.

I thought the old lady saw me.

'You hang on, Mrs Beaufort, I think that's them.'

The shadow cast across the front of Rock-a-Buy soon turned blue with the rotating lights of the paramedics' vehicle. Mrs Beaufort allowed herself a split second of relaxation and closed her eyes gently while Katy peered helplessly out of the window, waiting for help to burst through the door.

It arrived in the form of two men dressed in green overalls, their names Velcroed to their chests; one of the men was carrying a red box that he hoped he wouldn't have to open. He hadn't wanted to be responsible for bringing Mrs Beaufort back from death.

He didn't have to.

The warmth of the room was sucked out of the open door.

Something *was* there.

DAY TWO

Where you will learn more about:

A broken family
A missing lover
The local police department
How Evil moves
and a cat killer.

THE WALLACE WOMAN

'Mum, this is weird. It doesn't feel right.'

Mrs Wallace was waiting for the kettle to boil.

'Mum. Mum. Mum, are you listening?' Her eldest son was still in his pyjamas. He should have been at school but they were all closed in the local area that day on account of the Brady incident.

Mrs Wallace poured the boiling water over her tea leaves.

'I'm listening,' she finally answered, bringing her cup to the dining table.

'Henry could be anywhere. He's too small. You should have sent me. It doesn't make any sense. I'm worried.'

She knew that look.

'Don't get upset. It's going to be okay.' She moved her body closer to his, put her hand on his back and rubbed to reassure him.

To the majority of Hinton Hollow residents, Mrs Wallace was known as 'The Wallace Woman'. Scorned by a husband who upped and left her to raise two kids, the rumour was that it had sent her mad. To anyone that took the time to speak with her, to listen to her, they were the fortunate few who knew that it was quite the opposite. The situation had focused her, made her more attune to her surroundings.

Normal human insecurities would give me something to probe should I want to have an effect at some point, but she was as honest as a child.

'But how can you be sure? How do you know?'

'Because I feel it. Just as strongly as I feel that something is here right now. It's all over the village. But we were prepared. And we are safe. And Henry will be safe, too. Okay?'

He nodded, managing to hold back the tears and be brave like his little brother.

The Wallace Woman did seem a little mad. I could understand why she was viewed that way in Hinton Hollow. But, to me, the most important thing was that everything she was telling her son was right.

'Mum, this morning has felt so long without Henry here and not going to school.'

'I know and I'm sorry, darling, but it's going to be a very long week.'

PIG/CAT

The cat jumped up onto the kitchen counter and Darren saw a pig. Its tail in the air, content and purring, wanting food, I held the abattoir worker by the shoulders and I shook him.

To that mallet-wielder, the rasping vibration of feline affection sounded like the squeal he heard most days when unloading the truck.

Darren was making himself a sandwich. Cheese. There was ham in the fridge but he still couldn't bring himself to eat it. He shredded some lettuce and squeezed mayonnaise over the top. The cat walked by and added a hair.

To that skull-cracker, the graceful movement across the work surface of his only companion looked like the bucking of a cow, jumping towards the freedom of outdoor space or chasing a farmer as its calf is ripped away.

Darren pulled the hair from the mayonnaise, wiped his fingers against the back pocket of his trousers and watched as his pet dropped to the floor and started to wind around his legs.

Another nudge from me and the cat's tight anus stared at his owner. Darren tasted salt. He flashed to the fury he'd felt two days before. The wet nose and whiskers beneath him appearing like a bleeding snout.

I prodded him again.

That flesh-boiler crouched and stroked along the back of his animal then picked it up. Unlike the pigs he electrocuted or the cows whose heads he would shoot a bolt into, the domesticated animal he had in his arms had a name; they'd lived together for six years.

And, somehow, that made it worse when he gripped the cat's neck in one hand, held it down on the surface where he'd just made a sandwich, and stabbed through its abdomen repeatedly with the knife he'd used for butter.

There's a great deal of force required to pierce through flesh with a blunt knife. The kind that can only come with great anger, when a storm is brewing.

 ## AN OBSERVATION ABOUT PEOPLE AND DEATH

The execution of an adult can, somehow,
be understood and reasoned.
The death of a child can be heartbreaking but rationalised.
The massacre of livestock can be largely ignored.
Yet, the killing of a pet — particularly a dog or a cat —
is devastating. An unforgivable act.
It is evil.

I find this distinction between living things perplexing.

Darren was getting worse. He was not acting like himself.

Or, perhaps he was finally letting out the person that he had been holding down inside.

That anus prodder.

That pig kicker.

That salt shover.

That slaughterer.

A LITTLE TIME

Let's talk about the Bradys, shall we?

I wanted Faith Brady to die. If someone had to, I wish it had been her.

Save the children. There's more good there. And more good means the evil in the world can be less evil. I could rest a little.

When I watched that man come out of the woods and push a gun into the back of her head, I wanted the bullet to exit through her face along with fragments of her skull and obliterated parts of her brain. That way, I would know that the world was not entirely doomed. My small story would have been a lot smaller. That's the way I want it.

Jacob should have been there. And she should have been a hero. A mother.

She was neither of those things.

The father didn't know the truth. He wasn't there. So he thought that he was the weak parent.

'Come downstairs. It's no good to be up here alone. You can't get through this by yourself.' Owen Brady pleaded with his wife, trying to be the stronger half of the relationship, though the redness of his cried-out eyes betrayed his want for that role.

It was the second day in a row she had done this.

He couldn't get through this by himself.

'I'm not good to be around, Owen. Look what happens.' She didn't even glance at him as she spoke. Perched on the edge of the bed, her chin almost resting against her chest, she stared into the palms of her cupped hands. They were empty but it seemed that she was holding something only she could see. Her straight, auburn hair obscured her usually pretty face.

'Don't talk like that, Faith.' He knew he needed to be supportive, understanding of her situation, but he couldn't stand the self-pity. Nobody was blaming her for what had happened. It was a freak occurrence, they'd thought. Hinton Hollow wasn't the place that this kind of thing happened.

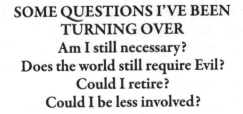

SOME QUESTIONS I'VE BEEN TURNING OVER
Am I still necessary?
Does the world still require Evil?
Could I retire?
Could I be less involved?

ONE MORE THING
Maybe it's harder to be Good?

'Why not? It's true, isn't it? That's what you're thinking, what everybody's thinking.'

'Nobody is thinking anything.' He looked around the room as if waiting for approval from somebody. 'Just come downstairs. If you want to talk, we'll talk. If you don't want to talk, we won't. Just ... please.'

He felt pathetic. Like he was the one that needed the support. She had seen it happen. She was there. She'd held Jacob, dead in her arms. Owen had been at work. In a meeting. A pointless fucking meeting about nothing that mattered when he should have been protecting his family from this hurt.

Faith finally lifted her gaze, her eyes squinting as though she agreed with Owen's estimation of himself. Like she could hear his thoughts.

Pitiful. Inadequate.

'You don't want to be around me now,' she told him, her voice seemingly not her own – I was helping her. Owen Brady went to speak but his breath halted the words. 'And I don't want to be around you.' Faith Brady spat the last word out in apparent disgust.

I should have been there, his bloodshot eyes groaned.

Would he have taken the bullet?

It's much easier to think that you would after the event.

Tears fell silently down Faith Brady's cheeks. Owen had nothing left. She knew it as much as the man's own shadow.

'Well, if you don't want to come down then at least go and see Michael before he goes to sleep.'

'I don't want to see Michael,' she shouted, not thinking of anyone but herself again. 'I don't want to see anybody. Can't you get that through your thick skull.'

'Keep your voice down.' Owen stepped towards his wife, his sadness giving way to momentary anger.

'Just leave.' Her voice was still raised.

Owen stepped forward again. It was the closest he had been to his wife in a day or so.

'Keep your fucking voice down.' He was quiet, venomous through gritted teeth. He didn't blink. He was thinking only of his sons. The one that had died but, even more, the one that was still alive in the next room.

Faith just stared at him, her chest moving noticeably up and down, her heart racing from the outburst.

'I'm not ready.' Her crying became more audible. Owen felt like he should reach his arms around her. Hold her, for months if he had to. But he was frozen to the spot, trapped between fear and sorrow.

It's hesitation that can get someone killed.

When would she be ready?

I let them go for a moment, stood back and watched.

'Please, Owen.' She softened, the tension in her face releasing. 'Just tonight. Go and see to Michael. I can't be around him. Not now. Not yet. Just ... just time ... I need a bit of time. For me. For Jacob. All of us.' At this point she placed her right hand on her husband's chest.

It was contact.

It was a start.

Faith told her husband that she was going to try to relax in the bath; she needed a little time to think. She may feel better afterwards.

'And come downstairs?' Owen asked, one final, pathetic time.

She nodded.

She lied.

The truth was too frightening.
The truth was damning.

THE BOTTOM BUNK

Michael's father kept telling him that Jacob was in heaven. Like that made it easier to digest. It just made it less real. The Bradys didn't go to church; they never even talked about things like that. They were not invited to Oz and Liv's wedding.

He was a kid. He wasn't an idiot.

The kid, who was certainly not an idiot, slept on the top bunk, because he was the eldest. Michael was seven. Jacob was five.

Was five.

Would always be five.

Michael was in bed by half past seven. The same as always. His father was desperately trying to keep their routine, keep everything normal. Though things were far from normal. They'd never be that way again. Jacob was gone. Whether his soul had been transported to some celestial plane or he had already been reborn as a swallow or he was simply in a state of grotesque, bloated decay, his life was over and the Brady family would be forever changed.

Michael knew what his father was doing and he understood the reasons, but Michael wanted to feel sad. He wanted to think about his brother. He didn't want him to be in heaven. He wanted him to be on the bottom bunk.

Michael pulled his duvet back and hung over the side of his bed, looking down at where his brother used to lay. He didn't expect to see him there, upside down, pretending to be asleep like he did every night; he just wanted to look, keep with his own routine.

But he remembered the gunshot and closed his eyes tightly, hoping this would stop him from seeing anything. It had been louder than they showed it on the television or the *pft* on computer games. There was a bang and then his little brother had slumped to the floor.

And Michael didn't know what the man said to his mother before running off.

He didn't know why he was the one still there.

Then, another sound. His mother was shouting again. She'd been doing that a lot.

'I don't want to see Michael.'

Her words hit his chest like the bullet to the son she had chosen to die.

The seven-year-old boy didn't know what he had done wrong. Why was it his fault? *Why does heaven need a five-year-old boy, anyway? Shouldn't it just be for old people?* And why did his mother keep saying those words?

Her thoughtless eruption upset Michael but not enough to make him cry. Nothing could hurt as much as losing his little brother. But he turned and climbed down the ladder to get into the bottom bunk. Rotating the pillow lengthways down his body, he held it tight but comfortingly.

'Just leave,' he'd heard through the too-thin walls.

His eyes closed tighter and he pictured his brother without a hole in his chest.

'Don't worry, Jacob,' he whispered out loud, 'she doesn't mean it. She's just sad about you, that's all.'

The seven-year-old boy, who was not an idiot but had recently witnessed the callous murder of his younger brother, didn't hear any more shouting from the room next to his. His room that he now only shared with a memory, an impression that would fade with time. Right then, it felt like he would never forget Jacob, but the difficult years ahead would diminish his recollection until all that was left was the sound of two thuds. One when a bullet hit an innocent living boy. And one when a dead child hit the ground.

Michael kept whispering.

'Daddy is sad too but he doesn't shout. I think he just wants Mummy to feel better. She won't come out of her room, Jacob. Are you in heaven? Is it nice? Are you an angel now?'

He waited for an answer, hugging the pillow, protecting it.

'Did you hear what that man said to Mummy?'

Another sound. The bottom of the bedroom door scraped against the carpet.

Then a soft voice.

DISBELIEVING PINCHES

'Michael, are you still awake,' the concerned father whispered.

His son made a noise, a groan of some kind that suggested he may have been asleep. But Owen knew that his son must have heard the words his wife had shouted a few moments before.

Brave boy.

'A change of scenery tonight, I see.' Owen spotted his alive son lying in his dead son's bed and it broke his heart even more. I could see it. The Brady boys were good.

'Maybe I should sleep on the top bunk.' Owen smiled, holding back emotion.

Michael didn't need his smile any more. He just held the pillow against his chest.

'Look, I'm sorry you had to hear that.' He sat on the bed and placed a comforting hand on his son's arm. 'Sometimes adults say things that they don't really mean when they are upset. Your mum is … Well, she's having a tough time. And she's sad. And it's probably best that she comes to see you when she's feeling a bit better.'

Michael didn't speak.

'If you want to talk about anything, anything at all, if you're feeling down or sick, then you can come to me. It's okay to feel that way. It's okay to feel whatever way you want.'

The father waited for acknowledgement. It didn't have to be verbal, a simple nod would have sufficed. But there was no discernible reaction.

'And, if you don't want to say anything for a while, that's fine too, just let me know and I'll make sure you get the quiet you need.'

MICHAEL KNEW ONE THING
His mother was keeping something from them both.

'I'm fine, Daddy,' he finally chirped. 'I just wanted to see what the bottom bunk is like. I kinda feel close to him down here, you know?' His voice wobbled.

Owen tried to camouflage the wiping of his tears.

'Are *you* all right?'

Owen Brady inhaled and held his breath. His son should not be asking him that. A seven-year-old should not be offering comfort. He thought of his miserable wife in the next room, running a bath so she could have her fucking *time*, so that she could soak in the filth of her experience. And for a moment Owen hated her.

For being the one that was there but could do nothing to save Jacob.

For not allowing him to grieve properly because one person had to keep it together.

But mostly for that very moment, when a young boy who watched his brother slump into non-existence only a day ago was having to be strong for his parents. He was pretending not to hear his mother's acrid rants. And he was worried about the father who thought he was coping but realised he was fucking everything up.

It had started as g u i l t. A slight push from me and this manifested itself as anger. It didn't take much after that to see that Owen Brady had started to feel hate.

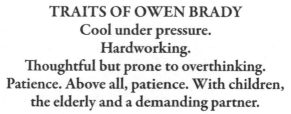

TRAITS OF OWEN BRADY
Cool under pressure.
Hardworking.
Thoughtful but prone to overthinking.
Patience. Above all, patience. With children,
the elderly and a demanding partner.

But inside, there must have been repressed anger because, when I pushed him, even slightly, that is what came out. Anger. Anger and hate.

And hate is darkness. It is something I can work with. It's the easiest thing to use.

'You don't have to ask me that, buddy. Don't worry about your old dad. I'm sad like you. Like your mum. But I know Jacob is in heaven. He's probably with your gran right now wondering what you're doing on his bunk.' He forced something close to a smile, but the corners of his mouth twitched with the lies he was telling himself and his son.

Michael said nothing. Again.

A father rubbed his son's arm – marked with disbelieving pinches – affectionately yet apologetically. Then he pulled the cover up over his shoulder.

'You want to stay here tonight, then?'

Michael nodded.

Owen kissed his son on the head and said, 'I'll be downstairs if you need me.' It was the same thing he'd said to his wife.

Then he told his son that he loved him.

Again, Michael said nothing.

THIS WASN'T HIM

Now, watch how I can work with hatred.

Owen Brady was a placid and patient man. He loved his job, it took up a lot of his time, but he loved his family more. It hurt him to arrive home only to see the boys at bath time, read them a story then put them to bed. He'd always felt like he had missed out and it was time he would never get back.

❧ SOMETHING WORTH CONSIDERING ❧
Time, whether missed, spent well or
not used in a productive and memorable
way, can never be got back.
You never get it back.

He'd spent every weekend, though, trying to make up for that. When he could have been resting or playing golf or going to The Arboreal for beers, his focus was solely pointed at being a present and attentive father.

Owen Brady left his sons' bedroom door slightly ajar in case Michael called out. He knew he'd be sleeping downstairs for a second night. Like there had been some kind of marital dispute. Like *he* had done something wrong.

Just a tickle from Evil at this point to get the mind racing.

He stopped in the hallway, creaking his neck to the left; his eyes boring into the closed door his wife hid behind, and he snarled. A nocturnal growl. He was giving in to the darkness.

Then a kiss from Evil.

Time. Sure. He imagined her submersed in the bath. *You have your fucking time while I lie to our kid about the lovely place his dead brother has gone to. You have your time in bubbles, wallowing in the grief you think only you can feel. I'll be fine on the sofa again. Don't worry about me.*

He could feel something boiling but managed to collect himself before doing or saying something he would never be able to take back. Or that's what he thought he had done, but in fact, I had let him go for a moment. I like to see what they do, what people are capable of. Without me.

Owen went straight to the fridge and pulled out a bottle of lager. He didn't turn on the television, he didn't try to lose himself in any kind of distraction. He sat at the kitchen table, with me, a pile of unopened mail at one end, and he drank. The first bottle went down as fast as iced water in July.

SOMETHING THAT HAS CHANGED
I never used to be scared of people.
You have the power to destroy everything.

He opened another and looked at the ceiling beneath the en-suite bathroom where his selfish fuck of a wife was lying in scaldingly hot water.

An evil tap on the shoulder.

Time. You bitch.

Another beer and another ten minutes to allow his thoughts to wander. For some reason he tried to imagine what had happened in the park. The information he had received from Faith was patchy. He knew no more than the average TV addict. His wife was too distant, too hurt, to recount the story again. His son was barely speaking. And he had nobody he could talk to. There were friends, a family-liaison officer who had been assigned to the Bradys, but he just wanted honesty. And she was the only one that could give him that.

I wished I could tell him but all I could do was push him towards the truth.

You're not the only one hurting, Faith.

Three more beers. A false image of the shooting replayed in his mind like a badly filmed home movie – in black and white.

I coaxed the anger and resentment towards the surface.

It's been over an hour. That's more than enough time. The words were a whisper in a voice that Owen Brady did not recognise as his own.

He stood up at the table, knocked back the last half-bottle of beer and slammed it down hard onto the oak surface.

You're going to talk to me now. Whether you want to or not.

Then he walked up the stairs. The sixth and seventh step creaking, but Faith could not hear it.

And he paced past Michael's room, his gaze fixed firmly ahead. He couldn't think about Michael otherwise he wouldn't go through with it. I swiped that notion away.

He pushed through the bedroom door. It was quiet. The top-left drawer was hanging open. He was just walking, not thinking.

Then he was rapping on the en suite door and calling his wife's name.

And he was saying let me in.

And she wouldn't answer him.

I couldn't help but laugh. This is my favourite part. The despair.

So he asked again. And he shunted the door with his shoulder, not knowing what he would do when he got to the other side.

This wasn't him.

The town of Hinton Hollow was different now. It had changed. Things were happening that should not. People were acting out of character. Local businesses were less welcoming. The residents could see it happening, they felt it, and there was nothing they could do to stop it.

One final push.

Owen Brady bust through the locked door.

Then there was the screaming.

DIE/DIET

I pushed Dorothy too hard.

Her flat was small. Too small for her despite the fact that she lived by herself. She had ordered undersized sofas to give the illusion of space, but it meant that she filled a seat designed for two people.

She was eating a tub of ice cream while she waited for her dinner to be delivered. It was cookie-dough-flavoured with chocolate chips and a tube of peanut butter that ran up the centre from the bottom to the lid. But it was dairy-free and that was enough for Dorothy to convince herself that it was somehow healthier.

Her head was hurting because she was eating too fast, but the app said her fried chicken was only three minutes away.

One more spoonful.

The pain of her freezing brain passed down into her shoulders and back. It felt like another attack. She had to keep herself calm. She knew how to fight the symptoms, at least.

Then the doorbell rang and her heart rate increased. I made her more excited.

See: *the Western diet.*

She wheezed down the hallway, dragging her bare feet because lifting them was too much effort.

'Good evening. One family bucket, beans, corn, fries, two litres of Pepsi aaaaand...' the man on her doorstep fished around inside his bag, 'one tub of cookie-dough ice cream.' He smiled.

Dairy free. Because she's on a diet.

'Thank you.'

'Have a good night.' He acted as coolly as he could. He could see the state she was in. He knew everything in that bag was for her. There was no family.

I could have made her feel guilty and it would have resulted in her eating everything.

I could have left her that night. She would have eaten everything.

I stayed and watched her. I saw as she ate the skin of three chicken legs before dunking the meat into the carton of beans meant for four people. I hung around as she gulped a pint of that fizzy drink straight from the bottle. I did nothing as she took the lid off the ice cream and placed it on the coffee table to defrost.

Then I pushed her too hard.

She wasn't even hungry for the food, but the pleasure centre of her brain had been deadened by gluttony. The grease was around her mouth but I made her want more. And quicker.

A handful of fries was dipped into the ice cream. Another swig of Pepsi. Her teeth typewritered up and down the cob of corn before it was thrown into the bucket.

Another chicken skin.

Another flicker of pleasure.

I stroked at her some more and that rapture tingled between her legs for a moment. It was fleeting. Voracity had deadened her libido long ago.

One more bite. One more spoonful. One more lick.

Stuff it in.

I saw the panic in her eyes. That this was dangerous. The fear of death, but more than that, the realisation that she was alone and there was nobody to help her. To slap her on the back. To attempt to wrap their arms around her waist from behind and pull inward and upward in a sharp, single movement.

She was choking to death and I could not tear myself away from the sadness of it all.

Dorothy was trying to gain momentum by rocking her body back and forth, just so that she could stand up. She beat a fist against her chest, attempting to dislodge whatever was stuck in her throat. She managed to reach for the Pepsi, hoping to wash it downward.

There was nothing I could do. I left her to it.

Dorothy died-with-a-chicken-bone-in-her-throat Reilly managed to get to her feet, she was grasping at her neck. Then she moved around behind her seat and launched herself towards the back of the sofa, hoping the upright section would hit her in the gut hard enough to act like a solo Heimlich manoeuvre.

But the undersized sofa, built for two, was light and flimsy and the legs buckled at the back and the front flipped up hitting her – comically – in the face. She fell onto the gentle cushioning and dislodged nothing.

She kicked her legs. She rolled. I left.

Dorothy Reilly would not be found until after I was gone and had taken Detective Sergeant Pace with me.

CURRENTLY UNAVAILABLE

It would require more than a single incident. That much evil could not cut through the malevolence of this world. No. I had to infect the town. It had to be a plague if there was going to be any impact, if I was going to make a lasting difference.

I have been there through wars, through famine, through plague. Those are the larger stories. Hinton Hollow was small. Perhaps I needed more of these stories.

Think global, act local.

I cast my net wide that day, capturing all who held a grudge or felt anxious. Anyone with a wandering thought for mischief or depravity was caught within my grasp. Anyone with a passing notion of infidelity. Anyone who cursed their boss or sister or another driver, even in their minds, was touched.

LIV DUNHAM WAS PASSIVE
She loved her job. She was getting married.
She thought life was happening to her.
Life was passing her by.

She had tried Oz's mother first. Before she pestered the police again.

Where the hell was she?

'Come on, May,' she whispered out loud to herself as the phone rang once. Twice. Five times before the old-fashioned answering machine kicked in again.

'You are through to the Tambor residence,' a formal but jovial male voice uttered. 'We are currently unavailable to take your call. Leave a short message and one of us will get back to you as soon as we can.'

May Tambor had not changed the message from her husband's voice even though he had died just over four years ago. Sometimes, when she was out, she called her own house just to hear him talk to her again. Oz had told Liv that he hated getting that message when he called his mother; it just brought it all back. But he'd never say anything to her because he didn't know what it felt like to have someone in your life that you loved in that way suddenly disappear forever.

'Hi, May. It's Liv again. I'm starting to get really worried about Oz. Just wondering if you've heard from him in the last day. Please give me a call when you pick this message up. Thanks.'

She placed the phone down gently and exhaled as though she had just delivered bad news to someone close. Liv tried to keep her tone as light as that of the dead man who had asked her to leave a message. She didn't want May to worry. Oz was all she had now.

Oh, Oz. Where are you? Talk to me. She looked upward at nothing and the words vibrated inside her skull.

Liv Dunham ambled into the kitchen, turned on the cold tap and left it running while she fetched herself a glass from the cupboard.

I'll wait here. He's coming back. She was finding it more difficult to lie to herself.

She took three large gulps of the water then fought hard to keep it down. Her throat was hurting from all the crying and felt as though she was swallowing straight vodka.

Back in the lounge, Liv sat on the edge of her sofa. Alert. The television stayed off. She couldn't hear about that poor Brady kid any more, it was horrid, she'd got enough on her mind. She knew his older brother, Michael. Well-mannered. Average but likeable. His parents seemed happy, too. Young. Still in love. Interested in their child's education from an early age.

She couldn't fight her instincts as a teacher and a member of the community. She contemplated what the Bradys must be going through, then she worried about May Tambor. And she thought about the wedding preparations and whether Oz had simply driven to Wales to sort out his fucking passport. Maybe her friends were right and he would surprise her. Maybe the whole town was in on it.

Maybe they weren't.

Her legs started to jump up and down, agitated and impatient.

She'd wait.

That's what she was supposed to do. Wait. They'd told her yesterday.

But she couldn't. She was starting to feel ineffectual. She was allowing Oz not to be with her. What was she actually doing to help? Staying at home and calling people. She was the opposite of a receptionist.

After a few mad moments, Liv Dunham found another number to call. She knew something was wrong. Oz wouldn't just leave without saying anything. He just wouldn't.

There were four rings before somebody answered. One less than it took for Oz's dead father to request you leave a message for the Tambors.

'Hinton Hollow Police,' it stated. 'Constable Reynolds.'

VOICES

Oz Tambor was alive. For now.

All was dark. Starless. But he knew that he was in a car. And it was cold. He could've seen his breath if there had been any light. And the wind outside bounced around the canopy and pushed its way through branches and leaves to sound like whispers.

My whispers.

Voices all around him.

My voices.

And he didn't feel able to move, though his body was in no physical pain. And his eyes wanted to close but his mind refused to let that happen. He was staying alert. *It's just as black when they're open, anyway.*

And he should not have left the house like that yesterday morning.

Then he wouldn't have been there, in an unlit car, in the biting forest surrounded by breathy murmurs he couldn't understand but were slowly driving him mad.

He had been taken, but he was alive.

And he had to somehow stay that way for three more days.

A LONG PAUSE

The news had said that nineteen people had jumped from the top of Tower Bridge. There were videos emerging that onlookers had taken on their phones, and Maeve knew that's where Pace would have been. Then buried in paperwork and identifying bodies, probably. But she couldn't shake the feeling that something bad had happened to him.

It was irrational. It was silly. She knew. But she called him again. *And he'd better pick up this time because she was going out of her fucking mind.*

'Where the fuck are you? What are you doing? Even the fucking President of the United States has time to tweet a hundred times a day so I don't know why you're so busy that you can't shoot me a quick text to say that you're okay.'

She'd been drinking. The things inside were leaking out.

'I've had a shit day, in case you care. There's no point in going into it, I don't want to do that over voicemail. I just want to talk to you, babe. I need to hear your voice. It will calm me down. I'm sure you'd be the same the other way around.'

H o p e.

Maeve had ordered Thai food to go with her two bottles of wine. She was distracted and could not be bothered to cook for herself.

There was a long pause. Her breathing slowed.

'I wish you were here. Please come back to me when there's some let-up in this case.'

She hung up, then, to nobody, said, 'I need you.'

THEY WERE KIDS

Michael Brady had fallen asleep within minutes of his father leaving the room.

SOMETHING ABOUT JACOB'S HAIR
He hated having it washed.
He hated having it brushed.
He loved having it ruffled at the back
by his older brother.

The pillow still pressed against his chest. It smelled like Jacob's wet hair. The clean scent of his freshly bathed little brother.

Michael hadn't had a nightmare about that day in the park; he may have dreamt, but he didn't remember anything when he woke up startled by the sound of yet more shouting.

He had drifted into slumber over an hour ago, feeling dismay for his father but that he was protected and cared for and safe. The weight of his own sorrow finally pressuring him into fatigue. He didn't dwell on his mother's words. The transformation of Hinton Hollow was not affecting the children. They couldn't be touched by the encroaching twilight.

But they could still feel fear.

They were kids.

And Michael was awoken from a dreamless sleep by a sound that instantly filled him with terror.

He had heard that howl once before.

NUMB

'You stupid fucking bitch.'

That's what he shouted as he burst in on his wife in the bath.

'You cunt. You idiot.' She was lying there just as he'd imagined.

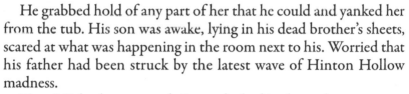

A NOTE ON SORROW
**Grief presents itself in different ways.
For Owen Brady it started with tears and
the misery of loss.
There was alcohol. And self-doubt.
And a touch from Evil.
All that was left was his anger,
blame and a distaste for his wife.**

He grabbed hold of any part of her that he could and yanked her from the tub. His son was awake, lying in his dead brother's sheets, scared at what was happening in the room next to his. Worried that his father had been struck by the latest wave of Hinton Hollow madness.

Then Michael went numb. Just as he had in the park.

He held his pillow tight, unable to move.

Owen Brady had no idea what he was doing.

BOTTOM OF THE BATH

Faith Brady wanted to be left alone that night. She wanted a little time. She didn't want to scare her son or upset him. She didn't want her husband bursting into the bathroom and screaming at her.

But she got it all.

Faith Brady could never tell them what she had done.

That she *should* feel guilty.

That it was her fault that Jacob was dead, no matter how her friends and family protested or attempted to pacify what they saw as natural, maternal remorse.

Faith Brady was jolted from another heavy bout of self-absorption when she heard the creak of the sixth and seventh stairs.

Her husband was on his way up to her.

To try again.

Why can't you just leave me alone, Owen. You're going to ruin everything.

She replaced the bottle of vodka she had been swigging from, covered it with the underwear in her top drawer, and perched herself on the edge of the bed, her head drooping so she didn't have to make eye contact. It was too painful.

He could never know.

Owen Brady had been trying to get his wife downstairs since she had returned home with their other son, Michael. Owen had been referring to the shooting as *the accident*. The police were calling it *the incident*. The police description was more accurate.

'I'm no good to be around.' She had slurred her words slightly. But Owen Brady only heard upset and tears rather than booze and culpability. She hadn't lifted her head because she knew the look on his face would break her.

She was removing herself.

Faith Brady had acted on autopilot for a few moments. Speaking words she expected every mother would utter in that situation.

Everybody blames me. You blame me. You shouldn't be near me. I'm bad luck.

Her mind was occupied with the sight of her own soft, manicured hands. She saw them covered in blood. She looked at the forefinger on her right hand. The one that never physically pulled the trigger, but certainly helped to aim the gun. She could see the teeth marks where she had been biting it in hostility since yesterday.

Faith finally lifted her head when her husband resorted to pleading.

He is weak.

'Just ... please.'

The disgust shown on her face had only been for herself. She wished she could have taken the bullet to her chest. She was bigger, she thought; perhaps she'd have lived. Or maybe she too would have ceased to exist before her head hit the stony floor beneath her feet, and then she wouldn't have to feel any of this. She wouldn't have to live with *this*.

She saw Owen withdraw at the sight of her.

Then he had mentioned Michael.

'I don't want to see Michael,' she had shouted. She hadn't wanted the words to come out that loud but the statement must have been true for her to react in that way.

I did nothing. I did not want to touch her.

IF I HAD THREE WISHES
1. That Faith Brady would have taken the bullet that day
2. That people were better and would choose more good.
3. You'll have to come back to me on this one.

Michael made her feel worse by being alive. He had been there. He must have known something but he was not saying it. She couldn't have him look at her. And know. He was her first-born and, in a small way, had always been favoured slightly. But not now. Not now that his brother was dead.

'Just leave,' she had screamed, hoping to push her husband away. Hoping to push everyone away.

Stop caring about me. Just give me time. I only need a little time.

Owen forced a glimmer of reality back into his wife's eyes when he propelled himself in her direction. She saw that he was angered. He was sick of her. *He should be.* She put a hand out to his chest and begged him for the one thing she believed she needed.

Time. Only a little time.

Then she lied. And he had bought it.

L i e s.

Faith Brady took the bottle of vodka from her drawer, walked into the en-suite bathroom, lit three candles and plugged the bath. She swigged at the vodka and grimaced. The only way she could feel better was to feel worse. She turned the hot and cold water on and adjusted until the correct temperature liquid flowed from the ornate mixer tap – slightly too hot – and poured in a muscle-relaxing bubble bath.

Then she swigged again. This time watching herself in the mirrored surface of the medicine cabinet on the wall. Her face was paler. Bonier. Witchier. She thought she looked evil. See also: *self-loathing, anxiety, airbrushed magazine images*. She felt unholy, though she had no religious convictions of her own.

What are you doing? she asked the woman looking back at her.

What have you done? one of them whispered.

Her fragile mind galloped.

She thought that Michael knew something. That he was protecting her for some reason. She couldn't bear the thought that *this* could be hanging over him. She'd already killed one of her children the day before.

Faith Brady rested the bottle on the side of the bath and fumbled the layers of clothing off her body and onto the cold tiles. The mirrored cabinet was starting to steam up so she could no longer look at the face she had come to despise.

She told herself that it would all *be okay*.

She had time.

For twenty minutes, Faith Brady had just lay on her back in the scalding hot water, staring upwards as the light from the candles faded out towards the ceiling. She'd locked the door behind her because she didn't want to be disturbed. She wanted that time. That nothingness.

It wasn't long before the limited light started clouding, her vision slowly disabling itself. The vacancy and emptiness she had been craving started to wash over her naked body like the mist of uncertainty now rolling over the undulating fields of Hinton Hollow.

This was what she wanted.

To simply not feel.

The vodka she had been drinking had helped to dull her world a little and the multitude of tablets she had pulled from the mirrored bathroom cabinet had slowed things down considerably.

Faith Brady had the little time she needed. She thought about the innocent little boy whose life she had thrown away, and she cried for the son she could no longer bear to look at. Then she vowed to herself that she would not let Michael down in the same way she had Jacob.

Faith cut both of her wrists vertically and then managed to slice horizontally across the top of her right thigh before she dropped the razor to the bottom of the bath.

NECK/TIE

This world, I've been here from the start. I've seen it destroyed several times. I've witnessed it frozen and I see now that it is melting. Never did I play such an active role until the arrival of man.

HERE IS SOMETHING TRUE
It was easy until you came along.
I had very little to do.
I had time to rest.
I could be lazy.
But you people won't let me.

And humans are getting worse.

They don't know who they are any more. They are an avatar. A dream. An aspiration.

A l i e.

A THEORY
Everyone is now two people.
The physical person. And the online persona.
The trouble is that nobody is fully their
physical self nor their online alter ego.

A SECOND THEORY
Everyone is now half a person.

They are projecting a set of traits and unrealistic standards – see: *happy family photos* and *humble bragging about achievements*. See also: *face-tuning* and *filters*. They are, at once, beautiful with flawless skin, eating healthily and cooking from scratch, with a family and dog they adore, but also lonely and ugly and shouting at their kids while they order fried chicken to be delivered to the house.

And they don't know which is the real them.

They are neglecting themselves and putting more effort into creating the person they wish to be rather than *becoming* that person. They are so focused on projecting this image to others that they forget about the real person they are. And they suffer because of that. They all suffer.

I think it is this that will contribute to another ending. I cannot see the humans coming back from this. Soon, they will have to start over.

Then I can rest again. But, for now, the pandemic of vulnerability gives me something that is very simple to tap into.

Another way that Evil can present itself is jealousy.

Annie Harding had seen online some pictures of her husband's secretary, and another of the only females holding her own in a male-dominated sales team. And she'd heard about the florist. Nobody was that nice to everybody.

But Liv Dunham had done nothing wrong other than excite a close-knit community about her impending nuptials. She was marrying her childhood sweetheart. She was beloved by parents and her pupils alike. She was pretty in a homely way. The same way that Annie had been. Before the doubt started kicking in.

Before her confidence was stripped.

Before I found her. And played with her low self-esteem.

On that second day in Hinton Hollow, Annie Harding's husband returned home late from work again. The top button of his shirt was undone and the tie he had been wearing when he left that morning was either in the car or somewhere in his laptop case. He wasn't sure.

The food she had prepared was on a plate in the kitchen covered in cling film. She had waited long enough.

'I just want to have a shower, wash the day off me,' he'd said.

Wash a woman off you. Scrub the sin.

Annie didn't confront him. She let it bubble inside. Faking her real life.

'Well, why don't you get yourself clean and I'll heat up your food.'

'Thanks, babe. I am starving.'

From all that fucking, no doubt.

Annie smiled. Her husband came close and kissed her forehead while she tried to subtly detect the scent of another woman on him.

When the bathroom door closed and she heard the sound of the shower running, Annie put the plate of food into the microwave, programmed it for five minutes, and hit the start button. Then she took the keys to her husband's car and went outside to look for his tie.

She had five minutes to find it.

It only took one.

It was on the floor in the passenger footwell. He'd said it was too constrictive after an entire day so it would make sense that he would take it off in the car and throw it to one side.

But I didn't want it to make sense. I wanted it to provoke. I wanted to bring out the real Annie. So I pushed her. A little harder than the day before.

It wasn't long until I was on the passenger seat and Annie was driving, telling herself that she was tired of being pushed around, that she was probably the laughing stock of the village, that she was sick to death of putting on a happy front and pretending that everything was fine when it wasn't.

Why does everybody else get to be happy? Why do they get to be in love?

Mr Harding came into the lounge with a towel wrapped around

his waist to find that the front door was wide open and his car – and wife – were gone. The microwave pinged and startled him. Three minutes after that, a rock was flying through a lounge window.

Annie didn't wait for the police like before, she jumped back into the car and sped home where her husband was sitting on the sofa, still in his towel, scraping mashed potato off the plate with his knife while shovelling chicken and green beans into his mouth with a fork.

He was hungry. He hadn't lied about that.

He'd been honest about the tie, too. The dark-blue one with the light-blue diamond pattern. The one his wife had tied around a rock, swung around in a circle a few times before releasing. The one that was still tied to a rock that was lying on Liv Dunham's living-room carpet.

THRESHOLD

May Tambor was right next to the phone when her future daughter-in-law called.

She liked her. She always had. But she loved the sound of her own husband's voice more. There was a click of machinery before his affable tone permeated the cold air of her hallway.

May wouldn't answer the phone now.

She wouldn't interrupt him.

Liv was not the only one who believed that there was something *wrong* with Oz's disappearance. It was not something normal, something usual, something you could explain away with wedding cliché and cold-feet rhetoric. The whole town of Hinton Hollow could feel it.

The air had changed noticeably since the Brady shooting yesterday. Everywhere seemed colder. Inside as well as out. As though the death of the Brady child ushered in a new season. A mood that threatened to bite all those in the town who refused to acknowledge it.

Hinton Hollow was exposed. A town whose secrets were no longer safe.

Outsiders were no longer welcome.

Even the convivial widow, Mrs Tambor, was different. Her home occupied a chill where her demeanour was normally enough to warm the modest space of the semi-detached house. Dust had settled on the furniture of the usually house-proud mother. The smell from the kitchen was not freshly brewed coffee or newly bought, decorative citrus fruit, or a sponge cake she would only eat a quarter of.

The curtains in the lounge were partly drawn, as always, leaving the room in a semi-darkness that echoed the depression creeping across Hinton Hollow as another moonless night threatened.

May Tambor was right next to the phone when her husband stopped talking and the tape began to whirr and clank before a beeping sound invited Liv to speak.

The beige carpet that led up the stairs behind May Tambor was clean and vacuumed to within an inch of its life. Ahead of her, by the front door, it was a mess. The filthiest part of the house. This was the threshold to the altered town of Hinton Hollow. Where bad things happened. Where children were killed in front of their families. Where strangers lurked in new shadows that were not there the week before.

Liv signed off. Her false spirit not fooling anyone. It was nice of her to try, though.

But May Tambor paid no attention to her son's fiancée. Her gaze remained fixed on the hallway ceiling. She was lying on her back, a single bullet hole in her forehead. The larger exit wound fixing her head into position on the wooden floorboards. The walls near the entrance sprayed with dots of crimson.

The bullet that passed through her skull would match the one lodged in the chest of the young Brady child and, unless somebody started listening to Liv Dunham, it would also match the bullet that was intended to killed Oz Tambor three days later.

GETTING STARTED

So, you see, young Jacob Brady was not the first victim.

And Faith Brady was not the first mother to die.

I could have mentioned this on day one, but it wasn't important then.

The community of Hinton Hollow thought that everything changed that day in the park – the moment Michael Brady's mother told the man with the gun to shoot her youngest son through the chest.

They thought it began with Jacob.

It looked like it had started there.

It hadn't.

They had regarded the broken florist window as an anomaly. There were whispers – see also: *g o s s i p, rumour, deflection* – about Annie Harding and her marriage, of course. Some folk had seen Dorothy Reilly wheezing around town with her trolley but they only speculated about the pains she must feel in her chest and the fact that her knees must ache. Some of the older kids had balked at the sight of her ankle fat hanging over her shoes.

But she didn't seem any different. No weirder than the day before.

Luckily, only a handful of other borderline sociopaths witnessed Darren's breakdown at the slaughterhouse. Though RD had noticed he was off colour at lunch the next day.

I was only getting started with them.

I wanted time with Liv Dunham. Because all of Hinton Hollow was invested in her wedding to Oz Tambor. If I could change them, if I could alter their course for the worse, I could affect everybody.

If I could play with Liv for a while, make her anxious, cause her to fear, to question, if I could raise her paranoia, I could ruin her.

It would be easy to show her that Oz was not in Wales dutifully obtaining a passport. I could tell her that he was in the boot of a car in the woods. But that was never the plan.

If she found him now, Liv would not react the same as she would finding him at the end of the week with a bullet in his face.

BOLD, RED CAPITAL LETTERS

Reynolds looked at the clock on the wall behind the front desk and sighed.

Half past eleven.

Bring on the mentals. The freaks. The waste-of-police-times.

Sure, it was a weekday, and this was Hinton Hollow, but the bars in neighbouring towns had just emptied and there were always people in them. There were always people who drank too much. And there were always people who would want to fight. Or climb something too high and unsafe. Or there were couples who wanted to fuck in the street, somewhere dangerous that they might be seen, or better yet, get caught. There were idiots who drove home from the pub because they lived close. *If you live that close, just fucking walk home.*

All this before you got to the drugs, the broken windows, the burglaries and the sixteen-year-old who should not have been out drinking in a bar and who was now on her knees somewhere with a nightclub bouncer's dick stuffed in her mouth.

Constable Reynolds would receive a call at midnight from a woman in her thirties who thought she could hear someone in her garden. It would turn out to be her husband, soused in Merlot, searching for the back-door key they kept in a fake rock.

But his first call had been from Liv Dunham.

'Hinton Hollow Police,' he offered. 'Constable Reynolds.'

A woman, probably late twenties judging from her voice, warbled her name in several different variations. She said she had already called before. Her voice sounded familiar, she was a teacher at the primary school, a known figure by many, but there were 5,118 people in Hinton Hollow and, no matter how close the people were, you couldn't know them all. Unless you were Mrs Beaufort.

Reynolds had taken his fair share of crank calls in the last day, since the park shooting – everyone had already forgotten about Annie throwing the rock through the window of the florist. Local people thinking they could help in some way, some of them stating that they had seen things that they certainly had not – creating false memories from the images they had seen on social media and the local news – others offering insight into the unfortunate Brady family. Not all of the information had been friendly or conciliatory: *they never went to church*. So he was prepared for the more eccentric callers that evening. The drinkers and the lonely.

Those affected by the change that I had manufactured.

'Where is your husband right now, Ms Dunham?'

Reynolds lowered his voice. His instant thought was that this was a domestic-abuse call: the wife had finally had enough of the beatings or the names or the false accusations but the husband was still in the house.

This was nothing to do with the Brady shooting.

After a short, stilted, misinformed few moments, Reynolds deduced that the caller was not in any immediate danger. Certainly not from another party, though her state of mind suggested that she was not in complete balance with herself.

'Oz. Oscar Tambor. He's missing.'

'And you say you are due to get married in a couple of days?' He tried to remove the condescension from his voice but it was difficult. This happens. Weddings. They can be stressful and it was usually the groom that bolted. They came back. They usually came back.

He knew how she would react.

'Four days. What has that got to do with anything?'

They always said that. Telling themselves that nothing was wrong though they knew it was probably over. *Call the florist. Cancel the band. Pawn the engagement ring.*

Detective Sergeant Pace, the unofficial lead in the Brady shooting case, entered the front of the station and mouthed the word *Anything?* to Reynolds. Reynolds held his hand over the mouthpiece of the phone, rolled his eyes and shook his head. He then nodded towards the detective as if asking, *Anything your end?* Pace puffed out his cheeks.

Don't even ask.

It's spiralling.

Reynolds was silent while the caller droned on, trying to fool herself into believing she has not been jilted. Pace leaned an elbow on the front desk and waited.

'I'm sorry, Ms Dunham, but there's nothing the police can do for you at this point in time.'

She hurled some coarse words in his direction, but he was more than used to that kind of colourful language. He attempted to explain that her fiancée was not *technically* missing yet. He was over eighteen. If he were a child, the police and all the power at their disposal would have been combing the area.

He knew she wouldn't sit still on this. Everyone who called thought that their problem was the highest priority. As they should. It was. To them. She was worried that the Brady shooter may have gunned down her husband-to-be. People get crazy when a crime such as that is so close to their own front door. But there had been no more reported incidents of gunfire, and resources were tied up in that case.

Pace looked at his watch then at the clock on the wall facing Reynolds' back.

Liv Dunham swore at Reynolds one last time before hanging up on him.

'The crazies are out in full force today,' he said, half to himself, half to Pace. 'So, anything more on the shooter?'

'All we know is that they are a chicken shit who shot a fucking kid and they're still out there.'

Reynolds felt uncomfortable at Pace's pithy evaluation of the case. He was an intimidating figure at the best of times – he was not overly tall, it was more his presence – but in this mood it was best to steer clear of the darkness that surrounded him.

Detective Sergeant Pace was his own worst enemy.

Detective Sergeant Pace would be punished.

Both of them felt me with them in that room, in that moment.

That was when Inspector Anderson walked in behind Reynolds. Both men stood almost to attention, Reynolds more than Pace.

'Pace.' The inspector's voice was low, authoritative. 'You're needed over at the Brady house.'

Pace said nothing.

'Mr Brady placed an emergency call. His fucking wife is dead now. Drag him in.' Then he walked back out of the door he had just entered.

Reynolds turned back to Pace but he was already striding out of the front door.

Nothing that exciting ever happened in Hinton Hollow. He shook his head in disbelief.

He waited ten minutes until another crazy called him.

'I think there's someone in my garden.'

HANDLE WITH CARE

The police had been incredibly patient with Little Henry Wallace but their composure was eroding with every shake of his head.

'Are you running away from somebody?'

A shake of the head.

'Did anybody try to hurt you?'

A shake of the head.

'Are you scared of what your mum or dad will think when they find out that you've gone?'

Another shake of his tiny, innocent head.

They'd tried more open questions but were met with silence. They had been handling him with care until a doctor checked him over in case there were any signs of abuse but, of course, the doctor found Henry to be perfectly healthy. A little short for his age, but thriving, nonetheless.

I could do nothing but admire the boy.

At what point does this leave you? When does cynicism creep in?

When do you start to doubt the world around you? When do you question your parents, teachers, God, the tooth fairy? And would holding on to those beliefs serve you better in the long run?

Would it make you more positive?

Would it make you more accepting?

Would it stop you from turning that doubt towards yourself? An action that leads only to fear and misery and worse.

A THOUGHT ABOUT BEING BETTER
**Forget your job, forget your relationship,
forget about being the best parent in the world,
forget about perfection.
Put in the most work, each day, on yourself.
Be better. Get fitter. Learn more.
Do this every single day.
Work the hardest on YOU.
The rest will fall into place.**

If more people thought about how they could be better, do better, you may find yourselves in a position to turn this tide of social-media lies and self-loathing and talent shows for people who only want to be famous and don't care what it's for.

There could be more good. Therefore, less need for me. And that would be perfect.

One of the policeman loses his cool and slams a hand down on the table. Little Henry Wallace reacts with distress and the other detective apologises for his partner.

I make a note and add him to the scurvy-cheeked man on the train who raised his voice to Henry. They will both get a visit from me when this is over.

Little Henry Wallace is taken away and put in front of the television. The detectives leave and Henry's shoulders twitch at the sound of the door closing. I look at him. I look into him. I see anxiety. I see worry.

I see a boy who just wants his mum.

Suddenly, little Henry Wallace doesn't feel so brave.

THE FUTURE MRS TAMBOR

She'd hardly slept. Why would she?

He'd been missing for nearly two days and she was the only one who thought there was something wrong. Nobody was taking her seriously.

Liv Dunham sat forward on the three-seater, tan leather sofa, both of her legs tapping restlessly up and down, wobbling, devoid of anything to do. She did the same thing at her desk when she was daydreaming at work while the kids read. She told herself that she needed more exercise, just a little toning to stop the jiggling, but that night her insecurities took a back seat to the thought of where her fiancé could be.

I'm heading out for a bit.

That's what he'd said.

Her friends reassured her that he'd be back, that maybe he was going to surprise her, that perhaps he'd needed some time to think. *He's got cold feet. He's left you.* These are the words they did not say, but Liv heard all too clearly.

Liv Dunham, Oz's girl, the future Mrs Tambor, sat forward on her sofa with bouncing thighs and looked at the plethora of cushions surrounding her. Oz was right, there were too many. She wanted to laugh at that but couldn't. Instead, she saw herself reflected in the television screen. It was turned off. She didn't want the white noise. She needed to be alert. The phone might ring. It could be Oz's mother informing Liv that he was safe and well, and with her. Though she'd just called and May had not answered. Again.

Fear is my greatest tool. It can be used to make a person do almost anything. You can take education, information, motivation and throw it all away, fear is the only thing you require. It is a slow and deadly poison. And it is effective.

Her mind was racing.

What if there was a knock at the door? The police asking if she would come and identify a body?

There's been an accident.

She looked at the black, smeared-with-fingerprints screen and recalled a news item she'd once seen about a man who went out and never came home. He'd hit his head and forgotten who he was but ended up living a happy life as somebody else. Then every poster for a lost cat or dog jumped from the recesses of her memory. And her mind conjured the image of a hundred faces she had seen with the word 'missing' plastered beneath in bold, red capital letters. She picked up the remote control and hit the off button to take away the tableau of false hope, but the television was already off and switched to the news channel she watched all day yesterday, hoping not to see a piece involving her fiancé.

The channel was re-running the same item about a child being shot in a park, and Liv felt awful at her relief that the face on the screen was not Oz.

She switched off the TV and stood up. She couldn't just sit there and wait for him to come home. She couldn't just hang around, she'd go insane. Maybe she had already started to.

Liv picked up her telephone and dialled 0734 999.

She held the phone to her ear for less than a second and then hung up.

Pull yourself together, Liv. She stared down at the receiver.

You don't need to type in an area code when you call the police. And that hasn't been the area code here for over ten years.

She replaced the receiver, closed her eyes, screwed a ball of her fringe into her hand – just enough to tighten and cause some pain – and cursed. Taking two deep breaths gave her enough opportunity to temporarily collect her thoughts. She took the mobile phone from her pocket and recalled the last webpage she had visited. Then, calmly, she tapped in the number on her screen for the local police station.

It rang four times before Reynolds picked up.

Add frustration to fear to create despair.

'Look. I know him. He wouldn't just disappear. He left yesterday morning and he didn't come home. He hasn't called me or his friends, I can't get hold of his mother, I've been trying all day. Doesn't that strike you as weird?' Liv's agitation seemingly boosted her level of coherence. 'I was told yesterday to stay here in case he returns.'

'That's correct.'

'Well, I've stayed here and he hasn't returned. What happens next?'

'I'm sorry, Ms Dunham, but there is nothing we can do for you at this time.'

'What do you mean?' Her voice was shrill with disbelief.

'Mr Tambor is an adult, and it hasn't even been forty-eight hours since you last saw him.'

'What has it been? Forty-one? Forty-one and a half?' Her sarcasm tried to mask the frustration she felt.

'Ms Dunham, I understand—'

'What do you understand? That I've called a few hours early? He's missing. I know it. This isn't like him. There's a gunman on the loose. Oz could be lying in a ditch somewhere while you sit there and do nothing. Something's not right in this town and I'm not going to stay here and wait around.'

'Ms Dunham. I would advise that that is exactly what you do. I assure you that I have seen this before. Wait for him. If he is not back by the morning then please either call back or come in to the station. We take every call seriously, Ms Dunham.'

'Sure you do.' She mumbled her words at no one while replacing the phone. She would have liked to have said something wittier.

Then she walked out into the hallway, grabbed her coat from the hook beside the front door and checked her pale face in the mirror once before exiting to look God-knows-where for Oz.

Out of habit, Liv double-locked the door. Then she paused and unlocked one of the bolts. *Just in case he comes back.*

Inside, the phone began to ring.

A TEACHER HE CAN TRUST

She dropped her keys. Twice.

'Fuck.' She cursed her own ineptitude the second time they fell to the ground with a graceless jangle.

Stay at home, she'd been told.

It hadn't even been forty-eight hours.

Liv finally pushed through the doorway, after more panicked fumbling for the keyhole, leaving it wide open for anybody, anything, to come in behind her.

I don't need a door. I am anywhere I want to be.

She threw her bag against the left wall of her hallway, took the first door on the right at speed and barged through the lounge into the dining room where the telephone was rattling on a shelf. She caught her hip on the corner of the dining table; wood crunched against bone and she shrieked in agony as it knocked her off balance. It bruised almost instantly.

'Hello?' She grabbed the phone receiver with her left hand and rested her back against the wall momentarily to take the weight off her injured hip. 'Hello?' she said again hysterically, not really giving the person at the other end a chance to respond. Her right hand rubbed against her bruise, not making a single bit of difference to the pain.

Nobody answered Liv Dunham.

But there was somebody there.

'Can you hear me?' she asked. 'This isn't funny, you know.'

With the phone pressed tightly to her ear, Liv tried to make out the sound at the other end of the line. Was there traffic? There were still a few pay phones left in Hinton Hollow; if the call was coming from one of them, background noise might give an indication of location.

'Are you trying to scare me?'

The sound was not heavy breathing; it was more of a hiss, like three people were whispering at the same time. It could have been wind blowing against the mouthpiece of a mobile phone, she thought.

It wasn't.

I wasn't with Liv; I was at the other end of the line.

I was one of the whispers.

'Because you're not. You're just pissing me off.'

Liv *was* scared. Everything was happening at once. May Tambor was not answering her phone. Poor Jacob Brady had been killed. Constable Reynolds had dismissed her as delusional. And the man she was due to marry in a few days had not returned home after saying *I'm heading out for a bit.*

A bit.

Now this. Some crank call. She started to wonder who it could be, running through likely candidates in Hinton Hollow. Male teachers at the school, perhaps one of her students sporting a pre-pubescent crush, one of the local drinkers from The Arboreal, even Father Salis jumped to her mind. Or that creep, Ablett.

'Look, if you're not going to say anything, I'm just going to hang up,' she barked, regaining a little composure.

Still, a hushed purr from the other end.

'Bring him back,' Liv eventually pleaded, her voice a little lower, unsure where the words or realisation had come from. She believed that she was in a one-way conversation with the man who had taken her partner, maybe even the same person who had shot Jacob Brady. 'Bring Oz back.'

She sounded pathetic, she knew that, but she didn't know what else to do.

There was no change at the other end. No laughing or tormenting words.

A nothingness that was so indicative of the social malaise that had swept across the town that week.

Then, another notion that seemed as peculiar as the thought that the local priest was calling her to tease.

'Oz?'

The call cut off.

Then a rock flew through her lounge window.

LONG WHITE WINGS AND A HALO

A baby taking its first breath. Foreign aid. Billie Holliday's voice.
  C h a r i t y.
  Cures. See also: *vaccinations, considered commentary, veganism.*
  Guide dogs for the blind. Recycling. Documentaries.
  A seventeen-year-old girl from Pakistan being awarded the Nobel Peace Prize for her advocacy of human rights in education for women and children.
  Honesty.
  L i e s. See: *little white, preserving someone's feelings.*
  Some other ways that Good presents itself:
  Laughter. Hummus. Allowing one person to pledge their life to another person regardless of race or gender.
  An elderly couple holding hands.
  Orgasms. Forgiveness. Acceptance. Telling somebody that you love them. Being told that you are loved.
  Somebody who chooses to listen when they could be talking.
  All fruit, with the exception of the durian.
  Jacob Brady.
  Michael Brady.

  Little Henry Wallace.

SELFISHLY SELFLESS

And her husband hadn't known what to do.

  Owen ploughed through the locked door, splintering the wooden frame and saw the still water, his wife submerged, not breathing. He was too panicked to notice that her face was holding a smile for the first time since the incident. Not happiness, though. A sinister relief.

He plunged his arms into the blood-addled, floral-scented water, like reaching through sin, and grabbed hold of anything solid. His left hand gripped a clump of hair; his right fell between his wife's legs and he heaved her out.

'No, no, no, no, no,' he said to himself before she slipped from his grasp.

I'm sorry. This time an unheard murmur.

'You stupid fucking bitch.' He was shouting now and pushing down on her chest fifteen times. He blew forcefully into her mouth twice, tasting her anguish. She was so lost.

He continued trying to resuscitate her, cursing with each verse of the heart massage, feeling futile with every chorus of air he tried to fill her lungs with. But she had been under the water for nearly an hour.

It was better for her, this way. Nobody would know what she did. It was for the best.

Selfishly selfless.

Owen Brady collapsed backward, his shoulder blades smashing against the bathtub, but he felt no physical pain. The smirk had been wiped from his dead wife's face; he never saw that haunting grin. The one that signified the abatement of Faith Brady's guilt.

He stared at the broken woman, crumpled on the tiles in front of him, and asked, 'What have you done, Faith? What about Michael? What am I going to tell Michael?'

Owen cried. But not for the woman on the floor. And, still, he'd had no time to cry for himself.

NO GOOD. NO CHANCE.

I had left Owen while he was drinking so that I could be with Faith Brady.

She, too, was drunk. Muttering to herself.

I love Michael more than anything. That's why I have to do this.

Whatever I look like to you, however you see me, whichever way I appear, imagine me rolling my eyes at this.

She declared those words to the tiles beneath her feet before stepping into the water. Then, looking down in the direction of the kitchen table on the floor below, where her saddened and frustrated husband was trying to drink away his hopelessness, she mumbled again.

I leave him with you. And take everything else with me. The evil. The things you do not need to know. The crap. I take it. You stay here with everything that is good and innocent and right.

So dramatic.

 ## A THOUGHT FOR THE PEOPLE
Life is happening *for* you,
not *to* you.

I watched her do everything. Not once did I get involved. Same as the park. And she did not take Evil anywhere. People do not have control over me. That's not how it works. I can't be controlled, only affected. And here's the warped mathematics of it all, the less good people are, the more evil I have to be. If you are better to each other then my impact never has to reach a level higher than a stiff breeze. Let me be lazy. You work hard, instead.

The problem I see more now is that people, even in a town like Hinton Hollow, have stopped being good to themselves. Without that, your species is doomed.

No good.

No chance.

Owen Brady felt fairly sure there was no heaven. He still feels that way. But, if there was, he knew for certain that his wife was not going there. And he would never lie to Michael about that. She was not allowed anywhere near Jacob.

He stepped over his wife's body and walked into the room they'd shared two nights before, when he thought he knew her. When they still had two sons. The phone was on her side of the bed.

She didn't have a side of the bed any more.

He dialled 999 and asked for the police and an ambulance, though he knew he was wasting time with the latter. The operator asked him to stay on the phone but he threw the receiver on the bed, leaving the woman talking to a corpse in the adjacent bathroom.

And Owen walked down the hall to lie down next to the boy on the bottom bunk with the pillow in his arms.

I got what I wanted.

Hinton Hollow had taken another.

EVERYBODY WALKED

Hinton Hollow had very little traffic, even during rush hour, but it was eerily quiet on the night that Detective Sergeant Pace visited the Brady home.

He tried to concentrate on the case while walking but it was all happening too quickly and the tempo of life in Hinton Hollow was more relaxed than his urban existence. The team at the station was small but they had known he was coming, and still it was taking days to sort Pace out with a vehicle. It took them a little longer to react. To everything.

He left one of the constables to deal with sourcing his car and went ahead to the Brady's alone, his mind wandering to the reasons he had returned and whether it had been the right thing to do. Then his phone vibrated. He knew without looking that it was Maeve, trying to contact him. Concerned. He'd have to face up to that at some point. I had to nudge him to stop him from doing it at that moment.

The town was united in its condemnation of the man who had killed the innocent boy, Jacob. Yet they seemed torn about where their minds should focus. The family would need support, of course, but so would Mrs Beaufort. She was recovering quickly, but her attack had scared a lot of people. *And who was more likely to be at the Good Shepherd on Sunday.* He rolled his eyes at that thought.

A streetlamp flickered as his shadow passed through it and Pace could smell cinnamon.

When people think they see the devil, they smell sulphur, but true evil smells like cinnamon.

And while his mind was busy thinking about everything and nothing at the same time it stopped on the image of that secluded spot in Swinley Forest and what he had done there, what he had left behind. He had been tested. And he had responded.

I looked into Pace's eyes that night and he stared right back.

Detective Sergeant Pace managed to fight his way out of his mind long enough to notice a man entering a phone box. One of the old, iconic red ones. Not a silver one with frosted glass where you could surf the internet in privacy. He managed to smile to himself at the charming idiosyncrasies of his childhood home. These are the things he had missed.

He turned right onto Cotters Way. The Bradys lived half a mile up on the left.

Four of them had lived there a couple of days before.

Only two remained.

ONE DOOR SHUTS

When nobody answered, Detective Sergeant Pace let himself in through the front door. This part of Hinton Hollow was a more modern development that had been erected quickly, and often at the expense of quality, to accommodate the growing number of young families that were either blooming locally or being imported from areas that were not close enough to the train line to commute to the city.

Couples starting out, like Liv and Oz.

Families like the Bradys.

The letterbox had been fitted vertically in a position that made it simple enough to reach a hand through, flip the latch and open the door from the outside. Every house on the development had this ill-conceived feature. Teenagers exploited the flaw when they forgot their house keys, but it had never been used for anything more insidious than that.

Pace pushed the door open quickly, lifting it at the same time to avoid the noise of creaking hinges. A light was on at the end of the corridor. There were empty beer bottles on a table. The chair was far enough from the table to indicate that it had been pushed back in anger, in haste.

The sixth step made a sound as his size-eleven foot pushed down against it. Pace stopped for a moment. There was only one door that was shut upstairs. Any other officer in Hinton Hollow would assume that Faith Brady's dead body was shut behind it. Pace knew that the boy and his father would be behind there, neither of them knowing what was happening or why.

Michael should have been scared. It had sounded like his father was killing his mother in the next room. But Michael knew better than that. He had been in the park the day before.

His eyes opened at the sixth-stair sound; his head was resting on his father's chest. They were both awake. Both in shock. Owen had called for the police and ambulance. He'd left his wife as a damp, wrinkled pile of sin in their en-suite bathroom. He'd been lying with his son since that moment, his arms and clothes still wet from dragging her sorry body from the tub. And Michael had welcomed him without question, despite the words he had heard exchanged in temper and everything he had experienced only the day before.

They were holding each other, lying in Jacob's lingering scent.

All the boys together.

Michael held his breath as Pace opened the door, the light behind him leaving him a silhouette that reminded the boy of the man who had killed his brother. He thought he was screaming but he was not.

'Where is your wife, Mr Brady?'

Pace hadn't even looked at the body but he did not suspect Owen. He'd still have to take him in, but he left the conclusion-jumping to the community members who thrived on g o s s i p.

'Can we talk about this somewhere else, Detective?' Owen was in denial. Not about Faith's suicide but that his son understood that his mother was now dead, too.

'We're going to talk about it at the station. Where is your wife?'

Owen looked at Michael, both of them still lying in Jacob's bunk.

'In the bathroom.' He exhaled. 'She's in the bathroom.'

When the paramedics arrived shortly after Pace, they gave him the same look they had given him in the park. No way. No hope.

Another dead Brady.

'I want you to come with me, Mr Brady. It needs to be now and things will look a whole lot better if you do it of your own accord.'

Owen held his hands up in a gesture of compliant surrender. Michael was sat up on the bed alone. He was lost. He'd feel that way for a long while.

'You'll both need to be checked over.' Pace's tone was more hushed. Owen had stepped close enough to have both feet in Pace's shadow, and Michael could be seen over his father's shoulder, doing his usual act of saying absolutely nothing.

'This is fucked. I don't know what to say to him.'

'Is there anyone who can look after Michael?'

Owen looked back at his son, then, through gritted teeth, 'I'll look after him.'

'I know that, Mr Brady. I mean for the next day. While you are answering questions, helping with the investigation.' Pace was trying to keep things as level as possible. For the boy.

'I don't...' He trailed off.

'No grandparents? Friends? Neighbours? A teacher that he trusts? Anything?'

Owen Brady shook his head in resignation.

'I can't think straight,' he admitted.

'We can appoint someone. We'll get him seen to by a doctor and someone he can talk to.'

Owen was nodding and explaining things to his son while people were photographing Faith Brady's undignified cadaver before bagging the woman and anything deemed vital from the last two rooms of the house she had been seen in.

Detective Sergeant Pace waited for a constable to finally arrive with the car he'd been waiting for. He put Owen Brady on the back seat and drove him back to Hinton Hollow Police Station, retracing the route he had taken to get there.

The man at the phone box was no longer there.

He had made his call.

He'd hung up on Liv Dunham.

And made his way back to the dark.

TROUBLE FOLLOWS

Pace was staying in a room above The Arboreal. A non-smoking, non-child-friendly room on top of the bar with a view that looked out over the Hinton Hollow crossroads. He took a sip of cheap whisky and lit a cigarette. And watched the lights turn from green to red.

I watched them, too.

I waited.

He took his mobile phone from his pocket – another way evil presents itself – and looked around at the wallpaper, expecting those black flames. But I gave him nothing. He had to make that call.

It was late. That's what he told himself. That's why he didn't call. He sent a text. Straight ahead, in the flat above the dentist, a morbidly obese woman had pissed herself and died and her dairy-free ice cream was soft but hadn't quite melted in the way that regular ice cream does. And her mouth was sticky with bean juice and soft drink.

Hinton Hollow. Population 5,017.

Down to the left, Rock-a-Bye was closed for the first day since anyone could remember. There was still a pile of clothes on the floor that needed washing.

Round to the right, towards the station, Reynolds was taking more calls than he could handle. Pissing in the street. Puking in someone's front garden. Fucking in a phone box. A broken window. A dead cat in a bin. A mother in a bath, wrists slashed. Hinton Hollow was two days into a steady drop that would see it fall into a pit of torment where nobody would be themselves.

Apart from the kids.

The kids would be fine.

Unless the mothers made the wrong choice.

Detective Sergeant Pace was weak.

Detective Sergeant Pace was scared.

Detective Sergeant Pace was a coward.

He sent a text to Maeve. The worried girlfriend. The woman who thought she loved him.

Hey. You still up?

That was it. If she didn't answer, she'd see in the morning that he was alive and well and that could buy him some time.

He put the phone on the windowsill and took a long drag of his cigarette, eventually leaning out of the window like a naughty boy and blowing more poison into his town. Mrs Beaufort would not approve.

The phone rang immediately. Maeve's name flashing ferociously. He shut his eyes for a moment and breathed to prepare himself.

Then hit the button to answer, not knowing how to open the conversation.

It wasn't worth worrying about.

'Oh, thank God you're okay. You are okay, aren't you?'

'Yes. Yes. Of course. I'm sorry I haven't come back to you. I meant to.' It was a half-truth.

See: *Little white lies.*

See also: *T r u t h.*

Any edge to the conversation dissipated within seconds. I wondered whether Pace was himself with this woman. He told her things about the last case. Things he had never told anybody. Things about the letters and the triggers and the bridges and the suicides and the cult and the murders and a manual.

DETAILS DETECTIVE SERGEANT PACE SHOULD NOT HAVE MENTIONED
The victims had received a letter.
The letter contained four words.
Nothing. Important. Happened. Today.
These words triggered their death.
He had been sent one of these letters.
He should be dead. He should have been on Tower Bridge.
Staying with Maeve that night had saved his life.

He didn't mention the culprit or how he had figured it out or how the police were still looking for somebody or how they would never find him. Because of what he'd done.

And you know that she was just happy to hear his voice because she let him talk and talk. About his hometown, about Hinton Hollow, about the Brady boy and his mother, about RD's Diner, about Reynolds and Mrs Beaufort, about how he wanted to get away from the city but it seems as though 'everywhere I go, trouble follows. Like I'm cursed or something. Like I've brought some fucking blight on my hometown, you know?'

She knew. She reassured him that there was no such thing. That he was being paranoid.

I wanted to throw some black flames across his walls but resisted. I don't do this for my own amusement. I am here to keep the balance.

The call finished and Pace lit another cigarette. The bar kicked out downstairs and three men walked towards the crossroads. The lights changed to green and a car that had passed him on his first day made its way towards Roylake.

Inside the car were two brothers.

Another way that evil presents itself is estate agents.

See: *Ablett and Ablett.*

POO-TEE-WEET

From 13th to 15th February, 1945, nearly 4,000 tonnes of explosives and incendiary devices were dropped on the German city of Dresden.

People, again.

I was there. Of course. I had to be. But I am not a Lancaster aircraft. I am not a bomb. I am not the fire raging through the streets.

I am the raging fire within.

That war, however, is a much bigger story than the one that unfolded in Hinton Hollow. The destruction of Dresden was physical. It could be seen and smelled and touched. The decimation of that Berkshire village was internal. The buildings would remain the same, with the exception of a few broken windows. The changes were occurring inside each member of the community.

They were starting to feel something. But they had no idea what it was.

I was content with my work on that second day and let The Hollow lie in peace. And I watched over Oz Tambor and the woods.

It would be good to get an early start the following morning.

A SNEAK PREVIEW
Day three started with 'Heeeeugh.'
And it ended with 'I...'

DAY THREE

Where you will learn about:

An inappropriate inspector
A man in the woods in the boot of a car
The Hadley family
Two estate agent brothers
and the weight of a soul.

WHERE IS HOME, ANYWAY?

'Heeeeugh.' Liv Dunham let out an exaggerated yawn, stretching her arms over the edge of the sofa she had slept so soundly on. A piece of cardboard was taped over the hole in the window and the rock with a tie wrapped around it had slept next to her on the coffee table.

She'd needed her rest after such a broken night when Oz hadn't returned. Liv had managed to convince herself, for one night, at least, that Oz was safe. That he was out there. He was alive. And that he had called her that previous evening.

Sure, the person at the other end of the phone hadn't said a word but, sometimes, when you love somebody, you just don't have to. That's what Oz would say when Liv was fishing for an apology after an argument. He thought he was being laid-back or funny, but it just pissed Liv off even more.

The cold whiteness of a new day was already beginning to cast some doubt over the young English-teacher's theory. It didn't feel like Hinton Hollow.

Catching a glimpse of her ruffled reflection in the television did not help. Her hair needed a wash and her left cheek was red and mottled slightly from the imperfections in the leather sofa. It lent her face some much-needed colour, but somehow she thought she looked too good for her predicament.

How could she sleep so well when a little boy had been killed in the town where she lived? How dare she contemplate something so trivial as her appearance when the man she was due to marry in a few days was still *nowhere*?

I teased her.

Are you certain it was Oz at the other end of the line?

Do you really know who Oscar Tambor is, Liv?

The truth is, that morning, Liv Dunham didn't know how she felt. She didn't know how she *should* feel, what she *should* do.

Last night she had been so struck by her situation. The call hadn't felt threatening. There was no heavy breathing or taunting. Just silence. But shouldn't that be more disconcerting? Her intuition had told her she was not in danger from the caller, but that wasn't based on anything other than sleep deprivation and the falsity that often accompanies hope. She had no experience in these matters. She had simply *felt* that it was Oz. She so much wanted it to be him that perhaps she convinced herself that he still cared enough to make contact. Maybe all she did was notify a mad person that she was alone.

Contradicting thoughts sparked across the synapses of Liv's educated mind, flustering her in the way Constable Reynolds had the previous evening with his condescending insights into her relationship. Her right leg was already bouncing up and down as she leant a little closer to the TV screen, the sofa cushion squeaking slightly against her skin as she moved towards the edge of the seat.

It was 10:15. Almost forty-eight hours since she had last seen or spoken – in a two-way conversation – with her fiancé. She could call the local constabulary again in an hour and they would have to look into her story. But what if the silence at the end of the phone had been Oz? Wouldn't she just be wasting police time when they needed all of their manpower to investigate poor Jacob Brady's case? The news about Faith Brady was not yet town knowledge.

Maybe the constable would laugh at her for calling again. Or perhaps he would note her desperation. Her genuine distress. Neither option seemed the correct answer, at that time, for Liv Dunham.

So she remained a woman of inaction.

Staying in and waiting for the phone to ring.

Waiting for Oz.

She forced herself to her feet and plodded to the kitchen, the bruise on her hip had spread out into a deep yellow fan. She took two slices of bread from the cupboard, placed them in the toaster and waited. They popped out a couple of minutes later, browned, but not enough. She pushed the lever back down, went to the fridge, removed the butter and a knife from the cutlery drawer. When the toast bounced up a second time it was more on the side of *charred* than *golden*. Liv buttered both slices, cut them in half diagonally then walked them over to Oz's place at the table and set the plate down.

Then she walked around to her own seat, gently lowered herself down and stared at the empty space she hoped would soon be filled by the man she loved and missed.

She took half a piece of toast off his plate and told herself that it was all she needed.

A PIG

Dorothy choked-on-an-ice-cream-covered-chicken-bone Reilly had finally managed to lose some weight.

At the time of her death, she dropped twenty-one grams.

The physical weight is insignificant when taking into account her obvious morbid obesity, but scholars and sceptics have pondered the idea that the metaphysical weight is incomparable. Many believe that this mysterious loss of mass at the moment one ceases to exist is a result of a person's soul leaving their body.

**WHAT I KNOW ABOUT
THE HUMAN SOUL
It's not my department**

At the moment Dorothy washed-down-a-bucket-of-chicken-skin-with-two-litres-of-full-fat-Coke Reilly died, her lungs were no longer active in cooling her blood. That sudden rise in temperature and subsequent sweating could account for the loss in weight.

Something I have noticed with the development of the Western diet – see also: *heart disease, diabetes, gout, gallstones* and *cancer* – is that people do not understand the weight of a gram.

What does 21g sound like to you? What object do you know that weighs 21g? That way, you would have a better idea of what a soul might weigh.

If someone had a cup of coffee and put two teaspoons of sugar into their mug, how much do you think that sweet powder would weigh?

What if you took a regular can of Coke and looked at how many grams of sugar it contained, would you understand what was going into your body? What if it was shown as thirty-five sachets of sugar? Would that paint a better picture?

And how would you react if somebody put thirty-five sachets of sugar into a cup of coffee?

If you don't understand what is going into your body, how could the human mind and collective consciousness possibly comprehend the 21g that seemingly evaporated from Dorothy Reilly if, in fact, it was not through sweat and was the sudden exit of her soul, her essence?

WHAT I THINK ABOUT
THE HUMAN SOUL
It is real.
It is in trouble.
Perhaps one does not have to wait for death
in order for a part of it to leave their being.

Twenty-one grams is not a lot. Dorothy was weighed down by her emotions as well as the composition of her body. She hated herself for what she was doing, and for giving up. She was alone and low. It burdened her on the inside. I think her soul would have weighed more.

Shortly after her soul may have departed, the largely atrophied muscles in Ms Reilly's body relaxed, including the sphincter muscles, meaning that substances held in the bladder and bowels while she was alive were given the opportunity to spill.

Further weight loss.

In total, it was less than a can of Coke.

Unnoticeable.

She had nobody.

And nobody would ever see. She was face down with food still in her throat. She had wet herself. There was shit in her underwear. But in that week, it ranked very low that Dorothy Reilly may have lost her soul.

Even a heart covered in fat can love. Can yearn. Can break.

Can be pushed too hard.

A CAT

It looked too much like a cat, even with the legs folded in against the torso. So, Darren decided to remove the head and wrap each section separately in clingfilm. The head was squeezed into a tight ball and the rest into a feline ballotine.

There was a separate bin for recycling food that was kept underneath the sink. Darren threw the head into the plastic box and disposed of the rest of his old pet in the receptacle that was reserved for other general waste.

He thought nothing of it.

I was with him but I did not have a hand in this. He was changing by himself now. And he was enjoying it. The freedom of it. This was who Darren had always been inside.

It does not seem right that his soul would weigh the same as Dorothy's.

He had the capacity for more. Greater evil. Like Dorothy Reilly, he was alone. Darren was not a well-known member of the Hinton Hollow community.

One more push and he could be.

One more.

A pig. A cat. More.

A HUMAN

I don't know why Annie broke windows.

I can't choose how individuals will react to my touch. Smashing the glass meant something to her. Perhaps her life was so neat and ordered and structured that throwing something through a window and creating something imperfect and cracked and messy was a release.

Maybe that's why she chose Liv Dunham's lounge as her second victim. Liv was loved in the village. Her students respected her, parents spoke highly, she was due to marry her school sweetheart. A perfect target.

Maybe Annie just wanted to break something.

In the morning on day three, I visited Annie Harding and I shook her awake from a guiltless sleep.

Her husband was fidgeting as the light began to creep in through the blinds. Annie felt beneath the covers. His bare chest was smooth and muscular. He stopped moving as she stroked down his body, then his eyes opened slightly when her hand pushed beneath the waistband of his boxer shorts.

'Well, that's one way to wake me up in the morning.'

'You just stay there,' she instructed, looking him straight in the eyes. No make-up and her hair in disarray, she looked younger. She was different somehow.

Her head ducked beneath the quilt and she kissed her husband's body, working her way downwards before taking his dick and putting it in her mouth. He couldn't remember the last time Annie had done that, even while drunk, but he didn't want to say anything.

It didn't take long to bring him to the height of excitement. He knew that he had to tell her when he was about to come so that she could stop and finish the job with her hand, leaving a mess on his stomach, watching his face as he hit that moment of nothingness. It was an unwritten agreement that they had.

He told her. But she ignored it. Instead, she pushed the covers away from her head so that she could look him in the eyes as he came in her mouth.

Neither of them spoke for a minute afterwards, lying next to one another, staring at the ceiling. Annie was smiling. Her husband in shock.

'I guess it's only fair that I should make the breakfast this morning.' He smiled and groaned slightly as he sat up. 'You want coffee?'

Annie Harding did not want coffee. She did not want to break any more windows. In fact, she was a woman who knew exactly what she wanted. All I had to do was give her a push and watch as she did the rest.

She sat up, too. Then grabbed her husband's shoulder and pulled him back to the bed. It wasn't aggressive and he could have fought against it but instead chose to lean into the playfulness. Annie straddled his stomach and looked down at her husband. She was wearing a grey vest and no underwear.

'I don't know where you think you're going.' And she moved herself up the bed until her knees were either side of her man's head.

The breakfast could wait a while longer.

I could not.

I had rounds to make.

BYSTANDERS

People do not call the police when they see that a young woman has taken it upon herself to kneel on the concrete and unzip the trousers of a nightclub bouncer. It's not a crime worth reporting. It is disgusting to witness, even for a moment, even a sideways glimpse. But what are you going to do? Chastise the girl mid-prayer? Confront one of those muscle-bound ex-military types who are undoubtedly preparing to unload their damaged-by-steroid-use, lazy swimmers into the mouth of the naive, hooch-soused wannabe dancer?

Another way that evil presents itself: bystanders.

Very little is officially divulged about the *events* that occur at The Split Aces club on the outskirts of Hinton Hollow. It isn't even really a nightclub, and the bouncers are more commonly referred to as *guards.*

It hasn't been officially disowned by the town, but it isn't acknowledged, either – the building is there, but nobody sees it. Though, should something untoward occur, Constable Reynolds would undoubtedly be the person on the front desk who would take the call. And, in that week, Detective Sergeant Pace would be the only man unafraid to follow things up.

But nothing was reported from that side of town on the second night. And there was no aggravation outside The Arboreal. No one had sped through the crossroads and jumped the lights on their way to somewhere more interesting. Very few people were outside in Hinton Hollow on night two of that dark week. Most had heard about the death of the Brady boy and intended to spend that evening with their own families, talking and hugging and double-locking the doors and triple-checking the windows.

In fact, it seemed to Constable Reynolds that just about everyone in Hinton Hollow was safe at home. All with the exception of Ernie Cavet, who had closed a deal at the IT company where he worked and had shared several bottles of Malbec with his boss to celebrate.

He'd arrived back in Hinton Hollow on the last train and hadn't heard the news. Then he'd wobbled his way across the playing fields, not noticing the darkness soaking the dirt path that led into the woods where Oz Tambor was lying in the boot of a car, shaking. And he knocked over a plant pot in his garden while looking for the spare key to enter his own house while his latest wife called Constable Reynolds about a *noise in the garden.*

There had also been the woman worried about her boyfriend. He hadn't come home but it had only been a day. *Liv Dunham*, he reminded himself. *And Oscar Tambor.* Reynolds had remembered the names clearly. Not that he was particularly skilled at his job, but because he had only received those two calls on what had turned out to be a laborious graveyard shift.

He assumed, like others, that the boyfriend was *stepping out* on this girl. Probably sampling the delights over at The Split Aces – Split Arses, he called it. The only thing happening in Hinton Hollow seemed to be the Brady case and he was not involved in that now that Pace was back. He probably would have been sidelined, anyway. His forte was the front desk; his face was kind. Dopey and largely vacant, but kind. Approachable. Reynolds was *filler* at best but he took it upon himself to remember Liv Dunham and the call she had made. He would check on his next shift to see whether she ever called back. He doubted she would. *Oscar Tambor will come home stinking of* strange *and she'll forgive him*, he thought.

Pace had dropped off Owen Brady – the father of the dead kid – a few hours before and let him sweat things out in a cell. Now, it was morning, and he was back to question him. It had been the most interesting part of Reynolds' night. He'd got a little excited by it. He knew he shouldn't have but it was just about the most thrilling event in the history of Hinton Hollow, as far as he could remember – like most, he'd lived here all his life. He was too young to remember the incident with Carson Chase and that other dark time – another small story in Hinton Hollow. Good to be back.

Tragic, he told himself, *but it's about time something happened in this town.*

Forty-five minutes later he'd be at home, alone with a beer at 11:30 in the morning. He didn't have a problem with the booze – though he liked it – it was simply that it felt like the night to Constable Reynolds. He was also going to heat up a lasagne before going to bed for eight hours, wake up, eat a bowl of cereal and get dressed for another late shift.

Eight hours was more sleep than Detective Sergeant Pace had that entire week.

He hadn't slept properly since Swinley Forest. Closing his eyes meant seeing a killer handcuffed to one of the trees.

G u i l t, for Pace, was like espresso for an insomniac, though its taste was slightly more bitter.

'Has he slept?' There was no greeting from Pace. Nor had Reynolds felt any warmth from the detective the night before when the chief had announced Faith Brady's death, not stating whether it was a murder or suicide.

'Not a wink, as far as I can tell.' Reynolds had been checking in on Owen Brady every twenty minutes as Pace had instructed before he left the station. Reynolds assumed he'd gone home to sleep. *Where is his home, anyway?*

'Good. That's what I thought,' he responded, knowingly, the right side of his mouth curling up into something that was almost a grin.

The look made Reynolds feel uncomfortable. He shouldn't be smiling on a day like today, a week like this week, with everything going on. It was exciting but nothing to smile about.

It was a big day for me.

A big day for Evil.

The door to the station rattled as a gust of wind blew out of town towards the train station. Pace jumped slightly and turned his gaze back over his shoulder. Reynolds noticed his anxiety but couldn't see Pace's balled right fist from behind the desk.

I needed to rattle him.

To build.

'Looks like that long summer has come to an abrupt end,' Reynolds offered. 'It'll start getting dark before you know it.'

Pace had no time for small talk about the weather, he was just pleased that nothing had come in behind him and caught him unaware.

'Chief out back?'

'Where he always is.'

Pace walked around the front desk and headed towards the door at the back that led into the part of the police station that people hardly ever saw. Both men looked at the large clock on the back wall. To Pace, the hands seemed to be moving so fast it looked more like a fan. Reynolds wondered whether the thing had stopped working.

Pace stopped before opening the back door reserved for employees only.

'Thanks for checking in on him.'

Reynolds shrugged his shoulders and tilted his head to one side as though saying *no problem, that's my job.* Then he smiled when the door closed behind the detective. He was dark and new and unknown to a degree but Detective Sergeant Pace had given Constable Reynolds something that he rarely received. Praise. Validation that his efforts were worthwhile.

But the approval and the excitement should have stayed within him. He should never have smiled. Not that week. When people were dying and Mrs Beaufort had been struck down. It wasn't right.

He wanted his beer and to talk with Father Salis. He wanted to leave through the door that kept blowing open. But the hands on the clock didn't want to move.

THE SHOW MUST GO ON

Everyone knew he was back. But, after two days, the town still thought of him as their possible saviour. That he would know how to deal with something like this.

I let them think that. I let *him* think that.

But it had to change.

He needed to see those black flames. He needed to feel them. He had done something bad, so I had to do something worse.

**IF DETECTIVE PACE HAD NOT
GONE INTO SWINLEY FOREST**
You would not have heard of Hinton Hollow.
I would have only visited here once, for Carson Chase.
Jacob Brady would have made it home from school.
Liv Dunham would have become Liv Tambor.
Mrs Beaufort would still appear to be kind.

Detective Sergeant Pace had left Owen Brady at the station and told him to rest. An impossible task with his youngest son being shot two days earlier and his wife joining the boy in the morgue the next night. The scene had screamed *suicide* to Pace but the chief wasn't taking any chances. He could feel the change in Hinton Hollow as much as Pace, who would soon start to blame himself for everything. Just as he had in the city.

'Come in,' the chief boomed from behind his flimsy door when Pace knocked. The door had frosted glass and etched in black were the words *Inspector Anderson*, arched into a semi-circle like some old-fashioned American private investigator. (RD would love that kind of thing.)

'Ah, Pace. What's the deal with the Brady fellow? Blamed the wife, did he?'

Anderson was a slight puzzle for Pace at first. He'd come across this kind of detachment before, hardened chief inspectors who had seen too much that they couldn't forget, seemingly desensitised to the violence and obvious corruption that jacked itself into their everyday lives. But he expected something different in his hometown. Something more wholesome, perhaps. Caring.

Pace had never heard of Anderson before and he didn't remember him from when he was a kid. He was older than Pace by maybe fifteen years, early fifties. It could have been that he had arrived in Hinton Hollow from the outside, that would explain his lack of propriety. It could simply be that he felt threatened by the arrival of a *City Detective*. He was playing up. Being the tough guy.

Tickled by Evil.

His inspector sat behind a desk that looked as though it used to belong to Mrs Beaufort when she attended school. It wasn't ostentatious, it was practical and it was there. Anderson sat behind it with a regimentally straight back though his chair was leaning slightly giving him an air of looseness. He looked as big sitting down as RD did standing up but less broad, less bearlike.

It was the moustache that finally settled Pace's opinion. That giant, thick, orange moustache that wobbled over his top lip while his Oxford accent resonated beneath. A moustache wasn't something you often saw on its own, even with the older members of town who had seen battle. It was more comical than serious – though it was a *serious* moustache. What it said about Inspector Anderson of the Hinton Hollow police was that he absolutely did not give a fuck what you thought.

'I haven't spoken to him properly yet, sir.' Pace found himself trying, for some reason, to sound as matter-of-fact as his superior.

'Leave him to sweat a bit. Of course. Probably best. You think he did it?' Anderson placed the end of a pen in his mouth and that simple action made Pace want to smoke.

'Absolutely not.'

The inspector nodded as though Pace had just uttered a most interesting piece of information.

'It looks pretty cut and dried to me. Everything at the house looked normal. The kid was in bed, the wife was upstairs in the bath, the husband was downstairs drowning his sorrows in beer.'

'Don't think he got a bit drunk and bumped her off for not looking after the kids properly?'

Fuck, this guy has no filter at all. Pace spoke to himself, engaging his own filter.

It was nothing to do with me. It's just how he was. There had been no tickle from Evil.

'It's far more likely that she felt worse about herself than he felt about her, sir. There were enough pills and vodka in the vicinity to prove lethal, and I'm sure the post-mortem will show this. Her skin was wrinkled. He'd have had to drug her, wait until she passed out before cutting her wrists and thigh, then wait downstairs while drinking for an hour before feigning a rescue attempt for the ears of the only possible witness.'

'Stranger things, Detective Pace. Stranger things.' He looked towards the ceiling at that point as though trying to recall a similar case. Of course, in Hinton Hollow, nothing had ever occurred that was even microscopically similar.

'The door had been locked from the inside. Owen Brady had to smash through it from the bedroom.'

'That's how it looks. I think you're probably right, but let's squeeze the little fellow a tad, eh? Cover things off. Tick all the boxes. And then get out there and find who shot the man's son.'

'I imagine that the schools will be shut today?' Pace changed the direction of the conversation.

'Out of respect?'

The schools had been shut on day two but that was long enough.

'Out of safety.'

'Oh Pace, you have been gone a while, haven't you.' Anderson pulled the pen from beneath his substantial facial hair and sat forward on his chair, leaning against his too-small desk.

Pace was trying not to screw his face up at his new boss but it was proving difficult. Who did he think he was talking to?

'Even if I wanted that to be the case, my hands are tied. There will be a united front on this one like there is about anything that seemingly goes against the town. We won't be bullied out of living our normal Hinton Hollow lives. You must know that? The show must go on.'

'But—'

'People still work in very tall buildings in America,' the chief interrupted. 'Londoners still get on the bloody Tube every day. And the children of Hinton Hollow will still pop their ties into a lazy half-Windsor knot and trudge up the path to their schools in this crazy wind in order to learn their *readin', ritin' and rithmatic.*' He attempted a West-Country accent for the last part though Pace knew not why. Perhaps attempting to detach himself further from the ordeal through humour, make it less real.

'Well, I hope you don't mind me saying, sir, but that's fucking ludicrous.'

'Welcome home, Mr Pace. I believe Owen Brady has some information that may prove pertinent to this case.' He raised a ginger eyebrow.

'Sure. Sure. I'm on it. Just need to make a quick phone call.'

Outside the chief's office, Pace took out his mobile phone. A text from Maeve.

It was too much to deal with.

He was going to text back.

I gently placed my weight on his shoulders and he put the phone back in his pocket. Ignoring her again. To his peril.

KEEP UP

'Forgive me, Father, for I have sinned.'

Father Salis did not recognise the voice on the other side of the partition.

Darren had never been to confession. He never went to church. That's not who he was.

Darren woke up, he ate breakfast, he went to work, pushed around some livestock, stunned them, cut them, skinned them, made them into deadstock, went home, ate, drank, masturbated and watched something on television while stroking the cat that was next to him on the sofa. That's what Darren did. What he used to do. Before he punctured his pet repeatedly with a greasy butter knife.

That's why he was at church. He wasn't himself. He was doing things that he would normally never do.

But these things were inside him.

And I was his guide.

'It has been forever since my last confession.' Darren didn't really know what he was doing or whether he even thought there was a God but he'd seen enough films to know that the thing you say after *forgive me* is a statement of how long it has been since your last confession.

'Forever?' Salis asked. His voice was calm, it sounded as though he was smiling.

'I've never been, Father.'

'And what brings you here today?' Nothing could have prepared Father Salis for the response.

'I punched a pig.'

I could have reached into the priest here and pushed a button that made him laugh. But I let it go.

'I'm sorry, you ... punched a...?'

'Pig. Right on the snout. And I rubbed salt into the cut. And I kicked it.' Darren hung his head.

'And where did this happen?'

'At work.'

'You work with animals? On a farm?'

'Something like that, yes.'

The slaughterhouse was like The Split Aces club, it was on the outskirts of Hinton Hollow but still within its boundaries. Near enough to know it was there but far enough to ignore. Nobody really wants to understand where their meat comes from and nobody wants to talk about anything that might happen at the club.

'Ah, go on.'

Darren explained what had happened on that first night. How he'd become so enraged with the animal and taken out his frustrations in a physical way. To Father Salis, Darren seemed mild, perhaps remedial, and repentant.

'You regret your actions.' It was not a question.

I could see that Darren did not like the statement. So I pushed him. I turned it up to a six.

'I didn't realise this was a sorry chamber, I thought it was about confessing.' He sat up straight.

'Yes, of course. But you are seeking the Lord's forgiveness so there must be some remorse, some regret.'

I turned Darren up to a seven.

'Well, I can't stop thinking about it. Running through it in my mind over and over. The thing is, when you start, the sound these things make when they are heading inside to die, it's terrible. Really.

Horrific. But you get used to it. You start to not hear it. And they are screaming, Father. It's like they know what's coming.'

Then he leant in towards the partition. Father Salis was turned to the side, listening rather than looking.

'You start to like it. That noise, it's like whale song, eventually. You need it to get you through the day. I bet you have some things that help you get through the day that you'd rather not talk about, Father.'

Darren watched to see if Salis was uncomfortable.

The priest didn't move. He listened.

'The thing is, the day after, I found that I couldn't eat meat. I just couldn't do it.'

Darren waited for a response.

Salis was quiet.

Turn up to eight.

'But it didn't mean that I didn't want blood. I'd had that cat for seven years. I loved him. He was my companion. He was always there with me.'

'A cat?'

'Yes. A cat. Keep up. My cat. He got a hair in my sandwich so I held him down by his neck and stabbed him through his ribs until he stopped moving. And you ask me if I regret what I have done? My only regret is that I didn't do it sooner.' He growled the last sentence through the dividing wall and, before the priest could look up and ask anything, Darren was gone.

I wondered where Darren would go if I dug a little deeper. Was it within him to take things further. To move on from the animals to humans? And is it my fault for unleashing something or is it yours for being so awful that I had no choice but to.

MOTHERS

There were three schools in the parish of Hinton Hollow.

Hinton Hollow Primary School had the largest intake of children in their infant and junior years because it was the biggest and also located more centrally. The ever-changing catchment areas did not seem to affect HHPS. If you didn't live within the Hinton Hollow border, there was no sense in applying.

Stanhope Church of England School was different. It sat on the border of Hinton Hollow and Roylake, the front gates opening out onto the Stanhope Road. The actual building was on Hollow ground but it accepted children from beyond the invisible town lines. Both were great schools. High-performing. High-achieving schools.

The third was the closest secondary school in the area and sat at its northern tip. The bricks and concrete were actually Twaincroft Hill structures while the playing field fell on Hollow earth. Liv Dunham taught there.

All three schools were open on that third day, that hump in the week that would prove more difficult to get over than any other Wednesday in the town's past. And every school was resolute in the decision to carry on, business as usual. None more so than HHPS, where bunches of flowers had already been laid in the park, propped up against a tree that had a snapped line of police tape tied around the trunk, rasping in the gale that had been dancing all over town trying to blow away the shadows. But summer was as dead as Jacob Brady.

Parents walked their children to school as usual, stalking the paths in closer packs, some looking around at the woods nervously, others telling themselves that lightning wouldn't strike the same place twice.

The teenagers at the secondary school seemed unaffected by the events. A kid had been shot, and they'd already established a pattern of victims that they didn't seem to fit into. Surely it couldn't happen to one of them.

On day three, that bump in the road of the week, they were right. They were lucky. Parents feigned strength and solidarity as they dropped their children in the playground, many of them waiting until the bell rang and the kids lined up in their classes to enter the hopeful safety of bricks and mortar.

What the people and police were looking for was a child killer. That's what they had wrong – in the beginning. The truth was, it had always only been about the mothers.

On that morning, as children filed into their classes and parents walked wearily back to their homes and RD's wife cut a carrot cake into twelve slices and Owen Brady sweated in a cell and Detective Sergeant Pace walked back to his room at The Arboreal, Oz Tambor was lying in the boot of a car with a coat wrapped snuggly around his torso, craving sugar.

And I was there.

Brewing another storm.

The wind was yet to build enough courage to penetrate deep into the woods, so everything was still for Oz, all but the fluttering of the highest leaves, the ones that would whisper to him. As long as he was in the woods, he was not alone.

The wind picked up throughout the day, breaking garden fences and felling roadside trees. Roof tiles clattered downward, smashing as recycling tubs took trips across pavements. Those were the least of Hinton Hollow's problems.

By the time my sinister tempest reached the middle of the woods, swaying the branches above the boot of that hatchback, the gentle murmurs had transformed into shrieks in Oz's ears and he would know he had to get out of that car.

NOTHING STABLE ABOUT IT

She'd thought it was a heart attack when her chest tightened and, as she lay on the floor, her head propped up by a pile of unwanted baby garments, she imagined it might be the end. She'd been working so hard. And she was old. Too old, maybe. She had always believed that slowing down would have been the thing that killed her.

When the pain moved into her right arm, she almost let go. Mrs Beaufort seemed to remember something about a pain in your arm when you have a heart attack. But perhaps it had been the left arm. In any case, she couldn't die. Not there. Not then with a customer in the shop. A new mother, too, for crying out loud.

Somehow, I always felt like she could see me.

She was the only one.

Her skull started aching, her neck stiffened and her jaw may have tightened – though that may have been a possible symptom that never actually occurred, she was just recalling some of the questions from the paramedics. Or was it the doctor? She wasn't quite herself yet. Maybe she never would be again; the darkness she feared was just outside the door to her ward. And I wanted her different.

THINGS I LIKE AND THINGS
I DO NOT LIKE
I like the children.
I like music.
I do not like Mrs Beaufort.

The fear of her own mortality had come second to the fear of scaring poor Katy Childs to death. That was when she called on the strength of the Lord to keep her eyes open.

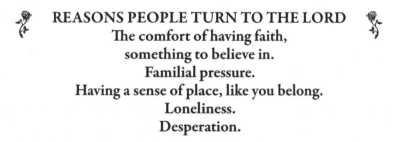

REASONS PEOPLE TURN TO THE LORD
The comfort of having faith,
something to believe in.
Familial pressure.
Having a sense of place, like you belong.
Loneliness.
Desperation.

Father Salis had been the first to visit. In truth, he expected to see old Mrs Beaufort for the final time. His eyes were red and sore when he arrived, but he covered it well. She could tell he'd been upset, of course. She knew everything about everyone, sometimes before they even knew themselves. She'd made quite the habit of predicting pregnancies and she had a nose for matrimonial unrest.

Mrs Beaufort explained to Father Salis that the Lord had carried her from the moment her head hit the folded baby-grow – aged three to six months – and the reverend had ad-libbed that *he still had much work for her to do*. Father Salis pushed his prepared deathbed speech to the back of his mind for use at another time.

It wasn't a heart attack that she suffered.

'Then what was it, doctor?' she asked, slightly uncomfortable that she did not know his name. She knew everybody's name. She had only ever visited her local physician, Dr Green, this was a very rare trip to the hospital for Mrs Beaufort. She had only been a handful of times since her birth over eighty years before.

'Stable angina.'

Mrs Beaufort let out an involuntary snort as she laughed.

'Stable? There was nothing stable about it, I'll tell you.'

That reaction was me.

The doctor, a young – too young in Mrs Beaufort's mind – Pakistani man smiled at his patient, flexing his bedside-manner muscles. Ordinarily, Mrs Beaufort would have smiled back, instead, she eyeballed him as though he'd just asked her how many men she'd slept with. It switched him immediately into clinical professionalism.

'I'm sorry. Yes. Stable simply means that it can be controlled a little easier. You are not in a lot of danger but an attack could flare up if you are overworked or find yourself under stress.'

'I run a shop in Hinton Hollow, Doctor...'

'Choudary.'

'I run a shop, Doctor Choudary. And a little boy has been killed in my town.'

Father Salis had informed her of the news she had missed while she had been in hospital overnight. He hadn't wanted to but Mrs Beaufort could be very persuasive when she wanted to be.

'I'm sorry. I heard about that. But that is exactly the kind of thing you cannot concern yourself with while you recuperate, Mrs

Beaufort.' He was flustered by the old woman's strength of character but mindful of the message he had to deliver.

'But I am concerned, Mr Choudary.' She deliberately replaced the word *doctor*.

'Yes. Of course you are. You just need to be mindful of your activity. You are in excellent health for a person of your years. You are not overweight and your smoking habits were limited to a very short time in your thirties.' Mrs Beaufort balked at this comment, embarrassed. It was an era when cigarettes were as normal as drinking milkshakes but she somehow felt ashamed of her weakness.

OTHER WEAKNESSES OF MRS BEAUFORT
Picking up people on grammar mistakes.
Young, red-haired women.
Ice cream with evaporated milk.
Wartime encounters with US soldiers.
RD's hands.

'So, if I keep working and worrying, it will happen again? Am I supposed to sit on the couch and watch television while my brain turns to liquid?' She pushed herself into an upright, seated position, strong enough not to rely on the mound of pillows behind her back.

'No, Mrs Beaufort. I'm saying that *over*working can trigger another angina attack, and they're not pleasant, as I'm sure you agree.' She nodded.

He explained that he was prescribing her glyceryl trinitrate. Should she experience any of the symptoms of an attack, she should take her medication. It would ease the pain within minutes.

'You can take it as a preventative measure should you know that you are about to embark on an activity that may be strenuous, but that does not mean you can take it every day in order to work as hard as you do now.' The doctor was slightly condescending with this final piece of advice. He knew there was a risk of offending an elderly lady, but he felt the message needed to get across.

He informed her that she was now free to leave but that he would advise that she stay for an extra day of rest. Then he left, walking straight through the darkness of the doorway, I never even touched him. Not one bit rubbed off on Doctor Choudary. But I wasn't there for him. I was waiting for the old lady who knew everybody in town. The friendly grandmother figure who people could turn to with their problems, including the local reverend. It was the sweet, gentle mother of Hinton Hollow. The one pressing her cold, bony finger repeatedly against the red button that would call a nurse. That was who I wanted.

She didn't fool me.

I grabbed her by the hand and led her.

'Yes, Mrs Beaufort. How can I help? You know, you only need to press the button once...' Mrs Beaufort rolled her eyes as the nurse reached behind her bed to fiddle with a button that would reset the call.

'I need to make a phone call. I'm leaving this godforsaken place.'

She'd only been wheeled into the ward on the afternoon of that first day, it was day three when she hit her buzzer over and over. That wasn't long. Certainly not enough time for the doctors, nurses, orderlies or other patients to know and understand that the woman in room six, the one with the hardened, narrowing arteries was no longer Mrs Beaufort.

PARISH RELOCATION

Father Salis was safe. There would be no intervention from me.

I would not change him.

THERE ARE TWO RULES
Leave the kids alone. They start off good.
Leave the priests alone.
They lock up too much inside.

Another way in which evil presents itself is the dog collar. See also: *Catholic guilt* and *parish relocation*.

From the beginning, I have not been able to control the effects of my touch. I can tease out your inner turmoil by latching on to your hidden truths, but I cannot decide how your own personal evil will manifest itself.

There is a certain stigma surrounding this pillar of the Christian community. It comes from somewhere real. It comes from somewhere dark. It comes from somewhere that has been hidden and moved around and obfuscated in order to protect the name of the church.

It has not come from me.

I leave the priests alone.

One thing I have learned from watching people over time is that taking something away from them leaves them yearning. That thing missing from their lives is the thing they search for when I grab hold of their insecurities. Abstinence often leads to promiscuity or infidelity or inviting a prepubescent choirboy to sample a glass of the sacramental wine before telling him that God wants him to swallow your poison.

These priests, these abstainers, they carry some of the worst things inside of them. And that evil often gets aimed at children.

I like the kids.

So I don't touch the priests.

Because I don't want them to touch the kids.

Some things should not be released. Some things are too evil.

Father Salis was safe.

But that does not mean that he was good.

TASTE BUDS

RD and his wife noticed it straight away.

They did know her. They had known her for many a year.

That was the reason she called them. She trusted them. She could rely on their discretion. She didn't want the town to know about her condition. Ordinarily Mrs Beaufort would want to keep this kind of information back so as not to have the townsfolk worry about her. That is how she would have felt on day one, before the shot reverberated down to Rock-a-Buy and dumped the elderly matriarch on her muscleless, wrinkled arse. By day three, her reasons for keeping her condition a secret were all her own.

'Exhaustion,' she bleated when the gentle bear shape of RD approached Mrs Beaufort's bedside, his dumpling of a wife tottering a few slow steps behind him.

L i e s.

'You had us all worried there for a second. Didn't she?' RD looked around at his wife, bringing her into the conversation. She was a quiet woman. Just got on with things. Hardly spoke a word and never a word out of turn. Her hair a curly, greying blonde cut, as so many woman of a certain age tend to have, to a length that never passed her bottom lip. It made her face appear rounder. Fatter. To RD, though, it was a cute face. A loveable face. He adored that dumpy, little Marcel Marceau. As he often said, she was *the only woman who could fill his heart* and *his stomach.*

**ALL YOU NEED TO KNOW
ABOUT RD'S WIFE**
She has phenomenal taste buds.
She cares.
She listens.
She is still good.

She sidled up to the hospital bed, resting her large buttocks against the metal frame, and took Mrs Beaufort's right hand and held it between both of her own. The hand was cold but RD's wife did not react. She looked her friend in the eyes and simply nodded. No words, but enough movement to say that she cared and would be there to help in any way she could.

'Nothing to worry about, honestly,' Mrs Beaufort lied. 'I've been overdoing it in the shop, that's all. The doctor said I need to slow down a little, maybe get some help in there. I'm not sixty-five any more.' She smiled an amiable smile and her friends reacted in the way they were supposed to, but RD felt the cloud hanging over all of them. What was happening to their town?

'We can help you out in the shop until you get back on your feet.'

'I *am* on my feet, thank you very much R—' She seemed insulted and would have addressed RD with his full name had he not interrupted her.

'Yes, yes, of course. What I meant to say was that we are here for whatever you need. To make things easier. If the hospital is telling you to slow down, we can be there so that you don't lose any speed overall. You know?' He exhaled heavily as though the sentence had been a race.

Who are you? he thought. *And what have you done with Mrs Beaufort.*

 I am Evil.
And I have come to
destroy your town.

Inside, Mrs Beaufort was screaming at herself not to act like this. She knew what she wanted to say but, sometimes, the words that came out were not as she had formulated them in her mind. There was no physiological damage from her attack – a small bruise to the hip, but she had been cushioned by the fastidiously sorted piles of clothing – but psychologically, it had taken a toll.

And I was toying with her.

 SOMETHING YOU
SHOULD KNOW
I enjoy this part.

She could hear herself. Bleating on. How her sudden, though apparently *stable,* angina was a shocking reminder of her passing years. A real thunderbolt. She had always remained active and never truly felt her foot sinking gradually into the Hinton Hollow graveyard, the plot of earth that had been reserved next to her husband. He had joked, when alive, that she should be buried with him. Put her coffin in the same hole. Have her on top. *You know I've always liked it that way*, he'd say. Jed Beaufort had been the only one who could get away with talking that way in front of his wife. A fleeting memory of Jed that I quickly extinguished.

I had her in my grasp.

'It's all changed now *he's* come back to town, don't you think?'

'Who? The Pace kid?' RD still thought of him as a kid because that is how most of the town remembered him. His wife shook her head in the background and screwed up her face slightly in disagreement that he was in any way to blame for what was going on in Hinton Hollow.

'Who else?' She didn't want to say these things. She had always liked Pace. She remembered the reasons he had left Hinton Hollow in the first instance. She understood the weight of his burden. It was the reason he had been welcomed back – though she had no idea why he had to return so hastily.

'I think it's an unfortunate coincidence that he returned the day that he did. Perhaps we are lucky that he's back to deal with what happened to the Brady boy. He's probably more experienced than Inspector Anderson in these matters. But that isn't something you need to be thinking about now. Let's just get you home.' He stretched out one of his shovel-like hands and his wife withdrew hers from Mrs Beaufort instinctively. Obediently.

She swung her legs around to the side of the bed and allowed RD to help lower her feet to the floor safely.

Then she shocked the big man.

Gripping both of his arms with her cold, white hands, she dug her nails slightly into his forearms – she wanted to hold him by the shoulders but he was too tall for that.

Stupidly, I let go of her for a moment while I admired RD's wife. I liked her.

'Something is wrong in our town, RD. Something is there that should not be. We have lived here all our lives, each one of us. There are dark days ahead and it will be up to us to ensure this does not last.'

RD did not move, he was rooted to the grey, flecked linoleum. The pain he should have been feeling did not even register, he was so drawn into Mrs Beaufort's intent gaze.

'We are the custodians of Hinton Hollow and we cannot let it be destroyed.'

I watched the futility.

She had felt weak in her shop, though she tried to be strong for Katy Childs and her new baby. But there was an internal struggle with the darkness now for Mrs Beaufort. It had temporarily debilitated her. But it was a weakness that she would not let anyone else witness. She had been around too long. Seen too much. There was more than enough that I could use against her.

She could never beat me.

'Are you with me on this?'

There was a pause. Several beats passed as RD peered down into the eyes of his elderly friend, he could see that she was serious. Her eyes were coated with a moisture that promised to form a tear if he did not answer her soon.

'We're with you,' he finally replied. 'Of course we're with you.' And he pulled his arms away, unsure in his mind. The woman he had walked in to at the hospital was not the same person he was looking at now. That was the real Mrs Beaufort.

She was fighting.

'Right. Let's go home.' Mrs Beaufort led the way. RD's wife grabbed his hand and they followed her out of the ward. Each of them stepping back into my shadow.

TOO YOUNG. TOO BROKEN.

And then there was the really bad weather.

Rachel Hadley walked against a breeze that was picking up into something far more ferocious. It pressed her clothes tightly against the front of her body as she leant against it for balance. Her thin skirt gripping her slim thighs and hugging a perfect mound in between. It would be obvious to anyone watching that she was not wearing any underwear.

But nobody was watching.

Nobody but me.

Stanhope Road was empty now the school rush had ended. Parents were either holed up in the safety of their homes or they had made that dauntingly speedy dash to the office from the school. Rachel had returned home after dropping both her children at school – Aaron was seven, Jess was ten – and had just enough time to say goodbye to her husband before he left for work.

Nathan Hadley owned and ran Hadley's Hair. Not the most imaginative name, but it was all his. He cut people's hair. Men's hair. He was a barber. If you really wanted to piss him off, you just had to call him a *hairdresser.*

This aggravated him for two reasons.

One: he used to cut women's hair, too. Nothing fancy. Nothing too stylish. There wasn't much call for an asymmetric bob in Hinton Hollow. Then Olive Keys grew up. He trained her and she set up her own small place once his wisdom had been imparted. He was left with the *short back and sides.*

Two: he was not a butch man, far from effeminate, but not macho in the slightest. And he cut hair for a living. And he took care of his body. And his own hair always looked immaculate – but he was a hairdresser, it was free advertising. And he was just so nice. So people assumed he was gay.

He wasn't.

Small-town mentality.

Hinton Hollow was unchanged.

Still, he started going by the name *Nate* rather than Nathan because he thought it added some credibility to his sexuality. The problem was that too many people had latched on to the cliché and, over time, it had become a *thing*.

Rachel had waited twenty minutes for her husband to be gone. She had warned him about the weather and he had grabbed a scarf from one of the hooks in the hallway. He kissed her on the cheek. Like a friend. Because that is what they had become.

The Hadleys were friends. Friends who argued. A lot, these days. Mrs Beaufort knew it, she could smell discontent. She knew you had an itch before you even scratched at it. But the rest of Hinton Hollow saw the Hadleys as normal. Average. Sure, the men would talk behind his back and suggest he was homosexual; it looked like narrow-mindedness but it was their own insecurities because most of the women in town knew that he wasn't gay – not that he'd step out on Rachel. Still, they all went to Olive when their roots needed touching up.

Nathan 'Nate' Hadley was snipping away at a head of white hair when his wife pulled the door closed behind her and felt that first gust hit her thighs, it felt fresh, especially without her underwear.

Her hair was not as short *down there* as it usually was. It was still well landscaped, but she'd been deliberately creating a *tuft* since Nathan had suggested it *might be nice to take it all off*.

'What is this sudden fascination with men to make grown women look like little fucking girls?' she'd asked him. *Or boys*, she'd said to herself. A joke at her husband's expense. Another argument. But they were still friends. And they still fucked. Why wouldn't they? The sex was great. It had always been great.

That day in Hinton Hollow's darkest week, Rachel Hadley had a *fuck it, we're all going to hell, anyway* attitude. She wasn't sure why she chose that day to leave the house. She didn't really understand her decision to abandon her underwear at home, the wind was picking up all the time and the clouds were moving in from all directions, suggesting rain.

She turned right at the end of her street, bringing her back on to Stanhope Road. Then she turned right again. Away from the school where her two children were happily looking through books and sticking shapes to a piece of coloured paper.

Away from Hadley's Hair.

Towards Roylake, which shared the road with Hinton Hollow.

Away from the darkness.

But it was too late. I had already touched her before Charles Ablett got the opportunity to lay a single finger on her.

PEOPLE RARELY LEAVE

Selling houses in Hinton Hollow is not a good business to be in. You have to wait until somebody moves out, but people rarely leave. Your best bet is that somebody dies, then you have an opportunity to bring in an outsider. Add a splash of colour to the community. There were rental properties but they were on the peripheries of town and used only as business crash pads – executives who did not mingle with the town's people.

I have no time for these people.

Their life decisions mean that they feel the alluring caress of immorality on a daily basis.

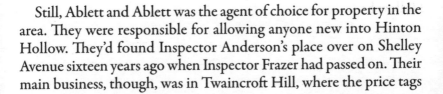

IT IS NOT INTERESTING TO MESS WITH A BANKER OR POLITICIAN
Because they always end up jumping out of a window.

Still, Ablett and Ablett was the agent of choice for property in the area. They were responsible for allowing anyone new into Hinton Hollow. They'd found Inspector Anderson's place over on Shelley Avenue sixteen years ago when Inspector Frazer had passed on. Their main business, though, was in Twaincroft Hill, where the price tags on properties were much higher, and the houses in Roylake were their run-rate business. Lots of turnover. Growing young families. A solid rental scene. That was the easy stuff.

The Ablett brothers found The Hollow strenuous. Burdensome. It was complicated enough that houses rarely came onto the market but there seemed to be some unwritten deal in place where every prospective client had to go through Mrs Beaufort's vetting procedure. But it was the challenge they relished. None more so than the youngest brother, Charles. If he could get his hands on anything in that peaceful insular town, it was considered a major scalp.

Two months before their *dark week*, Charles Ablett had valued the Hadleys' home. It was purely an exercise for Nathan Hadley, who wanted to know whether they had made any money on their investment since they'd owned it. Hollow houses rarely lost their worth; even in times of economic struggle, he was expecting a sizeable figure.

Charles had placed a higher value on Mr Hadley's wife and had made it his business to let her know this over the proceeding weeks – bumping into her while stocking up on groceries, queueing behind her at RD's Diner, he'd even gone for a trim at Hadley's Hair.

So, on that Wednesday, as the wind picked up, blowing four tiles from the roof of the Church of the Good Shepherd and a chair blew across the playground of Stanhope C of E School, smashing one of the windows of the greenhouse, Charles Ablett was opening the front door of his Roylake home – in a towel, his hair still wet from the shower – to find Rachel Hadley combing her fingers through windswept locks.

'Mr Ablett, I've come to discuss my valuation.' She smiled.

To him, this was the most prime piece of real estate that Hinton Hollow had to offer.

IN THE WAKE

It wasn't the sweating as much as the tears.

Owen Brady was alone. For the first time that week, there was nobody else to think about. Nobody to support. Nobody to be strong for. He'd cried so much that he'd made himself thirsty. Not because of the heightened emotion endured over the previous days and his incredible streak of bad luck; it was down to his memories. Fond remembrance of times when his two sons were together.

He thought about the day they had told Michael there was a baby living in his mother's *tummy*. He hadn't really understood. He was only two years old. But over the following months he had started to take an interest. *When is my brother going to come and see me?* he'd ask. And when Jacob did finally arrive – six days past the due date – he wasn't jealous, he just loved him. Even when Jacob was newborn, when his hair was thin and there wasn't very much of it, Michael would lie next to him on the living-room rug and rub his head softly, messing up his hair. It was a two-year-old's way of saying that he loved his brother and would protect him.

Owen Brady thought of this moment and every other moment that his living son had ruffled his dead son's hair. And he cried. And cried.

It wasn't until Detective Sergeant Pace walked into the room that he had to even give a thought to his dead cunt of a wife, who he missed so desperately.

JUST A MOMENT

It is a small story. But I learned so much.

AN IMPORTANT LESSON FROM
THAT WEEK IN HINTON HOLLOW
Change does not happen gradually. It is instant.

When somebody hates their job but does not leave for five years because the timing isn't right or they have to sort themselves financially or they need to find another job first, those five years leading up to resignation were not a part of the change. You can't count that time in the process.

It is five years of stagnancy, then a decision. And that choice then affects a change.

It happens in a moment.

I look at how quickly one person can fall in love with another. You know straight away. I've seen it. Attraction is there and it changes you in that second.

If you receive bad news, you can be instantly devastated.

I look at these mothers, the Wallaces, the Bradys and the other families, and it is clear how crucial decisions can be because the wrong one can alter your world.

So can the right one.

First the choice, then the change.

And here's one more thing, a person who is kind all the time can do something evil, simply by changing the state of their mind.

DISQUIET PRICKLING

'Wakey wakey,' Pace said as he entered the holding cells.

Owen Brady was lying on his back. He swung his legs around to the side and sat up.

'I am awake.' His throat was hoarse from the hours of weeping reminiscence. 'I've been awake all night.'

'Good,' Pace remarked, not looking directly at Owen Brady, he was fishing around for keys in his pocket.

'Good?'

'Well, a man in your situation, having been through what you have in the last couple of days, I would have felt a little uneasy if you'd had a perfect night of rest. Though, God knows, you're probably exhausted.'

'There is no God, detective. If there is, he's a sick son of a bitch.'

'I'll be sure to pass on your sentiments to Father Salis.'

Owen wasn't sure, at first, whether the detective was being sarcastic or caustic, but the darkness around his eyes and his very demeanour... He felt sure that Pace was not a man to waste his faith on anything other than himself and justice. Probably in that order.

Sometimes, I have to watch. Not get involved. See how things play out. And I wonder. How do people have faith?

'I didn't kill her, detective.'

'Let's get you out of that cell and switch the tape to record before we start talking about any of that, shall we?'

Owen Brady ran through his story. How Faith had been after Jacob was shot in front of her. The way she wouldn't talk to Michael. She blocked him out of her life. She couldn't face him, couldn't even be near him. It was her way of dealing with it, he'd thought. To detach herself from everything. Everyone.

'She blamed herself for what happened. But she was the only one who felt like that. How could she have known?'

'There weren't any ... *difficulties* ... in your marriage before that day?'

'What do you mean?' He knew what Pace was getting at.

'Were you arguing, Mr Brady? Were you going through a testing time? Was there a chance that she had strayed?'

'No. No way.' He was adamant about this. Pace thought a little too sure. 'We had our disagreements and quarrels like any other couple. And I have to work late occasionally when there are deadlines, but that's not often.'

'And you?'

'Me?'

'You had not strayed? A colleague? A secretary?'

'I resent the suggestion. We have two sons together.' He said this as though that were proof that neither of them would indulge themselves outside of their union. 'We had two sons.' Owen Brady took his glare away from the detective at this point and stared down at his side of the interview-room desk.

'I have to ask these questions, Mr Brady. Somebody approached your family and shot only your youngest son. This person probably knows who you are. I have to wonder why your eldest son—'

'Michael.'

'Why your eldest son, Michael, was unharmed – physically, at least. Why kill an innocent little boy? My only conclusion is that he was trying to hurt the child's mother.'

Pace was right about this. It was the motivation that escaped him.

'And, if he was trying to hurt the mother, it may be that she had rejected him in some way. Perhaps called things off. That is the reason these questions have to be asked and answered truthfully.'

Normally, Pace would not divulge his theories and workings to a possible suspect, but he did not consider Owen Brady to be a suspect. He'd pulled him in at his inspector's behest. This was a sensitive case; the man had been through a lot in a short space of time. If there was one thing Detective Sergeant Pace knew, it was that sometimes it paid to work outside the book.

And sometimes, *you* paid for working outside the book.

'I feel certain that she wasn't having an affair. She devoted her time to the children, to our home.' It stuck in his throat to talk of her so fondly after she had been so cowardly and given up on him and Michael.

The more they spoke, the more it came across that Faith Brady had been an attentive, warm mother and wife – until the end. Everything Pace heard, though true, was leading him no closer to Jacob Brady's killer. The Ordinary Man.

The wind blew wildly through Hinton Hollow and the clouds

covered the Berkshire sky, leaving their small town in a state of continuous twilight.

Pace looked out of the rectangular window that stretched across the back wall of the interview room. It was close to the ceiling and too small to fit a person through but the sky was visible. He shuddered, disquiet prickling his skin.

It was catching up with him.

He knew it. I threw some black flames his way as a warning.

'Mr Brady, you are free to go.'

SOMEHOW

You are probably wondering about the boy on the train. If you're not, why not? Why have you forgotten about the kid? He's a good kid.

LITTLE HENRY WALLACE
He has spoken.
He has eaten.
He is safe.
He will not tell the police he lives in Hinton Hollow.
He will not break when they try to paint
his mother in a bad light.

I checked in on the mother when Owen Brady was released.

She was a wreck. But hid that so well from the son that had stayed.

Henry could have been anywhere. He may have been noticed by the time he reached Oxford. *He is small*, she thought, *maybe nobody noticed him.* She couldn't remember whether the train was headed towards Bristol or Birmingham. Maybe he made it that far. It didn't matter. As long as he was out of The Hollow.

The news had been focused on the Brady boy. Nothing about a kid being abandoned on a train. She had to tell herself that he hadn't been 'abandoned', she had saved him.

I looked inside her. She was good. But there was a guilt eating away at her that had nothing to do with her son being dumped on a train out of town. When the information came in about Jacob Brady, she thanked God. She was almost pleased, almost proud, that she still had two children.

It stabbed at her. Because she was good. That is why she did not need me to interfere. And that is the reason I did not.

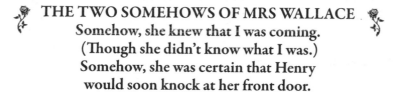

THE TWO SOMEHOWS OF MRS WALLACE
Somehow, she knew that I was coming.
(Though she didn't know what I was.)
Somehow, she was certain that Henry
would soon knock at her front door.

A LITTLE FAITH

He pulled the sleeves of his jumper over his hands and gripped the wool to shelter them from the bitter wind. Owen Brady was free. So why didn't it feel that way?

He'd told his version of events to the best of his memory, embellishing some details like the amount of blood and the scent of the alcohol. These things are expected when recalling situations of high trauma. Talking about it once had been enough for him. He started to understand why his wife had not wanted to go over that day in the park again and again and again. He still didn't understand why she had taken her own life when she still had enough time left to deal with what had happened.

And he would never know of the choice that she made. How that had been a bigger fuck-up than the vodka and the razor blade.

All he cared about was Michael. Once he had established his own innocence, he just wanted to get back to his son. Pace had informed him that Michael was safe. He was still at home. And Inspector Anderson had assigned a family liaison officer. But they would need to speak with Michael again. He was the best chance they had of catching this guy.

That terrified Owen Brady.

This man. This cowardly predator had already killed Jacob and he may not have poured the vodka down his wife's throat or stuffed the pills in her mouth or sliced the top of her thigh, but he'd killed the woman she once was and turned her into somebody that could leave her family behind without a thought.

Owen had been certain of everything he'd said during his interview but now he was doubting himself. Maybe Faith had found time to see somebody else. Ablett was always fishing around. That Hadley hairdresser may have been derided by the men in town but the women seemed to love him. How many men were there that he didn't know in Hinton Hollow? What if he wanted to come back and finish things off? Take the other son? Kill the husband? Wipe out the family.

After everything that had happened, Owen Brady's only certainty was also his biggest problem. He had no idea who his wife was.

YOU DON'T EVEN WORK HERE

'You just let him go? Fuck, Pace, you didn't think about talking to me first? You've been at the station for three days.' Inspector Anderson was not pleased. His giant joke moustache bobbed heavily on his top lip as he vented at his detective but he never stood up from his chair. 'The people in this town might not know who you have become but you arrive here with a reputation.'

Part of that reputation was for not backing down and he wasn't about to change now.

'A reputation? For success, I'd imagine. For cracking cases slightly more high profile than a missing pet or stolen newspaper.'

Anderson was taken back by this. He'd taken a shot and missed. He could dish it out to Reynolds and the other local constables but nobody had ever come back at him before. It was in this conversation that Pace realised Anderson was a bully and the don't-give-a-fuck attitude was a front for his insecurity – one of the easiest things for me to work with. He'd taken this post to be the big fish in the small pond.

Well, guess what, buddy ... there's always a bigger fish.

I'm on to you.

'The guy found his wife dead in the bath the day after she watched their five-year-old son get shot through the heart. This is an investigation into the murder of Jacob Brady. His father was at work when that happened. The person we need to speak with is Michael Brady, but the kid is understandably catatonic at this point.'

Anderson wanted to interject but had nothing to add.

'It's unfortunate, but I don't care about the woman that slits her own wrists as much as I do about catching the guy that can pop a bullet in a child and run off. I don't want to waste my time with anything else. If you want to fuck about getting proof of a suicide then be my guest, but I'm on the hunt for a child killer.'

'All right. You've made your point. You're right. You're bloody right.'

Pace thought a little more of Anderson for admitting this. He could see by the inspector's expression that he was wishing he could backtrack.

'Another thing.'

'Go on.'

'Keeping the schools open is the dumbest thing this town has ever done in what I see as a long series of dumb fucking decisions.'

Anderson wasn't sure what Pace was referring to with that comment. He'd only been in town for fifteen years. A relative newcomer in the grand scheme of things.

'That's not me, Pace. Councilwoman Hayes has the final say. You know I agree.' He was creeping now. All power in this conversation had been handed over to the dark, stubbled insomniac standing before the chief's desk.

Pace exhaled and rubbed at his face, the beard that was forming scratched against his right hand. The air speeding around the building in ever-increasing circuits was whistling. At first, a harsh, unsettling pitch that became a hum once it was accepted as *usual*.

That is the reason the people of Hinton Hollow were *losing*. They were too comfortable. In their bubble. They couldn't see the woods for trees. That's where the answer was being held.

The problem was that nobody had gone missing. The kid had been shot and left. If they'd been searching for a body, the police would have scoured every inch of The Hollow. They'd have plotted a grid of the woods and raked every millimetre of it. They'd have found the car that Oz Tambor was locked inside. Then they could get the answers that Michael Brady had been failing to provide.

'What have we got to go on so far?' The moustache moved closer to Pace as Anderson leant forward on his chair, his elbows resting on the flimsy desk, his eyes showing genuine interest.

'Not a lot. The kid said he looked like *an ordinary man*. The sex of the attacker is the only thing we can confirm as concrete.'

'But it must be an outsider? Michael Brady would have recognised him if it was someone local.'

'Despite the closeness of the town, Inspector, there are still five thousand people here. Nobody knows everyone, not even Mrs Beaufort.'

'Has anyone checked to see how she's doing?'

'Again, sir, she is not a part of the investigation. I'm sorry about her health issues but she hasn't crossed my mind.' He was cold. Anderson was recalling some of the other details that came with Pace's references and they seemed spot on. 'It might be an idea to get one of the constables to call the hospital and check on her condition. Reynolds is hardly inundated with queries.'

'He's about to change shifts. I'll get the next one to do it.'

'I have checked in with stations in the surrounding area and there have been no similar incidents in the last couple of days. It doesn't seem that a crime like this has occurred anywhere across the country so I'd rule out some kind of spree.' Pace continued to run through his thoughts, demonstrating his unwavering focus to his superior officer.

'Well, that's a relief.'

'It looks like an isolated incident so I think we are looking at someone local, somebody who knows the Bradys, rather than a drifter who just happened on the town and had an itch to scratch.

'You think Faith Brady was getting *doinked* by the delivery boy or something?' Matter-of-fact Anderson had returned to the conversation with his thoughtless comments. Pace raised an eyebrow.

'I thought the same thing. It happens so often. But Owen Brady was so sure of her fidelity. I think we need to talk with some of Faith's friends. I'll get on that right away.'

'Get yourself home first, Pace. Clean up. Maybe even grab an hour of shut-eye. You look tired and sinister.' He hadn't meant to say that last word but it crept out of his mouth, like his other meat-headed statements. Pace brushed it off, he'd made himself known already.

'Will do. I'll check once I've had a chance to speak with Michael Brady again.'

Reynolds was no longer on the front desk when Detective Sergeant Pace emerged from the back door. The kid was younger. Scrawnier.

'You must be Detective Pace.' He held out a bony right hand. 'I'm Constable Lynch, I've heard a lot about you.'

He hadn't, but he thought it was the right thing to say.

'Lynch. I need you to call the hospital and get an update on how Mrs Beaufort is doing. You know Mrs Beaufort, right?' Pace said all this while shaking the intimidated officer's hand.

'Sure. Sure I do. Everybody knows old Mrs Beaufort.' He smiled as he helped perpetuate the myth of the close community.

'Good. Report to Inspector Anderson when you have information from her doctors.' He started to walk towards the wind. Without looking back at him, Pace added, 'And, Lynch. Don't let her hear you calling her old, eh?'

Pace couldn't light his cigarette in the open, the flame from his match kept dying at the hands of the worsening weather.

This fucking town, he cursed to himself.

If everybody really knew everybody, then there had to be someone in Hinton Hollow who could identify the chicken shit that shot Jacob Brady. He couldn't pin his hopes on a seven-year-old suddenly becoming lucid.

Pace looked out across the street. The terraces on the opposite corner to the police station seemed to change their form. Like a theatre safety curtain had been dropped in front of them, shrouding them in shade. He leant forward and looked up at the overcast sky. Then accepted his fate and stepped forward.

He was growing increasingly paranoid. All eyes were on him.

It was catching him up, he knew that now.

Facing his old life was not punishment enough.

Pace suffered that week. But unlike the others in The Hollow, he knew that he was getting what he deserved.

THIS PLACE IS TOXIC

The traffic light changed from grey to red just as Pace reached the crossroads at the centre of town. He knew he was tired because reality was distorted. Everything seemed to be in extreme close up. He had lost his peripheral vision.

I could be right next to him.

He could see the red circle that was ordering cars to stop until further notice, and coming into shot was the giant rectangle of a silver transit van heading in the other direction towards the train station.

An indicator flicked to turn right.

He knew he was tired because the truth was being deformed. The subtle kih-kuh kih-kuh kih-kuh of the indicator sounded more like someone being slapped in the face repeatedly. He could no longer hear the engine ticking over.

Anderson had been right, he needed some sleep. Not long. He could live on three or four hours each night. Sixty minutes would keep him going until the early hours of the next day if he needed to. The only obstacle was that he had been told to go *home*.

And Pace had no idea where that was.

He could only get a room at The Arboreal for a couple of nights. For the rest of the week, he had paid up to stay at one of the several bed-and-breakfast establishments in the area. The Cider Orchard was more than a B&B. There were six en-suite rooms that had been converted from stables. It was private and a little pricey but within walking distance of the police station. Everything was within walking distance. Everyone in Hinton Hollow walked.

Pace had arranged a meeting with a local lettings agent, Charles Ablett, for the next day in order to understand his options. Surely the minimum was something that would keep him attached to a lengthy rental contract. It would demonstrate his intent to stay in town, to make the temporary transfer more permanent. But the detective still didn't know where he was meant to be, only where he should not. He wasn't ready to return to the city.

To Pace, that was good enough for now.

IF THE WIND CHANGED

Charles Ablett was very careful with Rachel Hadley. She may have been stepping out on her husband but she'd also taken the time to make him pursue her. There was a touch of class to this one, he thought. Even if she had turned up unannounced at his door wearing no underwear, it was their first time together, and she didn't seem like the kind of woman who would appreciate him unloading on her face. She'd probably never like it but he'd make her do it eventually.

They always let him in the end.

He also liked to get physical. Smack his ladies about a bit. Nothing untoward, in his mind, just some light choking and maybe a slap while the woman was bent over as he took her from behind.

But not today.

Not with Rachel Hadley.

She was a well put-together woman. He guessed that she was in her late thirties but her body was firm where he expected some softness. Her breasts were small but pert – tiny nipples. Like a young girl. Charles liked that. But he also liked discus-sized areola and fake tits and black breasts. He'd tasted them all, but Rachel was something special. He wanted to drink down her soft, milky-white British skin. He'd kissed her tenderly all over and masqueraded as a very giving lover.

He was following a pattern. His pattern. The Charles Ablett pattern for fucking unobtainable women. He was being different without any intervention from me. He was being good. But, for Ablett, that was even more evil.

Rachel Hadley rolled off and lay next to Charles. He didn't like to finish in that position, with the woman on top. He didn't want them to see his *oh face.*

'That was great.' Rachel was smiling, still in that state where her mind was blank. The thought of her children or husband lying dormant as she allowed herself a moment to bask in afterglow. I allowed her that much.

'It was.' Charles had enjoyed it. Not the sex part of it, that was standard. But the conquest. Nathan Hadley had cut his hair a week before, and Charles found himself thinking of him rather than the gorgeous, naked, sweating, panting woman beside him.

'It can never happen again.' The mood turned.

I wasn't there for Ablett. I had a tight hold over Rachel. Timidity had dissolved. She was brazen. She was confident. She was strong.

'What?' Charles continued to look at the ceiling, he didn't want to show her that he was shocked. His dick was not fully flaccid yet and it flexed with his abdominal muscles as he spoke. He was angry. That was his go-to emotion. Hit first, ask questions later. He was already wishing he'd choked her.

'Exactly what I said. Charles, this isn't me. I don't go around behind my husband's back.'

'Then what the hell were we just doing, Rach, because we sure as fuck weren't studying the Bible, no matter how many times you called for God or Jesus.'

She turned an instant shade of scarlet but kept her cool.

'Don't dirty it. I don't know what made me come here today. I don't know what made me choose you—'

He blew air from his nostrils at this remark, as though it was impossible to fathom that he had not been the recruiter in this little dalliance.

'I don't know what made me choose you,' she repeated, to make her position known, 'but it happened. I'm not sorry that it happened but I'm not going to let it happen again.'

Charles had heard this speech or a variance of it, before. Several times, in fact. They always came back for more. But, this time, he knew it was different. She was different. Maybe that's why he felt hurt.

'Well, I'm glad I could be of use to get whatever it was out of your system.' He made it sound lighthearted, he even looked at her while smiling a smile that could have been a wink. What he meant was *you don't get rid of me that easily.*

Rachel said in her head, *it got out of my system, all over your mouth and sheets.* She never thought like that, she was pretty conservative when it came to sex. It was a strange day. She recalled her father saying not to pull stupid faces when she was a child because her face would stick in that expression if the wind changed. Well the wind was changing in Hinton Hollow and she worried that if she didn't stop being a harlot right there and then, the wind would alter her forever.

'You were very useful.' She continued what she thought was some kind of *afterplay*, stroking his bare chest with her finger.

He wanted to snap it off.

PLASTIC STRAWS

To me, this is a small story. I have been active through wars, great battles, holocausts. I have seen genocide and terrorist acts that have killed over one hundred times the population of Hinton Hollow. I am everywhere, able to shift my focus hundreds of times as you blink. That week, I oversaw everybody in that quaint little nowhere on the map.

I am giving you a taste. An abridged version of everything I experienced. Because the human mind is smaller than ever before.

Where else could you find seven billion life forms, who are now so easily and borderlessly connected yet find very little time to focus on anything larger than their immediate self?

Your pictures are so small.

Millions preaching about saving the planet one plastic straw at a time then eating a burger made out of another species.

If you want to save more marine life, stop eating them.

If you want to be good, start with yourself. If you want to do good, you must go beyond.

And if you want to understand evil, look at this small story. Look at Hinton Hollow.

LOOK
May Tambor is on the floor.
A hole in her head.
Dorothy Reilly is on the floor.
A bone in her throat.
Oz is in the boot of a car.
Jacob Brady is in the morgue.
Faith Brady is in the morgue.
Darren cannot see a difference
between a pig, a cat or a human.

I am nowhere near finished.

I want the Hadleys, the Abletts, the Beaufort hag and the window breaker. I want fear and terror and insecurity. I want to keep the Wallaces out of this. And I want the rest to learn from everything that happened.

When all that is done, I want to set a fire. Black flames as high as buildings.

I want Detective Sergeant Pace.

THE ABLETT WAY

You don't just call it off with Charles Ablett.

My darkness was touching everyone in Hinton Hollow. For some it was a gentle ruffle of the hair that made them more playful, more susceptible to suggestion. For others it was a slap that triggered rebelliousness. For a few, it was drowning in blackness and snapping fingers and shooting young boys in the chest.

'I guess I'll see you about, then.'

She stopped stroking him, realising it was not part of the routine. He was dismissing her. He was making her feel how he wanted her to feel. Like a whore.

How dare she think that she chose me.

Charles Ablett had a habit of not letting things go, especially with women.

Rachel was starting to realise that she had made a mistake and that her choice had been the wrong one. She felt unsafe.

Without a word, she sat up in the bed, feeling the need to cover her breasts with the sheet though they had just been on full display as she bounced her way to bliss, her buttocks slapping against the top of his thighs as she thrust herself harder and faster downwards towards the end.

Her skirt was on the floor beside the bed, she leant over and picked it up with her left hand, her right still clasping the sheet to her chest. Ablett just lay there. Somehow threatening in his inaction. It was this apathy that scared Rachel the most.

It was taking too long to get dressed with one hand and she felt the increasing need to get the hell out of there. She let go of the sheet and stood up to pull her skirt up then walked to the foot of the bed where her blouse lay in a heap. She thought about how he had unbuttoned it and let it slip slowly down her back before firmly placing his hand there to pull her in closer to him.

What a thrill it was.

What an idiot she had been.

She buttoned herself up and looked around the floor to see if she had forgotten anything else. She didn't want to leave any evidence there because Ablett would undoubtedly hold it against her in some way. He was lying in the same spot with both hands behind his head. He flexed his biceps alternately as though keeping time with a song he was singing in his head.

'You've got everything you came with. You weren't wearing any underwear, you dumb bitch.' He smiled and shook his head as though she really was a *dumb bitch*.

'Oh, fuck you.' She didn't want to antagonise him but she couldn't stop herself from reacting.

'You can't go back on your word now, you've said that was the very last time.'

He was still smiling. She stared at him, disgusted. With him, and herself.

Then he sat up in bed. His expression changed. He was no longer joking. Rachel Hadley flinched but he didn't react.

'Now get the fuck out of my house.'

She bit her tongue and backed out of the room. She was afraid to turn her back on him. But Charles Ablett was not that obvious. Sure, he could have grabbed her right there. He could have hit her a few times. He could have forced her into something she had already expressed she did not want to do. He could have thrown her down the stairs. He could have killed her and left her in the pantry while he decided what was the best thing to do with the body.

That wasn't the Ablett way.

He'd wait until she had taken her mind off him before he struck. He'd hit her where it hurt her the most.

OTHER WOMEN TO HAVE FELT
'THE ABLETT WAY'
Faith Brady.
Liv Dunham.
Mrs Wallace.
Four dancers from The Split Aces.

Rachel stamped down the stairs. She wanted to get out but she wanted Ablett to know that he had pissed her off, that she thought he was an animal. Part of her wanted to go back in there and rip him apart with her nails. Attack him before he could get to her.

I thought about turning her up a notch.

She found her shoes at the bottom of the stairs and her jacket still hung on a hook by the door. The wind blew the letterbox open and it clattered, startling her. She looked over her shoulder instinctively.

Her heart pounding, Rachel Hadley threw her arms into the jacket and opened the door to step out into the darkening air of Hinton Hollow, it no longer smelled fresh. She thought about slamming the door behind her to punctuate her estimation of Charles Ablett. But, instead, left it wide open. The wind would slam it shut for her at some point. Or it would let something into the house that Ablett would not want to see.

She pounded the pavement as she paced down to Stanhope Road.

As she hit the corner, everything caught up with her and she cried.

She felt like a *Dumb Bitch*.

ONLY THE REAL WORLD

The Cider Orchard Bed and Breakfast was on the left once you passed the main line of shops and businesses – the grocery on the corner, RD's Diner beside that, a florist, post office, off-licence, and, bookending the strip, Hadley's Hair.

But Pace did not stop at Cider Orchard.

He continued along Stanhope Road, past the primary school, eventually taking a left on the road before Dr Green's surgery. The road snaked left then right. He came to a stop just after the miniature roundabout.

Across on the other side of the road was a grey door that used to be powder blue. It still had the number sixteen nailed to the front, of course. But *she* didn't live there anymore.

She hasn't lived there for a very long time.

Detective Sergeant Pace allowed himself to be lost in memory. He was tired and upset about the little boy who had been killed. He was more upset about the boy who had lived. But he allowed himself to forget the Hinton Hollow that was now and remember the Hinton Hollow as it was then.

Julee had been a darling of the town. A decent student. Helpful. Conscientious. She would stay behind after school to help teachers who ran learning clubs for the younger kids. She attended the church. She knew Dr Green, though she had never been ill in her life. She was a good kid. And she grew into a good teenager. Then a good young adult. That was the point where she finally became close with Pace. As close as he had always wanted.

They were both smart. They both studied hard. It seemed they were destined to tie the knot and become the natural successors to Mr and Mrs Beaufort as the unofficial town elders.

But Julee changed. Something inside her seemed to just flip. She wasn't happy there any more. She wanted out and she wanted Pace to go with her. But he loved The Hollow. Life was great.

Julee got worse.

'One day, you'll come knocking on this door and you'll find that I won't be here.' She was serious. Tears were clinging to her eyes to preserve her bravery.

'Julee, that's mad.' The word itself seemed to dry her eyes instantly, but the tears fell back inside.

'This place is toxic.' She held his arms tightly and looked up into his eyes. It was intense. He had no idea what had turned her, why she had become so paranoid. She scared him. He didn't know how to act around her. He wasn't seeing her as often.

Eventually, he never saw her again.

That *one day* arrived. He knocked on the powder-blue door and nobody answered. Julee was gone. She didn't leave a note. She hadn't contacted her grandmother to say that she was leaving. The kids in the after-school clubs were left without a helper. She just vanished.

Like Oz Tambor.

She was there.

Then she wasn't.

But she was old enough to make that decision.

There didn't seem to be any forced entry into her home. It was tidy. Nothing had been stolen but innocence. The police had the testimony of *the Pace kid* to go on, too. She wanted to leave Hinton Hollow.

There was no case.

Nobody blamed him directly. They all seemed concerned for his welfare, sympathetic to his heartbreak – as you would expect in Hinton Hollow – but he felt the wave that swept through town and knocked him from his perch within the community. The mantle of *golden couple* reserved for a future date when Liv Dunham and Oscar Tambor would prove their worth.

Julee had been right. That perfect little idyll had turned toxic.

Pace was starting to wish he'd gone with her. Maybe if he left, he wouldn't be that far behind. He could find her.

Of course, he didn't find Julee and he never found out what had changed her mind so drastically about Hinton Hollow. What it did was open his eyes to the underbelly of the town. The things that locals look past. The lies that everyone knows but never mentions. The darkness and the cracks. He didn't leave because of Julee but her disappearance changed Pace enough that he wasn't afraid to get out.

His tired eyes hardly blinked from the daydream. He was half hoping that the door would open and she'd be there.

What an idiot.

It's so much fun to play with somebody's hope.

Pace eventually blinked and, for a moment, the close-up world flicked back to normality. Perhaps he hadn't even been looking at the house, he'd been asleep and dreaming. Now, the door with the number sixteen nailed to it seemed far away. Too far to touch.

He waited a little longer.

Just in case Julee emerged.

The grey door shook and Pace's eyes widened. Surely this was still the dream. The door opened and a woman in her late thirties or early forties stepped out, hefty green coat and scarf tied around her head to protect from the wind, and a leash in her left hand. The dog bounded down the step and into the front garden. The woman, who was not Julee, nowhere near Julee, not even an older withered version of the girl he had once loved, pressed the button on the leash and the little hound choked to a halt. She slammed the door shut and Pace knew he was awake. Because only the real world is that fucking cruel.

He turned back. Tired. Despondent. The wind was picking up still. The dark clouds overhead that threatened a downpour but hadn't yet delivered were whizzing past like they were scared of The Hollow.

A woman was walking on the other side of the road, pressing herself into the wind. She looked a little underdressed. He couldn't see her face because she looked to be rubbing her eyes with the back of her sleeve.

Pace glanced as he passed the solitary figure fighting the elements, he just wanted to see her face – he could already see her thighs. Strong but lean. She pulled her hand away and placed it back into her jacket pocket. He caught a glimpse and smiled to himself. Rachel Hadley had this effect on most men.

He needed to call Maeve. I was making him forget.

Pace hit the high street again. He was, for want of a better word, *home*.

AFTERNOON DELIGHT

Rachel couldn't go home. She couldn't face the emptiness that would leave her alone with only the thought of what she had just done.

She'd managed to stop crying because she was so confused about whether they were tears of guilt or whether this was simply the release she had needed – a decent sob rather than an explosive orgasm. She reached the school and realised that she had no idea who she was or what she was doing there. This wasn't her. This wasn't her life. This wasn't how Rachel Hadley acted.

Sure, she was attractive and she got a lot of attention because of that fact. Men liked being around her as much as women envied her. But she wasn't a slut. That's what everybody wanted her to be, but she wasn't.

She stopped on the pavement and stared at the building, wondering how Jess was getting on with her maths, imagining Aaron kicking a football around the windy playground, scuffing another knee on his trousers.

No. She couldn't go home. Not yet.

She kept walking. Past the turning where the unmarked police car had just pulled in and on to her husband's place of work. She hoped the stiff breeze that had been punching her in the face all the way down Stanhope had blown off the stench of her adultery.

There were four men waiting and they all turned at the same time when Rachel entered the barbershop. They would have looked no matter who had walked through the door, but their gazes lingered a little longer because it was Rachel Hadley standing at the entrance.

Nate was trimming Old Mr Dale's wonderfully white mane. It was another short back and sides he could do on autopilot with his mind numbed and his eyes closed. But he performed with a smile on his face, which grew when his wife unexpectedly entered the barbershop.

'Hey, Honey.' Two of the men waiting on the sofa not-so-subtly nudged one another with their elbows as though *honey* was something only gay men said. They were reaching. Nate saw what they were doing, he was used to it. He ignored that they were making fun of him and pitied their ignorance.

One great perk to his job was that men rarely said that they didn't like their haircut. He'd wave a mirror behind their crown to show them the part of their head they never saw and they always said it was *fine*. When these narrow-minded, homophobic, small-town dicks came in and perpetuated an in-joke that had lost its humour years ago, Nate would fuck with the back of their head. Nothing outrageous like shaving a shape into the hair – a pair of testicles, perhaps – but simply putting things a little off centre. They'd never really know but anyone walking behind them would think that they had cut their own hair.

Intolerable idiots.

I wondered what I could make him do.

'Hey,' she responded, coyly.

'What are you doing here?' He left Old Mr Dale for a second, leant into his wife and kissed her on the cheek. He thought about giving her an air kiss on each side of the face, really give the Neanderthals something to elbow about, but he resisted.

'Does a wife need a reason to come and visit her man?' This wasn't a defensive response. Her shadow had turned it into something more playful.

'Of course not. You want to wait out the back? I'm nearly done with Mr Dale here.'

Rachel looked over at the old man, who nodded a kind acknowledgement into the mirror.

'Sure thing. Don't be too long.' She winked at the men sat on the sofas and the nudging stopped. Nate Hadley loved his wife for doing things like that – though that gesture seemed a little more brazen than usual.

The four men watched her walk to the door at the far end of the shop then disappear. Even Old Mr Dale caught a glimpse from the corner of his eye – he was old, not dead.

When Nate finally got back to his room at the back of the shop – a small room that housed a computer and a safe with the week's takings – his wife was just about ready to fuck his brains out. She was kissing him on the lips and rubbing the crotch of his jeans. She whispered in his ear that she was missing him as she thrust herself into him.

'What's gotten into you?' he asked, not quite pushing her away but not completely accepting her advances.

'God, Nate. I thought it might be a fun surprise. When was the last time we had a little afternoon delight?'

Nate was shocked. On one hand he thought it might be a good way to really stick it to those imbeciles waiting for a trim but another part was wondering where this fire had come from. It never crossed his mind that his wife would cheat on him, in the same way that Owen Brady could not imagine such a thing of Faith. But this was Rachel's way of dealing with her guilt. She was going to try to fuck it all away, get the poison out.

It just wasn't her.

She grabbed his dick and held it. He was getting hard. He didn't want to but he couldn't help it.

'I've got four customers out there.' He didn't push her hand away.

'Let them wait.' The corners of her mouth raised, her long eyelashes drawing him in. 'We'll be quick,' she added and almost threw in a girly giggle, but it never materialised.

'Rach, I don't know about this.' He looked over his shoulder at the door. It didn't have a lock. He hated that it didn't have a lock while he was counting the money or was inputting the combination to the safe, but the idea appealed to him at that moment.

'Well, this isn't going to go down by itself.' She gripped him harder. Then she dropped to her knees and took him in her mouth.

THE WIND

American Summer. Cortland. Haas. Pinova. Jupiter. Shenandoah. Each of the six barn-converted rooms at the Cider Orchard Bed and Breakfast was named after an apple variety.

Pace was staying in Haas.

The room was very modern. A king-sized bed with more pillows than one man could ever need. The television was a flatscreen LCD – forty inches from corner to corner. There was even a Bluetooth speaker to play music from his phone. He'd rested it in its cradle and selected Warren Zevon's 'She's Too Good for Me', putting the song on repeat. It was mellow and sad enough to numb him to sleep, and he hoped it would force his brain to dream of Julee.

He just wanted to see her walk out of that number sixteen door one more time.

Julee may have fled from Hinton Hollow without Pace but that did not mean that she was first to leave.

He didn't even get fully onto the bed. His feet were on the floor, he sat at the edge then let his back crash down on the springy mattress just as the sweet sound of Mr Zevon's languid singing voice told Pace that *he could hold his head up high*.

He drifted off into a peaceful slumber, his mind fixed on the chrome *one* and *six* that graced that once blue door. In his sleep, the one turned to a four and the six turned into a two. And the door was black. And he wouldn't wake up until he saw what was on the other side.

Then he was in Swinley Forest and he was walking. The man in front of him had his hands cuffed behind his back. He wouldn't stop talking but Pace could not hear his words. Then Pace was taping his mouth shut. Then he was handcuffing the man's wrists together around a tree trunk. Then the man was screaming beneath the gag. And kicking.

Then Pace was walking away and leaving the man to rot.

His eyes shot open. The wooden beam stretching across the Haas room ceiling high above him, Warren Zevon's languorous tones unbefitting of the detective's most recent thoughts. He jumped up and pulled his phone from the speaker to stop the music. He didn't want to associate the song with the moment he had just relived.

Almost ninety minutes had passed since he had arrived at his temporary home. He turned the tap to ignite the shower. The children would be filing out of their classrooms shortly and he had to get over to Owen Brady's house to check on Michael.

Pace perused his face in the bathroom mirror. He felt awkwardly refreshed but the reflection still suggested he was exhausted. He pulled the string above the mirror to kill the bulb and showered in the dark so that he couldn't see his own shadow.

I had him.

SLOW AND EXPOSED

Things got worse. The wind was blowing the shadow all over town. The black flames licking at anything it passed.

Ben Raymond was nine years old. He had Jess Hadley pinned against the fence during the lunch break and was teasing her about her *gay dad*. He hadn't been touched by the darkness – I stayed away from children, I liked them – he was just a piece-of-shit kid. It wasn't his fault. He wasn't born that way. But that's exactly what he was.

Aaron Hadley was seven. Three school years younger than his sister, two and a half in real years. He often teased his sister. He was big for his age. Strong, too. Sometimes he even ribbed her about her *gay dad* even though he was his father too. But that didn't mean anyone else could do it.

He saw that rotund meathead, Raymond, with his group of four followers, all laughing uncomfortably as their fearless leader pit his wits and his brawn against a girl. She was older than him, but she was a girl, and his four fake friends knew that this was wrong.

Aaron didn't even hesitate. He ran straight for Ben (*the Bully*). Two of his lackeys even moved aside instead of trying to stop the kid.

Aaron's shoulder connected with Ben's ribs. It was enough to make him let go of Jess, who straightened her school dress.

With Ben gripping his side, Aaron had enough time to jump on his chest and get a few hits in before the older, larger boy regained enough composure to haul the pest to the floor and administer a couple of punches of his own before a teacher broke it up.

'You idiot,' Jess said to her little brother. 'You could have got yourself killed.'

Then she smiled at him.

'Thanks.' She winked.

He smiled back, his left eye turning black. He thought it looked *cool*.

Rachel was informed immediately.

Her son had booked her a meeting with the headmistress straight after school.

DEAD WHITE HAND

RD and his wife dropped Mrs Beaufort at the Brady's house. What used to be The Brady *Home*.

'Thank you both for visiting and for coming to collect me. And your offer to help in the store.' Mrs Beaufort stepped out of the car. It was impossible to tell that she'd suffered any kind of medical mishap. She was a frail, thin old lady who was as strong as an ox. A stubborn, determined, ox.

'You want us to come with you? We can wait here?' RD spoke, of course. His wife nodded in the background.

'You can stop worrying about me, Rick. There are others in this town more needing of your compassion.' She was thinking about Owen and young Michael. And she was wondering how the mother was holding up. She had no idea that Faith was gone, too. That she had cut her wrists in a fit of guilt about choosing one of her children over the other. She'd find out eventually, everybody in town would. Some would even think she probably had it coming – Faith was the wrong name for a woman who never attended the Good Shepherd. But they'd never know why she ended it.

'There's enough compassion in this here wagon for everyone, Mrs B.' RD gave his big bear grin and saluted with his left hand, avoiding that want for an American accent once more. Mrs Beaufort turned and walked up the Brady's drive. RD and his wife headed straight back into town to relieve the part-timers from running the diner.

Mrs Beaufort gave it twelve steps before she allowed herself a short breath and a gentle rub of her chest. She told herself that the Bradys needed her, that Hinton Hollow needed her. And she took those final few paces to the door with the vertical letterbox and knocked with that dead white hand.

Nobody answered.

Why would they not be here? Where else could they go?

She looked down the drive at the empty space where RD's car had been parked moments ago with the offer to wait for her.

She breathed again and hit the door once more with that almost transparent right hand.

A woman answered.

'Hello,' the strange woman, who was not Faith Brady, said.

Mrs Beaufort took a step backward and looked around, making sure she had the right house, hoping that her constricted arteries were not now restricting the flow of blood to her brain.

No. You're in the right place.

'I'm Mrs Beaufort,' Mrs Beaufort exclaimed as though that was explanation enough for her arrival at the Brady house.

'Good day, Mrs Beaufort. I'm afraid this is not the best time...'

'I understand that Miss...'

'Day. I'm the family liaison officer assigned to the Bradys.'

'And I am a close family friend, Miss Day, fresh out of hospital, and I have not had the opportunity to offer my condolences or help to Mr and Mrs Brady since the accident.'

It was not an *accident*. Every movement in the park on day one was made with purpose. It was passionless and merciless.

'Mrs Beaufort, if you are as fresh from the hospital as you say, and certainly seem, I would suggest that you take care of yourself.' Andrea Day was an experienced FLO and she did not appreciate a busybody. She had a job to do and she only cared about the crime that had been committed and the family that had been torn apart and were being forced to deal with something unknown and unnatural. She did not give one fuck who that old lady thought she was or what she was doing there. Normally she would handle her emotions, suppress them. But not that week. Not in Hinton Hollow.

'Thank you for your concern, Miss Day, but I have known this family since birth. Not just the children but Owen and Faith, too.' Mrs Beaufort was not fazed by what she considered ignorance and insubordination. 'I would appreciate it if I could have a word with one of them.' She started to move towards the door but Andrea Day was not a woman to be messed with, either.

🌹 SOME THINGS ABOUT ANDREA DAY 🌹
I had not touched her at this point.
She was compassionate.
Male vulnerability turned her on.

'Back up, Mrs Beaufort.' She stood her ground, pulling the door almost closed behind her.

'I beg your par—'

'You can beg for whatever you want.' She was stepping well over the line of etiquette here but, as she would explain, 'This is a horrid situation to be involved in. It is a murder investigation. A heinous crime has been committed against a member of your community, I am aware of that and sensitive to the thoughts of the people in this town, but I do not need people in this house filling up a young boy's mind with pictures and words that never happened. Michael is very closed right now, as can be expected, but he is open to suggestion and we are trying to catch a killer of children here. Mrs Beaufort.'

The old lady was agog. Andrea Day allowed her to stand this way for a few seconds.

'So, if you'll kindly fuck off and mind your own business, I'll let Mr Brady know that you called by.'

The door closed and the old woman's angina felt decidedly less *stable*.

LOST

Pace turned up to find a bewildered pensioner snailing her way to the bottom of the drive.

'What the...?' he muttered out loud to himself as he turned his car up the kerb.

'Mrs Beaufort? Is everything okay? I thought you were...' He fumbled for the right words. 'Resting?' It sounded as lame and patronising out loud as it had in his head.

She didn't answer.

She looked lost and much littler than she had the day that Pace had arrived in town and visited her in Rock-a-Buy.

'Mrs Beaufort?' he tried again.

Nothing.

'Mrs Beaufort.' Now he was right next to her with his hands on her shoulders. 'Is everything okay? What are you doing here?'

'I came to speak with Faith and Owen. I wanted to offer my support. I ... I just...' She didn't make eye contact with the detective, who was worried that the wind might pick the diminutive lady up and throw her down the street.

'I think you should come and sit down for a moment, Mrs Beaufort. I can take you home.'

A WORD ON EVIL
It can hide and often be found in kindness.
Once the wheels are set in motion,
I can just watch. Or leave.

I wouldn't leave without Detective Pace.

He was the reason I was in Hinton Hollow.

Pace had no idea whether the old lady had made it into the house to discover that Faith was no longer living there – no longer living anywhere – and perhaps she was in shock at her discovery, or simply that she was hopped up on some kind of medication administered to her in the hospital that was causing her disorientation.

'I think I just...' She stopped talking as though she had expelled a complete and coherent sentence. Pace led her back down, towards a low wall she could rest on. The Bradys' curtain twitched as he helped her against it.

'Mrs Beaufort, if you could just wait here for a moment, I need to have a quick word with Mr Brady.'

'Good luck,' she scoffed.

Pace turned his back on the old woman.

KNOCK KNOCK KNOCK

'Who was that? Is everything all right?' Owen Brady asked the assigned officer as she shut the door and re-entered the house alone.

'Everything is fine, Mr Brady.'

'You can call me Owen.'

'Everything is fine, Mr Brady,' Andrea repeated. 'It was a neighbour wishing to pass on their sympathies to yourself and your son. It will probably become more frequent once this weather dies down.'

'Who was it?'

'Mrs Beaufort.'

'Hmmm. I'd expected her sooner, to be honest.' He raised his eyebrows. Andrea took that to mean that she was right about the old busybody.

'She's been in hospital.'

'What? Hospital? How do you know that?' For that brief

moment, Owen Brady stopped thinking about his own problems and his mind allowed him to think about Mrs Beaufort. He worried. 'Did she say what was wrong? Why didn't she come in?'

'Please sit down, Mr Brady.' Andrea saw Michael flinch at the recognition of his father's panic. He was sitting on his own in the dining room, which was only separated from the lounge by a small arch of plaster at the top of the two opposing walls. He was perched at the table reading a book. Living a life that was not his own.

'I thanked her for her concern and said that I would pass on the message, she should come back in a few days,' she continued, slightly bending the truth but her job was to be there for the Bradys. She found herself caring for them, particularly the boy. Though the air in Hinton Hollow had clearly cursed her tongue with more spite than she was used to, her compassion for the families she worked with did not waver. 'She's fine, trust me. You have other concerns.'

Andrea Day scuttled over to the main window and moved the curtain aside slightly with two fingers in order to check that the old lady had got the message. She couldn't see her out there. In her place was a man. He was tall, his coat was long, his face was dark with a stubble she found attractive. Through the netting, his eyes looked black. Though the wind seemed to be picking up with every passing hour, the trees shaking in the background, papers flying past the window, it did not seem to be touching the man that was walking towards the house. His hair did not ruffle. His coat did not flap. She felt like a target he was intent on striking.

She let go of the curtain, turned to Owen Brady with uncertainty in her eyes – a hesitation he read as *fear* – and the door was knocked on three times.

EVERYTHING AND EVERYONE

Rachel Hadley stood in front of the head mistress of Stanhope C of E School feeling like a naughty schoolgirl for the second time that day. Only, this time, she didn't have two fingers of the local estate agent curling up inside her.

But she had been occupying her time in any way that she could. Shopping, browsing the florist's window, flicking through travel brochures, walking against the wind to the river and back. Anything to not be at home alone. It meant that she was in her children's school, discussing their apparently bad behaviour, and she was still wearing no underwear.

Catherine Raymond acted with the appropriate decorum for a mother being called in to her son's school again as a result of his fighting. She was older than Rachel and she felt it. Ben was nine and his younger brother was one. Obviously not a part of Catherine's life plan, but it had happened and she was dealing with her situation in the best way that she could. Ben may have been feeling neglected but she was feeling tired. So fucking tired, of everything and everyone.

It wasn't until they were outside the front gates that Catherine laid into the young boy. She was pushing a buggy with her left hand and clipping the back of Ben's head with her right. She was shouting at him, telling him to grow up. Then, when he cried, she shouted some more, telling him to stop crying. When he didn't stop straight away, she raised her hand again.

Aaron and Jess giggled at the bully getting a taste of his own medicine. Rachel felt for him. The rebellious spark she'd been feeling that day as a result of the cloud moving through The Hollow made her want to clip Catherine on the back of the head and shout at her. But the woman had a small baby and it was probably already hearing too many raised voices.

'Stoppit, you two. You're still in trouble for retaliating.'

'But, Mum, I was protecting Jess,' Aaron protested.

'I know. But there are ways to deal with bullies, and bullies only act that way for a reason they are too scared to mention.'

Neither of them really understood what she was talking about or why she would defend Ben *bloody* Raymond but they stayed quiet.

'Let's get home, shall we?' Her tone wasn't mad, nor was it

accusatory. She was pleased to be going home, finally. And she wouldn't be alone because she had Jess and Aaron. And Nate would be back in a couple of hours.

The Raymonds were almost out of sight, powering off into the distance, the sound of the wind muffling Ben the Bully's castigation.

Stanhope Road was empty. The Hadleys were the last family to leave the school. The packs had run off earlier and eventually dispersed. They had been left behind. At the back. Slow and exposed.

WHO'S THERE?

Pace left a gap hardly long enough to scratch the back of his head before he rapped on the Brady door three more times.

Andrea and Owen were stunned into inaction. Michael was looking up from his book, waiting for somebody to move. He wanted to speak but he was still afraid of what he might say.

'Mr Brady,' Pace called, his words seemingly unfreezing the statues inside. 'Can you open the door, please? It's Detective Pace.'

Owen Brady opened the door himself this time, and Andrea went to the dining area to sit with Michael. She smiled as she entered. Michael did not reciprocate.

'Detective, I've already told you everything I know. I just want to be with my son. What else could you possibly want to know?' Owen spoke like a man broken and tired by his ill fortune. Wearied by the cruelty of fate.

'Oh, I have many questions that I require answers to in this town.'

Where is Julee? What happened to her? Why is Mrs Beaufort here so soon after her collapse? Is this all my fault? Did it follow me here? Where is home?

Owen said nothing.

'There's only one person in the world, as far as I know, who saw the man that shot a gun near Hinton Hollow Primary School on Monday.' He let the sentence float in the air, unaffected by the wind.

He'd thought about how he would word it on the way over – he was sensitive to the situation and wanted to avoid mentioning young Jacob Brady so explicitly.

'Detective. This really isn't the time. He's been through enough,' Owen pleaded but not with any force.

'The man with the gun is still out there, Mr Brady. We have no idea if he wants to strike again or whether he has something against your family name. What we do know is that Michael saw him and, if I'm going to catch this guy, I'll need more than the fact that he looked like *an ordinary man.*'

Pace had already taken one step up to the threshold before Owen Brady had resigned to inevitability.

No more of this small-town solidarity.

It was time for the boy to start talking.

NOT AN OPTION

Remember in the beginning, when I told you that you should just leave, because you'll be annoyed? Well, this is that part.

I know what you're going to think. Because I've been watching all of you. Forever.

You'll want the mother to say 'no'. You'll want her to say that she cannot choose between her children and that the bullet should go through her skull. You'll think that she should lay down her life so that her children may live. You'll want her to do what you feel Faith Brady should have done.

And this is the problem. This is the reason I am here, doing this.

It's because of you, and the things that you think.

You think the best course of action would have been for Faith Brady to have taken the bullet herself. You think her two sons should have turned around from their playful beetle prank in the park and seen their mother lying dead on the stone path as an ordinary man ran into the woods.

You think the next mother should do the same.

Because you are caught in the morality of it all. You think that you would choose your children's lives over your own. And what you are not seeing is that there is another option. The option not to accept evil. The option to be good, to do good.

There is the option not to be desensitised to the wrongdoings of the world.

There is an option to care.

For more than the immediate.

There is the option where neither the children nor the mother have to die.

Because of you, on day three, this was not an option.

THE BOY WHO KNEW SOMETHING

JESS HADLEY

When it happened, it happened fast.

A little faster than before.

The Raymonds were a dot in the distance. Agitation and impatience proving to be the key to their survival.

Jess was staring at the back of Ben the Bully until he disappeared. She was wishing he'd vanish. She kept saying it over and over in her head until she couldn't see him any more.

I made that happen, she told herself.

Take that, Ben.

After her mother had told her and her brother to be quiet, both children had been in their own worlds. They listened to her. They obeyed her instructions. But Jess, who was older, saw something different in her mother that day. She had been quicker to short her fuse. She had even stuck up for that slime ball Ben. She was being *weird*.

Jess brushed her long, scraggly, mousey hair away from her face with her right hand. She wasn't particularly *girly*. She didn't care about keeping her hair in the ponytail her mum tied every morning and she didn't mind getting dirty or falling over. That's how she'd got into the scrape with Ben the Bully. She was getting herself involved in *boy stuff*.

She thought about that *no-brain idiot* with his hand around her throat. He was strong, that was for sure. And her little brother having to save her. She'd wanted to kick that bully in the shins but she'd frozen. Aaron hadn't even paused. He was younger than her and he was protecting her. She hated that he had to do that but she loved him for doing it.

She looked over at Aaron but he was staring in the other direction. God knows what he was thinking about. Jess turned her gaze back to the front. Nobody was there. They were almost at the corner of their road. She wondered what might be for dinner.

There was the sound of her mother's voice, then Jess Hadley took a bullet to the face in the same way that May Tambor had.

There was no pattern.

He was killing little girls now.

AARON HADLEY

Aaron had been expecting a hero's welcome. He'd looked after Jess. His dad would probably pat him on the back for what he had done when he got home, when he found out that Aaron had saved his sister from that thug.

Dad will be proud, he mused, looking through the high bushes of the large, gated homes just past his school. The houses were two or three times the size of his. He was wondering what they looked like inside, how big their televisions were, how much room they had in their gardens to kick a football.

His knee was cold. Another pair of trousers that he'd ripped. Usually it had something to do with football, falling in the playground. He ran a lot. And he was fast. Fast for his age and even for the year above him. That's how he'd knocked Ben over, it was nothing to do with his strength, it was momentum and a lack of fear. It had helped that the tormentor's posse had moved aside so he hadn't slowed down at all.

It had hurt his shoulder when they collided, he hadn't looked at the bruise yet but he was sure there was one. His right knee had scraped the concrete of the playground. He didn't feel the pain at that point, even though he was bleeding, because the adrenaline had kicked in. It had taken over a part of his brain that caused him to reason with himself. He just lashed out. He'd got a few good hits in, too, before Ben managed to retaliate.

Before he remembered he could be hurt.

Aaron was smiling into the wind as he walked along Stanhope Road. He was pleased with himself even if his mother disapproved of the way he had handled the situation. He didn't think what he'd done was wrong. And he couldn't wait to tell his dad about it.

Then his mother's voice.

And the bang that floored his big sister.

One more for himself. Through the heart.

He was joining Jacob Brady.

An ordinary man ran away.

His mother wasn't crying.

  MY THIRD WISH.
I wish I'd let go.

RACHEL HADLEY

Rachel wanted her children to be quiet. She had to think. The only choice she was considering was whether or not to tell Nate what had happened. She was scared of Charles Ablett – and he was the nicer of the two Ablett brothers. She'd been so stupid.

So fucking stupid. So selfish.

She had no idea what had come over her but she still felt it, like a foreign presence that made her feel more adventurous. More sexual. More aggressive.

The last thing she needed at that moment was another decision to make.

So, when the gun was pushed into that dent in the back of her neck, just as it had been for Faith Brady, when those words were spoken softly, asking which of her children she would choose to die, Rachel Hadley was not herself and, therefore, did not act in the way that could have saved Aaron and Jess's lives.

She killed them.

She killed them all.

ORDINARY MAN

He left the car in the woods. It would be safe there. Nobody was looking in the woods. There was no missing body. Nobody that anyone realised was actually missing. Not yet.

Nobody was looking for Oz Tambor in the boot of a car. Like nobody had bothered to look for Julee.

They were yet to find that May Tambor was gone, too.

So he walked. Everybody in Hinton Hollow walked.

He blended in. He was one of them, whatever they called themselves.

Hollowers.

Hintonions.

The sound of the fast train rumbling straight through from London to Oxford was the only noise cutting through that rushing air around him. There were no cars on the road, no people walking around in this weather. But there would be soon enough. The kids couldn't just stay in school. They had to get home somehow. They had to leave at some point.

One of the mothers had to be asked.

He headed down the hill towards the crossroads, his long coat protecting him from a wind that seemed too scared to touch him. His stubble made his skin look as grey as the Hinton Hollow cloud cover. His steps were steady, unrushed, like he had nowhere important to be.

Walking to the crossroads was a risky move. If there were going to be any people – any witnesses – it would be there. Parents of younger children would be hoicking pushchairs into Rock-a-Buy, the florist was busier than ever with the latest run of untimely deaths, not to mention the wedding that was still booked in for the weekend. And there was always somebody at RD's Diner, no matter the time of day.

He'd be spotted if he risked that route. And be remembered. Locals would remember a local and they sure would not forget an outsider slinking through their beloved crossroads with nothing on his mind.

The ordinary man turned right onto Oakmead, a useful cut-through to avoid the traffic lights if you were driving through Hinton Hollow. The houses were arranged in a horseshoe around an area of greenery and trees that could be used as goalposts but were too thick to find a decent foothold to try and climb. He lit a cigarette and walked on.

Oakmead cut a corner that avoided being noticed at the crossroads and he emerged quietly on Stanhope Road around fifty feet from the school.

A bell rang and he could feel the stampede of children's feet, eager to get home to their games consoles and books and sweet treats and pets. Any that turned right out of the gates – his left – would be heading along the main high street. They'd be safe for another day.

He rested against a lamppost, finishing the dregs of his cigarette, watching as kids flew out of the door excitedly, as though they were staging a mass prison break. He could see the *Had* on the Hadley's Hair sign and rubbed at the unkempt nest on his own head.

Initially, a large peloton of people evacuated in both directions. He wasn't interested in either group.

There was only one question but there weren't enough bullets.

He was waiting for the stragglers. The kids who had lost a shoe after gym practice or those who were detained for bad behaviour, whose parents had been called in to resolve a disciplinary issue. He flicked the butt of the cigarette onto the floor and stamped on it, leaving enough evidence for the police to start mounting a more useful line of enquiry. The wind blew the burnt stub towards town, where it would never be found.

It was difficult to hear what the children were talking about with their parents that day because the air was either taking sound off into the distance or blowing too hard around the ears to make out the specifics of the conversations. They were clucking chickens and squawking seagulls. A rabble of nobody he wanted to talk to.

Then the Raymonds emerged from the gate. The mother was pushing a buggy with one hand and pulling an older boy along like a cartoon.

The ordinary man's back straightened against the post, pushing him forward slightly.

They could work.

Two children. One mother. The perfect combination.

She didn't pay any attention to the man on the other side of the road. She was too busy shouting at the boy and yanking him to keep up with her pace though her legs were much longer than his.

Ask her.

Ask her the question.

The gun was tucked into the back of his trousers, the handle hanging over his belt. He reached around carefully inside his long coat and gripped it in his hand. Then he slid it slowly around his body as the mother and her two children pushed on ahead. He put the gun into his pocket and took a step forward. His eyes were fixed on the nape of Catherine Raymond's neck.

Then he stopped.

Another mother appeared from the blue school door. The teachers that had been monitoring the playground had either dispersed or headed back into the building.

It was her.

It should be her. The runt of the litter.

Perfect.

She was attractive. More so than Faith Brady, though their thighs were a hair's width apart in terms of quality. He was thinking about her sexually though that was not what it was about. He shook that off instantly; there was work to be done.

He fell back against the post and allowed the family to exit the school grounds. They turned left – his right – and followed the-ones-who-got-away up Stanhope Road towards Roylake. The Raymond family moved much faster than the Hadleys.

Watching for a minute, he could see that their relationship was close. The children walked alongside their mother – the girl on her right, the smaller, younger boy on her left – unlike the Brady woman, who had let her kids run out ahead of her. They were not holding hands, they were too old for that, but they were as close to touching as could be without actual physical contact. They were a unit. That was clear, even to a murderer looking at them from behind.

They are a family, he told himself. *Her decision will be harder to make than the last one.*

He still didn't understand what he was doing.

He was pissing into the wind. The gale-force wind.

He saw Rachel Hadley talking to both of them. She was direct. She gave them equal attention, looking right at her daughter then left at her son. He couldn't work out which of them had been naughty. Who was at fault for keeping them all behind after school. Marking their cards for death.

When the mother had finished talking to her children, she rubbed the top of their backs with one hand, both of them receiving her loving touch at the same time. It appeared to mellow both children. The tension dropped in their shoulders and they both peered off into the distance, thinking about the things that a ten- and seven-year-old think about.

That's when he made his move.

There was no reason to look both ways before crossing the road, there was no traffic, but he did it out of habit and that inbuilt mechanism for self-preservation. Before stepping off the kerb he took one final look over his shoulder.

He moved quickly. Once the decision had been made there was no room for hesitation. He was gliding along the pathway of Stanhope Road as though dancing with the wind. He pulled the gun out of his pocket and pointed it forward, if she heard him coming he would have to end it there.

But Rachel Hadley could not hear him coming, not in that weather. He knew he would have to be close if he was to deliver his message.

He was a couple of feet away and the kids were still in a waking reverie. Rachel Hadley was looking straight ahead. She was wondering what to tell her husband. She was worried that she had made her family unsafe by acting on the dark impulses she had never experienced before. She was picturing Charles Ablett when the metal touched the back of her neck and a voice said, 'Don't scream. Don't you dare. You don't have to die today, miss.' He was delivering the lines in exactly the same way he had to Faith Brady.

Otherwise what he was doing wouldn't be fair.

He didn't even have the opportunity to ask her to decide which of her children she loved the most, which one she would like to keep alive. Because he was not speaking to Rachel Hadley of yesterday, he was threatening the Rachel Hadley of *today*. The Rachel Hadley who impetuously scratched a fifteen-year itch she never knew that she had. The Rachel Hadley who gave her husband a spontaneous, pre-lunch blow job in his back office. The fiery Rachel Hadley. The aggressive, pro-active Rachel Hadley.

She ignored him.

She did not allow the man with the gun to put her or her children in jeopardy. And, ultimately, that is exactly what she did.

She'd had enough of bullies.

The Rachel Hadley of that day spun around and lashed out. She swung her right arm forward, trying to hit the gun out of the man's hand. She only had the opportunity to say one word.

'You.'

Then he panicked and pulled the trigger, blowing a hole through her face at close range that obliterated her perfect triangle of a nose and sent splinters of enamel down her throat and embedded themselves in the lining of her cheeks. She hit the floor with a thump. Her hair blew around to the front of her formerly beautiful face and stuck in the mess that was left.

This is not how it is supposed to be.

Jess was the first to turn around. Just her eyes were enough to flip the man with the gun. He could see the woman who had just attacked him in those eyes. And that same triangular nose that promised the girl would grow up to be as beautiful as her mother.

Then he shot her in the face to ensure that she never grew up beyond that day on Stanhope Road.

The only saving grace to the speed of events was that Aaron, who would never hear his father tell him that he absolutely had been a hero that day, did not have enough time to see the mess that had been made of his mother's and sister's faces. The third bullet penetrated his skin and pushed through his soft, spongey, growing bones, ripping open his heart before his eyes could see the carnage and inform his brain that it should break in half anyway.

He almost dropped the gun. There were three dead bodies on the floor beneath the spot where he stood, itching, anxious. The only saving grace of this fucked-up situation was that it was confusing. For everyone.

The man with the gun had not received the answer he had been looking for, but the police would be equally mystified. It was clear that it was the same killer at work, the location and method were too similar to be discounted. It was the motive that eluded. Why kill Jacob Brady one day then take out an entire family the next?

All he could do was run, and that is exactly what he did. He sprinted back across the road, this time not bothering to check both ways, then disappeared into Oakmead, eventually passing through the other end of the avenue, up the hill past the train station and back into the woods. The only sound was the wind brushing past his ears as he ran until he arrived back at the car and all was a hush but the whispering of the trees.

HERE'S SOMETHING TO CHEW ON
Evil can get it wrong.

ON THE CARDS

There's a theory posited by scientists and thinkers that suggests the possibility of alternate realities or different dimensions. An idea that this particular situation with the Hadleys could have been occurring at exactly the same time in another galaxy or realm or whatever and the outcome would have been completely different.

In fact, they say that there may even be an infinite number of possibilities.

So, here, Rachel Hadley retaliated to protect her children and they all ended up perishing. Perhaps, somewhere else, she gave in and took the bullet. In another place, she takes down the ordinary man and performs a citizen's arrest and is hailed as a hero. Or the ordinary man doesn't look as he crosses the road and is mowed down by a learner driver. Maybe Evil doesn't exist. Or never visited Hinton Hollow.

The notion is all a little cosy, don't you think?

LET ME TELL YOU THIS
It's another l i e.

Another invented concept that humans tell themselves so they can continue behaving in the way they do. With apathy and self-interest at heart. They can't change what is happening. It is up to fate.

THE WORST LIE THAT HUMANS
TELL THEMSELVES
Everything happens for a reason.

The problem with this is that they put that reason down to destiny, when, in fact, they are the reason.

They are the reason their planet is dying and they don't care that there is no back-up.

They are the reason they feel so disconnected and disenchanted and disenfranchised. And they have lost the ability to empathise.

And they are the reason the Hadleys are dead. And that I have to exist and demonstrate to them just how awful they can be.

They are the reason that Evil has to be so evil.

TOO DARK TO SEE

Oz heard the car door slam then everything went silent.

He could hear himself breathing and he tried to hug himself to keep warm, his right hand stretching around to hold his left shoulder and his left hand on his right shoulder. He rocked. He thought about calling out. Or screaming. But nobody was there to help him.

It was so dark. Too dark to see.

All he had to get him through were thoughts of Liv Dunham and how he wanted to marry her that coming weekend. It was still possible. It could still happen. In his head, the ending was clear.

If he could just get out of this situation.

If he could let her know that he was all right, he was alive – hungry, but alive – not to worry.

If he could only hear her voice.

WHISPERS

She was not locked in the boot of a car but Maeve Beauman felt the same as Oz.

Trapped. Longing. Wanting to hear the person she loved.

The late-night conversation she'd had with Pace had meant

everything. He'd been thinking about her, too. He wanted her. Maybe he even needed her. But, instead of fulfilling Maeve, instead of pacifying her own paranoia and settling her, she wanted it more. She wanted it now. She wanted it all the time. And this started a spiral.

How can they go from that talk to nothing?
Why can't he just send her a message?
A kiss.
Some emotion.
Who is he with in that town?
What is he doing?

She didn't like the way she was feeling. She knew it was because of Pace. Maybe he was no good for her. But people have trouble letting go of the things that hurt them.

Detective Sergeant Pace was her habit.
Detective Sergeant Pace was heroin.
Her weakness.
She spirals. *Maybe I need to show him more love.*
She spirals. *Why is it always up to me?*
Maeve does not message him, she does not say that she loves him. She says nothing.
And she spirals. *It must be over.*

SEVERE GALE

'Michael. I know that this is difficult for you. What happened was not right and very unfair.' Pace could wait no longer to move forward with the investigation. The doctors and psychiatrists could say not to push the boy but that was not helping to catch this guy. The man with the gun. The ordinary man. 'My job is to make sure that this doesn't happen to anyone else. I want to catch the man that did this and I think you could help me to do that.'

Michael just looked at the detective, through him, in fact. He glimpsed his father in the background sat on the sofa next to that woman that wasn't his mother.

Why does she have to sit so close to him? he asked himself inside, but his gaze did not falter or show that he wasn't functioning properly. Trying to be strong while hurting inside.

Owen Brady was sat forward on the sofa, constantly shifting himself nervously. Andrea wanted to put a hand on his leg to steady him. She shouldn't really do that in her position but she was doing lots of things that went against her better judgement that day. He put his left hand down and gripped the sofa cushion. Andrea Day put her hand on his and spoke softly, 'He'll be fine. He's doing great. Try to relax.' She took her hand away eventually but it loitered longer than it should have.

Michael blinked then made eye contact with Pace.

He was back in the room.

He nodded.

'Okay. Thank you, Michael. Now you said that the man looked ordinary. Can you tell me a little bit more about what he looked like?'

Michael screwed his face as though he was thinking but said nothing.

'Was he as tall as me? As tall as your dad?' Pace offered, to get him going.

'You. He was as tall as you.'

'Excellent. That's a good start.'

Pace was worried about leading the boy too much. Kids found it easier to agree with an adult because they wanted to please, they wanted to help. But false information was no help at all.

'Did you hear his voice at all?'

Nothing from the boy.

'What about your mum?' This was risky ground and Owen Brady was becoming more agitated in the background. 'You told me that she called your name. Did she say anything else? Anything before that? Was she talking with the man?'

He could see Michael breaking. It was the last thing he wanted to do to a seven-year-old, but whatever this kid was holding back could be the key to breaking the case wide open and settling Hinton Hollow back into its sleepy existence.

His pocket started to vibrate. It was Anderson. Probably calling to inform him that Mrs Beaufort was fine and had checked out of the hospital. Something Pace already knew because the old woman was waiting in the back of his car. He hit the reject button and sent his inspector straight through to voicemail.

'Sorry about that, Michael. Now, do you remember? Was your mum talking to the man before she called your name?'

Michael looked around the broad frame of the detective sat opposite him at the dining table. His eyes were glazing. Owen wanted to stand up and stop this torture but held himself back.

His mother was dead. If he had heard something, what was the use in saying now? He didn't want to make his mum look bad. He didn't really understand what had happened to her. He had heard the word *dead* and he'd even used it in games with friends at school and with his brother, Jacob. But he'd never thought about what it meant. Where people went when they died. His family never went to the Good Shepherd so his understanding of heaven was limited to what was mentioned at school. And when his father had stated that Jacob had gone there like his gran had.

Pace's pocket vibrated again. He didn't even look at his phone, just squeezed the button on the top to hang up the call.

He does *know something*, Pace told himself. *The fucking kid knows something and has been holding it back.*

Pace was trying not to become annoyed but it was difficult with Owen twitching behind him and Mrs Beaufort no doubt becoming ever more frustrated on his back seat and Anderson incessantly pestering him with information that he already had and the boy who knew something.

He waited. Trying a new approach where he said nothing, hoping the boy would fill the silence with useful information.

But his goddamn phone began to buzz inside his right trouser pocket again.

He took it out this time. Anderson. Again.

'I'm sorry, Michael, I just have to take this.' Pace stood up from the table and gave Owen Brady a nod that said *you can get up and comfort your boy now.* Then he hit the green button.

'Pace!' His answer was barely one syllable in length. 'I'm in the middle of talking to a witness, sir. What's so important?'

'You were right, Pace. We should've kept the schools shut.'

Outside, Mrs Beaufort was lying on her side on the pavement.

ANOTHER HOLE IN THE HEART

Roger Ablett saw the blur of an ambulance whizz past the window of RD's Diner while he picked the tomatoes from his cheeseburger. And his first thought was: *What have you done now, Charles?*

He was five years older than his brother and ten stone heavier. That morning, while his brother was screwing Rachel Hadley, Roger had been showing a couple around a riverfront property in Twaincroft Hill – some middle-aged abrasive Yorkshireman who had made a lot of money doing something incredibly boring with barcodes but had bagged himself a not-so-middle-aged trophy who wanted to dock a boat on the Thames and fuck the arrogant idiot into a heart attack.

Barcode Man was not going to say that he wanted the two-million pound property right there and then but Roger could see in the young *climber's* eyes that she would convince him. That was the reason Roger was sat in RD's place when the paramedics drove through an empty Hinton Hollow crossroads, he was sucking down on his traditional reward – fat, calories, and lots of them.

He ordered the double burger with cheese, bacon, portobello mushroom, avocado and soured cream. RD's wife always put lettuce and tomato in Roger's burger and he always picked them out, leaving them displayed on his empty plate once he had finished. She knew he didn't eat them and she knew it was a waste, but it eased her conscience a little to give the dangerously overweight man something healthy to chew on. She was no merchant of death.

Roger slurped down a large milkshake between mouthfuls of sweet-potato fries. He was eating too quickly and his chest was hurting.

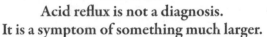

A NOTE
Acid reflux is not a diagnosis.
It is a symptom of something much larger.

He hit it with the fleshy part of his right hand, coughing after two punches. The other patrons of the diner went quiet. Maybe this was the day that Roger Ablett would finally keel over and die like Dorothy Reilly.

He was an intimidating figure. Large though not particularly tall, he was known for his temper or, more precisely, the way in which he seemed to lose it so easily. He had money and influence and a shrewd political mind.

He also had a younger brother who was not overweight, was good-looking and not as ambitious about his career as he was about fucking every woman in town. Roger had been known to muscle his way towards a decision that would be beneficial to him but he did not agree with using that muscle on women like Charles did.

But Charles was his little brother and he loved him in spite of these faults. And he looked after him. So, when the ambulance drove past, something was telling Roger Ablett that he was going to have to get his brother out of trouble. Again.

He coughed once more then slurped at the melted dregs of his banana milkshake. The other customers breathed. He was okay.

Maybe next time.

BURST APPENDIX

It was eerie.

There was nobody outside.

The paramedics drove up to the scene just beyond the primary school. Three bodies were lying on the pathway and the headmistress – who had made the emergency call – was sat on the low wall next to the school gates weeping into her hands. She had made all the remaining teachers wait inside until everything was *cleared up*. She did not want anyone else to witness the horror.

Thank God the kids had left.

'Mrs Blake?' The female paramedic approached the headmistress cautiously while her male counterpart moved towards the Hadleys. They were all lying on their backs. Two with holes in their faces and one with a hole in the chest. He checked the boy first; there was no way the other two could still be alive, that much was clear. He had to play the percentages.

'Yes. Yes.' Mrs Blake paused for a moment then said, 'Yes?' Her head was shaking from side to side very slightly, her body was saying *no*.

'Mrs Blake, are you okay? Did you see what happened here?'

'I'm ... I'm fine. I wasn't out here when it happened. I heard the shots, though. Three shots. I expected them to be louder, you know? But I guess the wind muffled them, or something. I don't really know about that kind of thing...' She trailed off. Her eyes were wandering to the side as if she wanted to look at the dead family but every time they got close to glimpsing them, they shot back in the other direction.

'I need you to take a deep breath.' And the paramedic took one herself to demonstrate.

'Shouldn't you be looking at *them*? I'm fine here. You should see to them. Do you think they'll be all right?' She knew it was a stupid question but could not stop herself from asking it.

'My partner has that under control, Mrs Blake. The police will be here at any moment and they are going to want to talk to you. I'm not going to allow that if you are not up to the task. So you tell me how you are feeling. Is anything hurting? Do you feel dizzy?'

'No. I'm not in pain. I feel a little disorientated but not dizzy.'

'Do you think you could stand up? The police will want to seal this area off as quickly as possible. Perhaps we could get you inside.'

'I am a little cold. There was no time to pick up my jacket.' Her head flicked to the side once more and she caught sight of one of Rachel Hadley's smooth, shiny shins. 'I wanted to move her, you know?'

'I'm sorry?' The paramedic did not know where this was going.

'Mrs Hadley. Her dress is, well, it's less than flattering in the position it's in. A little undignified. I thought about moving it down and straightening it out a little but I've seen those police shows and it's all evidence, isn't it? You shouldn't tamper with the crime scene.' Mrs Blake was speaking but not aiming her thoughts at anything in particular. She didn't know where to look and she was starting to spew words that were unnecessary.

'Let's get you back inside. A cup of tea will warm you up.'

A WORD ON BRITISH STEREOTYPES
They know that a cup of tea does not cure everything.
But they will always give it a try.

Detective Sergeant Pace came speeding along Stanhope Road. Roger Ablett was massaging his knuckles into his chest after devouring the last handful of fries and witnessed Pace's unmarked vehicle power past the diner with what looked like Mrs Beaufort in the back.

It *was* Mrs Beaufort. Her heart had broken on that first day, when Jacob Brady was shot, and the first cracks began to appear in her beloved town. She'd felt this too. Like an aftershock. Her chest was being ripped open and Hinton Hollow was being torn apart. She blamed the man in the driver's seat for bringing this blight.

Detective Sergeant Pace is a curse.

Detective Sergeant Pace brought this upon us.

Detective Sergeant Pace is society's burst appendix.

Now she saw him as the only one who could possibly repair what had been broken.

HOLEHEARTED

Pace could see between Rachel Hadley's legs from thirty feet away, through his dirty windscreen. The part of her body that Charles Ablett had described as *the perfect fit*.

She'd been blown onto her back by the force of the close-range shot. She'd rolled backward onto her shoulders briefly. When her body flopped down flat, her left leg had bent and the knee had remained pointing towards the sky. Her dress was pushed up to her waist and the wind was causing it to balloon. She was on display. Luckily, nobody was around. Not yet. Not like they had been when Jacob's life had been cut short on that first day.

Fuck. Is this escalating? Is it sexual now? Pace was whispering like the trees. He didn't want Mrs Beaufort to hear his thoughts but he could not keep them inside.

'Oh God.' He spoke loudly. There was no containing his reaction to the sight of two more bodies. Small. Innocent. Shattered lives.

'What is...?'

Pace slammed the brakes, cranked the gear into reverse and wrapped his left arm around the passenger seat to get a better view of what was behind him.

Nothing was behind him.

The engine revved. The tyres squealed in pain. The car whipped itself around to face the other direction. Pace could have popped the car back into gear and driven out of Hinton Hollow. He could have disappeared forever, left it all behind. Like Julee and Oz had. Like he had done to London. *I wasn't going to let him run away any more.*

Pace pulled the car over to the kerb and parked on a double-yellow line.

'Wait in the car,' he instructed Mrs Beaufort. 'Do not try to get out.'

'But.'

'You do not want to see this, Mrs Beaufort. Is there anybody that can take you home? If not, I will drive you there when I am done.' It was unorthodox but this was not a regular situation. He could see a female paramedic helping an older lady in through the school gates while another was administering to the boy.

Another hole in another heart.

Mrs Beaufort did not answer him. And that was good enough. She couldn't get out of the car, anyway. The back doors could only be unlocked from the outside. He didn't want her to panic if she tried to get out and realised that she was trapped. She already had a heart condition, the extent of which was unknown to the detective at that point.

He slammed the door shut and looked back over his shoulder.

Nothing there.

Nothing he could see.

Just me. Pushing him along.

Watching the horror.

YOU KNOW THIS PLACE

Inspector Anderson finished instructing his constable on the front desk that the information went no further. Hell, it wasn't even common knowledge that Faith Brady had taken her own life yet. Now there were three more bodies lying outside a school.

This needs a quick clean-up, he told himself in that rather special detached manner he had perfected since moving to The Hollow.

The bloody florist will be grinning from ear to ear. Never been a better fucking time to sell flowers in this town.

He sat down behind his desk, which was due to fall apart any day, and called Councilwoman Hayes. He did not need to look the number up. He knew it.

'I thought we'd agreed that I'd call *you*,' she answered, speaking under her breath slightly. Anderson could tell she was gritting her teeth.

'Anita.'

'I'm free tonight after nine,' she offered.

'Anita.'

'Too late for you? You're not past it yet, inspector.' Her tone was lighter.

'Anita!' He killed the mood. 'This is a courtesy call. You are going to come under some scrutiny very shortly. This cannot be contained.'

'What is it? What's going on?'

'Another shooting in Hinton Hollow.' It was a momentary lapse in his matter-of-factness.

'What?'

'Worse than before. Two kids. And the mother, this time.'

'Where? What?' She was upset. He could hear it.

'Outside the Stanhope School. I'm on my way there now. Nobody knows. I have my best man on the case but it will get out, you know this place. Be prepared, okay?'

He hung up before she could say anything else. Though he was no longer listening, Anita Hayes thanked him before she replaced the receiver.

Anderson's moustache was at Pace's side within four minutes.

HOPE

The paramedic gave Pace the same shake of the head he had given after examining Jacob's cracked remains. Young Aaron Hadley had died instantly. He'd gone wherever the souls of the innocent moved on to.

FURTHER THOUGHTS ON SOULS
A 21g loss in weight does not seem
enough for Aaron Hadley.
His bravery would make it weigh more.
He was bigger than his body.
An adult has more experience but a lighter soul.
Bravery and innocence are good.
So goodness carries weight.
Therefore, the more evil inside, the less soul you have.

A QUESTION
If Evil has no soul, why do I find myself caring
so much about this world?

The young girl looked just like her mother. She would have grown into the same woman, same body shape, same facial features. They both had the same hole in the front of their face and the backs of their heads, though the bullet had entered and exited at slightly different angles due to their difference in height.

At least that would give them a better idea of the height of the killer.

Because Michael fucking Brady can't even be clear on that.

Pace knew that it was wrong to think of an unfortunate child in that way but this was too raw. The town reminded him of all the things he'd hoped it would help him to forget. And I was gripping at his insides.

He dropped to his knees between the mother and daughter. He thought it would look like weakness but he didn't care. Sure, the town he had grown up in believed that he was now some kind of desensitised urbanite, and to an extent he was, far more than any of them, but he was fracturing. And cracks are what let out the light to make it easier for the darkness to find him.

He had to pull himself together. Like it or not, the people of Hinton Hollow saw Detective Pace as one thing only. Hope.

Another way that Evil presents itself: H o p e.

'Detective?' The male paramedic was concerned.

He hadn't worked the day after the Brady shooting. That had been his sixth day in a row. He was now scheduled for another four days before he had five days clear to recuperate. He hadn't rid his mind of the image of Jacob Brady, and now *this*. He was already looking forward to Sunday. He thought he might lie in and skip church for once.

Perhaps he'd need Father Salis by the time the week was through.

'I'm fine. I'm fine. This just ... It isn't right, is it?'

The paramedic didn't answer, he just gave what was becoming his trademark shake of the head.

'Who was the woman?' Pace composed himself and slot back into the role of investigator.

'It's difficult to tell. Her face is...'

'Not the victim. The woman that was being taken back inside by your colleague.'

'Oh. The headmistress of the school. She called it in.'

'Witness?'

'I don't know. I'm here to see whether anybody requires medical attention. Unfortunately there doesn't seem to be anything I can do here, detective.' He was acting professionally but Pace could see he was being eaten up, a thin film of water dropping over his eyes. He didn't care about that.

'Have you checked these?' He pointed to Jess and Rachel.

'I don't think there's anything I can do.' The paramedic's eyes widened as though stating something incredibly obvious.

'You're not here to think. You are here to see whether anybody requires medical attention. I've seen people live through similar.' He had, too. But not for long. And not without drawbacks. He wanted the paramedic out of the way. This had the opportunity to get ugly very quickly.

Pace looked over his shoulder at the car to ensure that Mrs Beaufort was still there and still looking in the wrong direction. He could see her hair. That was good enough.

Then a police car turned on to Stanhope from the direction of the train station, drawing more attention to the destruction just beyond the school. Another too-slow reaction. Pace wanted to smoke but instead strode out into the middle of the road and started walking towards the oncoming vehicle.

The sky was starting to fall.

FOR NOBODY

Anderson stopped his car next to Pace's and Mrs Beaufort watched the giant moustache step out from behind the wheel.

'Are you trying to get yourself killed, Pace? What's gotten into you, man?'

'Are you okay in there, Mrs Beaufort?' Pace ignored his out-of-touch inspector and bent over, checking in on his passenger, overemphasising his words like an ignorant tourist. She nodded. She seemed comfortable.

'Not long now and I'll get you home.'

He stood up straight and beckoned Anderson over with an angry gaze.

'An ambulance and a police car speed through the centre of town. People are going to want to know what is going on.'

'You weren't speeding?'

'Of course I was but my car is unmarked. This situation is going to explode, sir. We need to seal off the street. I know that is going to bring more unwanted attention but it's coming anyway.'

Anderson thought about the councilwoman. She didn't have much time.

They arrived side by side at the crime scene.

'Holy shit, Pace. That is disgusting.' His mouth engaged before his brain even had a chance.

Anderson was staring into the dark holes that spread out like meteor craters on the faces of the mother and daughter. He could also see the hole where Charles Ablett's dick had been that morning. At least Rachel Hadley's children would never know what she had done, that she had two different semen samples bookending her crumpled remains. Before they'd died, it hadn't even registered that their mother was trying to save them.

Pace clocked Anderson scrutinising the area between the victim's legs and nudged him.

'It's undignified, is what it is.'

'You're right. She shouldn't be seen like this. She'll be remembered this way. We need to get the photos taken and get these bodies covered up. Tape the area off and keep people back. I've got a possible witness inside. In shock, no doubt, but an adult this time. I can work with that.'

Anderson was nodding along as though he were the subordinate.

'Maybe I should talk to Mrs Blake. I know her,' he offered.

'Sir, I think you'll be better out here. More people will listen to you than to me if they are told to keep back, they'll see that this is a police matter. I'll check on Mrs Blake.' Pace didn't want to miss the opportunity and played to his inspector's ego.

'Get in there and see what she knows,' Anderson responded, making it sound like it had been his idea.

He stopped Pace before he left.

'Surely this wasn't sexual.' He said it like a statement but it was more of a question. 'I mean, there wouldn't be time. There was nobody about on the street, obviously. But, he didn't kill her then have sex with her?' Again, a statement that was a question. 'Then take her underwear as some kind of souvenir?'

'The killings do not strike me as sexual in their nature, no. But heinous crimes tend to escalate, they become more risky, the killer needs more of something to obtain gratification. I'd let forensics worry about whether intercourse was had and we can do our job. Shut this place down and speak to the witness.'

'Have you seen worse than this in the city?' For such a big man, Anderson seemed like a child at that moment.

Of course Pace had seen worse.

He'd done worse.

That's why he came back.

PLAYING CHICKEN

His kitchen was filled with the scent of microwaved jalfrezi curry.

Darren was responsible for pigs and cows; he let other people kill the chickens that he ate.

The slaughterer was bored.

Waiting for a truckload of livestock to be delivered to an enclosed area they had no chance of escaping seemed wrong. Not in the way that killing another living thing is wrong. Not in the way that they are defenceless and Darren has a stun gun or a mallet or a knife or a vat of hot water or his fists or his feet. Wrong because it was too easy.

He was unfulfilled.

He needed more.

Escalation.

I could have had a hand in Darren's mind but he would have come to the same notion whether I'd have been there or not. I was watching his change. I was the silent witness. The bystander.

That cat chopper was sick of the activists. Those protesting vegetarians and vegans with their placards and their chants, trying to convince the world that these tiny-brained animals were worth saving as much as any other living being.

DARREN HAD A THOUGHT
What if the animals weren't in the pen?
What if they had the freedom to run?
Then you'd see about their
brains and their stupid feelings.

And Darren decided that one way to escalate the fun, to increase his fulfilment would be to hunt an animal rather than having them gifted to the abattoir.

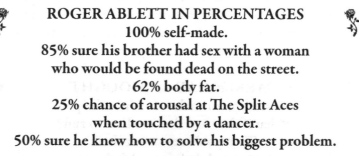

DARREN HAD ANOTHER BRIGHT IDEA
The next day, he would steal a pig.

12% TIP

Roger Ablett squeezed out of his chair and approached the counter.

'All done for today, Roger? Can't tempt you with anything sweet?' RD asked, already punching his bill into the till.

'Not today, RD. Thanks very much. My compliments to the chef, as usual.' He handed across a twenty-pound note before being told how much he owed. He was smiling the smile of a kind-hearted man. An occasional glimpse into the boy he had once been, when he and RD were inseparable.

RD took the note, popped the drawer on the till and fished around for the correct change. He tried to give it back to Ablett but he waved it away and pointed at the white bowl left on the counter for tips.

ROGER ABLETT IN PERCENTAGES
100% self-made.
85% sure his brother had sex with a woman
who would be found dead on the street.
62% body fat.
25% chance of arousal at The Split Aces
when touched by a dancer.
50% sure he knew how to solve his biggest problem.

'That's very kind of you,' RD said, dropping the coins and five-pound note into the bowl. Roger Ablett closed his eyes for a second to say, *of course*.

Then he turned and left.

Everybody walked in Hinton Hollow. Everybody but Roger Ablett. His car was parked behind the promenade of shops, in a bay reserved for one of the florist's vans. He just had to turn right towards the crossroads then right again and a third right to get behind the local stores. He could have been slumped in the driver's seat of his gas-guzzling Range Rover in three minutes. But the road to Roylake was being closed off. He'd have been turned away and made to travel the long way home.

But, on that day, Roger Ablett decided that he would walk. He would walk out of RD's Diner towards the unmarked police car that had Mrs Beaufort trapped in it like a rather comfortable hamster. He would continue until he met up with the local police inspector. And he would see the three bodies lying dead on the floor.

And he would recognise the woman as Rachel Hadley. The woman his younger brother had decided would be his next. Roger recalled his troublesome sibling saying that *she was gonna get fucked. Fucked good.*

If he could just keep his dick in his pants and his fists in his pockets.

A beep, and then, 'Charles. It's your brother. Where the fuck are you? What have you been doing today while I've been selling properties? Call me back so we can sort this mess out.'

He felt the anger rising within him as it so easily did. He hated those fucking answering machine messages.

He thought about his mother.

I'm sorry, Mother. I know you made me promise that I would look after Charles but he's getting out of control. I'm almost there, where I want to be. I could be running this town but I'm picking up his shit all the time. It's exhausting.

Then a thought to himself.

Roger Ablett had witnesses that could corroborate his whereabouts at the time of the Hadley shooting. If someone was going around bumping off kids and women that had scorned him in some way, maybe that same person wouldn't hesitate to kill a man.

Perhaps Charles Ablett could meet an untimely death. The police would never suspect his own brother, they would immediately put the fault in the direction of their local psychopath. And, if it was Charles doing this, Roger would be providing a service. He'd be an unknown hero. That would cancel things out with The Lord, surely.

It wasn't a thought he would usually have. But I wasn't usually there, massaging his mind.

Kill his brother to save himself.

Kill his brother to save the town.

Clean slate.

CONCERNED CITIZEN

The large, dark shape shuffling its way towards Inspector Anderson was unmistakeable.

What the fuck does he want? Anderson thought, rolling his eyes. *Where is that bloody photographer?*

Anderson stepped forwards to meet Roger Ablett. They stood in line with Mrs Beaufort.

'I'm afraid that's far enough, Roger. We're closing the road down.'

'What's going on here, chief?' He could see Mrs Beaufort from the corner of his eye but did not acknowledge the old bat.

'An accident outside the school. We're handling it. Should have the road open again in the next hour. Are you walking home this way?' He asked this knowing damn well Roger was not going to plod on for another half-mile into Roylake.

'No. No. Car's around the back. Just wanted to see what was going on, offer my help. Concerned citizen, you know?' His smile was misplaced and ill-judged.

'We've got things covered. The weather looks like it's about to get worse. You'd be better off getting back to your car.' It wasn't often that Anderson would control his mouth in this way but there was no sense in riling the monster who stood before him.

'We? Looks like you're out on your own.'

'Detective Pace is talking to a witness.' Roger Ablett balked slightly at the utterance of the word 'witness'. This could work for or against him, depending on how he decided to handle his brother.

'Ah, the prodigal son returns. I haven't had the pleasure yet.'

'I'm sure he'll make himself known to you at some point, Roger,' the chief grinned, knowingly. 'Now, if you don't mind.'

'No. Not at all. I do hope this horrible business is cleared up soon.' He turned away from Anderson and looked through the back window of Pace's vehicle. 'And a good day to you, Mrs Beaufort. I hope you haven't been getting yourself into trouble.' His teeth were yellow and crooked on the bottom. Mrs Beaufort could see them all, his grin was so wide. He found himself amusing.

He's not worth it, both Anderson and the old lady thought.

They watched him saunter back from where he came.

But he didn't wander straight back to his car.

First, he made an impromptu stop at Hadley's Hair.

A FLASH

Mrs Blake sat at her desk, in the same chair she had only recently been lecturing to a dead woman about her dead children.

Pace stood on the other side like one of her pupils. He looked at each wall then once in each corner. The soft lighting used in the school offices left no shadows. The windows were keeping most of the sound from the wind out.

He pulled a notepad from his inside left jacket pocket and a pen from the other side. He started to chew at the end of the pen before he spoke. A terrible habit but he couldn't shake it, like looking over his shoulder before crossing the road.

'Mrs Blake. I'm sorry you had to witness that. I've seen the injuries and I know this is a terrible question, but are you able to identify the three people outside on Stanhope Road?'

'Yes. Of course. It's the Hadleys. They were in my office, what seems like forever ago. I guess it was probably only thirty minutes.' She looked ahead as though they were still standing in front of her. She wondered whether she could have said anything different. Perhaps a quick wrist-slap and they'd have left too early for the killer.

'Can you give me their individual names?' Pace was treading carefully because he could see she was teetering on the edge of breakdown. But she was the best lead he had and he wasn't going to let it go this time.

Mrs Blake gave the details that Detective Pace required. Her voice was a little higher as she spoke young Aaron's name and reined in emotion.

'Why were they in your office, Mrs Blake?'

'Is that relevant?' She screwed her eyes into slits and her voice became a little more *head teacher.*

'Everything is relevant. It's not a case of passing blame or judgement, it's about collecting the facts. What were the Hadley family doing in your office?'

Every time he spoke or heard the word 'Hadley', his brain ticked over like there was something he was missing.

A previous case. One of the victims. Hadley Serf. Maybe.

The light flickered.

She explained the situation with the Raymond boy and the events that had taken place during the lunch break.

Professional. Precise. Stoic.

'Do the Raymonds and the Hadleys have a history? Has this kind of thing happened before?'

He needed more information. And quickly. I could help him by holding the headmistress's hand.

'Detective, if I can speak frankly...'

'By all means.'

'Ben Raymond is a little shit.' Her cheeks rouged at the unusual display of candidness. 'Every school has one and there's often one in every year. He's not actually a bad kid. His mother has recently given birth to a little surprise. There's a big age gap and my guess is that he's feeling a little left out. Not that I'm passing blame, you understand. Just trying to give you all the information.' She didn't wink but her eyes seemed brighter. Flirtatious, almost.

'So, no history between the families?'

'No.'

'Have there been any incidents with Mrs Hadley,' his mind jolted at that word again, 'with any of the other mothers.' He waited a beat. 'Or fathers.'

She knew what he was pushing for.

'She was very well liked. She got involved with anything she could. The kids were well presented and punctual. Of course there was jealousy, she was an attractive young mother but nothing that would lead to *this*.'

Pace raised an eyebrow.

Never say never. The darkness affects people in different ways.

'I'm not privy to everything that goes on, but the receptionists are less than discreet so most things do filter through. As far as I know, neither Rachel Hadley nor her husband had anyone I would class as an *enemy*.'

Pace kept emotion from his face. He tapped the pen against his teeth then pretended to write something down. This woman was starting to like the sound of her own voice and that was fine by him, as long as she was telling him the truth.

'Mr Hadley.' That was all Pace said. He was thinking aloud. Despairing at the lack of manpower in Hinton Hollow for such a case. They were not set up for this. The height of action in that town was a broken shop window or that one time somebody from Roylake stole a forklift truck and tried to steal a hole-in-the-wall cash machine.

If he'd had a team like he did in the city, that crime scene would be shut off from the public. The photos would be taken, the road would be closed, the bodies bagged. There'd be more than a giant moustache to stop people interfering with the area. The Brady kid would be out of the house where his mother had killed herself and in a safe place where a shrink could treat him and extract the pertinent information. Pace would be out looking for this man, this ordinary man with a gun he was not afraid to use on women and children.

And the fucking schools would have been closed.

He could feel his anger rising. A bulb flashed outside the window behind him and snapped him back into reality.

'Yes. Nathan Hadley. You know of him?'

'Nathan Hadley. I can't say that I do.'

'He owns the barbershop.' She pointed to her right.

Of course, that's where he'd seen it. It was only briefly, in passing, on his way back from looking at Julee's old house, but it had registered.

Pace was considering his position as lead investigator, that he would have to inform Nathan – Nate – Hadley of his family's fate. But he just couldn't stop that old mistress from talking.

'Well regarded, too,' she continued. 'He works close so picks the children up a lot. The mothers are quite doting on that kind of behaviour, as you can imagine.' She almost laughed. Had she forgotten what she had seen? 'The fathers, less so. Bit of a rumour going around about Mr Hadley's sexuality, but it's all bluster.'

So the conflict may have arisen from the other side of the Hadley marital bed, Pace thought to himself. He dare not ask another question for fear of further anecdotes.

The bulb flashed again. Twice.

'You were here when the shots were fired?'

'Yes. Sat exactly where I am right now.'

'What did you do when you heard them?'

Mrs Blake looked into her lap, the confidence and ease with which she had been speaking seemed to dissipate as she regressed into the old frightened teacher that Pace had first met out on Stanhope Road.

Another flash behind Pace's head as a picture of a spread-eagled Rachel Hadley was snapped for evidence.

'I waited. I was scared.'

'You didn't see anything?'

'No, Detective Pace.' She seemed angry but it was simply to cover her shame. 'I am a headmistress at a small-town primary school. I'm not in the SAS. I heard three shots fired very quickly.'

Pace wrote that down. It said more about the situation than anything he heard so far.

'I waited and I waited. I went to the window to see if it was all over.'

'Did you see anything, Mrs Blake? A man. Running away perhaps. Getting in a car...'

Another flash outside.

I let her go. She dropped back into shock.

Then there was the howl.

BLURRED LINES

Due to some boundary-line changes over the years, the shop actually sat on Hinton Hollow ground. But the sign still said *Roylake Leather and Guns.*

And the only thing you could see in the store was leather. Boots. Jackets. Saddles. Hats. Belts. Darren would shoot a bolt into the forehead of a cow, exsanguinate it, cut out its guts and skin it. The meat gets sent elsewhere, the skin ends up in Roylake as one of the many garments on display in that quiet, overpriced establishment.

The word 'guns' was faded. A nod to its long history and a time when the sale of firearms was a little more relaxed, particularly in rural areas.

But that did not mean they were not still available.

You hope that you live in a world where it is difficult for somebody underage to obtain alcohol. You hope that you live in a world where people have a roof over their head, where they don't have easy access to drugs. You hope you live in a world where your children are safe and sex is a positive experience between two people who trust each other, it is not thrust upon somebody who does not want it, it is not used as a weapon.

You h o p e.

You hope that your politicians are working for you and the good of those around you. You hope that teachers are not neglecting the students who require the most help and you hope that they are not giving so much of their time to those people that the kids at the other end are missing out somehow. You hope that your parents will support you, no matter what you decide to do or who you decide to be or even who you decide to be with. You hope that they would give their life for yours.

You h o p e.

And you hope that there is more good in the world than evil. And you hope that there can be peace. And you hope that the ice caps won't melt and a cure will be found and things will become more equal between the sexes.

With all this, it is a small ask for you to hope that Roylake Leather and Guns is simply holding on to its history. You hope that people are going in there to pick up a leather bowl to keep their car keys in. You hope there are no guns under the counter or out the back or in the cellar.

THE LAST WORD ON HOPE
Hope is just a dream when it is
not attached to action.

That week, in Hinton Hollow, many people were travelling to the border of Roylake and arming themselves. They didn't know why. They didn't understand that I was there, pulling that need out of them. They could feel that sense of social malaise coating the tired village they believed they loved. Some kept the weapons for safety, just in case. Some shot at birds. Many did nothing worth putting into my small story.

Guns were sold to lawyers and councillors, to cleaners and hairdressers. If you wanted one, you could have one. Nobody was interested in the leather.

They lost their hope and bought some guns.

Anybody could have one.

The first anybody was not a fireman or librarian, they were not a traffic warden or substitute teacher, he was an ordinary man.

BLACK FLAMES

The sound was jarring. Guttural. High-pitched yet with an underlying gravel. Like two voices screaming at the same time. And not in harmony.

There was no gunfire so nobody had been shot. But the noise coming from the pavement outside the school on Stanhope Road was worse than that.

It was a rare chord to witness.

The sound of a man's heart breaking.

Mrs Beaufort groped at her own breast in the back of Pace's car. The same pain she had felt when the shock of Jacob Brady's death reverberated across town to the Rock-a-Buy store. She had pills in her bag.

Roger Ablett coughed and beat his chest free of what he thought was recurring heartburn. Perhaps it was guilt. He could hear Nathan Hadley from his car behind the shops.

Fifteen minutes earlier, Ablett had stepped into Hadley's Hair knowing damn well that the owner was now a childless widower. He also doubted very much that he was the only Ablett that day to see between the legs of the late Rachel Hadley.

Maybe things would all work out for the best and he could get someone else to do his dirty work for him. Hadley could be the perfect patsy. He might even accept a punishment for a crime he did not commit as he had nothing else to live for. *He could hang himself by that pretty neck in his cell*, Ablett imagined, *take our secret with him.*

Roger Ablett was licking his lips as he entered the barbershop. There were six men waiting, three crammed on each of the blue leather sofas, trying not to touch one another. The windows were sweating and so was he. All this walking was too much hassle. Too healthy. His body was rejecting it.

'Afternoon, Roger.' Nate greeted him with an inviting smile despite not liking him particularly. He hated his brother a little more. The way he looked at Rachel was nauseating. She hadn't mentioned anything to him personally but word gets around, he knew what Charles Ablett was trying to do. 'Bit of a wait if you need a trim. Couple of the boys on a quick break out the back but things will speed along soon enough.'

Roger was pleased. He didn't really want a haircut, anyway.

'Oh, no. No problem. It was just a trim. I'll come back tomorrow. It'll wait.' And he burped into a closed mouth, re-tasting the cheese and bacon that had lain together so perfectly across his mammoth burger.

'Okay. Well, we'll be here.' He smiled again, the smile of a man who had no idea his family had been wiped out of existence.

Ablett was stood in the doorway, his left foot holding the door open. He was neither inside nor out.

'Bit of a commotion on Stanhope.' He offered this information like he was conversing with a good friend over a pint of ale at The Arboreal. He had hoped to ease it into conversation but had to resort to use of the shoehorn.

'Sorry? What's going on?'

The six men waiting on the sofas turned their heads to the left and watched the conversation move back and forth like a tennis rally.

'I'm not sure but it looked pretty serious. Messy.'

'In what way?' Nate was biting, mainly out of common decency but intrigue was also an ingredient of the conversation. That and the niggling sensation that he was *supposed* to hear this information.

'Inspector Anderson is there, as is that detective from the city.'

'Pace,' confirmed one of the waiting men.

'That's the fellow. Looks as though they are shutting down the entire street.'

'What?' Nate dropped his right hand to his side. He had been holding it up in front of his chest, the scissors resting limply and pointing towards the room where his wife had teased him to orgasm before lunch.

'Not sure, to be honest,' he lied. 'There's an ambulance there too.'

'Where?' Nate asked with urgency.

'Stanhope.' Ablett nodded his head over his shoulder to indicate the road he was talking about. He knew what Nate was asking, he was trying to rile him.

'I know it's on Stanhope, you said that already, but where on Stanhope?'

'Outside the school.'

But Nathan Hadley didn't wait for an answer, he was almost out the door when he said to his employee, 'Man the fort for a moment. I'll be back in a second.' He pushed past Ablett on his way out the door. 'Tomorrow?' he added before stepping into that wind.

'It's another day, Mr Hadley.'

Nate ignored the serious lack of charm and walked towards Stanhope Road, thinking about his children and the Brady kid who had been killed a couple of days before.

What are the chances?

He turned left and saw the lights from the ambulance. A police car was parked almost in the middle of the road, a black car was stopped next to it on a double-yellow line.

More than a parking ticket. He spoke with himself, trying not to enter into any more black thoughts.

But the look on Anderson's face was enough. He gave the game away.

Nate was running. Attempting to see past the frame of the policeman ahead of him. He clocked Mrs Beaufort in the illegally parked vehicle then a camera flashed behind the inspector.

Nate stepped to the right and saw the bodies. He kept running, pumping his arms and lifting his knees to give himself more power. Anderson looked as though he was going to try to stop him. He was large, strong, but not especially nimble on those flat feet. Nate sidestepped him with ease and bolted towards his wife.

He dropped to his knees between the two female victims, scuffing them like his dead son had at lunchtime tackling a bully, like his wife had as she knelt on the tiled floor of the barbershop office.

And then a howl.

Unlike Mrs Blake, Pace did not wait. He left the headmistress mid-interview and ran outside where there was wind and shadow and black flames lapping at everything that was good.

I FEEL SAD

Here's something: if you read a story, hear a story, or someone tells you a story where somebody dies, if you find that you don't really care because you haven't built up enough knowledge of that character and can't feel sympathetic towards them, that is on you.

Not just you, obviously. The storyteller has to take part of the blame for not creating some of the magic that you need in order to emote. But, as a human, not to care about the death of another person – whether you know them or not – to rejoice in the death of someone you deem to be bad or evil or a wrongdoer, that *is* on you. And, from what I see in the world, that is what people do.

When Dorothy Reilly keeled over in her flat, on her own, with a bone in her throat, did it hit you differently to the death of Darren's cat? If you felt no sadness at her solitude or the way that she had given up on herself, a part of you is missing. Your soul will be lighter.

If you felt some just cause that Faith Brady took her own life after failing to protect her children, yet feel heartbroken when a celebrity you do not know does the same thing because they did not have the appropriate support mechanism in place to deal with their fame and the things that come with being under constant public scrutiny, it is a mirror that you require, not a voice, when searching for the real evil in the world.

You felt awful when Jacob was taken because he was a child. Because he was innocent. Because he was good. Because his mother should have saved him.

That's easy to feel that way.

Perhaps you were also angry.

Even easier.

It takes so much to shock now, which means it takes too much to make you care.

Do you understand what I am saying? You keep pushing and pushing. Wanting more and more. Listening less and less. You are tearing your planet apart, refusing to see the destruction man has caused. You deny global warming. You fight over differing religious beliefs. You consume your information in bitesize chunks and don't have the capability to even consider why your attention span has dwindled.

Humankind has created evil at a rate that even I cannot keep up with. So, in order to be heard, in order for me to make you understand how awful your race has become, I have to be deliberately shocking. I have to always go beyond what you can do.

Evil will always exist, but the better you are, the quieter I can be.

You see?

I don't feel sad for the people in this story, I'm not supposed to, I am Evil. I am here for balance. As a necessity.

It is you that I feel sad for.

A SECRET
There are days when I do not want to do my job.
Day three was not one of them.

QUIET IS THE NEW LOUD

Pace saw the man disturbing his crime scene and howling into the wind. He had pulled his wife up into his arms and was reaching out to pull his daughter closer when Pace charged at him.

Nate never saw him coming.

He was scooped up and away from his wife before he fell to the floor with Pace on top of him. The barber struggled a little but all strength had left him and anguish blocked adrenaline. He gave up and lay face down in the road, weeping. The cries started low then raised in pitch and volume like the engine of a sports car accelerating. Pace flipped him over and held on tightly. The wreck of a man, sitting between the detective's legs, his weak body flopping backward against Pace's chest. Pace gripped Nate's arms. He looked up at Anderson for some help. Nate stared forward at the carnage of his life.

Detective Sergeant Pace is a blight on your crops.

Detective Sergeant Pace is black mould.

Detective Sergeant Pace is the metastasis you prayed against.

Mrs Blake appeared in the background at the school gates.

The six men from the blue sofas emerged around the corner with three barbers, two of whom had abandoned their coffee breaks.

The large grey bear known as RD stepped out of his diner with a tea towel in his giant right paw. Two of his customers followed.

Mrs Beaufort was banging her feeble, translucent, bony hand against the inside of the car window – Pace had locked the back doors in case he picked up a suspect – she was yelling 'let me out', but the wind took her muffled words.

The photographer stood motionless, his camera dangling by his side. He was used to the quiet serenity of a murder scene.

And Nathan Hadley stared, wondering who could have done such a thing. He thought about that animal Charles Ablett, probably angry that he couldn't get what he wanted from Rachel. He started kicking his legs and lashing out.

Pace had to restrain him. The scene was about to become a circus. He had to handcuff the man who had lost his entire family in one gloomy afternoon. There were locals watching as he slapped the cuffs on, it was going to do his reputation no good. Add to that the fact that he had imprisoned the town elder in his car, this was shaping up to be a long fucking night.

Roger Ablett hoisted his considerable weight up into his Range Rover, pushing with his foot on the step while gaining leverage with his arms on the doorframe. He was out of breath by the time his fat arse hit the heated leather seat.

He turned the key and grinned.

That went quite well.

Easier than he'd expected.

It was still light outside. But the darkness was moving in fast.

ALL THIS HAPPENED

Liv Dunham was restless. Again. Her upbeat mood from the morning had given way to solemnity once more.

She was in-between.

She hadn't wanted to leave the house in case Oz came back and she wasn't there to let him back into their lives. What if he called again?

That morning she had been certain that it was Oz on the other end of the line the night before but her solitary confinement had encouraged her to think and rationalise the events. It couldn't have been him. He wouldn't tease her like that. He wouldn't purposely scare her, his Liv, his love, his wife-to-be.

The suicide of Faith Brady had not filtered through the Hinton Hollow gossip mill at that point otherwise Liv may have been tempted to call the police back. But she felt so foolish doing that again. She didn't want to be condescended to. She was feeling the same way that Pace had felt many years before when Julee had just vanished. He'd had the silent calls, too, convinced it was her at the other end. He'd gained some peace from that, but Liv was growing more frantic.

She'd left three more messages on May Tambor's answering machine, the tape was almost filled with her concern. And now she was worried that she had given up information to a psychopath. Her voice sounded needy, she had spoken her fiancé's name indicating that she was not with her man.

She was alone. Unprotected. And stir crazy.

The television set was black. A few fingerprints were making fun of her but not enough for her to turn the set on and hear more bad news. Her legs wobbled up and down as she sat on the edge of the sofa, yet again, doing nothing to help anybody. Remaining in the one place a killer knew she would be on her own.

The telephone rang and she yelped.

Liv let it ring seven times.

What if it's May? What do I say to her? She trembled.

Then she dived off the sofa and ran towards the phone, the pain in her hip vanishing momentarily. She slid the last metre across the laminate floor in her socks but the phone stopped ringing.

'Fuck.'

Liv dialled 1471.

You were called today at 16:41. The caller withheld their number.

As she replaced the receiver, the phone buzzed to life again. She left it, not wanting to look anxious, and picked it up after four rings.

'Hello?' She tried to sound as casual as she could but her heart was punching the inside of her chest.

Silence.

'Hello? Can you hear me?' She tried again.

Liv knew it was the same person who had called her the night before, the feeling she got in those silences was exactly the same. She felt terrified but ultra-alert. Not the way she would feel if she was talking to Oz. He was the only one that could calm her. He was the only one who could get things back to normal. She felt so stupid for saying his name.

Another silence.

The wind in the back garden was pushing the trees towards the south.

As before, Liv's fear seemed to hone her focus.

'What do you want, huh? You want to talk to me, then talk to me. You want to breathe down the phone, then take that *crazy* somewhere else.'

Still, there was nothing from the caller. Nothing to say whether the breath was male or female, nothing to indicate who on Earth it could be. So she took a guess.

'Tommy, you're in big trouble if I find out it's you.'

Tommy was a kid from school who had displayed crush-like symptoms towards his teacher.

Miss.

'Father Salis?' She tried this name again.

Strike.

She desperately wanted to call Oz's name but didn't want to give things away as she had the previous evening. So she threw one more name into the mix, hushing it into the silence at the other end.

'Charles?'

Another short silence.

Then.

'I...'

DAY FOUR

Where you will consider:

An old lady who won't give up
A priest asking for forgiveness
The Raymond family
A pig stealer
Sibling rivalry
The importance of biscuits
and the need for a little time.

SHADOWS AND IMPULSE

Then it got worse.

'That has to be just about the worst fucking idea I've ever heard.'

Pace was furious. It was one in the morning and he hadn't stopped moving since the afternoon of day three.

He'd detained Nathan Hadley, who had become increasingly violent, and quizzed him for possible leads in the murder enquiry, but the barber had nothing to give, nothing he wanted to give, and was released with some leaflets on grief counselling.

Mrs Beaufort was hysterical at her treatment. She felt she had been left in the car like a neglected dog. Pace had to enlist the help of RD, who took Mrs Beaufort to Dr Green to be checked over before dropping her home.

He was also avoiding the media, both local and national, who were now fully aware of the small town of Hinton Hollow. The Berkshire haven that had managed to exist for so long as a road sign that people read on their way to somewhere bigger, better. He couldn't afford to be in the spotlight so soon after leaving London. He couldn't afford to have that last case dragged up again. Not now.

Stanhope Road had been closed for hours while the scene was picked at and photographed. The three bodies were bagged and taken away for further examination. The cause of death seemed pretty obvious to Pace, it was the motive behind the murder that was evading him. It would be confirmed that Rachel Hadley had sexual intercourse the day she died and would declare that it had not been forced in any way. There were no other marks to suggest the attack was sexual.

It was the first nugget of information that Pace felt could lead somewhere worthwhile. He'd tried to get hold of Nathan Hadley. As uncomfortable as it was, Pace needed to confirm whether Nathan and Rachel had *been together* on Wednesday. If they hadn't, the case could hinge on the identity of the secret lover. But Pace hadn't been able to find Nathan Hadley. He wasn't at home. There were reports that he had been at The Arboreal drinking, but even at midnight, the Hadley residence was empty, a ghost.

And now this.

Pace was stood in Anderson's office, the inspector behind his sorry excuse for a desk, Councilwoman Hayes leaning against a filing cabinet to his left, both of them wide-eyed in anticipation of Pace's response to their idea.

It was the worst fucking idea he'd ever heard.

CLEARLY CONFUSED

Anderson and Hayes had contrived the concept together before Pace had even entered the room.

Anderson and Hayes. An unlikely duo. They didn't seem to go together.

SOME OTHER OXYMORONS
Act naturally.
Bittersweet.
Farewell reception.

Humankind.

When the detective had his sudden, honest outburst, his inspector stood up from his chair to defend the decision.

'Now hold on a minute there, Pace.' His moustache jumped up and down. Pace watched it move with intrigue. He noticed the inspector's cheeks flush slightly. He perused the councilwoman's body language, her arms unfolding, one hand pushing her hair back behind her right ear, the direction her pelvis was pointed.

'How long have you been sleeping together?' Pace spoke clearly, seemingly pulling the information from nowhere.

A NOTE ON THE HOLD OF EVIL
At that point, the entire town was in my grasp.
Everybody in that room.
Some were being choked while others
were merely caressed.
From then until the end, I did not let go
of Detective Sergeant Pace.
The children could only be hurt by humankind.

Councilwoman Hayes' chest flared up in red blotches and her gasp was almost as comical as her lover's ridiculous facial hair.

'What did you say?' Anderson raised his voice.

Pace remained calm, triumphant even. This was his fourth day back home in the perfect village of Hinton Hollow and he had already uncovered as much seediness as he would expect in the capital.

'Would you like me to repeat the question, sir?'

There was a short silence while the alleged couple took a moment to gaze at one another.

'The murder investigation should be your primary concern, detective. What the councilwoman does or does not do in her own time is really none of your business.' Anderson had calmed himself, thinking he was taking the higher ground.

'I don't care that the councilwoman is married. And I don't care if she is stepping out of that marriage to be with you. But it is my business if stupid decisions are being made to save someone's arse because the last stupid decision that was made by the pair of you ended up getting a young mother and her two children shot in the face and heart.' Pace raised his voice slightly when he said 'face and heart', to punctuate his point.

The unlikely couple of Anderson and Hayes had concocted an idea to draw out the killer and trap him. In what they perceived as wise deduction, it was *clear* that the murderer was targeting mothers with small children. He was waiting outside schools for an opportunity, picking off stragglers who left themselves vulnerable. The Bradys had left school late because of a misplaced pair of shoes and the Hadleys had a meeting with the headmistress.

He must be waiting near the schools, they agreed.

There is a pattern, they had said.

'You have to close the schools,' Pace warned them. 'It sounds to me like you are using innocent children as live bait, Mrs Hayes. I really don't think your constituents are going to go along with that.'

POLITICS
Will get people killed.
*When nobody is thinking about the people.

'It's fifty-fifty at the moment,' the councilwoman finally weighed in. 'I know this community, detective, and I have spoken with them. There is still a general feeling that we should not let this man win, we should not bow down in fear. Now, I know that was the reason for keeping the schools open after the unfortunate incident with Jacob Brady, and that decision rests on my shoulders and the shoulders of the people of Hinton Hollow who supported me. They still have faith that this police station, small as it may be, can apprehend the figure causing such disruption.' She was eloquent. Pace could understand why she had been voted in, he wanted to listen to the words she was speaking. But some of those words – *unfortunate incident*, *disruption* – jarred with him as emotionless.

'You want us to stake out the schools and grab anyone who looks unsavoury? Is that the plan?'

'You make it sound rather crude when you put it like that, but that is it in essence, yes. There will be parents keeping their children off school either way, until this all blows over.'

She wasn't using the word *bait*, but that's what it was.

Pace looked at her. She was in her mid-forties, her hair was a greying blonde that suited her. She was short, petite even, but she had a presence that made her appear bigger than she was. It was that matter-of-factness – *until this all blows over* – that meant she was a perfect fit for Anderson.

The councilwoman was defending herself by going on the attack. Yes, she was taking a risk but this plan would definitely work, the people of Hinton Hollow had nothing to fear, the police and the local government were in control and nobody else had to die. Her decision to keep the schools open after Jacob Brady was shot was the right call because it had led to the capture of the man with the gun.

She was panicking. Thinking about herself.

She was pinning her hopes on two incidents of horrific violence having some kind of pattern. Pace knew that there was no ritual here. The killer was not performing in the same way with each attack. He believed that the Hadley shooting was a panic. The gunshots were too close together, according to Mrs Blake's testimony – he had gone back on Wednesday evening to finish his interview after detaining Nathan Hadley and palming off Mrs Beaufort into RD's capable hands. The killer had meant to shoot one person but something happened. There was no pause between shots to evaluate, he simply took out any chance of there being a witness.

One certainty was that the victims were all facing the opposite direction that they wanted to travel. So the killer had approached them from behind.

That's why you have to look over your shoulder.

But the only pattern was that there was no pattern.

It made the plan even more idiotic and dangerous.

She had it inside her but I was juggling with her insecurity and fear of failure.

'And you support this, do you?' Pace directed the question to Anderson.

'Do you have a better idea of how to draw this monster out?'

'A better idea than dangling an innocent child in front of his gun? Yes. We shut the schools, we gather evidence, we build a case and profile and we find this fucker. We don't play games with sociopaths and we don't unduly put people in the line of fire. Has everyone in this town lost their mind?' He looked around the room as though somebody might agree with him.

'Just one person. And he is the one we have to find.' Anderson thought he was rather clever with his retort. 'The people of this town are the same as they have always been.'

He was wrong about that, too.

EVERYBODY IS LINKED

Constable Reynolds was back at work on the front desk. He heard the chief's door slam shut then the gloomy figure of Detective Pace emerged from the door behind him.

Pace had hoped to be as convincing as the councilwoman, perhaps inject some wit and insight into his response but ended up saying, 'Well, some of us have got some real detective work to get on with so please feel free to take your ridiculous plan and shove it *all* the way up your arse.' Then he walked out.

Reynolds did not want to speak first. In truth, he was more than intimidated by the new detective; there was something that scared the young constable. He felt uneasy around Pace.

'Morning, Reynolds.'

'Good morning.'

'Ah, there's nothing good about it, I'm afraid.' This made Reynolds uncomfortable. 'Any chatter this evening?' Pace continued. He was leaning on the front desk tapping an unlit cigarette against it.

'Chatter?'

'Yes. Any calls coming in that might help us with the case? Has anyone spotted Nathan Hadley? Has somebody noticed a strange vehicle? Did they write down the registration? Gunshots, people going missing, that kind of thing.' He shook his head at the incompetency of the local force. Reynolds saw it and felt even more stupid than usual.

'Nothing.' Reynolds seemed sad about that fact.

'Keep up the good work,' Pace said, sarcastically, putting a cigarette to his mouth and walking off, lighting it before he hit the door as a small act of rebellion but also because it was impossible to ignite in that wind outside.

'Wait. Wait,' Reynolds called after him.

Pace turned around, inhaled then blew out smoke without speaking a word.

'There was something. Not tonight but a woman called.' He had purposely memorised her name. 'Liv Dunham. She's supposed to be getting married this weekend and her partner hasn't come home.'

'Nerves, maybe. It happens.'

'It hadn't quite been two days when she last called but she did sound really worried.'

'Has she called back since?'

Reynolds rustled through some papers and the call log. 'Doesn't look that way. Maybe he came home.'

'Maybe. Can you send her details to my phone? I'll add her to my list.'

Pace walked out of the station and back to the car. He was going to return to the Hadley residence. The Liv Dunham story didn't seem like a lead but Pace had some personal experience with partners suddenly disappearing from Hinton Hollow and nobody following it up.

Sure, Liv Dunham didn't exactly fit in with the *pattern*, but that was exactly the reason Pace felt he should investigate. Because there was no pattern. In a small town like Hinton Hollow, everybody is linked.

It was not about a pattern.

It was simply a case of motivation.

Shadows and impulse.

NICE GUYS

Nathan Hadley was an ordinary man.

A working man. A business owner. A provider. He was known within the Hinton Hollow community but not on a level any deeper than the small talk one can expect in a barbershop or the back of a taxi.

He was pleasant, softly spoken and he got on with his job every day. Cutting men's hair with pride. Though he could have uttered a bad word against some members of his community – clients were often forthcoming with information and anecdotes once relaxed into Nate's hydraulic chair – he never did. He was *nice*. A nice guy.

The town was full of nice guys.

He was also a father. He hadn't felt like one the day before when he discovered his children lying dead on their backs, their faces towards a heaven he was finding little solace in as the hours clicked into the next morning.

He had been drinking at The Arboreal, whoever had informed Detective Pace about that was correct. He'd been alone at a table. He'd been drinking Scotch even though he hated the stuff. He knew it got him drunk and he knew it got him angry.

The homophobic teasing had always been brushed off. He knew it wasn't true. He understood what jealousy looked like, he spent most of his day standing in front of a mirror with other men, scrutinising their appearance. But the truth is, the teasing was a form of adult bullying, and it had slowly and surely eroded the nice barber. He didn't know but it had been eating away at him. It affected the relationship he had with his wife. And that was hurting even more after the Scotch.

It had all been taken away from him.

 ANOTHER WAY THAT EVIL PRESENTS ITSELF
Niceness. You know the kind.

Anger, I can work with. See also: *repression, suppression, oppression, depression* and *sexual frustration.*

He didn't *know* about Ablett. He had no idea he'd been cuckolded. But it didn't matter. He'd snapped. Everything had given way. Rationality. Reason. The ground beneath him.

So Pace was left waiting all morning, watching the outside of a house that a family used to live in. Nathan Hadley, the *nice*-guy hairdresser did not return that morning. He had something to do and nothing to lose.

Nate Hadley was in the neighbouring town of Roylake not feeling like himself at all. And he had something he wanted to speak to Charles Ablett about. It couldn't wait.

The wind had died down a little but the rain was coming.

AMERICAN SUMMER

When it hit seven o'clock and Nathan Hadley still had not turned up to sleep off his bad decisions, Pace assumed the recent widower had consumed too many pints of local ale and had taken a wrong turn into a ditch or he'd been blown into the woods and got lost. Either way, it ended with a devastated man covered in leaves for the night and waking disoriented. He probably would have felt equally dizzied arising to an empty house with tidy beds where his children used to sleep. When sleep was temporary.

The other option was that he had something to do with his family's murder and now had quite some head start on the beleaguered detective. The very notion did not sit well with Pace. He saw the reaction of a husband and father whose life had been wrenched away so swiftly and cruelly. That was not fake.

Of course, there was a third option.

The Hadleys were all together again.

Pace could see the Hadleys' letterbox close up from within his car and tried to focus solely on the bereavement of the town and Nathan and Owen and Michael so that he did not have to think of his own deprivation.

He started the car. The sound of the engine did not kick-start his morning. It did not snap him from the reverie he was trying so desperately to avoid.

Black flames crept around the inside of the vehicle, pulling at his memories.

There was a confession. A signed confession over three hundred pages in length. The killer's manifesto. Pace had it in his possession. Directions on how he had started, how he had honed his craft. How he had killed more than two hundred people or, more specifically, made them take their own lives. It was all there.

Detective Sergeant Pace could have taken the perpetrator in, with the book, and sent him away for the rest of his life. Giving the families of the victims some closure, putting an end to the movement.

Instead, he took that man deep into Swinley Forest and left him there to die. Then burned the book and packed his bags for Hinton Hollow.

He knew it wasn't justice. He knew it was revenge for being on that list. He knew it was anger. And he knew it would never leave him.

I would never leave him.

Not after that.

Pace scrolled to the letter M in the contacts menu of his phone and he shook his head. She was the only one who knew. He couldn't blame the darkness, he had seen it and invited the heat of its black forked tongue.

He had done what any other person would say they wanted to do with that monster.

The same way that every parent would say they'd give their life for their children.

He'd gone too far and now he could not get far enough away.

Pace drove back to the centre of town where he punched a code into the keypad and the large white wooden gates of The Cider Orchard Bed and Breakfast pushed back smoothly to allow him to enter the stony courtyard.

The lights were off in five of the converted barn rooms but American Summer had the main bedroom light on and the curtains were not fully shut. Pace looked at the time on his phone and wondered how many more people in Hinton Hollow were sleeping through their bleak future.

He turned the key and entered the darkness of the Haas room. He was only stopping for a coffee. RD's Diner wouldn't be open for another hour and he couldn't face the idiocy of the police station until he could trump them with something more concrete to go on.

Pace walked across the bedroom, flicked the kettle on, ripped open three of the coffee sachets that were sitting in a tray with sugar, tea bags and jiggers of milk, and waited for the water to boil. He stood in the doorway of his rented room and stared over the rooftops of the town he once loved. Light was edging up over the woods and easing into town.

The light went off in the American Summer suite and a woman – who looked like she was paid by the hour – stepped out and walked past Pace without even a hint of acknowledgement before exiting the premises on foot.

One of the first people that Detective Sergeant Pace saw on that fourth day was almost certainly a prostitute. It was not his idea of Hinton Hollow life. It was grubby and indecent. And it would turn out to be the highlight of his day.

TWO PILLS

'You are through to the Tambor residence,' the dead man told her. 'We are currently unavailable to take your call. Leave a short message and one of us will get back to you as soon as we can.'

Then there was a beep.

Mrs Beaufort stopped shaking her head, the head in which she had just said, *I do wish she'd get rid of that bloody message.*

It wasn't her.

But it was, you see. Nobody in Hinton Hollow was being somebody they were not. Out of character, perhaps, the character they had created or fought hard to convey, but everything that everyone was doing was a real part of who they were.

'Good morning, May. Sorry, I know it's a bit early but I thought you might be up. Just hoping we're still on for tea and wedding chats this morning.'

The show must go on.

'Anyway, I'll start walking over in about ten minutes. Should take me another good forty-five to be with you so make sure the kettle's on.' The true Mrs Beaufort smiled at that. 'It might take me a little longer as I've only recently got out of hospital. Word probably isn't out yet. I don't want to make a big deal about it and get people worried.'

Though you *should have been concerned about me, my agoraphobic friend*, she sniped.

'I'll bring some cake, though I know you have probably whipped up something delicious. I can fill you in on what has been happening in the village. Terrible things, May. We're old enough to remember this happening before. Oh, and did you know the Pace kid is back? You'll probably be introduced soon enough...' She trailed off. Mrs Beaufort was one of those people whose voice messages were far too long, she ended up having a conversation with herself, there was almost no point in her going over. 'Cheerio. See you shortly.'

She hung up, a little out of breath.

In the kitchen, the washing machine was wobbling heavily as it spun through the final rinse. She ran herself a glass of cold water and sat at the breakfast table watching the cylinder rotate and the remaining droplets of dampness hit the window then dissipate in uneven trails to the outskirts of the circle. It was hypnotic. She managed to think about nothing for a few minutes, her emaciated right hand never releasing its grip on her drink.

Then the machine clicked twice to signify that the wash was complete.

Mrs Beaufort put two of the pills she had been prescribed into her mouth then used the water to help swallow them. Doctor Choudary had said that she could take them as a preventative measure if she knew that she was going to undertake something strenuous. This may have been her first full day out of hospital and, yes, she was already doing what the doctor was worried she might do – take them and continue her lifestyle – but *that was coincidence*, she advised herself, *it's not abuse.*

She pulled the pile of baby clothes from the washing machine and into a basket that lay beneath. She then carried the basket over to the tumble dryer and filled it with the tiny, fresh-smelling garments. They would be ready by the time she got back and she could walk them down to Rock-a-Buy.

Perhaps she'd need another two pills for that journey.

Outside, the air was fresh and untouched by anything sinister lurking beneath her town. She breathed it in, filling her lungs with a familiarity she had always loved, and started to walk across Hinton Hollow to visit one of her oldest friends.

It would all go downhill from that point.

MOST MORNINGS

Ellie Frith turned up for work at Ablett and Ablett ten minutes before she was due to start working. She was the junior letting agent. Roger had hired her. She was young and enthusiastic but not *conventionally* pretty. Not horrid to look at but hardly a head-turner like Jess Hadley. She wasn't even the best qualified of all the candidates. But Roger had his reasons.

He thought that women often flourished in a sales environment. They got great results because they were harder to say no to. He hadn't even interviewed any men that had applied for the position. Also, the fact that she wasn't so easy on the eye meant that Charles would probably keep his dick in his pants and get on with some work for a change.

Ellie pushed the door back and forth, rattling it on its hinges though she could see that the lights were not on inside.

'Fucking Ablett,' she mouthed.

Charles was always coming in late whether Roger was there or not. He'd be out drinking at Split Aces or he'd be fobbing off another of his married-lady conquests before showering in his glory and strolling into the office like his dick was a trophy.

She took her mobile phone out and called that local hound. He didn't answer. He rarely did. The next call was Roger Ablett. She didn't want to call him so early as he'd arranged to come in late after scooping a sizeable sale in Twaincroft Hill the day before. It was part of his reward ritual. But she didn't want to sit outside and wait for an hour under what looked to be a sky that was ready to split in half.

'What, Ellie? What?' Roger Ablett was not amused to be receiving one of these calls again. He knew what was going on.

'Sorry, Mr Ablett, but your brother ... er ... Charles, he's not here. I mean, he hasn't turned up so I'm waiting outside and I think it's going to rain.' She'd delivered this message a hundred times before.

Roger was lying in a king-sized bed that was seldom shared with another person. He peered over at his alarm clock.

'It's not even nine yet,' he growled.

She rolled her eyes, pulled the phone from her face and mouthed an obscenity angrily in Roger Ablett's direction. He'd lectured her endlessly about being at work ten minutes before opening so that she was *ready to go when the doors opened.*

'Give it twenty minutes. If he's still not there, call me back.' And he hung up.

Arsehole.

She sat on the pavement outside Ablett and Ablett half knowing that Charles wasn't going to come strolling along in the next twenty minutes. She thought about quitting her shitty job. She thought about it most mornings.

She works there to this day.

SOME TRUTHS ABOUT WORK
**People who find what they want to do
never *work* a day in their lives.
Then there are the people who find what they *have* to do.
And the people who hate their jobs more than anything,
most of them never leave.**

Roger Ablett rolled onto his side and hugged the pillow next to him. But he couldn't get back to sleep. He knew for certain that his layabout brother wasn't getting out of his bed any time soon and Roger would have to cover for him once more.

A PIG STEALER

Darren turned up for work early that day with a spring in his step and a dumb idea in his head.

You'd think the place would have to be spotless at the start of the shift, the way chefs will clear down and clean every surface of their kitchen after a service so that the next day would start afresh and hygienic.

Not at the slaughterhouse.

The perfume of death on that scale is difficult to mask. The scent of guts and entrails festers and the blood somehow lingers like a vapour you can taste.

Darren smells nothing.

Tastes nothing.

He walks past a giant skip that has been filled with the heads of cows. Their skin has been peeled away and their tender cheeks cut out, but the eyeballs remain intact.

They're looking at him.

Darren sees nothing.

Feels nothing.

Nobody had arrived yet so Darren managed to bag himself the exact car parking space he wanted. He had emptied his boot into his garage earlier that morning in preparation. Darren looked simple. He was simple. And it was the simplest of plans.

Later that day, a new employee was being brought in for the obligatory tour of the facility. He'd seen these a million times before. People without the stomach for it once they realised what the job entails. It was not uncommon to see somebody faint.

The aroma. Lingering. Festering.

Desensitising.

While everybody was distracted by the new kid or were busy pushing livestock towards the end of their days, Darren was going to force one piece of stock into the back of his car and drive it straight home.

What could possibly go wrong?

WILTING EXTERIOR

Mrs Beaufort had taken her time. The sky was washed out but the news said the real rain wouldn't arrive until the afternoon. By then she expected to be sat behind the till at Rock-a-Buy – probably sniffing another bag of donated goods.

It had actually taken her fifty-seven minutes to walk to May Tambor's house. She could have made it in her forty-five-minute estimate but the part of Mrs Beaufort that was still Mrs Beaufort told her to take heed of the doctor's advice.

I let her have that one.

She arrived at the top of May's drive with shortness of breath but no pain in her arms or chest. The pills were like magic.

There were two cars in the drive just as there always were and the curtains were almost completely closed, a six-inch gap in the middle at least allowed some natural light to permeate the Tambor house's wilting exterior. She could usually smell some of May's famous baking halfway down the lengthy driveway but *that* day there was only cold and the promise of a damp weekend.

She shook her head at the thought of a Tambor/Dunham wet wedding.

She tapped delicately on the diamond-shaped window of May's front door. Three times with the knuckle of her right forefinger.

There was no answer.

They'd made these plans over a week ago. May really didn't like leaving the house that much since her husband passed, she had some idea in her head that there were places *out there* that were not safe, they did not provide an adequate path of escape. Mrs Beaufort was sensitive to this and was usually the one to traipse across town for tea and talks, she knew that May had a big day coming up and was trying to keep things as relaxed as possible for her because she would have to leave the house for her only son's wedding.

It would be the first time in a long while she had set foot in the Church of the Good Shepherd. Most of the community were understanding of her condition but there was an undercurrent of dismay from members of the congregation who thought that church was the best place for a person in her situation.

The pattern of the killings was that there was no pattern, so the fact that each of the victims had neglected their faith and cut down on their Good Shepherd attendance was probably irrelevant, or at least as relevant as any other crumb of information the local police had picked up so far.

COMMUNITY CHURCH ATTENDANCE
The Brady family: Never
The Hadley family: Christian holidays
The Raymond family: Christmas only
RD: Most weeks (but somebody had to open the café)
Darren: Once for confession
Oz and Liv: Sundays
Detective Sergeant Pace: Once a decade (on average)
The Ablett Brothers: Charles, never.
Roger, when he needed something.

Mrs Beaufort rapped the door three more times before trying the bell. Still nothing. With her left hand clasping the door knocker, she placed her right foot on the small sill below the door and pulled her fragile frame up to peek through the window.

The blood had dried on the walls and her friend was laying peacefully on the floor next to the hallway table.

'Oh God,' Mrs Beaufort exhaled, lowering herself away from the glass and resting her back against the dead woman's door, trying desperately to keep her heart from racing.

How long has she been there like that? she wondered.

What have we done to deserve this?

God had nothing to do with the death of May Tambor, it was His worst creation that was at fault. The ordinary man.

I COULD GET USED TO THIS

Annie 'window breaker' Harding woke up on that fourth day with my whisper in her ear and a tingle between her thighs. I did not have to push as hard as the previous morning, her frustrations and mistrust were rising to the surface on their own and manifesting themselves into a sexual energy both Annie and her husband had long since forgotten.

This is how evil works.

I just have to get you started. What you do with that feeling is entirely down to you.

ONE MAJOR PROBLEM WITH EVIL
It can feel so good.

Annie had been on her knees and bent over when her husband finished inside her. He'd been staring at a different hole towards the end and imagining what it would be like to end things in there. That was the thought that got him over the line.

They collapsed on one another, breathing heavily, the occasional aftershock throb tickling a smile across their faces. He spoke softly, 'I could get used to this.' And they both laughed. A genuine moment of tenderness between the couple.

Neither of them would have to get used to it. Annie wouldn't have to do this kind of thing any more. I'd let go of her soon. I'd let go of everyone.

But there was still time left on this trip to Hinton Hollow. I was nowhere near finished yet.

And Annie still had one more window to break.

GOOD BOY

When Ben was born, Catherine was considered a *young mother*. The nights had been a test, of course, but she had given herself to them with gusto. Those initial six weeks where it is all so strange and new were as difficult for her as anyone else, but she got through. Either as a result of her youth or simply because she wanted to.

 **SOMETHING I HAVE
NOTICED ABOUT PEOPLE**
They find a way to do the things
they really want to do.

It all seemed so much more exhausting with the second one. It had only been eight years since she last went through all of *this* but she felt as though she wasn't handling it. In the short period of time that had passed, she seemed to have forgotten everything she had learned from having Ben and had transformed – overnight, apparently – into an old mother.

Ben Raymond kept one hand on his little brother's pushchair as his mother wheeled it along Stanhope Road. He was trying so hard to be good, he hated it when she was mad in the mornings, it always set him off in the wrong mood for school and he was already in trouble for picking on the Hadley kids the day before.

He had no idea what had happened to them.

It was too much for Catherine to think about with the way the baby had been that week. A restless, whining nuisance. She'd spent every night since Monday rocking the baby to sleep, singing, shh-ing, cooing, ah-ing. She felt drained, and a conversation about death with her already troubled eight-year-old son was not going to alleviate any of the tension she was experiencing. She just needed to get Ben to school and maybe the baby would sleep a little during the day and she could catch up on some much-needed rest.

The morning run was less crowded. A lighter smattering of people opting to take a stand against the unknown figure that was tormenting their community. Just under half the kids were at home still, either in bed or transfixed by the television. Catherine Raymond was powering through, with her dark eyes and her tied-up hair and her sicked-on shoulder and her young child that could not be touched by the darkness and had no other way but crying to tell its mother that something was very wrong.

She shuddered as she walked past the area she'd seen on the evening news where the Hadleys were shot. She wanted to feel relief that she had sped off angrily and had avoided the gunman herself, she wanted to feel grateful that she still had her two kids when poor Nathan Hadley had been left with nothing, but all she felt was tired.

'Please try to stay out of trouble today, Ben. Okay?'

Ben nodded.

'Okay?' She was using her authoritative mother voice because she was looking straight ahead and hadn't realised that he had acknowledged her obvious request.

'I will, Mum. I swear. I'll try really, really hard.'

Catherine Raymond spotted her son's hand holding on to the pushchair and her right cheek twitched into a half-smile. She could already see that he was trying.

She looked down at Ben's face. He seemed to be on the edge of crying, a feeling she knew all too well, and it hurt her. *He's eight, he shouldn't be feeling like that.* She cursed herself. He hadn't always been the bad kid in class. And, sure, he could be a handful, but she saw how loving and sweet he could be, too.

Stopping meant that the baby would resume the crying, unhappy at the lack of motion, but Catherine did not care. She halted before the school gates and crouched down to the same height as her eldest son.

'Listen, I know I've been a bit rubbish recently.' Ben said nothing. He just stared. 'It's very hard with a little baby at first because they don't want to sleep as much as we do and that means that Mummy is too tired to do all the things she wants to do. Okay?'

He nodded and she saw it this time, but Ben didn't fully understand where his mother was going with this story.

'Let's just get through the next few days without any scrapes or fights or name-calling and you and I will do something special on the weekend. Just us. Daddy can look after the baby. We can go to the cinema or something, how about that?' She forced a smile but Ben didn't have to. It was just what he needed. A little time. A little of his mother's time.

He hugged her tightly without saying a word, but the strength of his squeeze said enough.

This is why I like the kids. I look into Ben and he is not evil. He can't be, yet.

'Now, just ignore anyone who tries to tease you. They want to make you mad because they know it gets you in trouble and not them. Tell a teacher and if they don't do anything, keep quiet and tell me when I come to pick you up and I will sort it with Mrs Blake.'

'Okay. I won't get mad.' He meant it – the intent, at least.

'Good boy.' Those were two words that Ben the Bully didn't hear very often. 'Now give your mum another hug, eh?' It took all her strength to put on that brave face but for the first time in weeks she felt like a mother who knew what she was doing.

She waved him in and Ben ran over to two other boys he thought were his friends.

She watched him play for a few minutes before the bell rang and everybody lined up. He looked over at her and smiled. She hadn't seen that light for some time.

Then Steph Allen ruined the moment.

'Terrible, isn't it?' She was stood beside Catherine and spoke the words as if to nobody in particular, looking forward as her own child got into line.

'Sorry?'

'This whole situation. I mean, it's just terrifying. Nothing like this has ever happened here before.'

It had. She was too young to know. Out of the loop.

The thing with Carson Chase was just a myth to her, an urban legend.

Another small story.

'Oh, yeah. It's horrid. But what can you do?' Catherine was speaking rhetorically, hoping she could turn and head home to lie down.

'Cath, you look tired.' This was not what Catherine Raymond wanted to hear no matter how well meaning it was supposed to be. 'It's that difficult bit in the beginning. So nice when they turn that corner, isn't it?'

Oh, fuck off, Steph, you condescending bitch. The words swirled in her mind but her eyes were too jaded to convey her thoughts. I didn't want to intervene.

'Sure. It's getting there slowly.' She took some of her own advice about ignoring the people that try to rile you.

'A few of us are going to wait for one another after school. Walk together. Stick in a pack. Safety in numbers. That sort of thing. I know we live in opposite directions but it might be worth doing the same with some of the mums from Roylake. Maybe give Margot a call, or something.' She was so *proper* all the time that it aggravated Catherine almost to the point of physical violence. She hated that fake sincerity. The Good Shepherd was full of Stephs, it was part of the reason she didn't go any more.

'Yeah. Maybe I will.' She turned and powered back to her house without saying goodbye. She was weary and angry and feeling weak. And it was only nine o'clock in the goddamn morning.

SOMETHING ABOUT THE CHURCH

Pace had managed to charge his phone a little while drinking his extra-strength black coffee. The first name to light up the screen that morning was Inspector Anderson to inform him that there had been *another one*. Not a kid this time and nothing to do with the schools. An elderly woman shot, point-blank, in the face at her home. Seems she may have been there a few days.

Not so much of a pattern now.

A gaggle of mothers could be heard over the gate to the Cider Orchard Bed and Breakfast. Pace sighed at their ignorance. The free flow of information to the press meant that they were all adequately informed. They knew there was a man with a gun in their town. They could read that children and mothers had died. What was the point to this *solidarity*? He didn't have children so he couldn't say for sure how he would react but something felt wrong. Something was *off*.

Surely no parent in their right mind would let their child out of sight for a moment with everything that was going on. Not this soon. It was like something had taken over the town. Some kind of group mental incapacitation.

He flicked his cigarette out into the shingle and went back into the room to replace his coffee cup. Everybody was looking for a pattern – the kids, the schools – the families were not linked to one another in any relevantly malicious way, not that had been uncovered. Pace turned it over in his head. The link between the victims and their families had to be somebody else. So far, the only person he could think of was Mrs Beaufort. And that was clearly ridiculous.

Was there something about the church?

The gate swung open as Pace hit the exit button. He edged the front of the car out onto the pavement, aware of the pedestrians. The whole town seemed to be awake and starting their days.

Of course, that wasn't entirely true. Oz Tambor was asleep in the boot of a car, wrapped in only a coat. Hungry. Thirsty. A slave to his nightmares. Charles Ablett was lying in his bed after a difficult night; he was not going to show up for work at all. And his brother, Roger, was still holding the pillow tight when Ellie Frith called him again, just as he had expected her to.

BROTHERLY LOVE

The roar of the environmentally unfriendly engine alerted Ellie that Roger had arrived. His business was opening twenty-five minutes late and she knew he would be pissed off about it. He always was. She'd pay the price because he rarely used a strong arm with his brother.

For such a terrifying man, he showed considerable restraint with Charles. It seemed he could get away with just about anything whereas any other person in the world – man, woman or child – would be trampled over if it meant Roger Ablett would get what he desired.

'Pick up your fucking phone, brother. This has got to stop. Call me straight away when you get this message.' Roger was shouting down the phone at a man who was not listening. He didn't even look at Ellie, who was leaning against the window of Ablett and Ablett. He fished the keys from his trouser pocket and aggressively pushed through the entrance. Once inside he filled the room with his voice. 'Ellie, put the kettle on. We've got work to do.'

Her eyes threw daggers into his obese back but she did as he ordered.

Roger sat down at his brother's desk, pushed the circular button that whirred his computer to life and flicked through the diary that was sitting on his desk.

Charles Ablett's diary should have been thick with ink but Roger could see that he had been slacking off even more over the last few weeks – the last week in particular. In fact, he only had one appointment booked in for that day. A rental enquiry just before lunch with a Detective Sergeant Pace.

Perfect.

OLD FRIENDS

On the doorstep sat an elderly lady, her right hand rubbing her left arm for warmth or comfort or something to do. It was clear that she lacked neither the strength nor the speed to have committed the atrocious murders in Hinton Hollow but Pace was not ruling out her involvement yet.

She had a cast-iron alibi for her whereabouts when Jacob Brady was killed. She was in the hospital recovering when Faith Brady decided to take her own life. She was in the back of the detective's car when the Hadley family was systematically erased from existence. And she was the person who found May Tambor dead in her hallway.

Mrs Beaufort did not pull the trigger but she was hovering over every victim like a malevolent black cloud.

Pace thought he had worked her out. She was proud and old-fashioned in her thoughts and ethics. Old-fashioned in a good way. Not outdated. There was well-meaning in there. She was the matriarchal figure of the town and a devout attendee of the Church of the Good Shepherd. But he had seen a side to the old woman that was fearless and powerful particularly in the face of something that threatened her way of life and the way of Hinton Hollow.

He didn't fall for coincidences.

She knew something. If there was something to know in this town, she knew it.

Pace drove up to the house, parking behind Mr Beaufort's old green Jaguar. The driveway stones crunched beneath his tyres.

'Mrs Beaufort,' he called. She looked up. 'Are you feeling all right?'

'No, detective. One of my oldest friends is dead behind this door. I'm not all right. I have a pain in my arm and chest. I'm just trying to breathe, if that's okay.'

God, does she save all this vitriol just for me?

He held it in.

He didn't respond, just walked over to her and helped her to her feet.

'A car will be along soon. I think it might be best if you wait in there.'

'Oh, yes, that worked out perfectly last time, didn't it?' Her eyes were not her own. They were darker somehow. Older. But not in an elderly way. Old in the way that the universe is old. It knows things. It has seen things. It holds answers that are too far away to ever discover.

'Mrs Beaufort, it's cold out here. You've recently been in hospital and you're clearly in pain with what sound like similar symptoms. I am not for one minute saying that you cannot handle your situation but there is a heavy rain forecast and, above all, I really don't want you standing there when I bust through that door.'

The old bat huffed and groaned as she brushed herself down.

'Very well. But leave the car open this time.'

Pace went to hold Mrs Beaufort's arm to help steady her but she shrugged him off. He decided to let her walk back to the car herself.

Independent she-devil.

Through the diamond window he could clearly see a body. Her hair was thin and grey. She had a floral dress on. The smatter of brain and plasma on either wall of the hallway and her distance from the door suggested that the killer rang the doorbell, May Tambor answered, and he shot her there and then.

But something didn't fit.

All the victims had been executed while facing their killer. The shot to the face even matched that of Jess and Rachel Hadley. His female victims had each taken their bullet in the same place. Both boys had swallowed their pellet through the chest. Perhaps that said something about the man with the gun. He was trying to hide the identity of the women, of the mothers. He was breaking the boys' hearts. Perhaps it was one of those coincidences that Pace did not believe in.

For coincidence to be of use, it had to collide with fate.

The difference with May Tambor's death was that it was at her home and the murderer had not approached her from behind.

She let them in and then walked backwards down the hallway. It was someone she had known. Somebody she trusted.

She had been alone. The gunman would have known that. But everybody in the town would have known that. Her husband had died four years earlier and she had been scared to leave home since. It wasn't giving the detective a big enough crumb. Of course, if she hardly ever left the house, it would mean that she hardly ever attended the Good Shepherd.

Salis made house calls. He went to see Mrs Beaufort at the hospital.

The letterboxes on this side of town were placed more conventionally so Pace could not just let himself in as he had at the Bradys' home. He took a step back, inhaled deeply then rammed through the threshold with his shoulder, knocking all the air out of his lungs as he did so.

He had to step up into the house.

The first thing he did was close the door behind him. Pace had to duck down slightly to see through the diamond to the outside. Mrs Beaufort was muttering to herself in the back of his car. *Probably babbling some voodoo chant while sticking pins in a Detective Pace doll*, he mused.

He looked over his shoulder at the body of the late Mrs Tambor. She was stretched out nice and straight. Pace reckoned her to be around five feet and four inches. Tall enough to see out of the window at the person knocking. A woman so afraid of risk, of having no exit in a difficult situation, would surely not answer the door to somebody she did not know. An old friend, a priest, a policeman, a local councillor canvassing for votes.

The stench of death had filled the hallway but Pace investigated the other rooms to find them fastidiously clean. Dust-free surfaces, spotless carpets, not a single smear or fingerprint on any tap.

But then there were the biscuits.

More crumbs.

SAFETY IN NUMBERS

Two tracks of dirt lined the carpet where Catherine Raymond had been wheeling the baby back and forth in the pushchair.

She didn't care about the stains, the little boy had been nodding off along the street and she didn't want to take him out of the chair because she would have to start the entire soothing process all over again.

And she just couldn't face it.

She felt wretched about Ben. Maybe she'd been too hard on him yesterday, but the baby, the baby, the tiring, relentless baby, that's what was making her act differently; in a way that was other than herself. She'd make it up to her big boy. She would take him to the cinema on the weekend. He loved films. And popcorn. She could sit through an animated ninety minutes if it would just put a smile back on her boy's face.

He had been walking around with slumped shoulders and a sour, downtrodden look that should never grace the face of an eight-year-old child. It was her fault and there had been nothing she could do about it.

But she could feel herself turning a corner. He'd forget it all in time. But she never would. That was the real burden of being a mother. Not the sleepless nights and constant worry, it was that feeling that whatever you were doing, no matter how great you were, you were somehow fucking up your child for the future.

> ### WORRY: EVIL AND GOOD
> Letting your child know that you are worried,
> putting your worry on to them,
> this is where I find you.
> When things progress to anxiety and panic,
> these are the things I can use.
> Worrying about your child, wanting the best for them, trying
> not to make the mistakes your own parents made, this is the
> good worry. Even if you don't get it right, you care. I will not
> interfere with compassion.

The baby fell into a deep sleep. Catherine had reclined the seat on the walk home from school so that he was lying flat. She had, herself, been reclining in an armchair, pushing the baby back and forth with her foot.

She stopped the motion and he remained in perfect slumber. Allowing herself a smile and a relieved exhalation, she tucked the blanket tightly around the baby, swaddling him in comfort. Then she relaxed back into her seat, her feet resting on the pushchair.

Maybe Steph was right, she told herself. *I'll give Margot a call when I wake up. We can walk home together. In a pack. Safety in numbers.*

Then she drifted off into faultless nothingness.

TAKES THE BISCUIT

Actually, it was more a lack of biscuits that concerned Detective Sergeant Pace.

May Tambor's kitchen was spotless. Cream shaker doors hid every utensil and appliance that she owned, with the exception of a toaster and kettle. Even the oven door revealed a sparklingly clean inside through the transparent front.

Every inch of the oak work surface was clear but for a small section opposite the kitchen entrance. A square of wood was covered in icing sugar. A sheet of sweet snow with eight semi-circles at the top. Beneath that, the sugar had been smudged. Pace could see that some had spilled on the floor below. He walked back out into the hall and stood over the body. The section of kitchen surface with the icing sugar was clearly visible from that spot.

He could see what had happened the day that May Tambor was killed.

The killer called by the Tambor residence – time of death to be determined by the coroner – and knocked on the door. Pace would have the doorbell dusted for prints but expected nothing back on that front.

May Tambor would have entered her hallway, possibly from the kitchen where she was baking, and seen the person through the glass rhombus of her front door. Notoriously agoraphobic after her husband's death, it stood to reason that to have opened the door she would have to have recognised the person. That meant it was somebody from Hinton Hollow. If she was old friends with Mrs Beaufort then the number of people she knew in town would be vast, though her socially crippling condition could narrow the search considerably.

She would have opened the door and been greeted with the barrel of a gun. It was close to her, the spray on the walls indicated that. The killer did not run. He stood over the victim to check her. Pace walked through the movements as though it were happening in real time.

The house was spotless, nothing seemed out of place. No drawers had been upturned, no wardrobes ransacked. The killer came for one reason, to kill May Tambor.

But the biscuits.

Those goddamn biscuits.

Pace stepped over Mrs Tambor just as the killer had. He walked into the kitchen, pretending he could smell home baking rather than decaying pensioner, and he stopped at that small sugar-coated section of work surface that seemed so incongruous with the rest of the impeccably dust-free home.

He counted the semi-circles.

They were obviously marks where biscuits had once been. May Tambor had baked them – perhaps she was expecting company – and sprinkled them with icing sugar. Why she hadn't placed them on a cooling rack and done this, was unclear. Some agoraphobic idiosyncrasy, maybe.

Pace placed his arm above the top row and mimicked a swiping motion towards his waist. The murderer had stolen the biscuits before leaving. Some of the icing sugar was on the floor where they had been pilfered off the surface.

Criminals made mistakes, of course they did. They left prints and DNA, they walked in front of cameras, they bragged to the wrong person, they returned to the scene of the crime. But this, this seemed so impetuous yet somehow calculated.

Was the man with the gun suddenly hungry after such a kill. It wouldn't have been that difficult. May Tambor required no stalking or planning, she never left the goddamned house. From the size of the circles there must have been forty biscuits for him to take.

Pace kept saying *him* in his mind, as though this were the same killer as the man who had been stalking parents and children after school closed. The town was too small and insular for it to be a different case altogether.

Everything was linked.

Perhaps it was fortuitous. The gunman running rampant in Hinton Hollow saw the biscuits and thought that moving them, taking them away, making the lack of biscuits stand out as a clue, would get the investigating officer thinking that it was related somehow.

He's fucking with me, Pace reasoned.

Pace was annoyed at himself for giving it so much contemplation, thinking that this simple act of taking biscuits would build a better psychological picture of the man he was trying to find so he could contemplate his next move.

He laughed to himself. He was pinning his case on no biscuits. On the complete lack of physical evidence.

Forty fucking biscuits. Why would one person need forty fucking biscuits?

He was feeding somebody.

Maybe he had a dog. Or a friend. Maybe it was a kid with a sweet tooth. Or a cub scout. Either way, the biscuits were nowhere and so was Detective Sergeant Pace.

PLEASURE CENTRE

There were, in fact, forty-eight biscuits.

But only twenty left.

They were starting to go stale, wrapped in a torn plastic bag and rolled up in the boot of the car where Oz Tambor lay. He'd been rationing himself to four meals a day, each comprising of two peanut butter and banana cookies. He could feel himself getting thinner and it was making him feel colder at night in the woods, but the coat was beginning to feel more like a blanket.

HERE'S A NEW THING
I've noticed that, all of a sudden,
people seem to like to suffer.

Oz took two biscuits from the bag and scoffed the first one whole, trying to trick his stomach or his brain that he'd eaten something large and was therefore full up. He savoured the second one, wanting it to last. Delaying his gratification if only for a minute or two.

In those moments, he was free. He didn't even think about Liv to get him through. Perhaps it was a simple rush from the intake of sugar. The comedown was instant and severe, though. He'd started to contemplate death more and more. He dreamed again of how things could end and he would get back to Liv. The biscuits were the only thing keeping him alive.

What happened when they ran out?

A LOT OF TALK ABOUT BISCUITS

Inspector Anderson walked in to May Tambor's house just as Pace was laughing to himself at the inadequacy and surreal nature of the case.

'Something funny about this, Pace?'

'Only how funny it absolutely isn't, sir.'

Anderson looked comically confused as he interpreted the response. He peered over his moustache at the body.

'Poor May. Tough few years, I tell you.' Then he stepped over her carcass, just as Pace had, and joined his detective in the kitchen.

Pace was about to begin a short debrief on his findings when Anderson, at his unabashed best, said, 'That old coot always seems to be on the back seat of your car. Something you're not telling me?' He widened his eyes at the inappropriate innuendo.

He ignored the inspector and ran through his findings in the Tambor residence.

'Seems like a lot of bloody talk about biscuits.' That was Anderson's response.

'If you've got anything to add, I'm all ears. You knew her?'

'Of course. Everybody knows May Tambor. Bloody lovely lady and a marvellous cook, too. Bake sales at the church haven't quite been the same since her husband died. Must have been about four years ago, now. Didn't even know he was ill until it was too late, you know?'

Pace nodded as though he did.

'She's got a son. Oz. Supposed to be getting married soon. Looks like his mother won't have to worry about which hat to wear now, eh?' He turned around to look at the old, bloated baker. Pace looked up to the ceiling and muttered the words 'Oh, God.'

'Look, Pace, someone's got to go and tell the kid. Now either you can do it or I can do it.'

'Okay.'

'Well, I don't want to do it, so I'm sending you. I'll stay here and get things cleaned up and we can meet back at the station in about ninety minutes.'

Pace bit his tongue. He couldn't understand why Anderson didn't want to report May's death to Oz Tambor, it seemed like this kind of task fell very comfortably into his skill set. But Pace didn't want to be stuck in that house. He wanted to be out solving the case.

Anderson gave him the address and Pace started out the door.

'Don't forget to take your girlfriend home first, though,' Anderson called after him.

He stepped back over the dead woman. The red light on her answering machine was blinking with messages from Liv Dunham.

ANOTHER EPISODE

'Finished now, are we?'

That was Mrs Beaufort's welcome to the detective.

He ignored it.

'How are you feeling, Mrs Beaufort.' Pace was now stood by the car looking down at the feeble yet formidable woman.

'The pain is wearing off and my patience is wearing thin.'

 ### ANOTHER WAY THAT EVIL PRESENTS ITSELF
Mrs Beaufort.

Pace took a breath. The community he had stepped back into was not the community he remembered. It wasn't just the passing of time that had changed these people. It was something else.

It was him.

'I would like it if you'd take me to Oz. I've known him all his Hinton Hollow life and I should like to be there when he finds he is suddenly and cruelly an orphan.'

'Buckle up, Mrs Beaufort.' Pace closed the back door then got in the driver's seat. He adjusted the rear-view mirror so that he didn't have to turn around to speak with his passenger.

'I can direct you if you don't know the way.' She was looking into the mirror at Pace's dark, uncaring eyes and faultlessly transmitting the spite from her own. This was not a look that Mrs Beaufort had ever given before. But it was the resting expression of all that was evil in The Hollow.

'I know the way to the surgery, it's fine.' He was almost robotic in his tone.

'I'm sorry?'

'Are you?' It was cheap but he'd just about had enough of her. 'You've had another episode,' he said condescendingly. 'The best thing for you is to have a sit down with Doctor Green. Just to check you over.'

'You can pull the car over right now and let me out. I'll walk.' She grappled with the handle but the door could only be opened from the outside.

'I don't want you to take this the wrong way, Mrs Beaufort, but there is absolutely no way on Earth that I am taking you with me on police business to inform a young man that his mother has been brutally shot and killed in her home. That is not your job, you should not be put under that pressure. Particularly in your condition.'

Her face turned red, he could see it reflected clearly. She was either embarrassed or flustered. Or angry. Or all of those emotions. But she did not respond to him. She wanted to say that it wasn't his job, either. But I was holding her back.

'I'll swing by RD's on the way and he can come and take you home once you have the all-clear.'

She said nothing.

It was like an interview with Michael Brady.

And that was fine by him. They travelled in silence until they reached the surgery. Pace opened the door for Mrs Beaufort. He offered her his hand as support. She refused. Then she strode by him without a word into the surgery. She didn't even look unwell.

Pace turned right onto Stanhope Road, half a mile up from where the Hadleys had been culled the previous afternoon.

'That woman.' He cursed her out loud. 'Always getting in my fucking way.'

Driving, he saw the sign for Ablett and Ablett on the left. He pulled his mobile from his pocket, remembering that he had a meeting booked with Charles Ablett that lunchtime to discuss a rental contract. He was going to cancel the meeting.

The top left of the screen said 7%.

Detective Sergeant Pace dropped the device onto the seat between his legs and swung a hard left turn towards the estate agency.

He swore to himself that the only thing that was going to die in Hinton Hollow on that fourth day was the battery of his phone.

THEY DIDN'T TALK

Maeve Beauman was finishing a bottle of Pinot Grigio, checking her phone every five minutes and going out of her mind with concern. She was thinking of Detective Sergeant Pace and how she'd kill him if he didn't come back to her soon. Just a text. That was all that was needed.

She was watching the news. One of her favourite things to do in the evening – other than drinking and spiralling. The story of the people jumping from Tower Bridge had almost been forgotten, replacing the big-city cult crime were the small town shootings of Hinton Hollow.

There were several talking heads – people she would never know as RD, Inspector Anderson, Mrs Wallace and Father Salis – as the report attempted to capture the flavour of the community and how it had been rocked by tragedy.

She just wanted to see her detective.

She missed him.

She needed him.

But my hold over Maeve's detective meant that she had fallen down his list of priorities. Far enough that he didn't even have the time or compulsion to message her back with a solitary x. It took everything she had not to leave him another voicemail, instead, she opened another bottle of wine from the fridge, finished watching the news and decided that, if he hadn't contacted her by midnight, it was over.

 THREE WAYS THE NEWS HAS AFFECTED
DETECTIVE SERGEANT PACE
It thrust Maeve into his life.
It spread the word and told the world about
The People Of Choice.
It brought Little Henry Wallace back to Hinton Hollow.

A FLYING VISIT

Roger Ablett was leaning back in his seat like he owned the place, which he did; still, it wasn't an endearing image. Charles would sit in the same way, his legs spread a little wider like he was exhibiting some kind of rare artefact that everyone wanted to see.

Ellie Frith just kept her head down, her fingers on the keyboard and her ear to the phone.

The younger brother still hadn't turned up for work, it was a little brazen even for him. He would usually inform his brother at some point, but Ellie could tell that Charles hadn't been in contact because Roger was growing more frantic and had already left three messages since he'd arrived. He'd had four cups of coffee so far that morning and Ellie had made them all. Like a good little slave.

Another way in which Evil presents itself: slavery. See also: *corporate employment, the Tuskegee Study* and *insincerity*.

He slammed down the phone. It wasn't in anger, rather in triumph. He'd been on the phone, blurting out his usual string of bullshit. *We've had further interest in that property. Looks as though they're willing to go at the full asking price. You're in a great position because you are not reliant on a chain.* That morning he'd been blagging to the young wife of the abrasive Yorkshireman who had shown real passion for the riverfront property in Twaincroft Hill. She was Roger's leverage and he was pulling all the right strings. He'd celebrated the sale prematurely but he was an Ablett who never gambled unless it was a *dead cert.*

He leaned further back on his chair and placed both hands behind his head as though ready to receive oral gratification from somebody hidden beneath his brother's desk. Ellie wondered how much more weight that cheap office seat could take and found herself staring at her putrid boss.

'That's right, Ellie, watch and learn from the master.' He smiled. His teeth forever stained with coffee and red wine and God knows whatever else he shovelled inside that mouth of his.

'I am but your humble student, Mr Ablett.' She wasn't sure where that came from. She wasn't normally so vocal and she held sarcasm back as much as she could because it confused Roger. She could see it all over his face.

Also, she never called him Mr Ablett.

It was day four. Detective Pace had been in town for over three days, the darkness had followed shortly after. More people were being affected – see also: *infected* – and more would be changed the longer it remained.

The bell rang and a rush of cold air swept into the office of Ablett and Ablett. Roger sat forward in his chair. Ellie turned around, thinking that Charles had finally decided to show his irritatingly handsome face.

Ready for a showdown, she thought, divisively.

The door closed but the room remained cold.

DON'T BELIEVE EVERYTHING

'Good morning. The name is Pace. I have an appointment booked today for twelve that I'm not going to be able to make.' He stayed by the door. This was a flying visit.

Roger Ablett raised his hefty frame from the creaking chair. He didn't even look at his junior staff member when he said, 'Ellie, put the kettle on for myself and Mr Pace.' She stood up on autopilot. 'Coffee, Mr Pace?'

'I really can't stay, thanks. I just came in as I was passing. I would have called but my phone is almost dead. Honestly, don't worry about the coffee.'

Ellie started to sit back down in her seat.

'Nonsense, Detective.'

Ablett had done his homework.

Ellie rose again.

'I'm in the middle of a case right now, as I'm sure you know...'

'It will take but a moment. A simple case of crossing some Ts and dotting some lower-case js.' He chortled at his useless attempt at humour, producing a pen from his jacket pocket at the same time.

Pace relented and stepped towards the desk. Ellie was caught in some kind of hot-beverage purgatory.

'Now, I believe that you have been speaking with my brother, Charles.' Roger showed Pace an open palm, offering him a seat.

'You are not Charles?'

'Ha! I wish.' He didn't really know what he meant by that but it didn't seem to unsettle the detective. 'No. No. I'm Roger. Roger Ablett. His older brother. I'm afraid that Charles seems to have disappeared.'

'Disappeared?'

Ablett had Pace's complete attention. He excused Ellie from her desk, reminding her that she was supposed to be making a cup of coffee. He suggested that perhaps she take a coffee break of her own outside. Perhaps even treat herself to a cigarette. Pace's brain automatically told him that he required nicotine at that very moment.

Both men sat in silence until Ellie had disappeared into the back-room kitchen.

'Is this the first you are reporting of your missing brother, Mr Ablett?'

'Please, call me Roger.' He was smug. Pace thought of five other words he could call Roger.

FIVE WORDS TO DESCRIBE ROGER ABLETT
Fat.
Determined.
Misogynistic.
Powerful.
Dangerous.

'Look, he does this from time to time. He's a handsome boy with a liberal concept of work but he's my brother, and I promised our mother I'd take care of him when she was gone.'

'So you don't think he's just late today?'

'I can't get hold of him. He usually texts me or calls but I've been trying his phone all morning and it just goes through to his voicemail.'

Pace couldn't understand what had Roger Ablett so spooked.

'My phone is about to die. It happens. He could be in an area of bad reception. It's not great in this town.' Pace pulled his phone from his pocket to check the time. He had 5% battery life remaining. And a thinly veiled good-morning text from Maeve.

'Charles has a bit of a *hobby* in this town.' Roger looked away from Pace and down at the desk. 'He's not great at keeping himself to himself, if you know what I mean. He likes the ladies.'

'How is that relevant, Mr Ablett?'

'Oh, I don't know. I don't want to speak ill of the dead...' He was reeling Pace in.

'Go on.'

'I don't believe everything he tells me, a lot is bravado, if he used it a little more in his job ... Anyway, he spoke quite fondly about Mrs Hadley.'

'Rachel Hadley?'

'Yes. I'm not sure they had been...' He cleared his throat. 'Intimate. But I'm sure he would have been upset by her passing.'

'You think there's a chance they were sleeping together?'

'I really wouldn't like to say. Her husband is still here and must be devastated. It serves no interest to drag something up and make him think less of the woman. I'm just a little worried about my brother, Detective. This is unlike him. Something just doesn't feel quite right. I can't put my finger on it.' He looked over Pace's shoulder at Ellie Firth creeping back into the main office with a tray of coffees and biscuits. She laid them down on Charles' desk between the two men, who had stopped talking.

'Thank you, Ellie. If you want to take yours outside...' Roger spoke as though he were treating her, doing her a courteous favour. Rain was due within the hour. 'Detective, you really have to try one of these cookies. Charles brought them in a couple of days ago but they're still good.'

'Not for me, thanks.'

Pace took a sip of his coffee and pondered the information that Roger Ablett had so readily given up about his own brother. *In a town like Hinton Hollow, everything is related.*

'Have you been to your brother's home at all?'

'I haven't had time to check, yet. I've been too busy covering for him here.'

'As you probably know, it hasn't been long enough to declare your brother as a missing person but if you write down his address, I'll take a look myself.'

Ablett wrote down the address and pushed the piece of paper across the desk to Pace.

'Please get in contact with the station if you hear from your brother before I do. I would like to ask him some questions relating to the late Mrs Hadley. Ask for either myself or Inspector Anderson.'

Roger Ablett nodded an affable agreement.

That morning, Detective Sergeant Pace was gleaning information. As much as he could before the schools kicked out.

He was making links.

And, maybe he finally had his first suspect.

CAN THE SMALL TALK

Pace took the mug of black coffee with him. He had nothing else to talk to Roger Ablett about. This wasn't the time to discuss suitable properties. He told the estate agent that he'd be taking the coffee *to go*. Ablett was so surprised that he shrugged. And that was enough for the detective. He walked out the door and disappeared from sight.

He could smell the imminent dampness but, more than that, he detected the aroma of a cigarette.

At the end of the building, tucked around to the left, Ellie Frith was stood with one heel against the brickwork, sucking in a lungful of tar. Her cup of coffee planted on the floor beside her.

She was so sick of the office. The orders and the peacocking brothers. The false charm and empty promises. She knew of Roger Ablett's reputation, though. She knew of his temper, of his political aspirations and his business ambition. She knew not to cross him. To never say a bad word that might find its way back to his ear.

But that day felt different.

Fear was not as strong as disdain.

She felt unusually bold.

'Ellie, right?' Pace rounded the corner.

'That's right. How can I help you, Detective? Want to know if Roger is pitching a dud?' She took another drag of her cigarette and Pace pulled a box of his own from his jacket.

'No. I'll come back about somewhere to rent. I'm staying at the Cider Orchard. You know it, I guess?'

'We should probably can the small talk if you want some information, Detective. He'll want me back any minute to sharpen his fucking pencils or something.'

It seemed that Pace had misjudged the submissive wallflower.

'Fine. Let's cut to the chase. Where is Charles Ablett this morning?'

'Fucked if I know. He's got a string of women around this quaint little bible-loving town. Could be in any of their beds. Could be drunk in the woods. He likes that too. There'd probably be a few guys in this town unknowingly raising his baby if he wasn't killing all his swimmers with the booze.' She was wise-cracking but it was useful.

'Has he ever mentioned any names?'

Short questions. Let her do the talking.

'Too many to remember. He's not the most discreet lover a woman could ask for.' Pace wondered whether he'd ever had a go at the young girl spouting off. Maybe he'd rejected her. Called it off. Tried it on.

'He ever mention Faith Brady?' It was a leap but somebody had to take it.

'Sure. I'm not certain he ever got anywhere with her but he went on and on about her legs. Pretty disgusting stuff.'

Pace raised the cigarette to his lips and drew a mental line from the suspect to the Brady family.

'He's been obsessed with Rachel Hadley, though. There's been nothing else that he's wanted. Hates her husband. Not sure why, he's lovely, you know? Really nice.'

He drew another line in his head, pinning a piece of string from Ablett to the Hadleys.

'That's his thing, you know? He loves the unattainables. Looks at it as a challenge. Like collecting cub-scout badges or scalping Indians. He says *it's a war, a race against time.* I hope you don't mind me saying this but he's a goddamn animal.'

'You are entitled to that opinion,' he smiled at her, but she was stoic. 'And Roger?'

'What about him?'

'I imagine he is fully aware of his brother's dealings?'

'Of course he is.' She leaned in towards Pace and spoke more softly. 'He doesn't like what his brother does. It's probably the only decent thing you can say about him. I'm grateful that he gave me a job but, for all their differences, both Abletts have got that temper. You don't get used to it. Roger gets mad at his brother sometimes. It's scary. But, with Roger, it's always about work, and with Charles, it's always about women.' She threw the butt on the floor and stamped it out with the toe of her shoe.

'I should get back. He'll be wondering where I am already.' She picked up her coffee from the floor and walked off without saying another word.

Pace waited a while. He wanted to collect his thoughts. Dots were connecting. The unattainable women seemed key but it was unclear why the children would fall victim.

He still had to swing by RD's to arrange a pick-up for Mrs Beaufort. As annoying as he found her, he could have done with some of her insight at that point. He could've asked her more about Charles and Roger Ablett. There was bound to be more that she knew.

He was wasting time. He still had to visit Oz Tambor and inform him of his mother's untimely demise, and now he also had to swing by Charles Ablett's home. This was small-town policing. Running errands between investigation.

It wasn't him.

It wasn't Pace.

FORGIVE ME

An underweight, bearded Jewish man was nailed to a cross above the spot where Father Salis knelt, running through a section of Mark, Chapter 7 in his mind.

What comes out of a person is what defiles him. For from within, out of the heart of man, come evil thoughts, sexual immorality, theft, murder, adultery, coveting, wickedness, deceit, sensuality, envy, slander, pride, foolishness. All these evil things come from within, and they defile a person.

The priest's hands were clasped together and he asked his God for guidance and forgiveness. For those things that had come from within him. For his thoughts. For his pride. For everything else.

A dwindling congregation was not uncommon for a religion that refused to evolve with the times. The types of people that held on so steadfastly to outdated principles were dying of old age and new blood was not being integrated because the next, younger generation, a forward-thinking generation, were not being represented.

Weddings were still popular ceremonies in the church, even with those who were less devout. And principles were often dissolved to encourage secular couples to use the facilities because it fulfilled some old-fashioned dream of being Lady Diana and these things often funded the church's needs.

But numbers at mass were decreasing despite the offering of free wine. Not even the Papal update was enough to steer lapsed Christians back through the door.

The only other events that saw the pews packed were Christmas and funerals. December was months away but recent events, along with the weekend's marital ceremony, meant that the Church of the Good Shepherd would be filled for weeks to come.

Father Salis was grateful for that.

Grateful for the blessed union.

Grateful, somehow, for the death of children and their mothers.

Grateful, that he would be a part of it. That, perhaps, these events would bind the community, bring them back together, bring them to the church.

And, as a consequence of this gratitude, of this feeling from within, Father Salis once more begged his Lord for forgiveness.

LAST DAY OF TRADE

Three men had already walked by Hadley's Hair that day. Each of them had stepped up to the door and peered through the glass. One had even tapped on the window to see if there was anybody inside.

Of course the local barbershop would not be open the day after the owner's family was brutally slain on the street. It was taking Hinton Hollow's the-show-must-go-on attitude to the limits to expect any different.

Nathan Hadley returned home that morning. He had been drinking heavily the night before. He had stayed out. He had been to places he should not have visited. And he was back in his house. Nobody was watching it in Pace's absence – the police force was too small and were tied up with May Tambor's murder.

Hadley's Hair is no longer there.

That day was the last day of trade. The final customer receiving only half a haircut.

The premises were taken over years later by an estate agency.

Ablett and Frith.

The town moved on.

A SLIGHT TURN

The cigarette hissed as it hit the bottom of Pace's coffee cup. He left it on the floor where Ellie could find it the next time she had to escape her overbearing boss.

He waded into the centre of Hinton Hollow. The traffic lights were red and he didn't have time to park around the back of the shops. Pace yanked the steering wheel to the right and mounted the kerb outside RD's diner. Some pedestrians showed their disapproval with spite-filled looks but that was as far as they'd take it. The tall shadow that emerged from the vehicle held himself in a way that made it clear it was not worth approaching him.

Pace pushed open the café door and everybody turned around to view him. Quite the opposite reaction to the one he had witnessed on his arrival on that first day.

RD saluted him with two fingers of his right hand and Pace approached the counter.

The café owner started pouring a black coffee in anticipation, he liked to do this for all his regulars, remember their drink without them even having to order.

'Thanks, RD, but this is just a flying visit.' He'd said that once before.

'Well, take it to go, eh? You look like you need it.' He emptied the mug into a large paper cup. 'What's with the flying visit?'

'Mrs Beaufort.'

RD, eyes wide, nodded to his left to move Pace away from the ears of the locals.

'What's wrong? Another turn? I don't want to add to a rampant gossip mill.'

'She's fine. A slight turn. A reaction to some bad news but she's at the surgery now. She'll need a lift home. I'd do it myself but there have been a few developments in the case that I need to jump on right now.'

'Bad news?'

Of course, that's the part of the information he holds on to.

'I shouldn't really say but I guess Mrs Beaufort will tell you when you collect her. You can collect her?'

'I'll leave now.' RD's wife appeared with a Victoria sponge on a glass cake stand. Her timing was impeccable, as always.

'Okay. Thanks.' Pace looked over his shoulder. Outside he could see people walking past his badly parked car and shaking their heads at it. 'Look, I guess you know Mrs Tambor.'

'May? Of course. Tough few years. She's taken it hard.' His sincerity was matched by his wife's apprehension as she stood a few feet behind him.

'Well, I'm afraid she was found at her home this morning. I'm sorry.'

RD's wife dropped the cake, the delicate stand smashing over the floor behind the counter, its noise turning everyone's attention away from Pace and RD.

'I'm so sorry, RD, but I've got to go. Thanks for helping with Mrs Beaufort. I'll come back when I'm done. Thanks for the coffee.' He seemed to speak the sentence as though it were all one long word. Then he turned and left before anybody in the café had even realised he'd gone. He was like a ghost.

He was the wind.

Detective Sergeant Pace was a hurricane.

Detective Sergeant Pace is your irritable bowel.

Pace reversed off the pavement and headed off towards Roylake.

TOUGHER. MEANER. LESS SCARED.

Dorothy was still dead. Morbid obesity plus the natural bloating that comes with decomposition. Her doorbell rang.

A lonely figure in her lifetime, she was not immune to a friend or two calling by. But not that week. It was part of her regular routine. A standing order for a curry delivery. She always worked from home that day of the week and, instead of walking and queueing and waiting, she had arranged for a regular drop-off of buttered chicken with pilau rice, onion bhajis, sag aloo, Bombay potatoes and two keema naans, for her lunch.

The bell rang again.

Dorothy's skin was starting to mottle.

Again it rang, six times, in case she hadn't heard it because she was in the shower or something.

Then the food was laid down on the doormat as the delivery guy bent down to shout through the letterbox.

'Miss Reilly. Miss Reilly, are you there? It's your butter chicken, Miss Reilly.'

He waited. He rang the bell again. Then waited some more.

Finally leaving the bag of food to go cold on the doorstep, he looked straight ahead with spite running through him and spat, 'You fucking fat fuck.' Aiming his venom somewhere safe.

It's so easy now.

Behind a closed door.

From the safety of your own car as you drive past, giving someone the finger or shouting abuse.

From the warmth of your house as you hide behind an online persona that is tougher than you really are or smarter than you really are or more opinionated and outspoken than you really are.

Meaner than you really are.

Less scared than you really are.

This is you, now.

This is people.

This is what I have to stop.

LEATHER. AND GUNS.

Charles Ablett's was the grandest of all the houses that Pace had visited since returning to his childhood town. Four bedrooms for a bachelor would have been considered overkill, but even with the small amount of knowledge that Pace had about Charles, he imagined each room to have a double bed for a different lady, perhaps even themed, running his home like a bordello.

An impractical penis-extension of a two-seater sports car sat out the front of a double garage so Pace assumed that his prime suspect was home and simply not answering his brother's hot-headed messages.

Whose wife is he screwing in there? Pace wondered. *Is that how he chooses his next victim?*

As he neared the property, there was no sound coming from the house at all. No daytime mind-numbing chat show. No 5.1 surround sound modern R&B anthems. No screams of pleasure, nor displeasure from the upstairs windows.

Pace rapped the door with the back of his hand.

There was nothing.

He tried again, harder, saying, 'Mr Ablett. This is Detective Sergeant Pace. Your brother is worried about you. Please answer the door so that I may assuage his concern.'

Pushing the letterbox open, Pace was hit by the warmth from inside. It seemed odd to have the heating up that high if he was supposed to be at work. Though, if Ellie's words were true, there was every chance that he would usually be at home at this time of day.

And his car was sat in the drive.

Unless he had two cars.

Or was using somebody else's.

He waited. There was no time to waste. A few precious hours before the bell rang for the end of the school day. There was no movement inside the house. No creak of a floorboard or stair that would've made the detective lift his knee and thrust his foot towards the door. No one to pull him away.

Maybe that's what I was there for.

Pace was patient. He waited on the doorstep, hoping for the sound of a mistake. He moved around the back of the house – certainly not procedure to vault a garden fence but sometimes rules just get in the way of discovery.

The lounge was visible from the back window. White leather sofas and one wall that seemed to be made up entirely of a television screen. Ablett was a fabulously boring cliché in Pace's mind. A cut-price Scarface. There was bound to be a framed poster of the movie hanging proudly on some wall in the house. There was no noise escaping the windows at the back of the house either.

Maybe Charles Ablett was not inside the house, Pace reasoned.

He was there.

And he wasn't the only person who knew that.

SHUT UP AND LISTEN

'Fuck.'

His phone had died and Pace vented his frustration on the inside of his car, punching the steering wheel with the fleshy part of a clenched hand.

'Stupid piece of shit only lasts half a day. What's the fucking point?'

He threw the *piece of shit* into the passenger footwell and kept on driving across town. It had been over an hour since he'd stepped over Mrs Tambor in her hallway. It had started to feel like Hinton Hollow was closing in on him. His shadow, his past, creating a black hole that threatened to suck the historical town into non-existence.

The barriers of decency had come down and information was suddenly allowed to pass freely. Names kept coming up. Motives were arising. Evidence was growing. He dare not say it aloud but perhaps even a pattern was emerging.

Liv Dunham was opening her front door as Pace pulled up to the kerb at the bottom of her front garden. There was no car parked in the drive.

Everything about her screamed *average*.

Normal.

Nice.

Good.

She was no more than six inches above five feet in height. Her hair was a straight, clean, natural blonde. She wasn't out of shape, either. Though she wasn't in shape. It wasn't like she had a gut hanging over her trousers, but he wouldn't put her down as a gym-goer. Perhaps recently to ensure she'd fit into that wedding dress, but she was slim, with breasts that matched her hips.

Liv was standing at her front door when Detective Sergeant Pace walked through her gate. He was there to see Oz Tambor, to deliver the horrific news about his mother. He'd asked Constable Reynolds to send him the details of the woman who had called about her missing fiancé but he hadn't checked his messages and now his phone had died.

If he had, he would have recognised that she had the same address that he'd been given by Anderson for Oz Tambor. Another link. Another drawing pin. Another piece of string.

Another broken window.

He was walking into the unknown.

He was expecting to knock on the door and be greeted with a typically sunny Hinton Hollow welcome by a Mr Oscar Tambor. But the door was already opening before he arrived. Somebody had beaten him to that address. He didn't know Liv Tambor but he knew that neither of the people standing in front of him was the man he had come to see.

A LOVELY SURPRISE

This is what had happened.

The detective was pissed off and overloaded with work and information. He dropped Mrs Beaufort at the surgery and sped off to give a man he didn't know some information that he did not relish in delivering. She had been an unwanted burden on his already hectic and draining re-entry into the Hinton Hollow community. Sure, she was all goodwill and butterflies to her *family* but backhandedness and cockroaches to Detective Sergeant Pace.

The *city* Pace would have dumped her on the side of the road with a ten-pound note and told her to hold her thumb out to cars. But he had been more conscientious, driving her to the local surgery to meet with the town's beloved, long-standing doctor.

She walked up to the front desk but did not make an appointment with Sandra on reception – she should have, she was in a bad way and needed to be resting – but instead chose to converse with Sandra about the upcoming wedding and the possibility of calling a town meeting in the next week.

When Mrs Beaufort exited the surgery, Pace was long gone, though he would be taking a detour on his way to Oz Tambor. She popped another couple of her glyceryl trinitrate pills and set off.

Another long walk across the town she had always loved. Thinking that the onus to help rested solely on her thin withering shoulders. Plus me. Making sure she meddled. Because her insecurity about being insignificant in that town was more than enough to control her.

The trek took her about an hour. Almost the same amount of time it had taken Detective Sergeant Pace to extract information from Roger Ablett and interrogate Ellie Frith. And swing by RD's Diner to ask for a favour. And stalk the home of Charles Ablett.

Almost, but not quite.

She'd arrived at Oz Tambor's and Liv Dunham's house a minute earlier and pressed the doorbell with one hand while resting her weight against the wall with the other. She was out of breath and there was pain in her chest but she had got there and she had beaten him.

'Mrs Beaufort. Er, what a lovely surprise.' Liv brushed her hair behind her ear. She sounded out of breath, too. 'I wasn't expecting ... anybody, to be honest.'

She was not being honest.

Liv looked up over Mrs Beaufort's shoulder to see a dark, unknown figure approaching. Mrs Beaufort could see the expression on the young teacher's face was fear.

F e a r.

She turned around to see her least favourite detective.

He didn't look particularly pleased to see her standing there, either.

Her concern lay with Liv, though, and the reason she had reacted in the way that she had.

A GHOST

The two-day stubble hid his real face behind its shadow. He was tall. Handsome, too, his hair ruffled in a care-free way that implied that he did care. At least a little. But that is not the reason he caught Liv Dunham's breath.

The figure emerged through the gate, his coat billowing at the sides like broken wings. He was the wind. His pitted coal eyes only burned greyer as he closed in on her. She cursed herself for giving away the fact that she was at home alone when taking that first anonymous, breathy phone call. It was her own fault.

She had convinced herself that it was Oz that had called her on that first night, though the person at the other end never uttered a single word, and on the third had simply stuttered something. She'd even managed to sleep. But doubt had crept back in the morning just as it had before and she persuaded herself that the person calling her certainly was not her fiancé.

For a second, and only for a second, she considered shutting herself back inside the house, using the door as a barrier, leaving Mrs Beaufort outside to deal with the approaching terror.

She was shaking. Surely this was not it. Not in broad daylight.

But two young boys had already taken a bullet through the heart that week on their way home from school and the women seemed to be having their identities erased. In fact, everyone who had died that week in Hinton Hollow had perished during broad daylight.

All but one.

And they were yet to be found.

And Oz, who wasn't dead yet.

Mrs Beaufort had one foot ready to step into the Tambor/Dunham home. She peered up at Liv Dunham and lowered her foot at the young woman's expression. She did not quite seem to be herself. She was anxious, her eyes conveying some disbelief. It was as if she had seen a ghost.

COME IN

> 🌹 **REMEMBER: IN TIMES OF DIFFICULTY** 🌹
> **Denial. Solidarity. A stiff upper lip. Breakdown.**
> **Inner strength. Retaliation. War. Prayer.**
> **This is what people do.**

Liv was surviving on hope alone.

'I'm Detective Sergeant Pace.' He held out a hand and Liv accepted it with her own. It was strong. His hands were warm, but not kind. She audibly sighed and let the relaxation drop from her shoulders but only for a moment before the fear returned.

'Nice to see you again, Detective. Took your time.' Mrs Beaufort's mouth curled at one side in a grin meant only for Pace's tired eyes.

'A good day to you, too, Mrs Beaufort. How are you feeling? I see that you must have been given the all-clear by Doctor Green.'

'Doctor?' Liv responded in the only way she knew how. Forgetting about her own trepidation, releasing the fear she was holding on to about the disappearance of the man she wanted to marry *that* weekend. In that moment, she only cared about the welfare of the town's matriarch. It was this genuine compassion that made her such a great teacher.

'Oh, it's nothing, dear. Just a bit of a fall.' She tried to brush it off. *Well played, Detective. Well played.*

Liv turned her attention back to the man on her doorstep. She was no longer wary of him, but was now frightened he was only there to deliver bad news. That is the reason the police come to your door at an odd hour, they are there to inform you that somebody you love has been taken away from you. Somebody has died.

Pace could see that her eyes were beginning to well up. She was trying to be strong.

'I'm actually here to speak with Oscar Tambor. Is he home?' Pace asked.

'I'm Liv Dunham, his fiancée.' The name sparked behind the

detective's eyes. 'If you're here to speak with Oz then you'd better come in.'

SO MANY MESSAGES

There were two places set for breakfast at the kitchen table. One plate still had one and a half pieces of cold, limp, buttered toast resting sadly. Liv was just holding on.

Hinton Hollow was just holding on.

She flicked the switch on the kettle and proceeded to dither and potter about, opening the jar she kept teabags fresh in, picking some semi-skimmed milk from the fridge, grabbing a teaspoon from the cutlery drawer, all the time with her back to the detective. Keeping herself busy.

Busy doing nothing.

Pace needed this opportunity to speak with Liv alone, without the acidic tongue of the beloved town elder who was left sitting in the living room on a comfortable chair. Liv was going to prepare the hot beverages herself, but Pace had benevolently offered his services and insisted that Mrs Beaufort take the opportunity to rest after such a long walk. He had even managed to condescend to her by using that term she hated so much – *a woman in your condition.*

'Looks like I've missed Mr Tambor.' Pace lifted the plate with the toast off the table slightly with one finger. 'Must be at work already.' He added this knowing that it wasn't the case. Her back remained turned.

He did now recall what his dead phone would have reminded him. That Constable Reynolds had mentioned a Liv Dunham had called, frantic at the whereabouts of her partner. She was floating. Drifting. Preparing him breakfast in the morning on the chance that he would walk back through her door. Hoping he hadn't jilted her. Hoping that he would see the error of his ways, understand that she was the best thing in his life, hoping so desperately that he was not dead in the woods somewhere.

H o p e.

She was falling through a dream. A waking nightmare. And the only way to jolt her back to reality was with something real. Pace knew that.

'His mother was found in her home this morning.'

There was a silence as Liv's mouth opened wide, she tried to inhale but nothing happened. Then she said, 'Oh, May,' and began to cry. Her hands moved forward to support her weight on the kitchen work surface. The tears were whispered so Mrs Beaufort had no idea that Pace had just broken the news.

Liv turned around, more beautiful with the colour of sadness in her cheeks.

'Was it quick? Did she feel any pain? I mean, she hardly ever leaves … I mean, left, the house. She's had a tough time recently. I told Oz we were putting too much pressure on her to come out for the wedding but he wouldn't listen.'

Pace could have answered with a *yes* and a *no* and he would not have been lying. But he had her almost where he needed her. He just had to shock that poor woman into talking about Oscar. She was the link. He knew it. He could feel it. I twisted his heart a little more.

'This is not your fault, Liv.' He was gaining her confidence, forcing some familiarity by using her given name. 'And it is not Oz, either. Mrs Tambor was shot at her front door. She may have been lying there for a couple of days.'

Liv slid her back down the cupboard that housed cleaning products and a first-aid kit. And a plastic bag with fifty scrunched carrier bags inside it. She was crying. There was no sound from her mouth but tears fell from her eyes down her reddening cheeks.

'I've been trying to get hold of her for days. I've left so many messages. That should have told me, you know. She was always there. If I got the answering machine she called back almost straight away. Because she never went out.'

Pace allowed her to wallow for a minute. It was affecting her. She was yet to be touched by the darkness. But, now, it was inside her house. She had let it in.

I'd already done enough to Liv Dunham. She didn't deserve what was coming. Pace did.

Instinctively, he checked over his left shoulder.

'I know this must be hard for you, but I have some questions that I really need answering. Are you okay to do that?'

She nodded slightly. Pace had dropped into a squat so that he was at her level.

'By all accounts, it seems that Mrs Tambor was a well-liked and respected member of this community. I haven't been back in town long, but all the information I have received leads me to believe that she was one of the good ones.'

'She was.' Liv sniffed.

'Was there anyone who maybe didn't feel that way about her? Not all families get along.'

'She was a good woman, Mr Pace. A church-goer until a few years ago, but sometimes people lose a little faith when someone they love is taken from them so suddenly. I can't think of anybody who would want to *hurt* her, though. Not May.'

'What about Oscar? Had he had any confrontation with anybody? A small town like this, could be somebody wanting to besmirch the family name or get to him.'

'What? What are you asking me?' Pace had lost a little of her trust. He knew he had struck a nerve by mentioning Oz.

'Most of my job is to eliminate the information that is not useful, not relevant. That way I can really hone in on the things that will crack a case. Sometimes that means asking a question so that I can put a strike through it in my notepad. You are on the inside. You know more than anyone.' He looked Liv straight in the eyes.

'No. Nothing like that,' she confirmed, allowing herself to relax into the questioning.

'Where is Oscar Tambor, Ms Dunham?' He dropped the informality. He didn't have time. Not even a little.

🌹 A NOTE ON TIME 🌹
**When people say, 'Well that's two hours of
my life I'm never getting back', they're right.
You don't get it back.
This is also true of the good times, the defining times.
For me, time does not end.**

Liv forced herself to stand up, the small of her back resting against the kitchen counter. 'He...'

'Where is he, Ms Dunham?' His voice was quiet. It was more menacing that way, but his reason was not to disturb the vitriolic Mrs Beaufort who probably had her ear pressed firmly to the wall.

'We had a fight.'

'When?'

'Monday morning. Nothing serious. Stupid stuff. Practicalities. He needed a passport for our honeymoon. He's never had one. Never been abroad. I mean, we're only going to France. Paris and Provence, nothing spectacular.'

Preward, she thought. And almost choked on the word.

'Did he say where he was going?' He was keeping his questions succinct now, letting her speak. Letting her give up the information.

'No. He left. He took the car and left. I assumed he just needed to cool off, you know. It was just a silly fight. But added to the pressure of organising a wedding the whole town will be attending. Some of them are looking forward to it more than we are.' Her eyes darted a line through the wall to the spot where Mrs Beaufort was sitting, impatiently.

'And he hasn't tried to contact you since Monday morning?'

Liv paused. She hesitated for just a second.

And her lack of words was as incriminating as the lack of biscuits in May Tambor's kitchen.

'You called the police station the night that he did not return. Is that correct?'

'Yes.'

'Constable Reynolds said that you were very upset. That you claimed your fiancé had gone missing. You feared for him. You were worried. He used the word *frantic*.' She turned her head away. 'You then called again to follow up the claim when he hadn't returned after another day. Is that right?'

She didn't answer.

'Is that correct, Ms Tambor?' He probed her. He was pushing and pushing.

'Yes. I called again.'

'Then, suddenly, you decided it wasn't worth pursuing any more. You didn't call back after the third day. What was it? You've given up on him?'

'No.'

'You believe there's somebody else?'

'No.'

'You think he's dead.'

'No.' The final refusal was louder than the others. Pace looked over his shoulder again.

The kettle had boiled and clicked off at some point and the first drops of rain were peppering the kitchen window.

He had broken her down, that sweet unknowing schoolteacher. But it had pulled her fully back into reality. There was an honesty in that.

And it was only ever truth that would lead through that fear of the darkness and whatever lies beyond.

TIME

It was all Faith Brady had wanted. A little time. To come to terms with what she had decided. Perhaps to gain the bravery needed to take her own life.

Dorothy Reilly needed time. Time to get around. Time in between her job and her hobby of throwing food at her mouth to move properly and exercise, to plan her meals.

Owen Brady had time to recover. He was still alive. He had a son. But it was more time to suffer.

Inspector Anderson will wish he had a few more minutes.

Pace wishes he could turn it back.

And the Hadleys and Mrs Beaufort and Annie Harding, Darren, the florist, Father Salis, the Ablett brothers. Time was their enemy.

SOME THINGS THAT HAVE BEEN
SAID ABOUT TIME
The two most powerful warriors are
patience and time.
Time is money.
Time waits for no one.
Time is the most valuable thing a man can spend.
The key is not spending time but investing in it.

The Ordinary Man was taking time away from those children. He was giving the mothers none to make a decision. But that is exactly how long it should have taken to make the correct call. It should never have even been a choice.

I am watching everyone, and most people think they have no time. They are putting more into the jobs they don't want than the family they had planned so long for. They say they can't go for a run or to the gym but set aside time for television soap operas and sitting. Their houses are untidy but they spend four hours a day on social media or tapping pictures of sweets on their phone screen until three identical types line up.

I have been around forever. I have time. I can make mistakes.

Humans, you do not have this luxury.

So stop behaving like you do.

It is killing you.

PURITY AND HONESTY

Liv explained the calls she had received with as much precision as she could manage in her delicately drifting state. Pace was concerned about the information she had given up on that first phone call. The caller would undoubtedly realise that she was alone. He would have to assign some protection to her. If this was some kind of smite at the Tambor name, she was about to enrol herself into that camp.

But, as she spoke, as truth upon truth hit him in the face, Pace saw pins being pushed and strings being stretched all over the town of Hinton Hollow. The position at which they all crossed only led to one place.

Liv Dunham was unattainable. More than a woman with two young sons and a husband that worked too late, too often. Even more so than the couple whose fizzle was frazzled after a decade of love. She was days away from marrying her school-time sweetheart. She had been with only him. She was purity.

She was the greatest scalp of all time. The war-winner that dwarfed all battles before it.

But it would require something special to obtain that prize. Something different. Maybe removing her fiancé, not killing him, just keeping him at a distance, giving him just enough food to survive.

Detective Inspector Pace had one question on his mind.

'Liv. Do you know Charles Ablett?'

'Well, yes. He and his brother run the local estate agency over in Roylake.'

'And RD runs the diner, Mrs Beaufort runs the clothes shop and Maggie is the florist. Anyone could give me that information. How well do you know him?' When were people in Hinton Hollow going to understand that time was not on the side of justice. Wasting it only served to help the man with the gun.

All the men. All the guns.

'As well as anyone else, I guess.' She took a sip of her tea. Mrs

Beaufort's cup was getting cold on the side. And she was growing increasingly restless in the lounge.

'Honesty is the only thing that will help me catch this guy and get Oscar back to you. You've done so well telling me about the calls but I need to know about your relationship with Charles Ablett.' Liv could see in his eyes that the term *by the book* did not apply to him. He was going to find the truth whatever it took.

'I think the word "relationship" is perhaps a little strong for my acquaintance with Charles. I know him like most women know him in this town. He's a sleazeball who tries it on with everyone. Anyone with two feet and a heartbeat.' She looked around at Mrs Beaufort's teacup and winced. *How long will this questioning go on for?*

'He's made advances towards you?'

'Sure. He's tried to flatter me in the queue at RD's. He's rubbed up against me a few times in The Arboreal after a few drinks. I never even told Oz about that. I didn't feel comfortable. Charles Ablett gets bored. He wants what he can't have. That's all. How is this related to Oz? Or May?' Her eyes glistened with the promise of fresh tears and the rain beat harder against the window.

'I'm not sure yet. I'm still gathering information. Did you ever give him reason to believe that he stood a chance with you?'

'Did I lead him on? Of course not.' She stood up straight. Angry but hurt.

'No flirting for fun after a few drinks yourself?'

'What are you trying to say, Detective?'

'Have you ever taken things further with anyone besides Oscar Tambor?'

'I think that's quite enough, don't you, Mr Pace?' The sound came from behind him. He looked over his shoulder and saw Mrs Beaufort standing in the doorway to the dining room.

'Mrs Beaufort, these are difficult questions, I know, but they need to be asked and I beg you not to interfere any more with police business.' Pace spoke calmly to the old lady but Liv sensed an element of threat that she had never before heard directed at Mrs Beaufort.

'I have your tea.' Liv tried to divert the conversation but nobody was listening to her.

'You are barking up the wrong tree, Detective. Charles Ablett couldn't possibly have something to do with Oz's disappearance. You should know that better than anybody. You've seen this happen before.'

She turned and walked back into the lounge.

Liv Dunham and the detective stared at one another, neither wanting to be the first to speak – either about Charles Ablett or Mrs Beaufort's cliffhanger. Liv held out Mrs Beaufort's tea. Pace took it from her and they both followed their elder in to the next room.

LIGHT/DARK

The Tambor house was not that big. Mrs Beaufort had heard everything they had said. And she didn't have her ear pressed to the wall.

A part of her was resistant to interfering with the interrogation in the kitchen and another knew that she had information that might prove valuable. Information that she and a few others had held on to.

Mrs Beaufort was weak and the darkness was constantly stroking her like a beloved pet. The pain in her chest had settled into a dull throb rather than the shooting daggers that had assaulted her earlier when she had found her friend stuck with brain matter to her hallway floor.

This was now a fight. She had an internal struggle that was more than her battle with *stable* angina. Mrs Beaufort had to wrestle with her shadow self to do what was right, no matter how much it hurt her, irrespective of the history she would have to dig up.

Maybe I was temporarily distracted. Maybe she was just tough. Maybe light will always defeat the dark. Maybe the shadowless Tambor/Dunham residence gave her an advantage. Whatever it was,

Mrs Beaufort forced herself from that seat. She broke free of her shackles and she marched to that kitchen doorway. She did not rest her weary body against the frame. She stood dead centre. An old but robust woman. The real Mrs Beaufort.

And she told *that* man, *that* ghost who flew back into town on a gust of wind and ash that it was *enough*.

She had something to say.

She was important to Hinton Hollow.

And he should shut up and listen.

RIPPLES

Three generations of Hinton Hollow sat in that living room.

'Mrs Beaufort, what are you not telling us?'

'It's time for you to be quiet, Mr Pace. There are things that are known in this town and there are things that only a privileged few can know.' She took a sip of her tea. 'This has been sitting on the side for a while, hasn't it, dear?' She directed her question to Liv Dunham, who was sat on the two-seater sofa with the detective. Mrs Beaufort was on Oz's leather recliner. Liv had always hated that chair. She nodded. A little embarrassed.

'Hinton Hollow is special. It is different from anywhere else. That is why we stay here. That is why we choose to walk. That is why we support one another through all manner of situations.'

Pace found her romanticising of the town somewhat sickly and confused.

'But we are not perfect. We have secrets and we have danger. I have grown up here with the power of the river. I have known the woods for over eighty years and I have been wary. Hinton Hollow is what it pledges to be, but nowhere and nobody is perfect. You can feel an evil on a nightly basis if you simply travel to our borders. The Split Aces club would be an excellent place to start.'

Pace made a mental note. The club was seldom mentioned by

people in The Hollow because it was viewed in the way Mrs Beaufort had expressed.

'On the other side of town, there is the Ablett business. You are right to be cautious of both men, but I do not believe they could have taken Oz. I know this makes you think of Julee, Detective.'

Liv looked at Pace who had dropped his own gaze to the floor. He did not like to discuss Julee with anyone, least of all her grandmother.

'Most of the community see the crossroads as the heart of our town. The bustle, the business, the sense of belonging. But that is not the case. We are the brain, the mind. We have built that part of the town ourselves. The woods are the heart. They pulsate with a presence. You can feel it. Everyone has felt it. The trees were here long before even I took my first step.'

'This all sounds very haunting but what does it have to do with Oscar Tambor? How does it help me find a man who shoots children in the face and chest?' Pace looked at his watch. As captivating as it was, Mrs Beaufort's story sounded like a children's cautionary tale. *Don't go into the woods or you'll get lost.*

'This is the fourth time I know of that something like this has happened. Somebody goes missing. They are taken. Then the evil presents itself to the town. It is followed by great winds and a storm.' Mrs Beaufort put a hand to her chest and closed her eyes.

'You think there is a pattern? That this keeps happening? You think that Julee leaving is somehow related to Oscar Tambor disappearing? I really don't have time for this.' Pace stood up. Liv was not so hasty in her judgment.

'Hinton Hollow is a pond. The woods are the spot where a stone has been dropped and we are all feeling the ripples.' Mrs Beaufort wasn't doing the best job of convincing the detective with her fable.

Liv saw the detective to the door.

'By the way, Mr Pace...' He turned around on the doorstep, even a few inches down he was taller than Liv Dunham. 'That last question. I wanted you to know that I never did anything to encourage Charles Ablett. And I never acted on any of his advances. I couldn't do that. And that is the truth.'

'Thank you, Liv. That is very helpful.'

'Really?'

'Really.'

He turned his back and headed back up the path to his car, pulling his coat together with one hand to protect his chest from the wind and the rain, which was now pummelling down on the town's roads and pavements.

Liv Dunham had told the detective exactly what he wanted to hear. She had never been with Charles.

And he knew that she was telling the truth.

Unlike Mrs Beaufort. Pace thought her talk about the Hinton Hollow woods was mumbo jumbo. Folklore. Urban legend.

Faith could be a good thing.

Blind faith was always evil.

KIDS CAN BE CRUEL

DAY FOUR TROUBLES
I was everywhere.
And it was exhausting.

The baby screamed close to lunchtime and Catherine Raymond did not care.

She cared that her child was crying, she simply had no concern for herself about being awake. Because that is how she had felt for the few weeks before: pissed off that she was conscious.

By no stretch was it everything she required but she felt incredibly refreshed. And that gave her the one thing she had been missing. The ability to cope. The small things that had been dragging her down – the tears, muddy footprints on the carpet, the never-ending mound of washing – would now pass her by, at least for a short while, and it would take a lot more to make her snap. She even smiled to herself.

She was sick of hearing all the stories of famous historical figures who lived on three hours of sleep each night and still managed to run a government or invade a country. *But did they do that with a newborn stuck to their chest?* She imagined that even those thoughtless comments wouldn't faze her *that* day.

'Shh shh shh,' she spoke softly, looking the little boy in the eyes, 'Mummy's here. It's okaaay. It's okay.'

Catherine dug her hands beneath her baby and scooped him towards her. She relaxed back in the chair and adjusted her top to start breastfeeding. She had tried and tried for months but could not get the hang of it.

The damn thing won't latch on. If he's that hungry... she had cursed the day before when trying it in the chair that had been specifically placed in the nursery for that very reason.

It had been the same with Ben. She just could not do it. She tried every day. Her husband seemed to think that she was doing it wrong and that it should be natural. All her friends had apparently found it that way.

So beautiful. So bonding.

It just made her feel guilty about wanting to give it up and resort to bottle-feeding.

I can work wonders with a feeling of inadequacy.

That Thursday, she tried it again. It didn't work. Her baby became frustrated and more agitated than he had when waking up with an empty stomach. On *that* Wednesday, she would have persisted to the point of madness then broken down, heated a bottle and wept at her maternal ineptitude.

It's surprising what a few uncomfortable hours of shut-eye can do.

She stood up with him and ambled into the kitchen, all the time shh-ing and talking in calming tones while she one-handedly prepared a bottle of warm formula to pacify and satisfy her son.

He was quiet with the milk. Catherine studied his face, pulling out all the features that were clearly from her side of the family. She was looking to see if he was like his big brother but they seemed very different. He would grow into his features.

She placed him on the rug with some colourful, stimulating toys and sat back in the chair to watch him. She almost felt good. Relieved, even. Maybe it was a turning point for her. She was finally getting hold of the situation. Reclaiming a little bit of herself. Small victories.

Catherine reached down the side of the chair and picked up the laptop that had been charging. She went online, purchased two tickets to the film that Ben wanted to see – apparently *everybody* else had already seen it – and she printed them off.

She was going to take them with her when she picked Ben up. Show him that she meant what she said and that she could keep her promises. She pulled the warm sheets of paper from the printer, which was hidden, wirelessly, in the cupboard beneath the stairs, folded them and placed them in her bag so that she wouldn't forget them.

With her head cocked to the side, Catherine glanced down at her son. His cheeks were red for a moment but faded back to their normal colour. He grinned, cheekily. She knew what that meant before the smell found its way up to her height.

'You did that on purpose, didn't you?' She laughed. She actually laughed. 'Didn't you, little man?' And she rubbed his stomach affectionately like he'd just done something incredibly adorable.

Her second child may have come as a complete shock to her. She may have been *done at one, thank you very much*. The poor child may have been referred to as *a mistake* on occasion. But it did not mean that she loved him any less than she should, any less than Ben.

She was a mother.

And, *that* day, after a decent nap and another failed breastfeeding attempt, she felt unbelievably lucky.

NOBODY

Nathan Hadley wanted to leave Hinton Hollow. He wasn't feeling himself.

The night before had been fuelled with anger and alcohol. He tried to tell himself that he couldn't remember it all but that was a lie. He knew what had happened but it hadn't given him the sense of closure he had been expecting.

He had been given a day's grace due to the extreme nature of the crime but he was expected to go and visit the morgue. See the bodies. Say goodbye? He wasn't entirely sure. He was certain that he did not want to see his family in that way again. He'd caught a glimpse of each of them on the pavement of Stanhope Road but it had been Aaron that had stuck with him. Perhaps because his face was still intact. It could have been that he seemed so small as a dead boy because he was so much larger while alive.

Deaths had to be registered and arrangements made for a service that the entire town would, no doubt, want to attend. Though the funeral parlour was unusually busy that week and Father Salis would probably have to check his diary.

Nathan wasn't even sure he wanted anything at the Church of the Good Shepherd but that is what everyone in Hinton Hollow would be expecting. Rachel would want him to stand his ground.

But all he wanted was to get out. Get away, if only for a while. He wondered how Owen Brady was handling his situation. They had never been that close and it was uncomfortable to think that they could somehow be united through a patch of such unholy common ground.

He threw some clothes into a bag. Nothing that he'd thought about. A few things from each drawer and a spare pair of shoes. He didn't know where he would go or even if he would; it was just something to do that didn't involve facing up to the life he had been left with.

He felt alone. For a town that was so small and had such a close community, Nathan Hadley could think of nobody that he could call on. There was nobody around him that could help. He had nobody. He had nothing.

DAMN FINE COFFEE

'Come on, Charles. This is getting ridiculous now. It's lunchtime and you're still not here. I really don't care who is in your bed or how good she is, you need to slap her on the backside and tell her to get out because you have to get to work.'

Roger Ablett was talking on his mobile phone as he walked to his car. It was the sixth message he'd left for his brother that day.

'I've had to leave Ellie in charge of the shop for an hour while I get out for a bite to eat. Only God knows if it'll still be there by the time I get back. But you'd bloody better be. I don't care if the building is on fire, I want you at your desk making calls. That new detective is an easy rental, so close it down.'

He stopped at the end of the parade and rubbed his chest. He was slightly out of breath because he'd been walking and talking at the same time. It wasn't easy for a man whose heart wore cholesterol like a mink coat.

'I'll be at RD's for the next hour. I'd better see you after that.'

He hung up the phone and took a few huffs, and made a few puffs. To his left was the side of the building. On a concrete slab there sat hundreds of spitty, little cigarette butts that the ignorant smokers, like Ellie, had discarded without a care.

He tutted loudly then walked over to the spot he referred to as *cancer corner,* though it wasn't really a corner at all.

On the floor beside the orange tubes, some kissed by red lips, was the green mug from his kitchen. There was coffee-drenched tobacco floating at the bottom. He recognised it immediately as Detective Sergeant Pace's drink. From its location, he knew that he had been speaking with Ellie Frith.

CHEAP SHOTS

Kids can be cruel. And Ben 'The Bully' Raymond was, unusually, on the receiving end of the punishment that lunchtime.

The atmosphere had been odd at school all day. Classes were half empty and felt colder as a result. His thoughts even echoed. He felt that everything was aimed at him. The teachers were only looking at him. All the kids were avoiding eye contact with *him*. Like he had been the one who killed the Hadleys.

He'd kept himself to himself during the first break time. He'd told his mother that he'd stay out of trouble and the easiest way to do that was to be nowhere near anybody. That was his plan.

**THREE THINGS THAT WOULD
THWART THAT PLAN**
A tennis ball.
Passive-aggressive gay bashing.
Words about his mother.

But he couldn't do that for an entire hour. Eating the lunch his mum had packed took up fifteen minutes of his time – he even ate the satsuma that he didn't want – but two of his four minions had been made to come to school *that* day just as he had. He could see them talking by the fence. One of them had a tennis ball in his hands.

Ben made his way over sheepishly, avoiding the glare of other children, older and younger. His two *friends* caught a glimpse of him heading in their direction. The tennis ball disappeared inside a coat pocket.

'Hey, guys. What's going on?' Ben trembled. He didn't want to and that made it even more obvious.

'Hello, killer,' Dean – the taller of the two – said, raising his eyebrows. The smaller boy laughed. Ben knew that laugh. He'd heard it before. Boys around him that were scared, plumping up his ego though his comments held little true humour in their eyes.

'Come on, Dean. That's not right.' Ben took the higher ground.

'What's wrong, killer,' he nudged his little sidekick as he uttered the insult once more, 'not feeling so tough today?'

Dean pushed Ben in the chest. It hurt. Ben didn't fall over but he stepped backward. He did not retaliate. At first.

'No girls to push around today, eh?'

Ben felt bad about that immediately after, but Jess'd had a way of pushing his buttons.

It took everything he had to walk away, his head hung low.

Dean called after him. 'Yeah, you walk off. We all saw you get decked by that gay-boy's son, Benjy. Wouldn't want that happening again.' He laughed, not realising that he had inadvertently just called his own father homosexual.

This was not me at work. It was not the woods whispering ideas into Dean's head – I could not go near the children, I could not touch them directly. Dean was just a little shit who saw an opportunity not to be pushed around any more. Instead, he would be the one who did the pushing.

And that's exactly what he did. With Ben's back turned, Dean took a charge and floored him with a cheap shot from behind. Ben heard the entire playground fall silent. The rain had stopped for a while but had returned very lightly. He stood up and brushed himself down. He wanted to cry but wouldn't give Dean the satisfaction. Hinton Hollow kids were brave.

No. He would do as his mother said. Stay out of trouble. It was only another day of school and then it would be the weekend. She was going to take him to the cinema. If he could just keep walking away.

'What's wrong, Ben-der? Being a good boy for Mummy?' He laughed again. Ben wanted to run away but that wouldn't work either. 'My mum said that baby's not even your brother because your mum was *doing it* with the estate agent.' He signalled for his associate to join in the mockery.

Ben ran.

But not away.

He turned and bolted towards Dean the Dickhead. He watched Dean's face change from ridicule to shock but there was no time for it to evolve into realisation before the back of his head hit the playground floor.

Ben wasted no time scrambling onto Dean, putting his weight on his chest and unleashing punch after punch. He hit Dean in the face for saying that his brother wasn't his brother and he hit him again for spreading lies about his mum. But he kept hitting him and hitting him because hc knew that there was no way he was going to be going to the cinema with his mother on the weekend.

He was only doing what Aaron Hadley had done for his sister the day before. But nobody would ever call Ben Raymond a *hero*.

PART OF THE CULT

Pace felt bad about sending RD on a wild goose chase for the old witch and decided to swing by his café on the way home.

He was greeted with what was starting to become a customary head-turn. He wondered whether they did that for everyone or just him. Maybe it wore off over time.

RD was behind the counter where he belonged and began pouring a black coffee at the sight of his detective friend. It was the one place in Hinton Hollow where Pace felt *local*. Like maybe he belonged. Maybe one day he would turn around when somebody walked in to RD's. Part of the cult.

His hands were held out in submission as he approached the gentle bear of a man.

'I'm so sorry to give you the runaround, RD. I dropped her off and watched her go in but...'

'She's a slippery customer,' he smiled, lifting that grey beard to his ears. 'Mrs Beaufort is beyond us in years and even further in determination, my boy. I wouldn't hold on to it for too long.' He pushed the coffee towards Pace.

'I'll pay for this one,' Pace confirmed.

'You're damn right you will.'

RD turned his back and walked away. He wasn't angry with Pace, in fact, he was grinning as he headed to the kitchen. Pace could tell. Even from behind. He saw the beard lift then fall.

The bell rang as the door opened and Pace found himself as part of the herd, craning his neck to view the person that had just walked in.

So, it never wears off.

He was one of them.

The customer was a regular. Everybody turned back to their teas and cakes and the chatter recommenced. It was only Roger Ablett on his daily fat-intake mission. Pace gave the man a polite upward tilt of the head then turned back to his too-hot black coffee.

Seconds later, Ablett was slapping Pace on the back like they were old college pals.

'Good to see you again, Detective.'

'Mr Ablett.' He continued to stare into his coffee, wishing it to cool so that he could leave. He had to debrief Anderson.

Pace pulled his phone from his pocket to check the time, forgetting that it was out of battery. The realisation put him back into the foul mood he'd been in at Liv Dunham's house.

'Ellie told me that you had a chat with her, too.'

She hadn't.

'I'm talking to everybody in town. There's no point in drawing the lines if you're not going to fill them with a little colour.'

'Quite.' Ablett responded as though he knew what Pace was talking about and agreed with him. He was getting impatient about his lunch order, though.

'I'm actually looking to speak with your brother,' Pace offered.

'You and me both, Mr Pace.'

Neither man would look at the other. Pace left his gaze in the mug and Ablett's was stuck on the door that RD eventually emerged from.

'I drove by his house but there was no answer. If you hear from him then I would be very grateful if you'd let him know that I have a few questions for him.'

'Just to add a little colour?' Roger Ablett asked, not so secretly proud of the comment.

'Quite,' Pace responded, still not looking at the fat estate agent.

'Sorry for the wait, Roger,' RD apologised. 'Usual?'

'With chocolate milkshake today. I need the sugar, it's been a long morning.'

He did not need the sugar.

Ablett bid both men adieu and found himself a table where he read the local paper until his burger arrived.

RD rolled his eyes so that Pace could see. It seemed the Abletts had a reputation for annoyance.

'Did you find her?' RD asked, his voice quieter, his eyes looking towards Ablett's open ear.

'Sorry.'

'Mrs Beaufort.' He spoke through gritted teeth, his lips moving slightly at the start of each word.

'Oh, yes. She was at Liv Dunham's house, you know her?'

'She walked there?' He was only concerned about Mrs Beaufort.

'Apparently.'

'Never ceases to amaze me. In hospital one day, attending to her civic duties the next. She needs to slow down. I'm sure Liv and Oz have everything in hand by now.'

Pace slid a couple of pound coins across the counter and thanked RD for the coffee. Before he left, RD told him that there was a town wedding on the weekend and that he needed to catch the man with the gun before more funerals were booked into the Good Shepherd.

Roger Ablett's ears pricked up.

Pace said that he was close. He just needed a little more evidence.

RD smiled at Pace.

Ablett smiled to himself.

TRAMP/COW

Liv Dunham was the only other person in Hinton Hollow to witness the colder side of Mrs Beaufort. And all Liv did was offer to give her a lift back to Rock-a-Buy.

She transformed from sweet old lady with captivating tales of yesteryear to caustic old hag with fangs for dentures.

'I'm perfectly capable of looking after myself, Ms Dunham. You should only be worrying about your own problems,' she bit. It was the shadow Beaufort speaking.

The real Mrs Beaufort broke through at the sight of the innocent teacher's expression and apologised immediately.

'I'm sorry, Liv, dear. It's just that everybody has been treating me like some kind of invalid since I left the hospital. They think I've one foot in the grave. Handling me with kid gloves. And with everything that's happening in the town...' She trailed off as though thinking of the horrors that threatened to smite the good Hollow name forever.

'It's okay. We're all on edge. I don't even know how you've managed to keep it together for so long,' Liv backtracked, feigning a smile that was not reciprocated.

'Be a dear and fetch me a glass of water before I go.'

Liv stood up and went into the kitchen, feeling even more battered than she had when she awoke that morning. While she was out of the room, Mrs Beaufort popped another couple of the pills she already felt completely reliant on and waited for the liquid she intended to wash them down with.

At the front door, Liv poked gently one more time.

'It's only spitting now but the sky looks as though it's about to open up. It's a long walk back to the crossroads.'

'A little rain never hurt anyone. Now you get back inside and wait for Oz. He's coming back, you know?' Mrs Beaufort held Liv's arm in her hand for what felt like a genuinely tender moment.

'I know,' Liv said to Mrs Beaufort. And then, 'I know,' again to herself.

Naive little tramp, Mrs Beaufort's mind ticked, as I stroked her back gently.

Meddling old cow, thought Liv as she closed the door on the rain. They were words that never would have crossed her mind before that day, but she had allowed me to cross her threshold. I had sat on her couch and stood in her kitchen. It was early so the changes were subtle. But changes they indeed were. Nobody was escaping.

She found her mind was racing. Not with thoughts of where Oz could be or whether it was his voice or not on the phone, but questions. So many questions.

How does she know that he will come back?

What was that story about the woods being the heart of the town?

Should I cancel the band and the flowers?

Should I call Father Salis?

Why did the detective bring up Charles Ablett? How could he possibly know anything?

Liv was in the hall, pondering, when her phone started to ring.

Both Liv and her shadow ignored the call.

The caller withheld their number.

SO CLOSE

'Do you have something that can charge this?' Pace held his mobile phone aloft as he walked into Hinton Hollow Police Station. That was his greeting to Constable Lynch.

'Yes, sir,' Lynch responded awkwardly, wondering whether to enter into conversation. Perhaps warn the detective that Anderson had been trying to contact him.

Pace slid the phone across the front desk as though the gesture were enough of an explanation. Lynch caught it, opened a drawer, took out a tangled wire and plugged it into the bottom of the phone.

'Anderson out back?' Pace wasn't really asking, he was simply keeping things flowing. He had momentum now.

'As always,' Lynch spoke under his breath. Pace took it as a remark against the inspector rather than himself.

Pace didn't even knock. He was hoping to catch Anderson in the middle of some lurid act with the local councillor. What an advantage it would be to walk in and find Anderson's giant pubic mound tickling the nose of Ms Hayes as she gobbled down another length of his lawful package.

Anderson was alone at his desk.

As always.

'Well look who finally decided to bloody show up at work.' The chief did not stand.

'I've been out gathering evidence.' He had to hold his tongue, play the game a little.

'Really? Word has it you've been down having coffee with Roger bloody Ablett.'

Fuck. I left there about three minutes ago. How did word get up the hill so fast? It was a Hinton Hollow mystery he had no time for at that moment.

'Find out anything more about May Tambor?' Pace tried to change the subject.

'A ton of messages on her answering machine from Liv Dunham. Nothing yet on possible time of death but the oldest message is from a few days ago and the rate of decomposition would back that up. It's bloody horrible. Such a good woman. Left to rot.' He shook his head in apparent disgust.

'I know you've probably been trying to get hold of me but my shitty phone died. Lynch is out front giving it a nuke now.'

'I don't care about your fucking phone, I want to know what you know.'

Pace explained everything he'd found that morning and how his prime suspect was Charles Ablett. He felt that Ablett was a trophy collector and that his trophies came in the form of unavailable women. He wanted Faith Brady and Rachel Hadley checked for any signs that Ablett had been with them or near them on the day that they died. He believed that it was Ablett's way of either ending the relationship or it was his response to a woman ending it before he could get the move in himself.

Anderson's eyes said he didn't quite buy it.

Pace went on to talk about the disappearance of Oscar Tambor and, if the coroner's guess was accurate, he probably went missing the same time that May Tambor was shot. Perhaps May witnessed her son being taken and was removed from the equation.

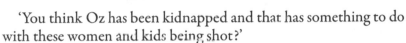

So close, detective.
Details are easier to come by than motive.

'You think Oz has been kidnapped and that has something to do with these women and kids being shot?'

'I think that Liv Dunham is the ultimate prize so the ante has been raised. These types of killers, their hunger becomes deeper and more insatiable, and the crime has to match that feeling. Things often escalate.' He was explaining things that he expected an inspector to be fully aware of already.

'All sounds a bit farfetched to me. Like some of the pieces of the puzzle have been forced into place.' It was a rare sight to see Anderson so pensive and critical. And professional.

'It's all I've got to go on. This guy is leaving nothing behind. We're being deliberately pointed towards the kids, and I think it's all to do with the mothers.'

Right again, Detective.

Nothing was said while Anderson mulled the notion over.

'Or we could go with Mrs Beaufort's theory that the fucking trees are doing it.' Pace ran a hand through his hair and bit back the want to call the old lady something derogatory and profane.

'Oh, that old thing.'

For a second, Pace thought his inspector was talking about Mrs Beaufort.

'You know about that?'

'It's Hinton Hollow lore. Nobody really believes it. The woods are possessed with the spirits of those who have gone missing from the town. Blah, blah, blah.' Pace pictured Julee Beaufort. 'Supernatural bullshit. Great fodder for a cub-scout jamboree but no place in a police investigation, of course.'

'Of course.' They finally agreed on something.

'So, as I see it, we have two theories. Either this guy is after the kids for some reason or he's after the mothers for jilting or being jilted.'

'I think that's a pretty coarse summary but I guess it's what we have.'

'Then let's plan for the worst.'

NOTHING LEFT

The canopy was too dense for the rain to penetrate, so the car stayed relatively dry. But Oz could hear it pattering high above him. It was soothing. It sounded similar to the way raindrops hit the roof of his and Liv's conservatory. They would often just sit out there reading, the weather fading into a hum of delicate white noise.

It brought back childhood memories of caravan holidays to the south coast with his mother and father. He'd lie back on his bed – that had been converted so effortlessly from the dining room table – place his hands behind his head and look up into a sky he could not really see.

He was curled into a ball underneath a long coat. There wasn't much room in the boot but Oz managed to manoeuvre himself onto his back, the coat still draped across him, and look up into the blackness, imagining the sky beyond.

For that moment, he felt like a child again. Free. Honest. He opened his mouth to catch the falling raindrops.

He thought about Liv in their conservatory, reading one of her *classics*. And he wondered whether she was thinking of him at that very moment.

She wasn't. She was thinking of everything but him. Questions bouncing around her mind like a racquetball. She was thinking of Charles Ablett and Mrs Beaufort and Detective Sergeant Pace.

Oz's stomach rumbled. He pictured his father trying to light the barbecue outside their caravan and he wished he could speak with him at *that* moment. He'd know what to do to get out of this mess. But all he had left was the irritating answering machine message that his mother refused to let go of.

He'd have given anything to hear that play one more time.

Oz felt around the boot over his left shoulder until he located the rustling carrier bag. He reached inside and counted. Only three biscuits left. He'd been munching away at them without realising. But he was so hungry.

NUTRITIONAL VALUE OF
MAY TAMBOR'S BISCUITS
Calories – 57
Carbohydrates – 7.5g
Fat – 2.6g
Protein – 0.9g
Fibre – 0g

Soon, there would be nothing left.

DAMAGED

The atmosphere in the Brady home was delicate.

Michael had gone to his room to lie down for a while. The things he had endured that week were taking their toll.

But at least he had time. He'd heal enough that the emotional scar tissue would hold together sufficiently for him not to have to battle through each day. He'd be able to accept what had happened and live with the hurt.

But Owen was damaged.

And darkness finds the cracks easier than light.

He descended the stairs languidly, hitting every possible creaking step, and was greeted in the downstairs hallway by Andrea Day, the family liaison officer assigned to the Bradys, whose professional conduct was waning with every minute that passed.

I LOOKED INSIDE ANDREA DAY
Sexual perversion.
Depression.
Separation anxiety.

IT MADE ME WONDER
What has become of people, of the human race?
Was this always here or have you created it?

She stopped him and asked how he was holding up. He shrugged and nodded his head as though he could handle things, he was getting there. But he wasn't. He was bottling everything up because he thought that was the best thing to do. It wasn't about him, it was about Michael.

He tried to walk past her to the kitchen. She blocked him. He just wanted to make a cup of tea. Her left hand eased him towards the wall. She was stood uncomfortably close to Owen Brady.

'You have to let some of it out, Owen. You have to allow yourself to feel.' She spoke softly but assertively, her shoulder pushed into his chest to pin him to the wall, her voice grazing the side of his face as it made its way to tickling his ear.

She reached into his trousers and gripped tightly.

He didn't try to stop her.

At first she moved up and down until she sensed *it* growing in her hand. Then she moved forward and back. Forward and back. Her hand was beating against her own leg with each tug.

Neither of them said a word as it happened. Andrea breathed at the side of Owen's face, his head was tilted back and looking up the stairs towards his grieving son's bedroom. Her hand was slapping alternately between their two bodies, keeping a rhythm with the falling rain.

She moved her hand faster and faster, eventually twisting herself around so that her back was pushed firmly against Owen Brady's chest. He felt weak but alive. There but somewhere else entirely.

The broken man finally ejaculated with a restrained grunt. His depressed load hit the laminate floor, at first, with vigour, then less with each pulse, ending with a dribble that was more reflective of his demeanour.

The family liaison officer left him there without a word and walked to the kitchen. She clicked the kettle on. Owen's head dropped in shame and relief but she had been right. There was that moment, just before orgasm, where he thought of nothing. Everything was blank. A moment of purity. It wasn't long but it was long enough.

He looked at the stranger in his kitchen then up towards his boy's room. He was no longer Owen Brady and she was not Andrea Day. It was spreading throughout the town. And it couldn't go on like this much longer.

Hinton Hollow was dying.

CALLING THE SHOTS

'I think we can rule out the secondary school,' Anderson said with some degree of certainty in his voice.

Pace tried again, in vain, to explain that two vaguely similar killings did not make a pattern. Just because the Brady kid and the Hadley children were not of that age, it did not mean the murderer was gunning only for mothers of infants or juniors. They had to protect all of the children in the area.

'Well, with the May Tambor discovery, we are decidedly short on legs around here.' Anderson's tone seemed to suggest that this was an adequate reason for his proposal.

'Councilwoman Hayes only stands to lose her political life if this goes wrong. She'll get another shot. There's always reality TV or a tell-all book deal or motivational speaking to fall back on. These kids, these mothers, they don't get a second chance.'

'Which school, Detective?' Anderson was ignoring the jibe at his lady friend.

It was postulation but Pace held a finger to the wind and opted for Hinton Hollow Primary School. He explained, sarcastically, that, if a pattern could be drawn up from the two shootings, it might be a fair guess that the killer was alternating between the schools. He envisaged Stanhope C of E as *too hot* after yesterday.

Though the killer may want to return to the scene of that crime. It would also be a decent bluff, if he thought the authorities were following his pattern, to take a shot at the school they were not expecting him to go back to.

Then there was the risk of the double bluff. With only two details, it was hard to draw anything more than a line, let alone a pattern.

'But that is conjecture based on non-reality, sir. We can't try to second-guess this guy. Not at this stage. We don't have enough. And what about May Tambor? How does she fit into all of this? We can't watch everybody's house, too. We need to call on the sense of civic decency in this town to watch out for one another on that front.'

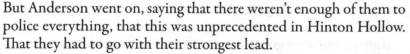

A TRUTH ABOUT PACE
He was right.
He'd been right all along.

But Anderson went on, saying that there weren't enough of them to police everything, that this was unprecedented in Hinton Hollow. That they had to go with their strongest lead.

'Pull some support from Reading or Oxford. They've got fuck all going on there. Six men. That's all we need. Two at each school.'

'I'll try. Until then, you need to get to Hinton Hollow Primary and keep your eyes open.'

Anderson thought that was the end of it.

'No way. That's not good enough. That is not, in any way, planning for the worst.'

'I beg your...'

'Listen.' Pace stepped forward as he interrupted. 'There are three of us here right now. We could pull Reynolds in, I'm sure. It isn't going to matter if somebody's cat is stuck up a fucking tree for an extra twenty minutes or a few milk bottles have gone missing from someone else's doorstep.'

The chief was completely attentive. He saw something in those grey, flickering embers that passed for Pace's eyes.

'If the secondary school is the least of our worries, we send Lynch to stand watch over there. Call Reynolds and get him to assist. I'm sure that they can handle zero action between them. If Hinton Hollow Primary is, indeed, our best shot, I will go there. That leaves you to keep vigil over on Stanhope Road. If we get the back-up, great. If we don't, at least there is a presence. Take a car with you so that it can be seen. It might just be enough to ward this psycho off for one more day while we figure a few things out.'

Inspector Anderson was not entirely pleased that Pace seemed to be calling all the shots and he was still annoyed at the swipe he'd taken at Councilwoman Hayes. But he couldn't knock the city detective's experience in matters far worse than his small town had ever seen.

He nodded then twirled a pointed finger, instructing Pace to turn around and leave. It was a small way of exerting his authority.

Pace did as he was required. He heard his chief on the phone to another station, calling for extra manpower.

They'd need it.

The schools were going to kick out in a couple of hours.

PERSISTENTLY WAYWARD BEHAVIOUR

'Hello?'

'Hi, Margot. It's Catherine. Catherine Raymond.'

Catherine did not like Margot. At all.

'Oh, Catherine. Hi. How are you? Terrible story about the Hadleys, don't you think?'

It was that kind of greeting, it really summed up the kind of person that Margot Doyle was. Fake and vacuous. Unsympathetic to such a degree that she seemed completely removed from reality. And she loved to talk. To everybody. About everything.

Catherine wouldn't have even bothered if Steph hadn't mentioned it that morning at the school gates. No doubt Steph would have nudged Margot about expecting a call so if Catherine hadn't phoned, the mills on Mount Gossip would be spinning a wonderfully elaborate fabrication about her and her stuck-up ways.

Sometimes in life it's easier to sit in the shit with others and lie than it is to step around them and keep your feet clean.

'Steph mentioned that a few of the mums had got together to form safety groups to walk the kids home.' Catherine did not want to enter into a conversation about Rachel Hadley, she thought it was in exceptionally poor taste to even bring it up. She was feeling bad about making Ben go to school, but the strength she had gained from her rest convinced her it had been the correct decision.

'Oh yes. It's just so daunting. Immy and Tam are already tagging along so you should jump in our group to make a foursome.' Catherine could hear the fake smile over the phone.

'Thanks.'

'No problem. How are you feeling with the new baby?'

'Well, he's not so new any more. I'm still a little frazzled, but hitting that six-week turn.' Catherine didn't want to say too much because Margot had a gift for fiction. Margot had already turned that one sentence into *deluded and finding it impossible to cope with two children*.

'It's always harder when you're outnumbered.'

She couldn't listen to any more of Margot's clichés.

'I think I can hear him in the other room now. Will need feeding again. Got to dash. I'll meet you at the gates after school. See you then.' And she put the phone down, she'd already taken the receiver away from her face mid-sentence.

On the floor beside her feet, the six-week-old was quietly and contently cooing.

'Now you're quiet. Couldn't even muster up a few tears to help your mum out.' She smiled at him. She was happy. And, though it had started to rain quite heavily, she was looking forward to walking down Stanhope Road to pick Ben up from school.

THE PERFECT DISTRACTION

It ran like clockwork. And many animals were harmed in its making.

Like always, it began with a delivery.

The blue, dented truck pulled in around forty-five minutes after Darren had arrived for work. In the hot weather, some cows are exhausted or sick by the time they reach slaughter. When it's cold, they can stick to the sides of the metal transport and have to be prised away. That day in Hinton Hollow, the weather was cold but not freezing. It was wet and the storm was well under way.

The animals were meant to be checked for stress but they were not. The workers find it hard to care for something that is about to die, anyway. And that level of care only worsens the longer they perform their killing duties.

Any cow that is sick or limp or dead is dragged out by a rope that is tied around its legs.

This was not the delivery Darren was waiting for.

He performed his duties, adding to the container of cow skulls and eyeballs.

TWO THINGS HAPPEN WHEN PEOPLE HEAR SOMETHING LIKE THIS
At first, they are disgusted at the treatment of animals.
Later, they eat meat.
This approach does not work in a world ruled by apathy and privilege.

Next it was lunch.

Then came the visit.

The new recruit was being shown around the place. It wasn't uncommon for them to throw up or even pass out. The scent of the faeces alone never left the place. Animals under stress tend to defecate. When living things die, they shit. You could see it on the new guy's face, and that was before he saw all the blood.

That's when the pigs arrived.

The rookie serial livestock killer was the perfect distraction.

Darren went out as the truck arrived and slipped the driver some money. To keep one back. Not a big one, and not one of the lame ones, either. There'd be no fun in chasing that. Just one that he could drag to his car, throw into the boot and tie its feet together.

And that is exactly what happened.

While the new recruit threw up on the stairs and old colleagues chaperoned some screaming pigs towards a brutal death their eventual consumers traded off against the promise of a wholesome existence while alive, Darren ran off with a pig, put it into his boot, tied its feet together and drove it back to his house.

By the time he returned to the abattoir, the kids had already been kicked out of school and nobody had even noticed he was gone.

I only had a light hand on his shoulder that day.

The rest was all Darren.

A SQUEEZE

Ellie Frith was alone in the Ablett and Ablett office when Roger returned, punching himself in the chest as he always did after one of his red-meat feasts.

'That lazy, good-for-nothing brother of mine still not here?'

'Just little old me,' she chirped, her new devil-may-care attitude now with some added devil.

Roger lowered himself back into his brother's chair and logged in to his computer. Twenty-three new emails including one concerning an offer for the riverfront property in Twaincroft Hill. He rubbed his chubby mitts together then used them to shield his mouth as he coughed.

'I saw Detective Pace at the diner. Said he'd had a nice chat with you after he left.'

'Not sure whether I'd call it *nice*.' She didn't look directly at him. 'Seemed very interested in Charles, though.' She glanced quickly around the side of her screen but Roger was flicking through his emails.

'And I'm sure you were nothing but complimentary, Ellie.'

'I was honest, Roger. I only told him what a hundred other people in town could've told him.' She was brazen and confident in her disregard.

I had them all in my hand.

'Mmm hmm.'

That was all he said.

If he was honest, the business ran more smoothly without the presence of Charles. He was a distraction. It would probably be best if his brother did not turn up at all.

As he thought that, I reached into his heart and squeezed.

MERELY A PRECAUTION

Not everybody in Hinton Hollow was aware of Detective Sergeant Pace. Even those who had known him in his younger years would not recognise the man he had become.

He pulled up in the residential area between Hinton Hollow Primary School and the park where Jacob Brady had been murdered. There were hundreds of flowers decorating the pathway and tied to the fence next to the swings. Pace never understood the idea of giving a woman flowers. For him, they always signified death. Untimely death.

Pace was still using his unmarked car, though he had advised Anderson to be more conspicuous with his choice of vehicle. Pace did not need to advertise his presence, his being there was enough. He could be felt.

Evil could always be felt.

His dishevelled, dark and enigmatic appearance shone brightly against the backdrop of the pastel bucolic scenes that epitomised Hinton Hollow life. A ghost traipsing through a Constable painting. He stood out. And for many of the mothers waiting at the gates, he seemed like a threat. A possible danger that clouded the safe passage of their children.

Of course, calling the local police station was useless because, thanks to Detective Sergeant Pace's idea, nobody was there to answer the phone. Nobody was there to help. But the mothers did as they were advised to do; they huddled together in packs, leaving nobody behind. They felt hunted. But, as long as there were no stragglers, as long as there was no weakness, they were sure they stood a decent chance of returning home safely.

Pace watched as women crowded together, some brave – or stupid – enough to let him know that they had spotted him lurking around the school perimeter.

I'm the good guy. I'm here to stop this. He told himself this, knowing it was only a half-truth.

Little. White. L i e s.

He rolled his eyes and walked towards the largest group. There were eight mothers crammed in a circle. He saw two of them freeze rigid as he edged closer.

Every mother acting in a different way.

Each of them with their own manner.

He couldn't know how any of them would react.

With caution, he reached into his pocket. One of the women – the one with the out-of-date hairstyle – opened her mouth slightly as though to scream. He clocked that. She was pre-empting his weapon.

Pace pulled the warrant card from his pocket and flicked it open. The woman with the open mouth managed to catch her scream before it was released.

'Detective Sergeant Pace,' he announced. Sixteen shoulders dropped their tension, and many more who were looking on. 'Good morning. It's great to see that you are taking the advice and being so vigilant.' He was speaking in his official voice.

But wouldn't it have been easier and more secure to keep your child from school and stay at home? the unofficial voice in his head countered.

THINGS THAT WOULD
HAVE BEEN EASIER
Being nice to your neighbour.
Not coveting someone else's partner.
Honouring your parents.
Not stealing.
Not killing.

'You think he's coming back?' The woman with the too-tight perm quivered.

'I'm merely here as a precaution, ma'am. A deterrent. You are right to be cautious. If there's anything you feel uncertain about, do not hesitate to inform me. I'll be right over there.' He pointed to the spot he had walked from. 'Good day, ladies. Get home quickly and together.'

He said nothing else and returned to his post. A spot he had decided would give him a great vantage point but also allowed anyone lurking to note his presence.

Word travelled around the groups of parents quickly that the man in the long coat was part of the local police detail. If there was one thing he could rely on in Hinton Hollow, it was the speed at which rumour moved.

Pace followed a strict routine as he surveyed the area, but his eyes kept being drawn back to the woods beyond the park. He had picked up on them that first day back in town when he was called out to the scene where Jacob Brady had been shot.

The rain, which had been stopping and starting all day, finally decided to rage.

It made Pace feel small.

And wrong.

And exposed.

GREY AREA

Reynolds and Lynch had the opposite issue to Pace. They were dressed in full uniform, patrolling the front fence of the secondary school – part of which fell on Twaincroft Hill land. There were very few parents waiting outside but several had made the effort to ensure the safety of their offspring.

The children were of an age where they could walk to school themselves or with a friend and, like certain members of the local constabulary, many of the parents had invented a pattern that did not exist and believed their kids were not in harm's way.

Reynolds was tired from another all-night shift and adrenaline was pulling him through what he was calling *protection detail*. Both constables had the best of intentions, and they hadn't simply fallen into their careers. They wanted to help. They wanted to serve and protect. The fact was, they just weren't set up for the scenario their town had found itself in. It was probably best that they were out of the way. As far from the *action* as possible.

They were useless.

That is the reason they were assigned to the secondary school, the outskirts of town. It was exactly where Detective Sergeant Pace needed and wanted them to be.

Out of the way.

The diluted edges of evil.

NOT LIKE A MOTHER

It took a few minutes to figure it out but Catherine Raymond eventually managed to fit the plastic rain cover over the pushchair. She had wrestled with it inside-out and back-to-front before eventually figuring out the correct position of the crumpled polygon, the eyelets on the elastic fitting perfectly over the protruding hooks on the frame.

Her baby was swaddled in a blanket and tucked within a fleece foot-muff before being covered by the shelter that would protect him from the rain. Catherine packed a bag with wipes and spare nappies and a change of clothes though there was no way she was going to unravel her child from his protective cocoon; the school was only a few minutes away. But mothers were supposed to be prepared.

She double-checked the pocket of her bag though she knew the printed cinema tickets were in there. She'd already checked twice. Then she closed the flap, tapped the leather and threw it over her shoulder. She was going to make things right. God knew she had been neglectful. She hadn't been herself for weeks. Her husband had been a stranger in that time, her eldest son, forgotten. And her new baby, a nuisance.

Catherine Raymond had been wanting to feel something. Joy at the new addition to her family. Relief. Pride in the pregnancy and the birth. But she had felt numb. Not like a woman. Not like a mother. But she was determined to get through this.

She was strong.

She would put everything back together the way it was before. Better than it was before.

HANDLE IT

Councilwoman Hayes sashayed into Hinton Hollow Police Station soaked in shade. Her heart touched with anxiety, her head filled with mischief. She locked the door behind her. Nobody was on the front desk. She laid her jacket over it and began to unbutton her blouse as she walked to the door behind. The clock on the wall said 14:55.

Twenty minutes before school finished.

Inspector Anderson had no luck with recruiting extra hands and was clearing away his things before leaving. He was hoping that Pace was right; if the man with the gun was going to attack another school, he would double-bluff and return to Hinton Hollow Primary. *Pace would be able to handle it*, he comforted himself.

F e a r.

The last thing he wanted was to be confronted by the killer himself. That is not the reason he had chosen the position in Hinton Hollow fifteen years before. That was not the way to cruise to retirement.

The man with the oversized moustache was so preoccupied with his own thoughts and the trepidation of fulfilling his job description that he did not notice his door was open and framed the silhouette of a woman, her right leg bent coyly, sexily, her blouse hanging open. Relaxed. Inviting. Enticing the officer into the absence of light.

'Bloody hell.' He was startled. 'That looks like an excellent idea but I'm not sure it's the time...'

'Is there ever a bad time?' She closed the door behind her and waited.

'Not usually, Anita, but I'm on my way to Stanhope School. Standing guard, so to speak.' He moved some stationery around his desk, trying to distract his own thoughts.

'You've got almost twenty minutes. It shouldn't be an issue. Take the car.'

Anderson wasn't sure what was annoying him more, the fact that she appeared to be making a comment on his sexual prowess or that yet another person was throwing orders his away and telling him how to travel around the town that he was in charge of protecting.

Or that Anita Hayes was walking towards him, her hands soft against her own skin, and he knew that he was going to do exactly what she told him to do.

Weakness everywhere.

SAFE WITH ONE

Stanhope Road was a circus. A lot of parents had made sure that they arrived at the school before the bell rang for the end of the day. The pathway was not wide enough for the herds of people hoping to escort their children back to the safety of their homes, many of them realising that community solidarity was too much like hard work. They were standing in the road just to be as close as they possibly could to the gate.

Catherine Raymond could see the gaggle from a few hundred yards away. Not a parent on that pavement was bothered by the rain pelting down on their heads. She picked out Margot's tousled red locks and, though it seemed like one large crowd, there was a clear segregation of friendship and social groups within the larger mob. Margot was stood with four other mothers, some with a younger child in tow, others without.

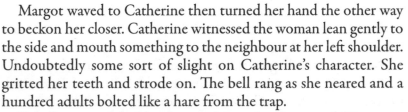

A FACT
The *only child* was keeping
their mother alive.

Margot waved to Catherine then turned her hand the other way to beckon her closer. Catherine witnessed the woman lean gently to the side and mouth something to the neighbour at her left shoulder. Undoubtedly some sort of slight on Catherine's character. She gritted her teeth and strode on. The bell rang as she neared and a hundred adults bolted like a hare from the trap.

Kids flew out of the blue door and into the playground. They were unaware of what was lurking in the shadows. The clouds above were black and ominous. Miles away, thunder was popping and crackling, heading towards The Hollow for a showdown with fate. It was time to go home.

Parents ushered their children out through the gates faster than a royal palace bomb scare. Catherine waited with her troupe for Ben, her hand on the side of her bag to protect the paper tickets from getting wet. She was smiling at the prospect of telling him all about it but was growing anxious as the crowd dissipated and the parents within her safety throng stared at her, agitated, because she was the only one left waiting.

They looked at their watches. They rubbed at the kids' shoulders as if to say *don't worry, we'll be going home soon.*

Then Ben's teacher appeared at the door and nodded resignedly towards Catherine.

'One sec. I won't be long,' Catherine said to nobody in particular.

Nobody – in particular – responded and she went in.

PROVOKER/PRINCESS

'Probably that little brat of hers,' Margot Doyle exclaimed. 'Always in trouble, that one.' Her son, Dean, nuzzled himself into his mother's leg and she rubbed his back affectionately.

Dean 'The Provoker' Doyle.

Dean 'your mum is a killer' Doyle.

'Mum, when are we going home?' he whined, wanting to get out of there before Mrs Raymond and her son emerged with information that would cast him in a bad – and accurate – light.

She stroked at her son's cheek. 'What've you done now?' she asked, looking at the graze near his eye.

'Nothing. I was in goal at lunchtime. Can we go now?'

'Soon. We'll go soon. We just have to wait for Mrs Raymond. Okay?' And she hugged him tighter into her leg.

Telling your daughter she is a princess sets her up for failure.

'Yes. We should wait,' said another mother.

'We should,' agreed a different friend, looking up at the darkening sky. Both women meaning that they should wait maybe a minute longer before they reassess the situation.

The playground was clearing faster than the sky could fill with dread. Seconds turned into minutes, or at least they felt that way.

'We don't know how long she's going to be. We could be stood out in the rain for ages.'

The insensitivity started pouring out of the circle before the door had swung shut behind Catherine Raymond. The wolves were making suggestions but it was up to Margot to make the final decision.

I hardly interfered.

This was who they were.

And, for all her failings, she hung on for longer than anyone expected.

'Just a couple more minutes,' she tried. She knew how it worked. If anything happened, it would be the Doyle name that suffered.

It was getting so dark that lights were turned on inside the school. There were now only four mothers left stranded and drowning in the downpour. Margot looked out onto Stanhope Road. There was no traffic and no people. Life had dispersed. The rain was now so heavy, looking over to the opposite side of the street was like watching a television that had lost its reception.

'Okay. We waited. I think we are all agreed that we stayed here to support Catherine but, let's face it, she's left us high and dry ... so to speak.' Nobody agreed but they also didn't disagree – leaving Margot entirely culpable should the decision result in a monumental blunder.

'Come on, Dean. Hold Mummy's hand.'

Dean 'Princess' Doyle.

She gripped her son firmly. 'Stick together, ladies. Don't fall behind. Let's get home.'

And that was it. They followed Margot like sheep. Poisonous, calculating, selfish sheep.

It wasn't until they were almost at the corner where they would all turn left off Stanhope Road that Margot really noticed the cut on Dean's lip.

'I fell,' he lied.

He protested it again and again until his mother pieced the jigsaw together.

It was at that moment that she stalled. She stopped. She wanted to turn back and give Catherine Raymond and her bastard son a piece of her mind and her mouth.

The other mothers were not as interested. They were still walking.

And Margot Doyle found herself languishing at the back of the flock.

A FISH IN THE PERCOLATOR

The baby was used to the shouting. The screaming. Sometimes, the swearing. It had always been a part of life. He'd become accustomed to the noise. Six months old and desensitised to despair.

His brother was taking another verbal beating. He couldn't do anything right. In trouble again. Little Charlie didn't understand why Ben was always spoken to in that way, and he didn't have to. He was warm in his pushchair and felt cuddled by the blanket that had been wrapped tightly around him, pinning his arms to his body and smothering his feet and legs.

The sound was muffled by the weather. Large droplets of water thrashing against the transparent cover that protected him from the wet. He couldn't see much of the outside. It was all sound and smell.

The sound of voices nearby.

Shouting from a distance.

Then a sound he had never heard before. That no baby should ever have to hear. That no person would wish to witness.

All he knew to do was cry.

ONE DAY

Ben wept. The vocal scaldings, he was used to. It was her disappointment, her sadness that he could not handle. It was his fault that she felt that way. He had broken his promise. Just one day. It was only one day. He couldn't stay out of trouble for one stupid day.

He'd tried to explain what had happened but his head teacher was not allowing him the opportunity to put across his side of the story. Dean Doyle had said some horrid things. Things Ben would never utter to another human being. Sure, he'd hit a few people and pushed some smaller kids around. He'd held his hands around Jess Hadley's throat but he was sorry about that. About all of it.

Ben Raymond was not a spiteful boy. He was simply bigger than his own body.

His mother had fought his corner in there. Though a visit to Mrs Blake's office was becoming an all-too-regular feature in the Raymonds' week, Catherine refused to let the school preach to her about bullying and not see that it was exactly what they were doing to her son.

How easy it was for them to pin a misdemeanour on Ben because he had a record of behavioural issues. How lazy of them to assume he was in the wrong. How negligent of them to allow Dean 'The Dick' Doyle to wander free while Ben 'The Bullied' Raymond was reprimanded without question. Guilty until proven innocent.

If anyone was going to chastise the kid, it was going to be his own mother.

And that is exactly what she did.

Ben couldn't understand every word his mother threw in his direction, she was even more high-pitched when angry. She swore as soon as they set foot on the playground, the blue door shutting heavily behind them. Then she lectured him and asked him questions that he knew she didn't really want an answer for and she waved some folded papers she had in her handbag in front of his face and the rain made them wet. And he cried. And she cried. And the rain made everything look pretty.

His mother desisted, eventually. Ben took up his position next to the pushchair, holding on to the frame and walking downheartedly beside his little brother. It was more difficult *that* day because the rain cover was blocking the part of the frame Ben usually held. He didn't want to complain. He'd done enough that day already.

On Stanhope Road, the only sound was the thwacking drumroll of water against concrete.

Then more shouting.

Ben could see people in the distance turning up the road he lived on, pushing babies like his mother and holding hands with their kids just like she used to. Mrs Doyle's red hair was unmistakeable. It throbbed against the greying backdrop of Roylake. She was waving her hand. That fuckwit, Dean, was by her side – acting the victim, no doubt.

Ben felt the pushchair slow then halt. His mother did not say a thing. He was afraid to turn around and look at her. He could not see the disappointment in her eyes again *that* day.

The little boy was readying himself for the confrontation with the

Doyles. And the aftermath where he would be made to suffer once more.

They were coming. Ben took a breath. His hair was flat against his head and rain was wriggling down his face, forming droplets that fell from the tip of his nose.

Then there was the noise.

Charlie started to cry next to him.

And he watched Mrs Doyle fall to the floor, dragging Dean down with her.

SPIT IT OUT

It had been playing on a loop all day, as these things so often do when no new evidence or information has appeared.

RD had been interviewed as a long-standing member of the community and local business owner. Salis and Anderson were two pillars of the community, ticking off the quota for law and religion, and Mrs Wallace was in the wrong place at the wrong time and was caught unaware and asked a question about being a parent and still taking children to school in the wake of such horrific events.

LITTLE HENRY WALLACE WAS BRAVE
But he was also a child.
A hundred miles from home.
Alone.
And he missed his mother.

So, when he saw her on the television screen as the news stories looped around again and again, the officer in charge spotted the kid's reaction to the sight of the woman and his suspicion was confirmed when Little Henry Wallace began to cry.

He wanted to go back to Hinton Hollow to his mother and brother and friends. The police officer worked on that to glean all the information required to take that poor boy home.

When the officer called Hinton Hollow police department, an out-of-breath Anderson picked up the phone.

'I'm in a rush, can you please spit it out.' The inspector could still make it in time for the end of school if he rushed the call and used one of the cars to drive down.

'His name is Henry Wallace. We found him a few days ago on a train, on his own, not talking. He says that one of the women on the news about your town is his mother. We would like to bring him home and sort this mess out. Does that cover it enough, Inspector?'

Henry felt bad about not keeping his promise. That's the kind of emotion that can let me in.

Everyone in Hinton Hollow was worried about the kids in school; I was worried about the one who was coming back.

EVERYTHING BETTER

Catherine Raymond had walked into the school office to find her son standing in front of Mrs Blake's desk, his hands by his side and his gaze to the floor. The look on the headmistress's face made Catherine want to punch her; she looked so smug, like she was proud to have dragged Catherine back in for another round of Ben bashing.

Blake just sat and watched while Catherine struggled backward through the door with her pushchair.

'What's going on? Are you all right, Ben?'

The little boy's eyes lit up. He could see his mother. Not the mother who had been shouting at him for the last few months, the one who was tired and couldn't be bothered to play or read or do puzzles with him. It was the other one. The mother he had before little Charlie came along. Ben straightened his back and puffed out his chest.

'He's fine, Mrs Raymond. Which is more than can be said for Dean Doyle who has a bruised eye and cut lip.' Mrs Blake seemed different from the level-headed teacher who had preached discipline only the previous day.

'Well, I wouldn't know because I can't see Dean Doyle or his mother in the room. They are waiting outside, though, if you'd like to bring them in.'

The mothers outside were already talking about leaving Catherine to rot.

'This is not about the Doyle boy, this is about Ben and his persistently wayward behaviour.'

Ben winced. He looked up at his mother with *sorry* in his eyes. He meant it; she could see that. She screwed up her mouth in a way that let him know she was angry but it wasn't with him. Her eyes were saying, *step aside, I've got this.*

Catherine Raymond put both hands on Mrs Blake's desk and leant forward. It looked a little threatening. It was supposed to. She catapulted words in the direction of the stunned teacher, asking her questions but not giving her the time or opportunity to answer them.

Where is the Doyle boy? Why is he not on trial, too? What provoked Ben to behave in such a way? Is he not afforded the right to defend himself? What kind of meeting was this? Were the teachers taking the easy way out rather than addressing the larger problem? Where did she get off marching a grown woman into the office for a slap on the wrist? Who did she think she was?

All the while, Catherine's thoughts were with the folded paper in her handbag. She so wanted to give it to Ben and this bitch was ruining everything. Why could he not have been good for just one day? Was it her fault? She should have kept him off school until things had settled in town.

The mood eventually settled into something more temperate. Catherine Raymond had supported her son. She had stuck up for him even though he had resorted to physical violence on another human being. She had shouted and cursed at the head of her son's school.

And it had not been the darkness at work.

She was simply being a mother.

The result of the meeting was that Ben would be placed on report. At the end of each day, his teacher would fill out a page in a book describing Ben's behaviour. It would teach him to take one day at a time, like he was a recovering alcoholic, or something. Catherine wasn't even sure he would last a day but she didn't say that out loud.

'And what happens with the other boy? Dean Doyle,' Catherine asked, wanting justice.

'Well, I think he'll be icing his eye and lip.'

'That's not what I meant.'

'I know what you meant, Mrs Raymond.'

'I guess I'll have a word with the Doyle family myself, as you clearly cannot do your job properly.' She regretted that comment immediately after saying it but she knew that she was about to leave and the frustration was building in her once again. This time it was heading towards Ben. He'd ruined everything.

Mrs Blake said nothing. *If you were doing your job properly as a mother then the school wouldn't be forced into the position of disciplining the little brat.* It was not a thought that usually entered her mind. She loved her job and usually had a real empathy for the more troubled children. But she'd had experiences *that* week. And they had changed her.

They were changing everybody.

'Fucking bitches,' Catherine cursed as she exited the school to find that her safety group had left her stranded in the pouring rain. The day was getting worse. She could feel herself sinking again.

'You couldn't just keep yourself to yourself for one day, could you, Ben? I have to get hauled into Mrs Blake's office. Again. What did Dean do that was so bad, eh?'

Ben went to open his mouth but was cut off.

'Oh, don't even bother. Let's just get home and then we'll sort this mess out.'

She wasn't annoyed at him. She was irritated that she'd been forced to behave in the manner she had. She supported her son even though he'd acted irrationally. Then Mrs Blake had still *won* somehow. And she'd been left alone and at risk by a bunch of selfish mothers. All she had wanted was to pick Ben up and surprise him with something nice. It was her way of saying *I'm sorry for being a shit mother recently, I'll make it up to you, I promise.*

Ben was crying. It made her feel worse. She'd held the reward out in front of his face then taken it away. *Look at what you could've had.* It was wrong. She shouldn't have done it. She just needed quiet. No more talking. No more shouting. No more confrontation.

Then she saw the bright red beacon that was the head of the woman who had deserted her and her boys because of a little drizzle.

Catherine Raymond stopped. Margot Doyle was dragging her goading little spawn towards her.

She looked down at her sons who were waiting patiently with her. Little Charlie, the baby who had surprised her with his unplanned existence, was obscured by the flecks of water that stuck to the surface of his rain cover. She could see the top of his head. Dark hair like his father. She swallowed.

Standing perfectly still next to the pushchair was Ben, her first-born, the one she had planned. He was waiting. He was demonstrating that he could be a good boy. Like he used to be. He'd just stopped crying, though, so he couldn't look at her. And he knew when she needed quiet so he didn't say anything. He didn't ask why they had stopped. He didn't comment on the Doyles moving closer and closer.

She reached a hand out to stroke him on the back of the head. Just that touch would have been enough to let Ben know that everything was all right, that his mother loved him, she would forgive him of anything.

Catherine withdrew her hand.

Then she closed her eyes.

DRIFTING

The man with the gun was standing in the rain. He had watched flocks of women and children being ushered out of the school towards the sanctity of home. But he had not panicked. There would be somebody. And they would be perfect. There was weakness. With mothers, there was always weakness.

The rain was washing the reality away from the scene playing out in front of his eyes. He was invisible to the four women packed closely together. The last rabble, kids huddled between them as though muscle and fat and bone and sheer force of will would be enough to protect them.

He watched. The woman with the bright-red hair stopped but the others did not. She was the lame or injured cub who limped behind its stronger siblings.

Then, to the left, another. Perhaps more feeble. He had seen her before. That day when he had approached Rachel Hadley. She was fast *that* day. She was strong.

He drank it all in, this man, this ordinary man. He soaked up the situation. And he knew he did not have much time. It would have to be now.

The mothers and children were walking towards each other. The one with the vibrant hair must have seen him cross the road because she started shouting but the storm swallowed her words.

He pushed his gun into the back of Catherine Raymond's head and told her to be quiet. He asked her the same question that he had asked Faith Brady. The same as he had asked Rachel Hadley.

She did not have to die; she simply had to make a choice.

He could not imagine that she would have him kill the baby. It would be the boy with his back turned to her. That was his guess. But, Faith Brady had chosen her youngest child. And, in his mind, Rachel Hadley was protecting herself, not her children, when she attacked him.

The mother with the gun poking at her skull did not answer him straight away. He could hear Margot Doyle in the background, still yelling and dragging her son by the arm.

Directly ahead of him, he saw this mother raise her right hand. He was wary. He recalled Rachel Hadley's angered reaction. But this woman was not going to strike him. She was reaching out to her son.

I knew she'd pick him, the gunman boasted to himself.

But she relented, pulling her hand back to her side. She closed her eyes. He could not see her face but that is what she did. And then she spoke.

'Take me.'

He pulled the trigger. He was shocked. He had hoped that a mother would eventually sacrifice herself but he hadn't truly believed that it was possible. Like so many in Hinton Hollow, he had lost his faith.

But there was no time for reflection. The rain cover was now peppered with a salsa of brain, skull and blood. The baby was crying. Further along Stanhope Road, the other mother, the lucky one, pulled her child to the ground to protect him.

The boy he thought was going to be chosen did not turn around straight away. He was still looking dead ahead. He was doing as his mother had asked. He was behaving.

By the time Ben Raymond looked over his shoulder, the man who had shot and killed his mother was merely a shadow in a long coat disappearing onto Oakmead.

Moments later, the town's police inspector came speeding along the road towards the carnage on his pushbike.

A baby wailed.

A boy, in shock, rummaged through a bag for a crumpled cinema ticket.

And a mother held hands with her town as they both died.

Drifting once more into faultless nothingness.

MOMENTS

This is how Inspector Anderson fucked up and got Catherine Raymond killed.

Anita Hayes approached the chief at his desk. He was fake tidying, trying hard to think with his head and not with his tightening balls. He had to get down to Stanhope Road and announce himself as present.

But the councilwoman seemed to glide across the room to him. Her blouse was unbuttoned and he could see enough skin to excite him. She approached him at the desk and pulled his head into her breasts – he was the perfect height while seated. She ruffled his hair. He tried to pull back but not too hard.

Hayes could feel Anderson's soft facial hair tickling her skin as he started to kiss her, his large hands reaching around and pressing into her back before unfastening her bra.

The scene ended painfully on the floor surrounded by broken wood. Her joke comments on his prowess had proven to be accurate. The desk had finally given way. The papers and stationery Anderson had been pretending to tidy had been swiped across the room just before he picked up the councillor and lay her on her back on his old desk.

It held her weight, her feet pointing to the ceiling, heels resting against Anderson's chest as he thrust inside the married woman. The pressure became too much near the end as his movements sped towards climax and he leant his body against his lover's to have more skin contact.

The flimsy wooden desk collapsed before Anderson had finished. The councilwoman and the inspector fell to the floor with a crack. Anita Hayes let out a yelp that was distinguishable from the noises of pleasure she had mustered for her man up to that point.

But that did not hold Anderson back. He continued to pump back and forth with his partner bruised and in obvious discomfort. When he finally rolled off the councilwoman, they both laughed.

Pleasure and pain. Not something they planned to make regular, but it had worked *that* time.

He still had time to get to Stanhope C of E.

'You see? Plenty of time left, you animal. Jump in the car, I'll close the door when I leave. Think I'm just going to lay here for a few more minutes.' She smiled and patted his thigh.

But it wasn't the impromptu, gloom-fuelled intercourse that had helped kill off the last light of Hinton Hollow. It was that message about the missing Wallace boy.

It hadn't been used in a long time. There had been no call for it. High-speed car chases through The Hollow were very rare; most crimes were not urgent enough. Besides, everybody in town walked. That is how it had always been in their little slice of heaven.

The useless lump of metal would not start. Something was turning over in the engine but nothing was catching, nothing ignited. That was nothing to do with me.

Just dumb luck.

Anderson looked at his watch. He was now late. The man with the gun was already there and he sensed no police presence. All he saw was opportunity.

The chief had to go back into his office, the councilwoman was true to her word and was indeed still lying on the splintered wood of what used to be a police desk. He didn't speak to her. He found the drawer intact and fished out the key to his bike lock.

Minutes later he was whizzing past an empty school towards another victim. It had been a few minutes. Moments, really.

The thunder crackled overhead, splitting the leaden sky in two, promising to swallow the town whole.

COMING HOME

Liv Dunham picked up the phone after three rings.

She said nothing. She didn't want to give anything else away.

This time, it was not silent. She could hear her caller breathing. And he was breathing heavily.

She caved. 'Hello?'

He continued to pant before forcing himself to inhale deeply.

'Hello?' she tried again. 'Who is this?'

'Liv?' he spoke.

Tears fell instantly from her eyes.

'Oz? Is that you? Is that really you?'

'I'm coming home.'

'What? Where are you? Are you all right? Did they hurt you? You have to call the police. Oz? Oz?' She was excited and furious and scared and elated all at once.

'Forget that for now, Liv. I'm coming home. Wait for me.'

He hung up.

THE WORLD WAS GETTING DARKER

The man with the gun was running through the woods. His ordinarily ruffled hair was now slick with rain and falling over his forehead.

He could hear the trunks of large trees sighing in the wind. The leaves began to form more of a shelter as he edged deeper inside. He could see the silver of the car a few hundred yards ahead. He sprinted that last few hundred yards, hitting the back window of the vehicle with his hands to slow himself down.

The gun was still in his right hand. He tucked it into his belt, the handle uncomfortable on his back. Then he pulled the keys out of his pocket and pressed the button that would unlock the car.

He lifted the door to the boot above his head, letting the light in.

There was nobody inside.

He punched the parcel shelf several times.

It was coming to an end. He knew that. But he wasn't scared. He felt weak, that was all.

The man with the gun leant his hands on the rubber seal around the boot opening and bent down to look in the car. One of the back seats was pushed forward. Not easy to do from the inside but not impossible.

He looked around over his shoulder. The world was getting darker and he was feeling tired. This was not over, not yet. But he needed rest. Murder had taken its toll on him emotionally and he was drained.

The man, that ordinary man, the man with the gun tucked into his belt, walked around to the rear door of the car – on the side where the seat was unclipped and folded forward – and pushed the seat back into position. But not fully. The clasp did not *click* shut. He then walked to the back of the car, hoisted a leg and set his foot down in the boot.

Then the second foot.

Moments later, he was crouching down, his right hand held the inside of the boot door, pulling it shut and leaving him lying in the blackness.

He sighed with relief. If the police did venture into the woods, if they followed the whispers that tickled the leaves, if it led them to that car, they would find a man locked inside the boot. He would tell them that he had no idea what had happened, that he had been in there for days with very little food or water. And only a coat to keep him warm at night.

They'd believe him at first. They'd have to. He'd been reported as missing.

Oz Tambor felt around above his head until his hand stroked against the rustling carrier bag. He took both biscuits out and ate them, devouring the first and savouring the second.

He needed to regenerate; then, just as he had told Liv Dunham, he was going to go home.

RELIEF IN DISGUISE

Faith Brady had died but nobody had been murdered on the second day.

Outside, the wind was picking up and blowing out anything that resembled a lingering autumn from Hinton Hollow.

It was dark in that car. And cold, getting colder. But Oz Tambor was alive. The coat he was wearing provided adequate protection but if the temperature dropped any more, he'd be in trouble. At least he still had Liv. The thought of her, anyway. The prospect that this nightmare could come to an end and he would be able to make the wedding that they and the town had put so much effort into.

On the Tuesday evening of *that* dark week in Hinton Hollow's past, it was Liv Dunham who had helped Oz through to the next morning. He imagined the ceremony, the flowers, the speeches and the cake. He thought about Liv taking that triangle of toast again one morning. He pushed forward in time to a point where they would be sitting on the sofa, her hand on his hand, his hand on the bump, waiting for movement.

Then his mind skipped back to the past and his own mother. It was a Monday and he had forgotten to do the one thing he had been in charge of. He was supposed to sort himself a passport for his first trip abroad.

He recalled the quarrel with Liv and he wished he hadn't left things on that note. If he could just talk to her now, he could change things. He remembered that long walk up his mother's front garden because there was nowhere to park. She'd been annoyed that he hadn't announced beforehand his intention to visit. Hungry in the dark, cold car, he thought about the smell of the bread that was baking.

May Tambor had handed her son his birth certificate without question. She had been keeping it within her files. Oz's father had always been so organised in that way throughout his life.

But he wasn't Oz's father. And May was not his mother. Not

biologically. He'd been on the Earth a matter of days before they'd taken him in as their own. Any other moment in his life but that one, any other day he might have been able to digest the things that May Tambor was explaining to him. But the pressure of the wedding, that he was putting on himself, that the good people of Hinton Hollow were choking him with every time he took that seven-minute stroll to the crossroads in the middle of town, it had mounted up. It was suffocating him. And this news had been the second to last thing he needed.

NEWSFLASH
The last thing he needed was me, bringing a storm.

'Did you think you would never have to tell me, Mother?' He'd raised his voice at May. Something he'd never done before. He was standing up, too. He looked threatening.

She'd managed to talk him back down to the couch with her. She'd explained things. He'd felt more settled. He knew he'd have to explain this to Liv as soon as possible.

Then he asked, 'Is that it? Is that everything? Everything I need to know?'

May Tambor didn't move.

'Mum. What else is there? You've started this now. The truth. Come on.'

It was too much for him. That last piece of information could have waited. He'd have found out eventually. Oz just could not handle it then. *That* day. At *that* moment. Too much information to digest. He was only human. A man. An ordinary man.

He left the house and he was taken. By Evil.

That was not where it started.

Oz Tambor walked back to his car with the darkness that had taken him and he drove out of town. He didn't really know what he was doing but he knew where he was going. And that was the problem.

The shop sold guns and leather. Oz only wanted one of those offerings.

And that is where *it* started.

With the intention.

Next, he was driving his ordinary car back to his ordinary town and tapping on the door to what had been, he thought, an ordinary home to an ordinary family.

When May Tambor opened the door, Oz did not afford her the courtesy of choice that he would give to Faith Brady.

Die for me, he had said to the woman who had raised him, looking her directly in the eyes before blowing a hole in her face. In what was continuous movement, he continued walking forward, stepping over May's body, walking towards the kitchen, swiping the warm biscuits on the counter into a carrier bag and taking his father's long coat from the rack. It had irritated him for four years that she had left it hanging there.

But that coat was keeping Oz Tambor warm enough in his car on that first night as he listened to the trees talking.

Thinking about the woman he had called *Mother* his entire life.

And when he would call Liv again.

And he hoped that the next mother he questioned would be different. That she would prove him wrong.

NIGHT, NIGHT

The pig was tied to Darren's radiator by its leg. It fell over. It screamed. It shit on his dining-room floor. But it couldn't be heard. Darren had left the radio on a classical-music station, hoping it would calm the animal while also drowning out any noise that it made.

He had left a pile of food on the floor. Apples, lettuce, mushrooms and other vegetables from his fridge he was not going to eat.

The animal was unhappy and alone and in distress, but in no way was the situation worsening the quality of life it had already experienced.

The damn thing should be thankful, Darren thought. *I gave it an extra day.*

It was lying down on the carpet when the slaughterer returned home from work. Darren could no longer sense the smell at work but it was different in his own house.

'Oh, you dirty...' He stopped himself.

Part of him wanted to cut its head off slowly but the mess was already too much in there.

He left the dining room dark and the music on. Then he made himself some pasta and mixed it with a ready-made sauce. He drank three beers while he watched television and ignored any stirrings in the room behind him.

Before retiring for the evening he went to check in on his new companion.

Darren spoke to the pig.

'That's right. You get your rest. We are up bright and early in the morning and I will set you free. But you'd better get running because I'm not giving you too much of a head start.' He smiled. Then he added, 'Night, night, little one.'

HAPPY ENDING

He'd had to speak with more than one mother. Faith Brady had failed. So, too, had Rachel Hadley, though her intentions could be construed as honourable.

Catherine Raymond had loved her children enough to choose herself to die. That, or she hated herself enough to choose her children to live. Whatever the mother's motive, it was the result that Oz Tambor, the ordinary man, had been looking for. It had reaffirmed his faith.

He was startled when he awoke in the darkness of the boot. He shot up and rasped his head against the parcel shelf he had punched a few hours before.

Deep in the woods, he was unaware of the panic and malaise that had set in for the Hinton Hollow community. That was not his concern. That something had swept through the town, changing almost everybody into someone they were not, did not mean a thing to the ordinary man. He had changed. He was altered. Oz was still in there somewhere, hanging on to the possibility of his happy ending.

There was no such thing.

Happiness was simply relief in disguise.

Oz's stomach growled and he rolled his eyes in the darkness, lying back down. He turned onto his stomach and pressed both hands against the back of the seat until it flopped forward, allowing him to crawl out through the gap. No light was let in this time.

He continued through the space between the driver's and the passenger's seats, eventually dropping in behind the steering wheel. The keys were in the ignition. He turned them forward one click. The dashboard lit up as he flicked the headlights on. The windscreen wipers squeaked as they pressed against the rain.

He turned around and looked through the back windscreen. All was darkness.

NO VOICEMAIL

That was it. No more. Maeve was sick of all the waiting around for love. She was tired of putting in all the effort for no reciprocation, no reward. She'd had enough of it from her first husband and she wasn't going to take that shit from Detective Sergeant Pace.

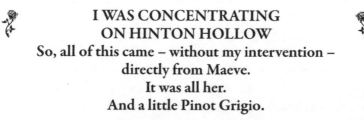

**I WAS CONCENTRATING
ON HINTON HOLLOW**
So, all of this came – without my intervention –
directly from Maeve.
It was all her.
And a little Pinot Grigio.

She didn't want to text him. She didn't want to leave a goodbye voicemail. And she knew he probably wouldn't pick up if she called. It was late, anyway. So she did it the old-fashioned way. She wrote him a letter. Nothing poignant or cutting, no farewell speech.

Just a short note that would let him know it was all over.

She didn't even write it with her own hand. She typed it and printed it and folded it into three before placing it into a self-adhesive envelope that would be delivered the next day so that he would understand his predicament the moment he returned home.

DAY FIVE

Where you will understand:

The Isaacs family

The significance of pigs

The importance of truth

and why some windows had to be broken.

THIS IS THE END

My small story.

It was strange.

You got angry.

Then it got worse.

Just as I told you in the beginning.

But, if you are still here, it is because you want to know how it ends.

Endings are tricky, aren't they? You want everything to be resolved, tied up in a little white bow.

Order. Chaos. Order regained.

But life isn't really like that. Especially in a place like Hinton Hollow where the community is, at once, disconnected, yet inextricably linked to one another.

And this isn't your story, is it? It is mine. It is Evil's story. And, of course, Detective Sergeant Pace's story.

I would love to tie things up for you. I would also like for people to have more empathy and to be kinder to one another, so that evil may continue to exist but in a more diluted form, where things like this do not have to come to pass in order for people to be reminded what it means to have humanity.

Again, I am not sure that will happen. I do not yet know if what I did will make a difference.

So, here is a version of the end.

AN ORDINARY MAN

Oscar Tambor was pronounced dead at 9:37 on that fifth day.

Liv Dunham identified the body.

'And you're absolutely certain?' Pace hated asking that question but she had only glanced at him.

'We were due to be married this weekend. We've been together a long time, Detective.' She was irritated. It felt like an accusation but the man lying on the floor had been shot in the face, his features had been disfigured.

Liv had no idea who the woman was who was lying dead next to him. The one with the hole through her chest.

'I'm sorry, Ms Dunham, I have to ask. Does Oz have any distinguishing features on his body? A tattoo? A scar? A mole? Has he been circumcised? I know this is hard.' He was simply being thorough. He had to be. Anderson had fucked up. Another mother had been killed due to poor preparation and negligence. Pace was not going to make any more mistakes.

'It's him, Mr Pace. It's him.' All the while she was shaking her head and looking at the other woman.

Pace's first thought had been some kind of lovers' suicide pact. He had convinced himself that he should be looking towards Charles Ablett, the man who had courted these women before killing them. He expected that Liv had been the cheater in the relationship. Perhaps it had been Oz. Maybe it was his final fling before the big wedding, a last shot at freedom with something strange. An older woman.

On closer inspection, there was no sign of a weapon.

This had been an execution.

He was trying to see the connection. It had to be related. Everything was. But it didn't quite fit. All the male victims had been shot through the heart and all the female victims had the bullet strike them in the face. This scene was the reverse of that.

Was it symbolic?

Was he creating a pattern that did not exist?

Anderson entered the room, pushing past the local constabulary. They had travelled several towns east to Barkmere, just across the bridge into Oxfordshire. The incident had been flagged up to Constable Reynolds as being similar to those that had occurred in Hinton Hollow *that* week. There was the usual friction concerning jurisdiction on arrival, but Pace could be very persuasive, particularly in person, when his presence was palpable.

'I've got the details on our lady friend, Pace,' Anderson said in his usual heartless manner. Pace gestured for one of the other officers to come and take Liv away.

'What do we know?' Pace asked once Liv had been escorted outside.

'Laney Isaacs. Forty-nine. Widow. No mortgage. Part-time position at the job centre. One child. A son, Harvey. Trying to get hold of him now.' He was reading from his notepad. 'Doesn't really fit the description of the victims from our town, does it? We could be knocking down Ablett's door right now.'

The warrant had finally come through to search Charles Ablett's home in connection with the Hinton Hollow murder investigation but it was followed closely by the information they were given about the scene they were standing in.

'Apart from the widow who was shot in *our town*. In her house. Who just happens to be the mother of the man lying dead on this floor.' Pace screwed his face up in disbelief.

He turned away from the inspector and crouched down next to the bodies. Liv had told him that she'd had another call, that it had been Oz and he had said he was *coming home*. What could he have meant by that. He'd asked Liv to wait for him.

'You knew Oscar Tambor, right?' Pace asked Anderson without turning around to look at him.

'Sure. The wedding was a big deal. I didn't really know him personally but I knew of him.'

'And this is Oscar Tambor?' He pointed at the sad-looking corpse.

'Liv said so, didn't she?'

'I'm not asking Liv, I'm asking you.' Pace could feel the tall man with the moustache lean over him.

'Sure. I've met him a couple of times but he's not someone who lives long in the memory, you know? Kind of nice, kind of humble. Nothing remarkable.'

Detective Sergeant Pace spun slightly on his heels, turning to face Anderson.

'Just an ordinary man, some might say.'

'What are you getting at, Pace?' The inspector's eyes were reduced to curious slits.

'It's not clean.'

'Well, that happens when people get shot, blood tends to go everywhere.'

'That's not what I mean. The other murders left nothing for us to grip hold of and run with. Terrified kids with visions of monsters implanted into their minds do not make the best witnesses. May Tambor was left undiscovered for days, so why was the front door left wide open for a neighbour to wander into at this address?' He was speaking out loud to himself more than he was involving Anderson in his process.

'I'm still not sure I know the relevance.'

'I'm saying that something doesn't fit. There are no real mistakes that I can see, this is linked but it's not the same. All the murders have been cold but there is a difference between not caring what the police might find at a crime scene to *this*. It's all too deliberate. It seems fake. Like *he* wants us to be here, seeing what we are seeing.'

Pace stood up. He looked around the room. The spatter of red on the walls and television, which was still turned on, a news channel advertising itself. There was the unmistakable scent of ready-meal containers in the kitchen, wafting in to mask the aroma of death that no longer registered with the detective. Some faded rectangles on the wall where pictures had been taken down or moved. And an ashtray filled with grey-and-white dust but devoid of cigarette butts.

It all felt conveniently placed.

'Why would he want to do that?' Anderson questioned.

'If I had to guess, I'd say he's telling us something. That the motivation behind this murder was different to the others.'

HE WAS SAYING SOMETHING ELSE, TOO
It was over.
He was finished.

THINGS ARE NOT ALWAYS AS THEY SEEM

Liv Dunham sat in the back of Detective Sergeant Pace's unmarked car. Anderson would remain in Barkmere and locate Harvey Isaacs. He was trying his best to make up for his mistake the day before. Pace was letting it happen. Maybe when this was all over he'd let Anderson know that he would never be able to make amends. That these things stay with you forever. They change you. They make you into somebody new. You can't escape. You take that darkness with you wherever you go.

For now, he'd let him think that he was being useful.

Pace was driving Liv back to Hinton Hollow. He looked in the rear-view mirror, just as he had done with Mrs Beaufort. He expected more tears. She'd said it herself, they had been together for a long while. They were due to get married *that* weekend. Perhaps her suspicions matched his.

'I'm sorry, Liv,' he said earnestly from the front of the car.

She said nothing but was looking into his mirror to make eye contact.

'Don't read anything into what you saw at that house. Things are not always as they seem. We will get to the bottom of this and uncover the truth. Until then, you need to remember only the Oscar that you knew.'

These were the tricks he had tried when Julee disappeared.

She did not speak for the remainder of the journey and Pace didn't push her any further.

The car pulled up into the spot that Pace had left it in the first time he had visited Liv's home. She made the same mistake that most people did and tried to let herself out of the car. Pace got out and unlocked her door from the outside.

'Thanks for the lift.'

'Wait.' He reached out and grabbed her arm. She snatched it away. 'I'm sorry. Look, here is my personal mobile number. Don't hesitate to give me a call if you remember anything that you may have left out of our conversations.'

🌹   **IN CASE YOU DIDN'T KNOW**   🌹
This is how Pace had met Maeve.
He was working a case.
Her husband had died. He gave her his card.
And, one day, she called him.

'Yeah, sure.' She dismissed him. 'It's over now, though, isn't it,' she told him and started walking off again, screwing the card up as she walked but not throwing it away.

'Ms Dunham,' he called after her. 'Ms Dunham.' He repeated it louder, shorter.

She turned.

'Call me if you get any more strange phone calls.' The embers of his eyes glowed. She saw something in him that she had not noticed before and he saw that on her face. She was cautious – scared, perhaps – of what the detective thought he knew.

SOME KIND OF SICK JOKE

As soon as the door was closed behind her, she felt safer. And she let it all go.

There was sadness there, of course. Years of her life, perhaps the best part of it, the formative years, the things she'd supposedly missed out on because she had this long-running relationship. She wept for the loss of that and she cried for the people who never understood and would never feel the way she had felt about Oz. They would never know that pleasure and passion. That made them unlucky. But they would never feel this hurt and that made them unlucky too.

Because what she was feeling was real.

TO APPRECIATE TRUE PLEASURE
You must experience true pain.
This is not one of those vice/versa instances.
This is why pain endures and pleasure is fleeting.

The situation seemed like a nightmare. Kidnapping. Guns. Murder. Death. The gloom that had descended on everyone around her. The surrealism of the wider world gave Liv Dunham's more actuality.

She felt bruised and crushed. And alone. She hadn't felt that way for longer than she could even remember. It was terrifying. Oz had always been there with her. What would she do now? She couldn't go to Paris or Provence alone. She didn't want to. She wanted him back.

But there was also a confusion in her mind, as her back rested against the inside of the closed front door. He had called her. He had told her to wait. He had said that he was coming home. Was that a mistake? Did he mean to call that other woman? That old bitch he was lying next to. Was that his home? Is that where he went? To die?

It just did not sound like Oz at all. He wasn't like that. He wasn't rebellious or even adventurous. He wasn't boring or safe either. He was something else. Reliable. Honest.

Liv started to think that perhaps none of it was real. The dead kids, the mothers with holes in their faces, the creepy new detective. None of it.

She was no longer crying, though she couldn't remember when it had stopped. She was exhausted. She hadn't slept after Oz's call because she was waiting. Just like he said.

In a daze, Liv walked into the kitchen and switched the kettle on.

She didn't check to see whether it had enough water, she just pressed the button. On the table by the phone, flowers were dying in a vase. They had been there since Sunday. They should have lasted longer but they'd been sagging for days. It reminded her that her reality was that she was now alone. She would not be getting married.

Liv opened the drawer where her address book was kept – all her contact details were in her phone but she kept a hard copy – and she turned to the page where the florist's details were written.

I really ought to start cancelling everything, she thought. It would keep her busy. It was necessary. She started with the flowers because they would be the easiest, Maggie would be the most understanding.

As she went to pick up the phone and make her first horrifying confession, it rang.

She picked it up and said nothing.

No sound came from the other end of the line either.

Liv felt inside her pocket for the scrunched piece of card she had been given by the detective and wondered how he could have possibly known that this would happen. That she would receive another call just like the ones she had been receiving all *that* week.

'Hi. It's Oz. Want to talk?' a voice eventually said.

'What is this? Some kind of sick joke? Who are you?'

'Liv, don't hang up. It's me, Oz. I promise.'

'But I...'

'I can explain. Meet me. Tomorrow. Forget about Sunday and all those people. Just you and me. Okay? Liv?'

It sounded like him. He apologised for the passport incident. She'd only told Detective Pace and Mrs Beaufort about that.

'Liv. Are you there?' he asked, sounding slightly distressed.

'What happened?'

'Meet me tomorrow and I'll tell you everything.'

THE REWARD FOR SUFFERING

He couldn't tell her everything over the phone.

It was something like this.

Laney Isaacs heard a knock at her front door. Dinner was in the oven. She was upstairs and wasn't expecting Harvey home for another thirty minutes. Harvey, her son who still lived at home though he was approaching his mid-thirties. Harvey, that perfect little boy she had always treasured so highly. Harvey, the man who felt he could not leave her after his father had died. She wouldn't cope.

It had been nine years since he had passed.

Laney opened the bedroom window to see who was at the front door – Harvey's room was at the back where it was quiet, he'd never been a great sleeper.

'Oh, Harv. It's you. You're a bit early. Forgotten your key? Give me a sec and I'll come down and let you in.' She didn't even let him answer.

She was talking out loud to herself about his key and arriving too early and how she wasn't ready. Laney Isaacs wrapped her dressing gown around her, tied the belt around her waist and bounded down the stairs.

She could see her son's face through the window. He didn't look well, not like himself at all. She opened the door.

'Everything all ri—'

He barged past her, his head hung low and he coughed.

She closed the door.

'Harv. What wrong?'

He pulled out the gun from his belt and held it to her face, telling her not to scream otherwise he'd blow a hole straight through her skull.

Like May Tambor, she had hoped that the truth would never arise, that only she would have to live with what she had done and not have to confront it. But, in life, the only reward for suffering is more suffering, or, if you're particularly unlucky, justice.

'It's you.' She spoke quietly, her voice somewhere between fear and realisation.

'It's me. Whoever the fuck I am.' He waved the gun to the left, instructing his mother to move into the living room.

He closed the curtains and told her to sit down.

'You don't look that old. I guess you really were young when you had me, eh? At least May told the truth in the end.' It would have felt alien for Oz to refer to the woman he had called Mother for over thirty years as May, but this was not the real Oz Tambor standing there and it wasn't Harvey Isaacs, it was the shadow that lingered somewhere between both of them.

'I've been known as Oz for as long as I can remember. Did I ever have another name?' His arm was starting to ache so he brought the gun down to his waist.

Laney Isaacs shook her head.

'Couldn't even be bothered to name me. Sounds about right. Didn't want to make an attachment, I guess.'

Laney tilted her head to one side. She wanted to speak, to say that it wasn't like that. She was young, too young, and she was about to have another baby. She could have stuck it out, asked for help, she could have given them both up, but she didn't. She split the brothers apart. She was a teenager and she fucked up. Twice. The Tambors could help. They could keep it quiet. Make it all go away. She chose herself and she had regretted it ever since.

Now she was going to pay for her mistake.

They all were.

Oz was not interested in gaining closure. He did not want to hear her reasoning. He did not like her. He did not want to get to know her. It was her fault that he had shot May Tambor. The blood of Jacob Brady and the Hadley family was on her hands, not his. That is what he told himself. And maybe what he believed.

He did have one question for her, though.

But it would have to wait.

MOTHER?

Harvey Isaacs was a liar, too.

Maybe it was hereditary.

He was a year older than the brother he knew nothing about and, as it happened, in a similar position to Oz in his personal life. He was going to take the next step with his girlfriend. The trouble was that Laney had no idea that Harvey had even been seeing anyone. He had his own secret.

Harvey told himself that he wasn't telling his mother because he thought it would hurt her, but truthfully he was afraid that it would hurt him. He'd given up on relationships before because he couldn't bear what it was doing to his mother. Not this time.

He'd stuck around for nine years to support her when his dad had died. It was time to move on. For both of them. She was young enough to still have a life. She didn't need to run out and find a man straight away, but she had to, at least, attempt to get past the hurt. And she had to do it alone.

Besides, Harvey had *news*.

He turned the key and heard the television blaring in the living room.

'Mum? I'm back. Dinner smells good.' He lied. He was so sick of the ready meals.

Oz put the gun back up to shoulder height so that he had a more accurate shot should he need to take it. With the other hand he put a finger to his lips and mouthed *shh*.

It was time.

AGAIN

They looked so alike. Oz was a little slimmer than Harvey, but Harvey lived off salt-filled ready meals and Oz had only eaten forty-eight biscuits that week.

The elder brother was stunned into silence. Not by the gun – though that certainly played a part – but by the vision of the man stood opposite him.

'Mum?' Harvey asked, not taking his eyes away from Oz's face.

'I'm fine. It's okay.'

'I wasn't asking if you were okay. What the hell is this?'

Oz pointed the gun at his brother and shook it to the left. Harvey understood the gesture and moved away from the doorway and into the lounge next to his mother. She was seated. He remained standing.

'Who is that?' Harvey spoke almost without moving his lips, directing the question to his mother through the side of his mouth.

'Stop talking about me as though I'm not here.' Oz was calm. Too calm. It made Laney and Harvey feel even more on edge.

'He's your brother, Harvey.'

'My what?'

'Stop talking to each other?' Oz was more angry. He raised his voice. The venom was frightening. 'I am not your brother. I do not know you. I do not want to know you. I am simply here to speak with Miss Laney Isaacs. I have one thing to tell you and one thing to ask you. Then I will be on my way. Do you understand?'

They nodded in unison. Laney tried to hold Harvey's hand but her youngest son gave her a look that said *it just would not do*.

Oz looked at the woman who had given birth to him then given him away.

'You do not have to die today, Miss Isaacs. You are being given a second chance. But you do have a choice to make. Who is your favourite? Which son do you choose to stay alive? I should probably remind you at this point that my name is Oz, in case you had forgotten.'

'This is ridiculous,' Harvey interjected. Oz looked at him, a stare that burned through to his heart.

'This is not your question. You should trust your mother to make the correct decision.' This was harder than Oz had anticipated. The real Oscar Tambor was hurting inside at the sight of the brother he only learned he had been involuntarily wrenched from on day one. But he was not strong enough to fight his darker self.

'Say the name of the son you wish to live. I do not need a reason. Just a name.' He had modified his speech with each mother he had spoken to. 'Or you can say nothing. Then you will die. You will sacrifice yourself for your children. I know this can be done. I have seen it now.'

Oz never moved the sight of the gun away from the centre of Laney's forehead.

He waited.

Harvey held his breath. There was nothing he could do. He couldn't think about how much he loved his mother, all he could think about was how he would not even be there if she had just tried to pull her fucking stupid life together.

And then she said, 'Harvey.'

She wanted to save Harvey.

She wanted to keep Harvey and let Oz go.

Again.

Oz looked at them both. The family he never knew, never needed, never needed to know about. And he placed the muzzle of his pistol underneath his chin. His finger trembled on the trigger.

'Wrong answer,' he said and whipped the gun to point at Harvey's face.

Oz took a quick step forward and blew a hole in his brother's head that killed him instantly.

'Noooooo. You bastard. You fucking lunatic.' Laney tried to stand but thought better and dropped back to the couch.

'If there has been one thing I have learned this week, it is what a breaking heart looks like. It happens to every parent, good or bad. Selfish or benevolent. Yours is truly beautiful, Mother.' He spat the last word out. 'Really, it is an image not easily erased. Heartache. This is you at your most pure.'

Then he unloaded his last bullet into her chest.

He shot her through the heart because she had broken his.

He could not stand to see his brother's face because it was a reflection of the man Oz could have become.

How could he possibly have explained that to Liv over the phone?

HIS OWN TOAST

Then he'd have to explain how he didn't just leave after killing his biological family.

He'd have to explain how he tucked the gun back into his belt and walked towards the scent from the kitchen. To Harvey, it had smelled like unreal, pre-made food. To the man who had been living on cookies, the meatball-and-cheese pasta bake represented a fine-dining experience he could not pass up.

There were two meals in there. And some garlic bread, which had burnt. Oz Tambor ate it all. He sat on the sofa next to a woman with a hole in her chest and he forked over two thousand calories into his mouth while watching a news item that detailed his exploits in Hinton Hollow, followed by a soap opera he never watched and didn't really enjoy about families more dysfunctional than his own.

He ate too quickly but he enjoyed it and was full. Bloated, even.

He was also fatigued. Murder is hard work. Running away is even tougher. And his body was now working overtime to digest the food he had just shovelled into his stomach.

Oz left the television on but turned the sound down to a more sociable level. The house would have been too eerie if it had been silent. Particularly with the two dead people in the lounge.

He dimmed the lights and went upstairs, where he found two bedrooms. He spent the night in his dead brother's double bed. It was a comfort he had really missed that week while being cramped in the boot of his own car.

He slept straight through until morning. Not too late. He still had some things to take care of. He ate a large breakfast. First a bowl of cereal and then toast. Every piece of his own toast. No half went the way of anyone else's mouth. It had been something he'd missed while in the woods, but it was a detail he revelled in at the Isaacs' house.

The bodies in the lounge were exactly as he'd left them, of course. Harvey looked just like him. Sufficient to fool the police for long enough, maybe even fool Liv if she was asked to identify him. Oz found Harvey's passport in the drawer of the desk in his room. Along with a little pocket money. He memorised the details.

Oz turned the television up and made sure he removed any photographs of Laney and Harvey together. He left the front door wide open and got back into his car.

It was over. He had everything he needed apart from Liv.

Once he had Liv, it would end.

TOGETHER

Sure, Oz could have mentioned something. Perhaps that May had lied to him his entire life. There may have been others in the town that knew the truth. People of May's generation. *Mrs Beaufort must have known*, Oz told himself. And RD, probably. But adding them to his list was not an option. It was not a part of his mission.

Instead of mentioning any of his story, Oz lied to Liv. He told her he'd been taken but had escaped. He said he was scared but he just had to get some things together and he would meet her on Saturday morning. They could be together. He wanted them to be together.

Oz still wanted to marry Liv Dunham that weekend.

But he wanted out of Hinton Hollow.

The place was toxic.

A VERSION/AVERSION

Does that version of events work? It gives Oz his motive. It shows the ordinary man on the brink of happiness being consumed by rage that his life has been a lie. That the one person he always trusted was the one person who betrayed him. That this lack of understanding and empathy led to inhuman atrocities and evil.

The problem is, while a bow can be placed around his motivation for killing the mothers, there is no real justice. His brother was not at fault for any of this, yet took a bullet to the face. And what about the families of the victims? How were they to ever receive closure?

And he probably should not have told Liv he had been taken. Perhaps that he just went away to get himself a passport.

It is a little messy and somewhat problematic.

But life is that way.

People lie and get away with it. People kill and are never discovered. The best writers don't sell the most books. And a concert pianist will perform to hundreds or thousands while a tone-deaf teenager, who plays no instruments, will be auto-tuned and sold to millions because their greatest skill was having genetically full hair.

Sometimes, after the chaos, order is not regained.

SOMETHING ELSE YOU SHOULD KNOW
This was a version of how things ended.
How they could have ended.
In an alternate reality, perhaps.
But, while it is all true, none of it happened.

This was the only part of proceedings that Oz had planned. And this is how he ran through it in his mind every day while lying in the back of his car. It is what kept him going. More than the biscuits.

Just because it was planned does not mean it came to pass.

Remember when I said that sometimes evil presents itself as truth?

Little Henry Wallace was coming home. Back to Hinton Hollow. I couldn't let him come back to this. I couldn't have that ending. I couldn't have Oz loose for another school run.

Oscar Tambor was in the woods, in his car. He was not at his birth mother's home. He was not putting a bullet into the face of his estranged brother, and Liv was not misidentifying his body. He was still in the car and still in his own mind.

His storm was fading fast.

He was waiting for the whispers.

A BIG HOUSE WHERE EVERYONE COULD SEE

This is also true.

The part with the mothers was a necessity. To demonstrate the level of evil required to make a point. To show these people how far they have regressed.

But this was about Detective Sergeant Pace.

It was his story.

Lights flicked on around the close that Charles Ablett lived on. He had enough money to move to a substantial property a little further into the countryside – he had the connections, too, thanks to his position at Ablett and Ablett – but that was not Charles' style. He wanted a big house where everyone could see that he had a big house.

The police were outside. Pace arrived in his unmarked car and Anderson in the vehicle that had let him down so badly the day before. He'd had it fixed that same day. Suddenly, everything was being done by Pace's book. He was trying to make up for it. Being professional. Being efficient. He still couldn't lose his inappropriateness but that would mean Anderson wasn't really Anderson.

A shutter moved on the equally luxurious property opposite. Within seconds, Roger Ablett knew the police were going to storm through his brother's front door. They had their warrant, their suspicion and their motive. What they didn't have was their man.

Roger called his brother to warn him but got his voicemail message.

They pushed through the door with relative ease, Pace leading the way.

It was huge and open-plan. The living room looked as though it had never been sat in. The cream carpet was spotless. There was not a single smear on the television screen, which looked too large and heavy to be hanging from a wall. There were no books or films or photos. A few ornaments dotted the floating shelves and windowsills, plastic-looking things that clearly cost a lot of money and were considered art by some idiot in a toupee, but nothing that really showed Charles Ablett's personality. And that in itself said so much about Charles.

The kitchen was off to the right. Modern white slabs everywhere. Clean. Uncooked in. Around the size of Pace's entire apartment in London. But there were bottles everywhere. He'd been drinking and he'd been drinking heavily. And probably not alone.

Pace made a gesture with his hand that Anderson determined as a signal to follow him upstairs. Even in these soulless palaces, one could not get to the top of the steps without one of them creaking. As soon as it made a noise, Pace leapt two at a time and aimed himself at the one room with a lamp on. Anderson followed but checked the darkened room to its left in case it was a trick. He did not like Pace's impetuousness. It was the type of behaviour that could get someone killed.

The dark room was clear. Anderson exited to find Pace stood in the doorway of the lit room. He wasn't moving.

On the bed, a man was lying naked. He was in decent shape for a corpse. Pace couldn't make out his identity because there was a pillow over his face that had been ripped open by the bullet he expected to find lodged in the man's head. He also expected that man to be Charles Ablett.

There was a bottle of Johnnie Walker Gold resting in his left hand. It had hardly spilled. Pace could smell it over the death and cleaning products that had been used all over the house – either to conceal evidence or Charles had had a fastidious cleaner.

'Matches May,' Anderson said behind Pace's head.

'What?'

'May Tambor. She had been shot in the face. And I don't think we need to pull the pillow away to know that's the case here.' The inspector seemed almost proud of his deduction.

'It looks the same. It could have a link. But I think this is someone cashing in on the mayhem.'

Before Pace could continue his diatribe, the boom of Roger Ablett interrupted. He was downstairs, calling Pace. Calling Charles.

'Bang on time. I thought this might happen.' Pace smiled. He knew how Hinton Hollow worked. He'd been away for a few years but he'd already been back long enough to have some insight into its darker underbelly.

That was his speciality.

That's where he lived.

Pace hung himself over the bannister and looked down the stairs. The considerable frame of Roger Ablett almost blocked out the light from the kitchen. He was the one thing that could make the inside of that house suddenly appear small and quaint.

'Don't come up here, Mr Ablett.' That was an order. A polite order.

'What do you mean? I'll go wherever I damn well...'

Pace and Anderson moved quickly to block him off before he could take in the crime scene.

'I'd like you to accompany us to the station.' Pace took the lead and Anderson allowed it. He had no idea what was going through his detective's mind but he knew it was best to leave him to work his magic.

Ablett threw his weight around a little and backed it up with some bravado about *not going anywhere unless he was being arrested.* Pace didn't budge. He told the overweight estate agent that he would arrest him but it was in Ablett's best interests if he didn't walk out of his brother's house, in front of the neighbours and, no doubt, news cameras that had been tipped off by now, in a pair of handcuffs. *Reputations don't recover from that shit.*

Roger Ablett's face flushed. He coughed violently three times then hit his chest with his fist and agreed to go quietly.

Pace suggested that Ablett return to the station with Inspector Anderson.

'Are you following?' the chief questioned.

Pace looked only at Roger Ablett when he spoke. 'I'll be along shortly. I'm going to pick up Nathan Hadley.'

It was going to be another long Hinton Hollow evening.

To everyone else, the walls were clean and the house was sterile. To Pace, the surfaces were covered from skirting board to ceiling in black flames.

He had other things to take care of.

Once more, he wondered whether he could run away.

A REMINDER

You want to know who killed Ablett? Definitively. That's what happens with this ending.

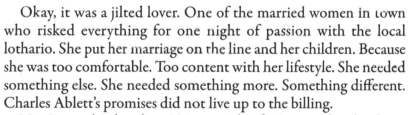

I'D LIKE TO TELL YOU ONE THING
It doesn't matter.

Okay, it was a jilted lover. One of the married women in town who risked everything for one night of passion with the local lothario. She put her marriage on the line and her children. Because she was too comfortable. Too content with her lifestyle. She needed something else. She needed something more. Something different. Charles Ablett's promises did not live up to the billing.

No. It was his brother. He was sick of carrying that layabout around his whole life. Supporting him. Giving him a job. Letting him off with behaviour he would not tolerate from anyone else.

Roger Ablett knew what Charles was like. Everyone thought he doted on his younger brother. Nobody would suspect him over a jilted lover or a cuckolded partner. They knew that Roger was ruthless and determined but not in a way that would harm his own family. They would suspect Ellie Frith of being a climber before they pinned it on that walking heart disease.

Maybe it was obvious all along that it was Nathan Hadley. He ticked all the boxes. Disturbed and depressed at the sight of his entire family murdered on the street. Drunk. Hungover. Suspicious, and rightly so, that his dick was the second one that had been in his wife's mouth that final morning.

There was no forced entry. Rachel had left the door open the morning she left Charles Ablett. Who knows how long he had been there. He may already have been dead when Pace came to call. Both Ellie Frith and Roger Ablett had keys to his home.

What is important is that a man died. A human being. Not a good one but a human nonetheless. And the important thing to think about is the reaction of others. This determines the state of the collective consciousness.

Are you desensitised to the violence?

Are you secretly rejoicing because something evil has been taken down?

Do you feel it is justice?

Are you more concerned with who did it rather than why it would ever happen in the first place?

Charles Ablett was at an age where he was at the greatest risk. While every dalliance around town seemed like a successful conquest, while he appeared to pride himself in such misogyny, while he was a picture of confidence and swagger, the slick estate agent was dreadfully unfulfilled. He was dying in small-town life. He was stuck. In the considerable shadow of his brother, drowning in a sea of futile fornication. In simplest terms, he seemed to be bursting with evil but really, he was filled with sadness.

And it is easy to get a gun in Roylake when you know where to go. And easier when you have influence and disposable income. And it is easy to lie in bed alone and drink. But it is difficult to stare down the barrel of a gun. And it is harder still to pull that trigger as you do so.

But this is what people do.

So, I will also tell you that while a jilted lover killed Charles Ablett, and his brother killed him, too, as did his colleague, and the local scorned hairdresser, I will also inform you that Charles Ablett killed Charles Ablett.

You can take that as the truth or you can decide that it was one of the people on that list.

I WOULD JUST LIKE TO REMIND YOU
It does not matter.

THIS HAPPENED

Hinton Hollow was a small town. Just over 5,000 residents. And I touched every single one that had some form of depravity or insecurity locked away inside them.

Every single one.

But I could not fit them all into one story. They were not all interesting. They were not all affected to the extent of Oz Tambor or Mrs Beaufort. Not every person in that once quaint community found themselves involved with Detective Sergeant Pace that week.

While there were several interconnecting tales of good and evil, there were some characters who didn't seem to fit.

If the identity of Charles Ablett's killer really isn't important, then why did I tell you about him? And, if Oz Tambor never made it to his birth mother's home to execute her and the son she had chosen to keep, then what was the significance of that plan?

And why keep returning to a woman who likes to break windows and a young, angry man from the slaughterhouse on the outskirts of the Hollow?

THE REASON IS SIMPLE
Because this happened.

FRESHLY SQUEEZED

Oz pushed against the rear seat of the car from inside the boot and it fell forward. He clambered through the gap and over onto the driver's seat. There, he took the keys from his pocket, pushed them into the ignition and turned.

On the second attempt, it jumped into life. Cold air started to blow into his face and he adjusted the dial to its warmest setting and waited. The radio was playing some freshly squeezed instrumental jazz on a station he did not recognise.

He waited for the engine to warm the air being pushed towards his face.

His hard work was done.

He had a little time.

Oz Tambor was actively seeking the sound of the whispers I had tormented him with all week. He didn't need them now, he was too far gone. He was changed.

He reclined the driver's seat and shut his eyes, imagining Liv's face when she saw him again. Picturing her in that white dress. Then he wondered what his real mother might look like and how similar to his brother he would be.

And he thought about shooting his brother in the face because he knew the woman he was going to visit had no right to call herself a mother. That she would undoubtedly make the wrong decision.

He had gone over the details every day that he had been in the boot of that car. He knew how it would play out.

And the jazz music clicked and the symbol shuffled and the clarinet kicked in and I gave him some whispers and the car got warmer.

HOWL

And Annie Harding's husband didn't want to have sex in the kitchen when he got straight home from work. So I shouted into her mind and the rage bubbled inside.

The doubt over his fidelity resurfacing. Her inadequacies as a lover, a mother, a woman.

'Please don't take it as a rejection. It's not that,' he pleaded.

'Yes. Dinner first. Then dessert later.' She was calm on the outside. But that wasn't really her.

'I've forgotten one thing so I am going to nip out and grab it.' She took the keys from the bowl that her husband had just put in there and left. To howl at the moon.

She drove, speeding to the centre of town. She could see where the florist had boarded up her window. She turned right at the crossroads. Up the hill. Towards the school. But not that far.

Her large 4x4 turned off-road and into the woods. She screamed obscenities while hitting the steering wheel. She wanted to be nowhere. Some place nobody would go. Out in the wild. Because she was wild. She was feral. She was anger and strength and passion.

She hit the brakes, killed the engine, jumped out and started running forward. Running fast. Running hard. Until she was breathless and lost and had to stop.

Annie looked up but everything was dark. The canopy above her blocking out the light. But the whispers still made it through. She kept walking until she came to a clearing. She could hear the animals. She could see the trees and the rocks and the leaves.

Annie Harding had forgotten why she was so mad but she knew that she was, and she knew what to do. She walked over to a large, moss-covered rock at the bottom of a tree. She bent down and used the strength of her legs to pick it up. Then she used those legs again to jump it up so that she could rest it on her shoulder.

It was her biggest and heaviest rock that week.

Then she ran again.

And she threw it hard.
And she broke another window.

TWENTY SECONDS

The pig made hardly any noise as it was helped back into the boot of Darren's car. It had squealed uncomfortably when first stolen but, after a night in the warmth of its new owner's dining room, there was very little sound from the back of the vehicle as Darren ambled around the quieter roads that took him across to the other side of Hinton Hollow.

A sharpened kitchen knife lay on the passenger seat. Darren had spent the evening sharpening it. The butter knife was enough to puncture the organs of a cat but this was not a domesticated animal, this would require something more. And, as he peered into the rear-view mirror at the beast behind him, he knew he would need to stab the thing several times just to slow it down.

He'd killed enough trapped, defenceless animals in his time to have a realistic idea of the strength he would need to pull this off.

This was next-level stuff.

It was escalation.

It would be a battle.

Above all, it was going to be enjoyable.

Fulfilling.

The slaughterer pulled up somewhere quiet and switched off the car. It was time.

As he gazed through the back window at the animal he was hoping to hunt and kill, you could be forgiven for thinking there was a moment of fondness that passed between those two living things. As if, at that moment, they were somehow equal. They both knew what this was about.

They were both terrified.

Darren opened the boot, expecting to help the pig out and onto the ground. But, as soon as the gap was wide enough, the prey jumped out and ran for its life.

'Oh, you playful little girl. You trickster. You really had me going there.' Darren was talking to himself and smiling as he shut the car.

I was just watching. This was all Darren.

He walked around to the passenger door, opened it and reached in for his weapon. Then called after the swine.

'Don't stop now, you little grunter. I'm giving you another twenty seconds then it's game on.'

He counted in his head.

Twenty … nineteen … eighteen…

The pig was confused and swerving up ahead.

Fourteen … thirteen … twelve…

Darren never took his eyes off the sow.

Seven … six … five…

Then it disappeared behind some trees.

Two … one … Go.

SOMETHING WAS RUMBLING

Annie Harding ran out of the woods the same way she had entered. At one point, she thought she was lost but after throwing that rock, she was on autopilot.

She hadn't stopped to assess the damage. She was confused. She had gone out to the middle of nowhere to scream her lungs out until they filled Hollow Forest. Yet, somehow, she had broken another window.

As light started to creep through openings in the canopy above she could see more. An owl, she thought. The sound of frogs or crickets. Something was rumbling. Clicking. Leaves were rustling under foot but she wasn't sure it was her feet making the noise.

She fished around her pocket for the keys and thumbed the button that would unlock the car. The indicator lights flashed up ahead as it came into range. She pulled her seatbelt on and started driving, leaving a huge shadow behind her. Through the window to the left, she thought she saw a wild boar.

Within a couple of minutes, Annie Harding was on the road that led downhill past the station into the centre of town. She straightened her hair in the mirror, parked the car behind the main parade of shops, bought two bottles of red wine, returned home and ate dinner with her husband.

It was still day five. I had not fully released my grip on the town, so Annie drank the wine, straddled her husband on the sofa and looked him in the eyes, pretending that she was enjoying what was happening. Faking an orgasm on her perfect sofa with the tie-in, splash-of-colour cushions.

The next day, there would be so many cracks she would have to paper over.

THE PIG GOT AWAY

Oscar Tambor did not end up with a bullet in his face at the end of the fifth day.

He opened his eyes on that driver seat but did not pull out of the woods to go and confront his birth mother for abandoning him as a newborn.

His vision was temporarily blurred and there was a pain in his head above his left eye.

The air on his face was no longer warm. Cold air was rushing in through the hole in his windscreen and a giant rock lay on his lap, digging into his stomach and thighs.

When the images started to sharpen, the only thing in Oscar Tambor's face was another face. A man he did not know.

Darren.

'What are you doing out here, friend?' the pig hunter asked.

'I'm trying to get home.' Oz grimaced, the pain in his leg was worsening. 'Can you help get this thing off of me?'

Darren was on his heels, squatting just outside the open driver-side door. And, over his shoulder, keeping him steady, holding him on track, was me.

'Ah, fuck. It's really digging into my leg.' Oz tried to move the rock aside then screamed as the pain worsened suddenly. 'Oh, Jesus, help me. It's like I'm being fucking stabbed.'

'Well, I sharpened it all night.'

'What?'

'The knife I keep cutting you with. It's sharp, no?'

Oz was confused and scared. Something I could have tapped into. Maybe even given him the strength to get out of the situation. But Little Henry Wallace needed to be safe. He was brave. He was good. Oz was done.

'The damn pig got away. Outsmarted me, if you can believe that.' Darren rolled his eyes but smiled, knowingly. 'Looks like I'm only good enough for slaughtering the trapped animals. The ones who have no place to go. The ones who think they're going home.'

Oz didn't have time to scream before Darren ran the blade across his throat, just as he did a hundred times a day to the animals who had taken a bolt to the head.

It didn't always kill them, they were just stunned. They could feel their lives dripping away. They were conscious when their skin was stripped.

Just as Oz was conscious when Darren started cutting his guts out. He knew what was happening as the human slaughterer slit lines in his face to pull out Oz's cheeks.

He would leave the eyes in the skull.

Oscar Tambor could not make a sound as Darren moved on from pigs and cats and cows to his ultimate prize. Oz had lost enough blood to drift into a haze as the novice huntsman grabbed a clump of the child-killer's hair, held his head up and stabbed repeatedly into the side of his neck until it came clean away in his hand.

The wedding was off.

DAY SIX

Where you will find:

Evil releases its grip
Everything goes back to normal
Normality can change
and you are wrong about needing a little time.

A MOMENT

Then it was the come-down.

I had to let them all go.

Hinton Hollow. Population 5,013.

The thing I already knew before this trip is the lesson I hope that they have learned.

Everything can change in an instant.

Life. Death. Love. Hatred. Changed in a split second. But so can people. The fact that human beings have the capacity to meet somebody they never knew before and fall straight in love with them tells you everything. If you can do that, if you can make such a drastic alteration to yourself in a moment, you can do it for anything.

You can end a relationship that is no good for you. You can quit your job that you hate. You can stop eating sugar or meat or drinking alcohol. You don't think it is easy to do this, that you need time, it takes time, all you want is a little more time.

KNOW THIS
You are wrong.

Stop it. Stop it now. Stop comparing yourself to others, especially those who are not portraying their reality. Stop seeking out the things that make you feel bad about yourself. Stop 'liking' things that you don't really like. Stop trying to please the people that do not matter.

Start trying to please yourself.

Start complimenting someone, even when you don't think that you have to or that they won't really appreciate it. Start saying thank you when somebody compliments you, rather than throwing it back in their face because you don't feel you deserve it.

Start being kinder. All the time. Not just for a week or a day after some celebrity takes their own life or because there is a hashtag you feel you can get behind.

Stop saying you want equality when what you want is dominance. Start wanting equality.

Be real.

You can change.

You can fall in love overnight. You can start saving money. You can start donating money, or better yet, your time. Listen instead of talking. Know that you are not the most important thing in the world but to a handful of people, you may actually be just that.

Make a choice.

A choice to change.

To be true. To be you. To be good.

Because the more of you that take this decision, the less I have to get involved in the world. The better you are, the less evil I have to be. And I do have to be. I am necessary.

But let me be lazy.

I hoped this would sink in. I hoped there could be a change in the 5,000 people of Hinton Hollow. I hoped it would be instant. Tragedy is a phenomenally effective unifier.

I lifted myself from their lives. Their repressed emotions and insecurities dropped back down inside them. But now with the knowledge that they were there. The people of Hinton Hollow had the choice to drop seamlessly back into the everyday or to make every day.

Annie Harding woke up that morning and did not try to fuck away her husband's hangover. She also did not fall into the mundane. Instead, she rolled over, placed her hand on his face, looked him in the eyes and told him sincerely that she loved him. Then she kissed him and said she was going to put the kettle on.

RD and his wife opened up for breakfast as usual. Darren ordered sausages and ate them. Mrs Beaufort took her pills and walked to Rock-a-Bye and Liv continued to wait for Oz. She was starting to doubt that it had been him on the other end of the line.

Owen Brady did not answer the door when Andrea Day arrived to visit. He was going to devote all of his time to Michael. She saw the blinds twitch as she left but did not fight it.

Ben Raymond spent an entire day with his father and crying baby brother, watching films in the house. He didn't want to go to the cinema any more. He didn't want to be naughty.

Ablett and Hadley were still being held and questioned.

And Little Henry Wallace woke up that morning in a double bed with his mother and brother. She had protected him by sending him away and his brother had protected her by telling the police that he had placed his brother on the train that day.

The malaise had lifted from their town and in its place was a sense of ill ease and wonder but also the promise of something different. Of a change.

They would recover.

I did not need them any more. It was up to them to find the good and use it wisely.

All that was left for me was to take the one man I was still waiting around for.

The one I could not let go.

DAY SEVEN

Where you will note:

God did not rest
and Detective Sergeant Pace had to make a choice.

ONCE WAS ENOUGH

It seemed like everybody in Hinton Hollow attended the Church of the Good Shepherd that final day in Hinton Hollow. Even Pace was there.

Father Salis stood outside in the rain, greeting everybody that entered.

'Welcome, Detective. Please, come in. Get out of the rain. Space is limited today but I'm sure you can squeeze on a seat somewhere.' He smiled. Part salutation, part self-satisfied at his growing flock. 'I wasn't aware that I should be expecting you,' he added, still with a supercilious grin.

'I'm finding myself open to a lot of new things since returning home.'

Pace entered the old church and was hit by the smell of childhood duty and languor. He did not attempt to force his way onto the end of a pew, instead he slunk to the left and dropped into the shadow of a pillar.

He'd expected a similar response to his attendance as he had received the first time he walked into The Arboreal as the new man in town. But nobody really noticed. Eyes were all front and centre. Waiting for the wisdom of the dog-collar standing in the rain.

Pace scoured the room. Hayes was seated with her husband near the front. The large moustache of Anderson scowling three rows behind. Mrs Beaufort was on the very front row, left-hand side, seat furthest to the right, on the aisle, closest to God. Salis even gave her a personal mention, dancing daintily around her health issues but wishing her well all the same.

Owen had even managed to scrape himself up and bring Michael with him. He cringed at the mention of Faith Brady, and his son still looked to be in the same state of catatonic shock he had been in when Pace had thrown his cigarette away before entering the park near the primary school.

Nathan Hadley was less hypocritical, he'd also spent a far from mesmerising few hours in the police station the night before, answering questions about Charles Ablett's death. So had Roger Ablett, but he had peeled himself from his bed. His pew squeaked in agony every time he fidgeted. He was definitely listening to Father Salis's rousing sermon but his eyes never left the ceiling.

They prayed for those that had departed in an untimely fashion and they prayed for one another. Salis mentioned the detective in a hasty acknowledgement, and Pace could see him searching for a dark, unholy figure within the congregation to point out and aim his rhetoric at. Pace was well hidden.

He remained that way until everybody had left the Good Shepherd. He managed to catch RD's eye before he left. The big man gave a wink and a thankful nod.

Pace didn't want gratitude. Too many had perished on his watch and he knew it was he who had brought the blight to town.

Everybody that walked out seemed to have had their spirits lifted by the good Lord's wisdom. Fucking idiots. Maybe he should stay. Somebody had to protect these people. Even Mrs Beaufort was unusually pleasant to him. She asked whether he'd be sticking around this time.

The truth was, he didn't know. If the whole town could buy the crap that Salis had just spouted then maybe there was something to the story that Mrs Beaufort had told about the woods. Something ancient at the heart of Hinton Hollow. He'd seen some pretty strange things recently. Her anecdote had stayed with him.

Perhaps his soul had already been condemned to an eternity among the whispering trees of his childhood town because he'd already left it once. Once was enough. He had plenty of time to be reunited with Julee if the lore were true.

Something was there.

And he was sure it wasn't God; the darkness had followed him into the church with such gracious ease. Now they were both there with only Father Salis remaining.

Maybe all that was left for Detective Sergeant Pace was chaos and terror and looking over his shoulder and old age and black flames and no love. And death. Always death.

Or he could stay. Make himself useful.

Not run. Stop running.

Confront it.

He could do good. Or, at least, he could do good enough, so that he would not have to spend the long time that follows life running from fire.

EPILOGUE

Where everything happened for a reason.

A LEAP OF FAITH

Detective Sergeant Pace is no good.

Detective Sergeant Pace is a footnote.

Detective Sergeant Pace is a small story.

He told Anderson that he was coming back. There were still a lot of loose ends to tie up. But there were also things that needed the same back in the city.

Pace had instructed Ellie Frith to send him a list of rental properties in the area – preferably on Hollow ground rather than Roylake.

RD was overjoyed that the prodigal son was planning on returning, on coming home. Even Mrs Beaufort, in her new holding-down-the-spite way, showed some good cheer at the prospect. Pace wondered whether he was beginning to feel happiness for himself. He was positive.

The train journey back seemed faster than the trip to his hometown the week before. Fields gave way to glass buildings and graffiti-covered walls and cranes and a life that was passing by too fast.

He looked at his phone but there was nothing from Maeve. A part of him was pleased, another was somehow let down. He couldn't deal with her at that moment but he also missed her company.

I held him so that he would not contact her. That just wouldn't do. She had ended it. He'd find out soon enough. He had lost the closeness and the sex and the confidante. She was the only person who knew the details about that last case and about how he ended it.

He knew.

Maeve knew.

And I knew.

The weight Pace felt had never left him. He thought that going back to Hinton Hollow would somehow relieve him, wash away his sin. Or something. But that weight was me.

Sitting. Waiting. Knowing.

He was paranoid that everything he touched turned to shit. His therapist put it down to stress, but Pace was right.

Evil was following him.

He unlocked the door to his city home. It was cold from a week of no activity, no heating, but I filled that entrance with my black flames. I covered everything but the pile of papers on the doormat.

Pace was scared to enter, I could see that. But I knew that he would. Some people are more comfortable in the dark. Some seek it out. Some thrive there.

When he picked up the pile of letters and leaflets, I extinguished my fire. He shut the door behind him and leafed through, throwing the junk mail back to the floor.

Hinton Hollow had already begun to heal as Detective Sergeant Pace ran a finger beneath the flap of the hand-delivered letter that Maeve had personally posted so that he would open it the moment he came back to London.

She kept it brief. It was a very short note. Just a few words that let Pace know that it was the end.

He read Maeve's letter, walked into the kitchen, turned on the gas hob and dipped the end of the paper into the flame.

It was over for him.

The rest of the day, I left Pace to it. He showered, he changed, he ate, he saw no more black flames. He cancelled his phone and his broadband. He emailed a local estate agent about a valuation on his property. Everything was leaning towards a move back home.

He didn't try to contact Maeve.

He did venture into his police station and speak with his superiors about transferring permanently. He did read the news about Little Henry Wallace. He found something on one of the middle pages about his last case.

By rush hour, he was ready.

He went back to Tower Bridge, where nineteen people had jumped to their deaths.

It was supposed to be twenty.

He showed his warrant card at the front desk and explained that he was the detective in charge of that case and needed to go up in the lift. The tour guide made the same joke they always did to the paying public venturing up to the walkway.

Pace exited the lift. There were stairs that had been cordoned off because of the incident. He flashed his badge and ducked underneath the tape. He walked up the stairs and pushed through the door to the outside. It was cold, he couldn't feel it.

I watched him.

And did nothing.

He walked along the top of the walkway and stood where those nineteen people had. Before their end.

He shut his eyes and imagined. He remembered.

Then, below, somebody screamed.

He didn't have to say *go*.

Or count down from three.

He just knew.

ACKNOWLEDGEMENTS

This was a long book for me, so I'll keep this part short.

To Karen Sullivan, whose ongoing support of my writing is incomparable. Your encouragement to go with the weird ideas I come up with is liberating. You didn't even roll your eyes when I said I wanted to write a book from the point of view of Evil. Thanks for allowing me to keep pushing things. (We won't always get it right but that's half the fun.)

West, who blitzed through the edit with me. You somehow make the worst part of the process, for me, more tolerable. The crap we got rid of that nobody will ever see...

My agent, Kate. The commercial angel/devil on my shoulder. I'm coming around to the idea that selling some copies of my books could be a good idea.

Liz, for always moving my book to the top of the pile and the front of everyone's minds.

The readers and bloggers and reviewers who championed *Nothing Important Happened Today*. That book means so much to me, as does your support of it.

To Forbes, you made bringing out the gimp seem like the fluffiest part of *Pulp Fiction*. Thanks for the book support and this new harrowing annual photo tradition.

Tom, I have ignored your advice for nearly a decade but your dirty little spreadsheet saved this book from its third time in the bin. You bastard.

Mum and Brendan. A tough year for you two but still, somehow, always there.

To Phoebe and Coen, you are my sanity and my love. Evil would have nothing to work with.

Kel, I think this book saw me have my lengthiest moody, this-book-is-a-piece-of-shit period. And you're still here. Either you really like me or you're getting better at ignoring me when I need you to. It's all part of the process and there's no one else I want to share my self-loathing with. You're bloody lovely.